ROSE
DHU

ROSE DHU

A NOVEL

MARK MURPHY

Published by GFB™, Seattle
www.girlfridayproductions.com

Produced by Girl Friday Productions

Cover design: David Fassett
Production editorial: Kylee Hayes
Project management: Sara Addicott

Image credits: cover © Shutterstock/Bruce Corn

ISBN (paperback): 978-1-967510-70-2
ISBN (ebook): 978-1-967510-71-9

Library of Congress Control Number: 2025916409

First edition

This book is dedicated to my parents, Jack and Peggy Murphy, who always believed in me, and to my wife, Daphne, my best editor and closest friend, who taught me the meaning of unconditional love.

Amor vincit omnia

PART ONE

DISAPPEARANCE

1

July 20

The Gold Surgery Team gathered in a tight knot in the Memorial Hospital surgical doctors' lounge. Hyped up on caffeine (coffee and energy drinks are plentiful in the OR), the interns and medical students had come in at 4:00 a.m. to pre-round, reviewing the labs and X-ray results on all twenty-eight patients on service so that they would be ready when their attending physician, Dr. Janie O'Connor, came in to run the list before the start of the day's surgery schedule.

It was now 6:50 a.m., and Maddie Mandel, the chief surgical resident, had called Dr. O'Connor for the fourth time. "It went to voicemail again," she said, staring at her iPhone in disbelief, as though the device were lying to her.

Maddie was an intense, no-nonsense "gunner," a fierce patient advocate who would not accept anything less than 100 percent effort. Pegged as a potential chief resident from the very first week of her intern year, Dr. Mandel was an early O'Connor acolyte. Now, Maddie was Dr. O'Connor's heir apparent and right hand. The Gold Team looked to her for guidance.

But today, she had none. The first case was scheduled for 7:00 a.m., and Janie O'Connor was nowhere to be found.

"We can't take the first patient back until I talk to Dr. O'Connor," Maddie said. "The attending has to be in-house."

It was July, the first month of the academic year, and all the interns and medical students were skittish greenies, unused to their new roles. Things would be very different for all of them in eleven months. For now, the absence of their attending physician constituted even more of an intellectual decapitation than usual.

Dr. Mandel pointed to Bill Kelly, a pale, freckle-faced intern, and flicked her index finger toward the preop area. "Bill, go tell the first patient that there's been a slight delay. And let the OR charge nurse know. I'll try to locate Dr. O'Connor. Maybe she's sick or had car trouble. Either way, we need to put a hold on things until I can track her down."

Dr. Kelly, who was only twenty-six and looked even younger, nodded vigorously and sped off.

Maddie was certain that Janie O'Connor was not merely under the weather or having car trouble. *She would have called,* she thought.

Maddie had to find a plan B.

Scrolling through her phone, she found the number for Dr. Malcolm King, a surgical attending who was not on ward duty this month.

He answered on the first ring.

"Dr. King? Maddie Mandel. I'm on Gold Team with Dr. O'Connor. We have a full surgical schedule today, and Dr. O'Connor has not shown up yet. I've been trying to get in touch with her, but I've gotten nothing back, and it's been nearly an hour."

Maddie and Dr. King spoke for a moment. Hanging up, she turned and faced the rest of the Gold Team. They were staring at her, wide eyed and tight lipped, as if they expected something cataclysmic to occur.

"Dr. King will be the attending physician for the service today. He's on his way down. We're going to run the list with him, and then we can start the surgeries," she said.

The entire team seemed to exhale in unison before scurrying off to the computers to finish chart prep.

Dr. King had given Maddie the number for Janie's landline, which she called at 7:00 a.m.

"Hello?" a sleep-caked voice answered.

Maddie felt a jolt of electricity course through her. "Dr. O'Connor?" she exclaimed.

"No, this is Diane, her sister. Who's calling?"

"I'm sorry to bother you this early, ma'am. It's Maddie Mandel, Dr. O'Connor's chief resident. You sound just like your sister on the phone. Is Dr. O'Connor home?"

"Hold on. I'll check."

There was a momentary pause as Diane put down the phone. A crow, or maybe a raven, cawed boisterously in the background.

Diane picked up the phone once again. "Her car is gone," the sister said. "She's not at the hospital?"

"No, ma'am," Maddie said. "We can't find her. Will you please have her call me if she contacts you?"

"Of course," Diane said. And then they hung up.

Maddie was worried. This unscheduled absence was very uncharacteristic behavior for her mentor and good friend.

Where are you, Janie? she thought.

2

They never found her.

On July 19, Janie O'Connor wrapped things up late at her office, then drove to her restored antebellum home at Rose Dhu, a riverside community on Savannah's Southside, where she had lived for nearly a decade.

But by the next morning, she was gone.

Janie's bed was made. Her car was missing. There were no signs of foul play. Only after Janie failed to show up at the hospital did people realize something might be wrong.

Janie O'Connor was formally declared missing after twenty-four hours. By then, it was Saturday.

That weekend, the case made the local evening news. Dr. O'Connor was well known and well liked in Savannah. A former collegiate soccer player at the University of Georgia, Janie was still a competitive athlete at thirty-six years of age. Her long predawn runs were legendary, and a meticulous attention to detail and unwavering patient advocacy had made Dr. O'Connor a role model for nearly every surgical resident in Savannah. An articulate and passionate spokesperson for women's health issues, she was a popular speaker at health forums in places like the Landings, the Ford Plantation, Palmetto Bluff, and other high-end retirement communities in the area. She was also a favorite source of interviews for Coastal Georgia television stations.

But what made Janie socially well known in Savannah was not her medical expertise. Instead, it was her boyfriend—or, perhaps, her *former* boyfriend, depending upon who one spoke to.

Janie O'Connor had been engaged to Phillip Carruthers for over a year. Widely considered Savannah's most eligible bachelor, Phillip was a striking thirty-eight-year-old billionaire, the scion of Savannah's wealthiest family. The Carruthers family's presence in Savannah dated back to colonial times. They were a tight-knit bunch, very active philanthropically, and there were buildings, streets, and even a midtown park bearing the Carruthers name. Phillip had taken control of the sprawling Carruthers business empire following the untimely death of his father, Anderson Carruthers, in a hunting accident a decade before. Fiscally savvy and equipped with a Harvard MBA, Phillip had expanded the family's pervasive influence dramatically over the years he had headed the company, and the family now had twisted its tentacles into a vast array of imports and exports, warehouse construction, and real estate ventures throughout Coastal Georgia. The Carruthers family was even prominent in the metropolis of Atlanta four hours north, where Phillip maintained close ties with the governor, who he frequently went hunting and fishing with. Socially adept and charismatic, Phillip was well known as a ladies' man, and his reputation as a dedicated bachelor was also well known. Seeing as Phillip showed up with a different woman on his arm at every social event, his nickname was Playboy Phil.

Janie's relationship with Phillip Carruthers was unexpected; their engagement was an absolute shock. When Phillip announced his engagement to Savannah's sweetheart, Janie

O'Connor, it ignited a societal firestorm. Playboy Phil was formally off the market.

The wedding was scheduled at the imposing, white-spired Cathedral of St. John the Baptist in historic downtown Savannah. For months, social media hummed with rumors and innuendo about the details. A gargantuan wedding party pavilion, designed by New York architect Archibald Hadid, was under construction on the Carruthers estate on Wilmington Island. Movie stars, a cadre of Atlanta-based entertainers and athletes, and a certain Tony Award–winning producer were all rumored to be attending.

But then, with plans well underway, everything fell apart.

Chatter about premarital discord began when construction of the wedding party pavilion abruptly halted. Shortly thereafter, the small army of florists, bakers, and musicians hired for the event was told to stand down.

The Savannah gossip mill raged, its rumors ranging from the merely scandalous ("Playboy Phil cheated on Dr. O'Connor with the wedding planner!") to the ridiculous ("I heard he was planning to force her to stay at home and just make babies for him!"). The scandal-savvy hive of Coastal Georgia society had never been more abuzz.

Right smack in the middle of this swirling maelstrom of innuendo, Janie O'Connor up and vanished.

Two days after Janie's disappearance, Janie's sister, Diane, was interviewed by Tina Baker, the charismatic anchor at Savannah's WKKR television station. By that point, the national news media had started to report about Janie's disappearance. Tina's interview with Diane was picked up by CBS, the parent network of WKKR, for a national prime-time broadcast.

Detective Frank Winger and his partner, Pepper Stephens, were the lead investigators on the O'Connor case. Savannah Police Chief Clarence "Gatehouse" Brown had said he needed his "best team" at work on the high-profile disappearance. Frank and Pepper had worked together for over a decade and had cracked many a high-profile whodunit.

But Frank had never seen a case quite like this one.

The night the Tina Baker interview aired, Frank picked up some takeout sushi at Hirano's. Dressed in battered blue jeans, a vintage Eagles T-shirt from the original *Hotel California* tour, and battered Tecovas cowboy boots, Frank did not look much like a detective. Most people thought he was a day laborer—if they even saw him at all.

"The usual, Frank?" said Keiko, the perky cashier at Hirano's.

"Of course," he said, grinning.

She dropped four containers of shrimp sauce and a pair of chopsticks into the bag.

When he arrived at the condo, Frank took off his reflective aviator sunglasses and dropped them on the table next to the front door, catching a glimpse of himself in the mirror in the process.

"Jesus," he muttered.

He was always surprised at his appearance these days. At forty-six, he saw that his once-black hair was now grizzled and streaked with gray, and his face was as creased as an old saddle. He'd grown the beard a few years back to try to look more distinguished. That had been Paulina's idea, of course, and he had not shaved it since she died, out of some vague respect for her memory. But the beard was flecked with gray, too, and Frank realized now that it just made him look even older, like one of the aging knights from some medieval drama on HBO.

Sushi had been one of Paulina's suggestions, as well. "You can't just eat pizza and hamburgers every day," she'd said.

"Sure I can," Frank had replied.

Paulina *had* convinced him to eat sushi, though. And he loved it now.

Frank didn't usually watch much TV, mainly local news and Ravens and Orioles games (*you can take the boy out of Baltimore . . .*). Still, it was readily apparent, even to him, that Tina Baker was too talented for the relatively small Savannah market. Poised and professional, Tina's questions to Janie's sister, Diane, reflected both her compassion and her razor-sharp intellect.

This story might be Tina's ticket to the big time, Frank thought.

"I understand you were living with your sister at the time of her disappearance?" Tina asked.

Diane nodded.

"And you actually saw her on July 19, the night she disappeared?"

"I did."

"What time was that?"

"She got home about 7:45 p.m., or maybe a little after that. It wasn't dark yet."

"How did she seem?"

"Perfectly normal. She made herself a turkey sandwich—I'd already eaten, since she'd gotten home late—and we talked a bit. I wasn't feeling well, so I took a sleeping pill and went to bed early. She said she was going to read some and turn in early herself. She had a big surgery day the next day."

"And you never saw her again?"

Diane shook her head. Tears filled her eyes. "By morning, she was gone—although I didn't realize it until a few hours had gone by."

Tina leaned forward, a concerned look on her face. "What do you mean?"

"I was still asleep when the chief resident called the landline around 7:00 a.m. It startled me—the landline doesn't ring much these days—and I was a little groggy when we spoke. Janie's bed was made, the alarm was off, and her car was gone, but that was normal. She gets up at 4:00 a.m. even when she's off and usually leaves before dawn every day. After I hung up with the chief resident, I fed Janie's dog, Boodles, took him outside, and made myself some breakfast."

"Why did the chief resident call the landline?"

"I guess they had not been able to reach Janie on her cell. Janie insists on keeping a landline so she can be reached if cell service goes down. That's the way she is. She always has a backup plan."

"And what did the chief resident ask you?"

"She asked if Janie was home and if I had seen her."

"What did you tell her?"

"The exact same thing I'm telling you. I tried calling Janie's cell and got no answer. I called our parents, but they hadn't heard from her, either. I walked all over the property here at Rose Dhu, thinking she might have been injured somewhere— Janie has about five acres, and we see water moccasins and copperheads sometimes—but she was nowhere to be found. I even went out on the dock and checked the kayaks, but they were all stowed. I then drove along her usual running route, thinking something might have happened to her while she was exercising. We sometimes see stray dogs roaming around the neighborhood, or even a few stray people, but there was no sign of her anywhere. Around lunchtime, I called the chief resident back, but she still had heard nothing. That was when I really started getting worried."

Diane brushed a few tears away, gently shaking her head.

"Do *you* think your sister would leave town without any sort of explanation?"

Diane shook her head vigorously. "Janie would never do anything like that. It's so unlike her. She's the most responsible person I know."

"What do you think happened to your sister, Diane?" Tina said.

Diane looked up, her electric-blue eyes red rimmed and swollen. "Something terrible, Tina. She's been kidnapped or . . . or . . ." Diane never finished the sentence, but her crumpled face said everything anyone needed to know.

Frank froze the streaming image and gazed at Diane's tear-stained face for a moment. She was wearing a fair amount of makeup, but there was a faint bruise on her neck and another at the angle of the jaw, below her left ear.

It may be nothing, Frank thought. But maybe not.

Frank unfroze the image, and the interview went to a commercial.

He picked up a legal pad from his desk and jotted down a few notes:

Diane saw Janie the night before at 7:45 PM
Gone by 7 AM Friday
Car gone/alarm not on (was it ever activated?)
Has dog
Cameras?
Relationship between Janie and Diane
Bruises on Diane's face and neck

When they met, which would be soon, Frank would have some very specific questions for Janie's little sister.

3

Frank called his partner early, before leaving the condo, to make sure he was still coming to breakfast.

"Hold on. I'm on the john," Pepper said.

Frank heard the toilet flush and shook his head. "Jesus. TMI," he muttered.

Detectives Pepper Stephens and Frank Winger were nothing alike. "Mutt and Jeff," Chief Brown called them. (Frank didn't really know who Mutt and Jeff were, but he got the drift.) They got along just the same.

"I know you guys have a lot of irons in the fire right now," Chief Brown had said when he assigned them to lead the Janie O'Connor case, "but I need you two on this one. It's big, and it's going to get bigger."

Pepper, in his mid-forties, was balding, overweight, and perpetually rumpled. Bespectacled, with bulging Billy Joel–like eyes, full lips, and a squashed nose, he looked more like an accountant than a cop. Happily married to Candy Stephens, *née* Durrence, from nearby Glennville, Pepper had three hyperactive school-age kids in private school, eschewed exercise ("no time for it"), loved Braves baseball and Miller Lite, and rarely took a vacation.

Most importantly, Pepper was the closest thing to a brother that Frank had ever had.

The two men met daily over breakfast at a throwback diner just off Paulsen Street, appropriately called the Breakfast Place. It wasn't fancy, but the food was good, the service was fast, and the bill was always cheap as hell. Also, they had amazing coffee.

Steam surrounded Pepper's florid face as he drank his first sip. "This is great, as usual, Lurlene," he told their waitress, who smiled at him.

Lurlene, their favorite waitress, was ageless, the sort of woman who could have passed for forty or seventy. She had a pencil behind one ear and an order pad in her hand, just as she had for two decades.

"I don't know how you can drink coffee when it's that hot," Frank said.

"His throat's been leatherized over the years. Right, Detective?" Lurlene said. Her voice was husky. Frank suspected that she smoked, although he'd never seen her do it.

"Is that actually a word?" Frank asked.

"It is now," Lurlene said. "So what'll you boys have? The usual?"

"Works for me," Frank said, folding up the laminated menu.

"Same here," said Pep, who hadn't even opened his.

Frank stirred a container of creamer into his coffee. He knew that *his* throat wasn't leatherized. Pep liked his coffee scorching, strong, black, and unsweetened, which made Frank a little jealous. Frank had to temper his coffee, moderating the taste and temperature to the point that it was almost tepid. He attributed this coffee intolerance to the time he spent in

Afghanistan, when the Army's regulation java was routinely bitter and god-awful, but in truth, he wasn't sure.

"So whaddaya think, Frankie? Did the good doctor skip town, or is she dead?" Pepper said.

"That's jumping the gun a little bit, don't you think?" Frank said.

"Well, it's probably one or the other. She either left town or she's dead."

"She could have been abducted," Frank said.

"OK, that's a possibility, too. Maybe aliens beamed her up. Maybe she was eaten by a gator. Anyway, she's not where she's supposed to be, that's for sure."

"Did you see Tina Baker's interview with the sister?" Frank asked.

Pepper nodded.

"How does Tina get our most important witness for an interview on national TV before we can even talk to her?" Frank asked.

Pepper shook his head. "She's got connections," he said, rubbing his fingertips together to emphasize the point.

Frank pulled his yellow legal pad from his briefcase and produced a pen. "I took a few notes from the interview," he said.

"You are such a dweeb," Pepper replied, grinning. He sipped some more coffee, fogging his glasses.

"The sister, Diane O'Connor, said that she saw Janie sometime the evening of July 19, before sunset. She estimated 7:45 or so. That correlates with when Dr. O'Connor's office staff last saw her; they said she left the office a little before 7:30 p.m. Diane went to bed shortly after Janie got home and awoke at around 7:00 a.m. on July 20, when she was called on the landline by the chief resident. By that point, Janie was gone. The residents at the hospital had started calling Janie's cell at 6:30

a.m., but she was not answering. I think we can assume whatever happened had happened by then. So we have a roughly eleven-hour range for her disappearance, from 8:00 p.m. July 19 until 6:30 a.m. July 20."

Lurlene walked up, tall and graceful, despite bearing two armloads of food. "Here ya go. One farmer's omelet with hash browns, a side of bacon, and one short stack with maple syrup, grits, and sausage." She set the plates down before the two men and smiled broadly, then winked at Frank before turning on her heel.

"She fancies you," Pepper said, watching Lurlene's trim form as she walked away.

"She does not," Frank said. "Her flirtation is a running joke between us." Frank flipped to the next page on the legal pad. "Anyway, here's how I see it: We now have a timeline. We know Janie made it home, so that's where we start. We need to check out Dr. O'Connor's residence pronto, to see if any clues were left behind. It looks like the last person to see her alive was her sister, who lived with her. We can interview her at the same time we visit the house. I know the house has an alarm system; the sister said so. But are there surveillance cameras? Did the neighbors see anything? That's all critical to find out."

"Sounds logical," Pepper said.

"We also need to interview Phillip Carruthers. He's the ex, and that makes him a potential suspect. Maybe the prime suspect."

Pepper rolled his eyes and shook his head.

"What?" asked Frank.

Pepper chewed for a moment, then swallowed. "It's just that anytime we deal with the Carruthers organization, we always have to go through Morris Shefter, and he's a royal pain in the ass," he said and took another sip of coffee.

"He's their attorney. He gets paid big bucks to be a pain in the ass."

"I know. He's just . . . He's difficult. Interviewing Carruthers with Shefter around is going to be a Saharan shitstorm."

"I agree, but we have no choice." He glanced down at the legal pad again. "Both of Janie O'Connor's parents are living. We'll need to speak to them, too. Also, any coworkers whom she was particularly close to, friends, acquaintances, et cetera. Did anyone hold a grudge against her? Are there any secrets we don't know?"

"There are *always* secrets we don't know," Pepper said, popping the last sausage into his mouth.

Frank wiped his face with his napkin and dropped it on the table. "Then let's go find them."

4

"No," Chief Brown said. "Not yet."

It had been a seemingly simple request: Frank wanted to bring Phillip Carruthers in for questioning.

"He's the ex-fiancé, Chief," Frank said. "That puts him near the top of our suspect list."

"Bringing him in will ignite a media feeding frenzy. You know that. And we'll have to deal with Morris Shefter," he said, echoing Pepper's concern. "That guy will eat us for lunch if we don't have all our ducks in a row beforehand. Remember when Phillip had that DUI when he was a teenager? Idiot patrolman didn't know who he'd pulled over."

"That was a real shit show," Pep said, nodding.

"That must have been before I was here," Frank said.

"Yeah, it was over twenty years ago now, but it seems like yesterday," Pepper said. "Shefter came into the hearing in his thousand-dollar suit with his pinkie ring glittering and intimidated everybody. Even the DA was afraid of him."

"The DA was Mike Devereaux back then. Ole Mikey left to take a leak right before the judge came in and never came back. Shefter faced off against the little pimple-faced associate he left behind and ripped that poor kid a new asshole. The associate resigned from the DA's office shortly after that and left town for good. Shefter ate him alive and spat out his bones. That's the sort of thing I'd like to avoid," Chief Brown said.

"That, and the media circus," Pepper said.

"Well, yeah. That, too. You need to let me do the groundwork for that before we set it up. Follow up on your other leads, and I'll work on the Phillip Carruthers piece."

Frank shook his head, frowning.

"Don't give me that look, Frank. Let me handle this my way."

"Roger that, Chief," Frank said with a relenting sigh. He left Chief Brown's office, closing the wooden door softly behind him.

Frank and Pepper divided the rest of the work to move through the interviews more efficiently. Pepper would speak to Janie's parents and coworkers, while Frank would head out to Rose Dhu to look over Janie's house and interview Diane.

They'd clearly have to tackle Phillip Carruthers (and Morris Shefter) later.

Frank drove his battered Hyundai down White Bluff Road. White Bluff was a typical suburban four-lane avenue at its beginning, lined with gas stations, convenience stores, and chain restaurants. However, after it passed the brick gates of the Windsor subdivision, White Bluff metamorphosed into something entirely different: a verdant tunnel that drove straight through the heart of a dense maritime forest. Frank realized he'd never driven down this portion of White Bluff before.

This place looks haunted, he thought.

The road's edge was crowded with an impossible tangle of vegetation. Although a few cheery rays of the afternoon sun dappled the roadway, the forest surrounding the road was draped in deep shadow, mist drifting among the trees.

When Frank turned left onto Rose Dhu Road, the forest

canopy finally opened, revealing a cerulean sky above and a broad grassy savanna stretching out to the Vernon River. Rose Dhu Road turned again, hugging the marsh's edge. Frank could see a pair of whitewashed shrimp boats bobbing at their moorings in the river.

Janie O'Connor had purchased Rose Dhu Plantation several years earlier. The plantation had been in the Houston family for over two hundred years. Infighting among the many Houston descendants had led to indecision and neglect as they lacked the resources or the will to maintain the property. As a result, the old plantation house, like the rest of the property, had fallen into absolute ruin.

The massive granite arch marking the entrance looked oddly out of place juxtaposed against the vast expanse of the marsh, a jumble of rough-hewn stone chunks, like the remnants of some long-forgotten castle. Its iron gates hung wide open, frozen in place. An abandoned guard kiosk fashioned from the same blocks of granite stood empty, windows gaping, the glass long gone.

After purchasing the property, Janie had gradually restored it, bit by bit and acre by acre, until it had achieved some semblance of its former grandeur.

The entrance to the driveway was marked by a simple wooden sign inscribed with *Twin Oaks*. Frank drove between the eponymous gargantuan oak trees and followed the path, which snaked among the moss-draped trees of the maritime forest for a bit before opening onto a circular driveway.

"Good God," he muttered.

The house overlooked the Vernon River from a long, sloping grassy bluff. The white home had black hurricane shutters, and its red metal roof was supported by four thick white columns that spanned a broad herringbone-patterned brick porch. Twin gas lanterns flickered by an arched cut-glass doorway. A pair of large cement planters, each containing a small fir tree, flanked the doorway. English ivy cascaded over the edges of the planters almost to the ground.

Frank rang the doorbell.

A deadbolt unlocked with a sharp *click*, and the door opened.

Diane O'Connor was a small-framed blonde with porcelain skin, high cheekbones, and brilliant blue eyes. Her posture was perfect and erect, like a ballerina's. She seemed to be wearing a bit more makeup than Frank would have expected for this time of day, but it was perfectly applied, and the bruise he had noted at her jawline during the television interview was now only a faint bluish smudge.

Frank immediately thought she might be the most beautiful woman he had ever seen.

"Hello, Detective. It was so good of you to drive all the way out here. Come in, please," she said, gently sweeping her arm into the house. Her voice had a faint Southern lilt to it, like half-and-half iced tea—just enough sugar.

"Thank you for taking the time to meet with me," Frank said, stepping inside.

An ancient Labrador stood close by Diane's leg, its pink tongue lolling sideways out of its mouth.

"This is Boodles, Janie's dog. He's a good boy," Diane said.

"Hey, Boodles," Frank said, scratching the old dog between the ears. His tail wagged enthusiastically.

A soaring central hallway shot through the house from front to back. A glass door that matched the front door looked out onto the river from the hallway's other end. An antique grandfather clock ticked on one wall; a graceful, curved stairway ascended upstairs on the other side. Antique sofas and tables lined the foyer, with colorful oil paintings of marsh scenes and fields filled with wildflowers hanging from the walls.

"This is quite an impressive place," Frank said.

Diane shrugged. "It was all Janie's doing." She laughed.

"By the time she bought it, it was rumored to be haunted. The place was an absolute wreck. Our parents wanted Janie to tear the house down and start over, but that only made her more determined to restore it. And even though it took *years*, she did it, both the house and the grounds. That's Janie for you," she said.

"She did all the work herself?" Frank asked.

"A good bit of it. The stuff she couldn't handle, she subbed out, of course. She started with the yard, which was the easiest. But she also became an expert in carpentry, wiring, masonry, and plumbing while she was rebuilding this place. She's always been good at everything. When we were kids, she was first-team all-state in soccer and basketball, class valedictorian at St. Vincent's, and was voted Most Likely to Succeed. She was a First Honor graduate and a Phi Beta Kappa scholar at the University of Georgia. She was the most outstanding surgery resident at UNC. Always the superstar." Diane shrugged and looked away. "Me? Not so much."

"I'm sure you can hold your own," Frank said.

"You've obviously never met my sister." Diane smiled faintly, then nodded toward the hallway. "We can talk more in the den," she said.

They walked across the foyer, Boodles limping along beside them step by step.

The den had a brick fireplace on one wall flanked by built-in shelves filled with family pictures, memorabilia, and antique books.

Opposite the fireplace, a pair of large picture windows looked across the yard, which stretched to an undulating plain of marsh grass and, ultimately, to the shimmering expanse of the Vernon River. A dock shot out, straight as an arrow, toward a red-roofed dock house perched at the water's edge.

"Have a seat and make yourself comfortable. Can I get you something to drink?" Diane asked.

"A glass of water would be nice. Thank you," Frank said.

Frank sat in a leather wingback chair beside the fireplace, looking across the river. Boodles took a seat next to him, curling up on the floor. Diane returned a moment later with a tall, clear glass of ice water.

"Here you go," she said, smiling. "I'm impressed. Boodles seems to like you, and he's usually a pretty good judge of character."

Diane sat down on a rust-colored sofa facing Frank. A glass-topped display table containing dozens of seashells squatted between them.

Frank took a sip of water and sat the glass on a coaster. "I appreciate your willingness to speak with me today," he said. "I know this is hard."

"It is. Janie and I are very close. When we were kids, Janie was the best big sister anyone could ask for. She protected me." Diane's eyes were downcast. She dabbed at them with her fingers.

"She protected you? How's that?"

"Janie never puts up with any shit from anyone." Diane blushed. "Pardon the language," she said.

"It's fine," Frank replied, smiling. "I'm a cop. I've heard plenty worse."

She looked up, her sapphire eyes locking with Frank's. "I was always skinny and a little insecure, but Janie never let anyone take advantage of me. Not once, not ever. When I was eight, this neighborhood bully named Tommy Wilkins pushed me down on the sidewalk. Tommy was fourteen, smoked, had a scar over one eye, and was mean to animals. All the kids in Ardsley Park were afraid of him. When he hurt me, Janie, who was about ten at the time, knocked his front teeth out."

Diane shook her head. "I really miss her."

"I'm sure you do. It seems like everyone who knew her does."

"We're all in shock," Diane said.

"I'm sorry to have to come here and talk to you about this on such short notice, but we are trying to find out what's happened to her."

"I'll help any way I can," Diane said, flashing a brief, pained smile.

"I'm going to get straight to the point," Frank said. "What do you think happened to Janie?"

"I don't know," Diane said.

"Did Janie have any enemies?"

She laughed. "Everyone who ever met my sister loved her," she said.

He raised an eyebrow. "No negative interactions at all?"

"None," Diane said effusively. "Janie did not have an enemy in the world."

"So if Janie had no enemies, what do you think happened to your sister?"

Diane shrugged. "I don't know, but I'd be willing to bet it had something to do with Phillip Carruthers."

Frank sat up, cocking his head slightly. "Why do you think that?"

"I'm sure you know they were engaged."

"I do. But the engagement was broken, right?"

Diane nodded vigorously. "Phillip was furious when Janie broke up with him. Mama had warned Janie that men like Phillip were used to getting whatever they wanted, but Janie always insisted she could handle him. Mama had wanted Janie to marry Dave Wommack, her boyfriend from undergrad and med school. No one was happier than Mama when Dave and Janie got back together after she left Phillip."

Frank felt the hair on the back of his neck stand up.

"When did the breakup with Mr. Carruthers happen?"

"A few months ago, back in February."

"And when did she and this Dave Wommack guy get back together?"

"Shortly after she broke up with Phillip."

He wrote this detail on his legal pad. "Were Dr. O'Connor and Dr. Wommack still dating at the time of her disappearance?"

Diane nodded. "You didn't know that? I thought everyone knew that."

"Our investigation is just starting," Frank said.

"Janie dated Dave throughout her time at the University of Georgia and medical school. Dave was like part of the family. Everyone always assumed they would get married. But when Dave matched at Hopkins and Janie matched at North Carolina, she broke up with him. She said they both needed to focus on their careers. After residency, Janie returned to Savannah. Dave showed up here a year later. We all thought they'd get back together after that. I really think that's what Dave had hoped, too, but it didn't work out that way. Janie was focused on her career and on redoing the house. She'd see Dave intermittently at the hospital, but by that point, she insisted that they were just friends. Phillip was the first guy Janie really went out with after she moved back to Savannah."

"How did Janie and Phillip meet?"

"She saw him as a patient. There were a few sparks, and things took off from there. She told me the story once."

—

April, last year

Staring out across the Vernon River through the large picture window in her kitchen at Twin Oaks, Janie O'Connor was washing sweet potatoes at the large granite-topped island in the center of the room. Diane was visiting for a few days from Isle of Hope. Sitting at the kitchen table, she grilled Janie about her new boyfriend, Phillip Carruthers.

"Does he hold the door open for you?" Diane asked.

"What difference does that make?" Janie said, shaking her head, a thin smile on her face.

Janie vigorously scrubbed a sweet potato with a vegetable brush, inspecting it for a moment before setting it down on a paper towel.

"Mom always says you can tell a lot about a man by the little things. It's not the gifts, you know. That's just money, and Phillip's a billionaire, so it's not like he's sacrificing anything for that. The more important thing is how he treats you. Does he respect you? Does he understand you?"

"He does," Janie said, crossing her arms in front of her chest. "Why would you ask that?"

"He's not going to try to make you stay home and have babies?"

"Why the hell would he do *that*?" Janie asked.

"Think about it. What's different about you when you look at all the other girls he's dated?"

"I don't *know* any of the other girls he's dated," Janie said. "And I really don't care to know them."

"Come *on*, Janie! You don't read the society pages?"

Janie shook her head. "I don't," she said.

"I don't believe you. You read *everything*," Diane said.

Janie went over to preheat the oven. "I read the Savannah paper, *The AJC*, *The Washington Post*, and *The New York Times* daily. I enjoy going over medical journal articles and even reading some trashy novels. But the local society pages don't interest me. They never have. I couldn't care less. That's something for people with more spare time than I have."

Even if just to herself, Diane had to admit that part of the recent distance between her and Janie had to do not only with

Phillip but with Dave Wommack, too. "Big Dave" had always been around when she was growing up, and Diane loved him like a brother. Dave had enjoyed joking around with Diane, cajoling her unmercifully as he tried to draw the shy teenage version of Diane out of her shell. Phillip was the polar opposite of Dave.

"Well, your boyfriend's nickname in Savannah society is Playboy Phil. And the difference between you and every other girl he's ever dated is that you are a well-educated professional. The other women have all been socially prominent bimbos looking to snag the good-looking rich boy. Your engagement to Phillip pissed off a lot of debutantes."

Janie snorted. "My apologies to the debs."

Diane washed her hands to help with the salad. "How did you two meet again? You never told me."

"He came into the office to get a cyst removed," Janie said.

"How romantic!" Diane exclaimed, fanning herself in an exaggerated fashion as she fluttered her eyelids.

Janie shrugged. "How else am I supposed to meet someone when I'm at work all day?"

"Church, maybe?"

"I'm not at church as much these days. You know that." Janie was grating carrots, her hands precise and efficient.

"So tell me—what was that romantic cyst removal visit like?" Diane asked.

Janie smiled at the memory. "Phillip had discovered a lump on the small of his back. In the exam room, he pulled up his dress shirt so I could see it. It was a benign nodule under the skin about the size of a blueberry. A sebaceous cyst. He said he could feel it whenever he tightened his belt, which bugged him, so he asked me to remove it. We were talking afterward, and he kept staring at me. Finally, he told me that I was gorgeous and said he wanted to ask me out. I told him that that was inappropriate since I was his doctor. 'I guess I'm going to have to find myself another doctor, then,' he said." Janie blushed. "And that's how it all started."

"I'm curious—what does Dave think?" Diane asked.

"Like I told you before, Dave and I are good friends, but that's it. He says he's glad to see me happy."

"And you believe that?"

"I do. Look, Dave was my first love. In many ways, I'll love Dave forever. But there's no future there. I've moved on with my life."

"Mom and Dad still speak to Dave all the time. They think of him like a son," Diane said. She began peeling a Vidalia onion.

"My relationship with Phillip is different. My heart beats a little faster when I see him. I enjoy looking at him when he's sleeping. Sometimes, I pick up his shirt and inhale his scent when he isn't looking. It sounds crazy, but doing that can make me just the slightest bit dizzy. I guess it's just the pheromones, but I've never experienced that sort of thing before. It's a totally different experience from what it was with Dave." Janie fell silent, staring off into space as she stood at the sink.

"Earth to Janie. Are you *daydreaming*?" Diane asked. "Who is this romantic replicant who has replaced my hard-charging, no-nonsense, balls-to-the-wall sister?"

Janie glanced over at Diane, who was now chopping up the onion. "Diane?"

"Mm-hmm?"

"Do you know how you always described your relationships? How you'd fall head over heels in love and become infatuated, and sometimes even obsessed, with them?" Janie asked.

"It's *always* like that with me, unfortunately," Diane said, shaking her head. "I'm a sucker for romance."

"Unfortunately? I was always jealous of you! I've never had that, not with anyone."

Diane put down the knife and dabbed at her eyes. "My

relationships with men are cyclical, Janie: All moonlight and rose petals at first, and I think, 'At last! This is the one!' The sex can be mind-blowing, but it eventually gets in the way of anything more meaningful developing. It always ends up tragically, with me being confused and hurt, and the whole relationship collapsing in on itself. It's the same damned thing every single time, cycling from supernova to black hole. I *hate* it." Diane's eyes were red and swollen. Her lip was quivering. "I just want stability, you know? Someone I can trust, someone who loves me just because of who I am, someone who will stick by me even when I'm old."

Janie kissed her sister on the forehead. "I guess people always want what they don't have," Janie said.

"Just be careful what you wish for, Janie," Diane said. "Unbridled passion isn't all it's cracked up to be."

—

Frank Winger found himself staring at Diane as she told this story.

He was distracted by her looks. He knew that was unprofessional, but he couldn't help it. He decided to just accept it and re-engaged his detective's brain to think through the timeline of Janie's disappearance.

Think about motive, means, and opportunity.

The next question just popped out of his mouth: "Who is Janie's heir?" he asked.

Diane blinked. "What?"

"Let me rephrase that: Do you know if Janie has a will? And if she does, could I see it?"

Diane blushed. "I don't know. I guess she does. It would be unlike her not to prepare for any outcome, including her death. We've never really talked about it, though."

"She's never been married, right?"

"No."

"No children?"

"None."

"So if she doesn't have a will, you'd stand to inherit all of this if she died, correct? You're her only sibling."

"I don't know. I guess so. Why are you asking this?"

"I keep an open mind to all possibilities. Most murders are crimes of passion. For anything premeditated, there's usually a motive. And most murders involve family members or loved ones." Frank glanced at his legal pad, tapping it with his pen. "In your interview with Tina Baker you said you didn't think Janie would leave town suddenly. Would she kill herself?"

"No!" Diane said with a gasp. "She'd never do that!"

Frank knew where he had to go next, but he was a bit reticent about the next steps. Diane seemed fragile, as though she were teetering on the edge of an invisible precipice. He didn't want to push her over it—but he needed answers, and there was no other way to get them.

He took a deep breath before continuing. "Well, that leaves us only a few options. If *you* were investigating this case, who would be your prime suspects?"

Diane's shoulders slumped. "Phillip Carruthers—and me, I guess. But I'd never hurt Janie."

"I'm sure Phillip will say the same thing."

She looked at him through narrowed eyes. "What are you getting at, Detective?"

Frank leaned back in his chair. "When you gave the TV interview with Tina Baker, I noticed a couple of bruises on you. One at your jawline on the left. Another was on your neck. They're not as prominent now, but I could not help but see them. Care to explain where those bruises came from?"

Diane looked at him, her lips slightly apart, but no words came. "I . . . well, it's just . . . ," she stammered.

"Ms. O'Connor, I'm not trying to be confrontational. Your

sister is missing. We need to find out what happened to her. I can't afford to leave any stones unturned."

Diane seemed to settle back in her chair, her eyes downcast. She smoothed out her dress and shook her head slowly. "Good," Diane said quietly.

She had folded her hands in her lap in front of her, and her legs were tightly crossed. Her lower lip trembled slightly. "What if I told you something that might tie Janie's disappearance to Phillip?" Diane said quietly.

Frank leaned forward slightly, staring at her tear-filled eyes. "I'm all ears, Ms. O'Connor," he said softly.

A torrent of tears flowed down Diane's face, which had broken into a million pieces. "After Phillip and Janie broke up, Phillip sent a man here to find Janie. That man raped me."

5

Fifteen Years Ago

When Frank was in Afghanistan, he tried not to think about dying, although it wasn't always easy. Death was always just over the next hill, often hiding in clumps of stunted bushes or crouched behind some ancient doorway. He found it best to light on a distraction: crossword puzzles, for example, or pulp fiction.

But then came the girl.

She visited the camp daily, selling fruit from her family farm. A tiny little slip of a thing, perhaps thirteen years old, she wore the same olive-colored niqab each morning. For the longest time, Frank never even saw her face.

Each day, she would push a small rusty wheelbarrow filled with pomegranates into the camp, selling them for a quarter each. Although the men did not trust her at first, she won them over with her gentleness. She spoke with a soft voice, in halting English, although her grasp of the language improved with each interaction.

"What's your name?" Frank asked one day.

"Amani," she said. "It means 'one who has aspirations.'"

"It suits you," he said.

Frank could see her greenish-gold eyes dancing behind her veil. He asked about her family, but she did not wish to talk about them much.

"My mother is dead," she said. "My father grows pomegranates with my uncle. My brothers used to help us, but now most of them are gone."

"Gone? Are they dead?"

"No. They have left," she said.

"Where did they go?"

"Into the mountains, before it was cold last year. They have not been home since."

Amani was hungry for knowledge. She was enthralled by the magazines Frank showed her from America (*The Atlantic* and *Newsweek*, primarily). Although she could not read many of the words, the pictures showed her things she could scarcely imagine in the arid, rock-strewn village she called home.

"Women in America can study?" she said one day as she saw a photograph of a female doctor.

Frank nodded.

Amani frowned. "Then what happens to their families? Who will cook and clean? Who takes care of the children?"

"Men and women usually help each other with the household duties," he said.

Amani clicked her tongue against her teeth, shaking her head. "My father would never approve of that," she said.

Then, one day, Amani did not come. When she finally did four days later, her beautiful greenish-gold eyes had a pained look. The joy had leaked out of them.

"What's wrong?" Frank said.

But Amani would only say "A quarter apiece" while holding a pomegranate in her tiny hand. She always wanted American money.

After several days of silence, Frank had had enough.

"Amani, are you angry with us? Has someone here cheated you? I can help make it right, but I need to know what is wrong."

"I have no quarrel with you. Everyone here is very kind to me."

"Well, what is it, then? What has happened to you?"

Amani's jaw was set. Her eyes had a faraway stare, as if she were looking at something she could scarcely believe to be true. "My father has a new business partner. He wishes to marry me."

Frank sat down on a crate in front of Amani. The day was hot and dry, as always, but suddenly Frank felt the dust of a thousand years in his mouth. "Surely your father won't allow that," Frank said.

"He *wants* it to happen," Amani said. "My father's new business partner is wealthy. Baba thinks the marriage will bind our families, like a ribbon wound tight around our wrists."

"But you are too young," Frank said.

"That's what I told Baba. I told him that American girls can attend school and get an education. He said that is not what God wants. He told me Americans are godless infidels who are all going to hell. It made me angry, and I spoke out against him. I told him he was wrong about you, that all of you were nice and treated me respectfully." She stopped. There were tears in her eyes. "I talked back to my father. It's a sin against Allah."

"That's not a sin," Frank replied.

Amani's eyes widened. "Oh, it is! It's one of the worst sins! That's why he hit me."

Frank recoiled. "You father *hit* you?"

Amani nodded slowly.

"Amani, take off your veil. Let me see your face," Frank said.

She looked down at her feet. "I cannot," she said. "It is not allowed."

"I need to see what he did to you."

Amani looked around and furtively lowered her veil, only for a second. Her face was bruised and swollen, her upper lip split.

"Amani, is that all that happened?"

She would not answer. Instead, she covered her face once again, then turned away from him and left, pushing the wheelbarrow ahead of her across the rock-strewn landscape. A pomegranate toppled out and rolled across the ground, finally coming to rest against a rusted, ragged-edged tin shed.

Amani never came back after that.

A week or so later, a thin young man with a pronounced limp pushed Amani's battered wheelbarrow into the camp. He had a scraggly beard and a deep facial scar, which slashed the bridge of his nose almost in two.

"Where is Amani?" Frank asked the young man.

The man gazed at Frank. His anthracite eyes gleamed, bottomless and unfathomable.

"The girl?" Frank asked again.

"My sister?" the man replied in perfect English. "She's dead."

Frank felt his gorge rise, but he swallowed it. Nausea sat in the pit of his belly like a jagged-edged stone.

"What happened?" he asked.

"She refused to marry the man she was betrothed to. That is forbidden. The man took her virginity so that she could never marry another."

"He *raped* her?"

The young man shrugged. "You Americans do not understand the ways of our people. She was *promised* to him. She would not yield to her future husband. Submission of the woman is the only way. Women cannot refuse their husbands in this manner. Even your Bible says that women should submit to their husbands in everything."

Anger boiled up inside Frank, but he held his tongue. "How did she die?" he asked instead.

"Amani slit her wrists," her brother replied, without compassion. "Killed herself. So now my sister is in hell, beyond salvation."

He then turned and left, his bad leg turning slightly outward as he trundled the battered wheelbarrow through the blighted landscape, as unconcerned as if he had been talking about the weather.

Frank had always hated rapists.

He hated them even more after that.

6

Present day

"You were raped?" Frank asked.

Diane nodded. There were tears in her eyes.

Frank sat back in the chair. "I'm so sorry to hear this. I don't want to sound insensitive, but did you know the person that did this to you? And did you report it?" he asked.

Her lower lip quivered. "I . . . It's complicated," she said.

They were silent for a moment after that. Diane, leaning forward, would not make eye contact with Frank. Her eyes were a million miles away.

And then she spoke. "After Janie broke up with Phillip in February, he was irate. He would call and text her over and over, at all hours of the night. He'd show up at her office when she was in the clinic. A couple of times, he parked his car here when she was due to come home, just waiting. It got even worse when she started seeing Dave again. Mama had warned Janie that Phillip was used to getting what he wanted, but none of us thought his obsession with her would be this profound. Jealousy just consumed him."

Diane shook her head. There was a distant, pained look in

her eyes. "One day, just days before Janie disappeared, this terrible . . . *man* showed up at our house. Right here. He broke in, barging his way into this place, a place he had no right . . ."

Diane shook her head slowly, her lower lip quivering. She was staring straight ahead, looking back into a past that only she could see.

"It was *awful*," she said, her voice a mere whisper.

—

July 14

Boodles jumped up and ran to the door. He growled at first and then began barking incessantly.

Diane glanced at the antique clock on the wall. It was a little after 7:00 a.m. Looking out of the bay window in the kitchen, she could see a deer and her fawn grazing in the yard in the early morning light, their tails flicking nervously.

"Oh, come on, Boodles," she said. "Leave the poor deer alone."

Living at Twin Oaks had not been Diane's idea. For the past ten years, she had kept her own tidy little cottage at Isle of Hope. Her garden was spectacular, and her view of the river was soothing (although she had to admit that the view from Janie's place was better). Diane's life at Isle of Hope had been predictable, which she liked. She had a good job at the public library, with predictable hours. It wasn't exciting, but it was orderly—and Diane, like her sister, thrived on order. After Phillip and Janie broke up, Janie had asked Diane to come to Rose Dhu and stay with her for a bit.

"I like having you around, and Boodles does, too," Janie had said. "You can stay as long as you like."

"A bit" turned into a few weeks, then several months.

Diane visited her Isle of Hope cottage several times a

week. She tended to the plants and checked her mail (she'd eventually get around to having it forwarded, but she was an unabashed procrastinator, as Janie always said). She figured she'd move back to Isle of Hope eventually, but she was very comfortable at Rose Dhu—and she truly enjoyed being around her sister again.

Janie and Diane had always been close. They were sisters, but they were also best friends. Ever since they were children, Diane and Janie had shared all their hopes and dreams. They watched *Say Yes to the Dress* together, swapped decorating ideas, and exchanged myriad books and recipes.

But that had all dried up when Janie and Phillip were dating. There had been weeks when the sisters barely even talked. Janie had found herself thrust into a different universe, going to society events in glittery evening gowns or flying to the Bahamas or Montana on Phillip's G4. He monopolized almost all of Janie's time when she was not at work and consistently limited Janie's interactions with her family. Phillip seemed to consider the O'Connor clan a nuisance, an annoying swarm of flies that must be constantly shooed away. He never warmed up to any of them even after he and Janie were engaged.

Diane had been surprised Janie had let that happen. *I guess love really is blind,* she thought, resigning herself to the inevitability of their separation.

So when Janie and Phillip broke up, Diane was neither surprised nor unhappy—and she was positively *elated* when Janie and Dave resumed their relationship. That fixed so many things, making all their lives much less complicated.

Most importantly, it brought the old Janie back.

Boodles was growling and pawing at the back door. *I don't see the deer anymore,* Diane thought. *Maybe the old boy just needs to go to the bathroom.*

She turned off the burglar alarm and opened the door. Boodles bolted outside, barking vociferously.

"Boodles!" she yelled, stepping out onto the back porch.

The man was a blur, coming at her so hard and fast that she had no time to react, no time to do anything. She barely even saw him.

Diane's head slammed against the door, exploding fireworks someplace behind her eyes. Her legs buckled, and she collapsed.

A heavyset brute dressed head to toe in camo and black loomed over her. "Well, you're obviously not that bitch doctor, but I suppose you'll do," he growled.

The man grabbed Diane by the shirt collar, dragging her back into the house on her butt. Diane, woozy and semiconscious, could do nothing.

Boodles was barking again, coming closer. The man pulled out a silenced handgun and fired a single shot. The bullet made a curious zipping sound as it tore through the air.

The old dog yelped once and fell quiet, collapsing into a heap.

Diane wanted to stop him, but the man was far stronger than she was. Her head throbbed. She felt a rivulet of a warm, sticky substance running down her face and into her mouth, metallic and salty.

She tried to think of other things: of God and sunlight and flowery meadows in springtime and anything, *anything* but this.

She could only see out of her right eye. She closed that eye tightly, trying to shut out the world, but it was no use: She could still hear him, smell him, and *feel* him, which was the most awful part of all.

Please, she prayed. *Please let it end.*

Diane lay there, her fists clenched into tight little balls, and prayed for a quick deliverance from this hell. She'd always been a good Catholic, faithfully attending church every Sunday and confessing every Friday. Today, however, the

Almighty seemed preoccupied with more pressing matters in the universe.

"I work for the Carruthers family," he said, his voice tinged with pride. "Do you know what that means?"

He leaned down so close that his lips brushed Diane's ear. Diane did not respond, saying nothing at all, but he answered his own question for her.

"It means I'm untouchable," he whispered.

At that moment, Diane had a nasty epiphany. The thought came to her in a sudden electric shock that jolted her good eye wide open. *He's going to kill me,* she thought. *That's why he's telling me this. He plans to make sure I'm not going to be around to say anything.*

Suddenly, there was a dull swatting noise, like someone striking a huge fly with a magazine—and then the man pulled himself away from her, his massive, stinking bulk abruptly lifted away.

"What the FUCK?" he roared, blood trickling down the side of his face.

Janie was standing in front of him, her right hand clutching a crowbar. She had hit him in the head with it, opening a nasty laceration right above the right eye that extended into his scalp.

Before the man could move, Janie struck him again—a golf swing this time, aiming for his crotch. The tire iron collided with his pubic bone with a *crack!* He doubled over in pain.

"Get out of my *house,* you asshole!" Janie screamed, standing over him.

She swung again and hit his knee, collapsing it inward. The man fell, struggling to pull up his pants, but he managed to get his right hand into one of the pockets, and then Diane saw it, gleaming dully in his fat, sweaty fist: the handgun, its dark steel gleaming against his pale white flesh.

"OK, bitch, let's see what you've got now," the man said,

grinning. He hiked his pants up around his waist and cinched his belt, keeping the gun leveled at Janie the whole time.

Janie's eyes narrowed into slits. "I know you," she said.

"What?"

"I recognize your voice. I know your *smell.* You're the guy who broke into my garage."

The man stomped toward her, his gun raised.

It was right then that Diane saw Boodles. The big lab, who was *never* quiet, had slinked through the open back door into the den behind the rapist, stalking his prey from the man's blind spot. Diane noticed the fur over Boodles's left thigh was matted with dark blood.

"I'm coming for you, bitch!" the man bellowed.

At that precise moment, Boodles lunged, fanged jaws open wide. The dog's mouth clamped hard on his right forearm and would not let go.

"Jesus Christ!" he yelled.

Boodles shook the man's arm violently, his sharp teeth tearing the skin and muscle clean off the bone. The gun skittered across the room, stopping beneath a nearby sofa.

"Aagh! Let me go!" the man screamed, wide eyed.

"Kill him, Boodles!" Janie barked.

The dog's furry legs splayed wide. He jerked his broad head back and forth, trying to rip the man's arm off.

Janie scrambled to retrieve the wayward handgun from beneath the sofa.

The man slammed his left fist into Boodles's skull, and the old dog yelped, releasing his death grip on his other forearm. The rapist held his tattered, bloody arm against his side. Boodles was growling at him, bloody teeth bared, his body coiled and ready to lunge.

Janie leveled the handgun at the man, aiming the barrel at his chest. "Get out of my house, or I'll kill you," she said.

Goggle eyed with pain, the man stumbled toward the

door. Blood welled up between his fingers, splattering crimson droplets across the heart pine floor.

And then he was gone.

Janie sprinted to the back door and locked the deadbolt. She dropped the handgun on the granite countertop and ran to Diane, who was sitting in a chair in the kitchen, her face buried in her hands.

"Let me see you," Janie said, kneeling beside her sister.

Diane, feeling her bloody face begin to swell, looked up at Janie. She was trembling all over. "That man—he said he works for *Phillip*, Janie."

"He doesn't work for Phillip." Janie shook her head. "I know just about everyone in the Carruthers organization, and I've never seen him."

"He told me he worked for the Carruthers family. He said he was untouchable."

Janie suddenly sat upright, staring off into forever. Her eyes had filled with tears. For a moment, despite all her pain, Diane felt sorry for her sister.

"Shit," Janie said quietly, shaking her head.

Diane stood up, trembling. A tiny rivulet of blood ran down the inside of her left thigh. Slowly, gingerly, she limped over to the bay window and placed her palms flat on the windowsill as she looked out across the river.

"What are we going to do?" Diane asked.

"I don't know," Janie said, shaking her head. "I truly don't."

7

Frank was stunned. He and Diane were still sitting together in the den, but it seemed like a different place somehow. The bright, sunny room now had a dark history, previously unseen, that seemed to poison the air around them.

"That all happened right here?" Frank stared at Diane. He glanced around the room. Boodles looked up at him and grinned, thumping his thick tail on the floor.

Diane looked away from him, eyes distant, but she nodded.

"And you never reported it?"

"I couldn't. I briefly thought about it after Janie disappeared, but I was too scared. With Janie gone, there would be no holding them back. If I reported it, I was worried the Carruthers organization might make me disappear, too."

"Did you tell anyone else about the assault?"

Diane shook her head. "Janie and I kept it quiet. Janie told Dave, of course, but that's it—and he promised he wouldn't talk to anyone else about it, because I insisted."

"Do you know where the man's gun is? You said he left it here."

Diane shook her head. "I haven't seen it since that day."

Frank looked at his legal pad. "You said Janie recognized the man, that he was the same guy who had broken into the garage."

Diane nodded. "She was certain of that. The garage break-in happened last fall, before Janie and Phillip ended their engagement. I don't remember the exact date."

"Do you recall the details?"

"Janie pulled into her garage after work one day, and some guy she'd never seen before was standing there in the dark. It freaked her out."

"Did the man attack her?"

"No. He just walked past her without saying a word, went right to the river, and she heard a boat motor cranking. Then he was gone."

"Did she call the police?"

Diane nodded. "That was before I was living here, but she got Phillip to come over, and the police came to investigate, so there should be a report. Phillip should remember it as well." Diane was trembling. "Janie finally learned his name, after he showed up here and . . . did what he did. His name is Trek Richards."

"Trek?"

"Like *Star Trek*. And he really did work for Phillip. He was not lying about that part."

Diane looked devastated, her eyes red rimmed. Her hands trembled as she brushed the hair from her face.

That's enough for today, Frank thought, standing up to leave. "Is there anything else you want to tell me—any other detail, even the tiniest thing?" he asked.

Diane pursed her lips, shaking her head slightly—but then she stopped, cocking her head. "Maybe one little weird thing, something Trek said while he was here."

"What is it?"

"I was half dazed, and I can't recall everything, but he kept talking to himself. In the middle of everything, he mumbled something about having to get on with things because he had a flight to catch. It was a weird comment, so it stuck in my mind."

Frank wrote that down. "I really appreciate your honesty and willingness to cooperate, Ms. O'Connor. I know talking about this isn't easy, but it may help us find Janie."

Diane looked up at him. "You think she's dead, don't you?" she asked.

"We don't really know, Ms. O'Connor. We don't have a body."

"They killed her. I know it," she said. She grasped Frank's hands in her own. "Promise me one thing, Detective. Promise me you won't let Phillip Carruthers get away with killing my sister."

Frank glanced at Diane. She was looking directly at him. Her cobalt eyes were like gemstones, so beautiful that he had to fight the urge to look away.

"I'll tell you this," she continued. "If Janie had never dated Phillip Carruthers, she'd still be around today. I'm a hundred percent certain about that. All the bad things in our lives have come from him."

8

Frank's interview with Diane O'Connor had bothered him.

He normally could emotionally dissociate himself from the people he interacted with at work. It was a self-preservation technique he'd learned in Afghanistan, and it was usually quite effective.

But Diane O'Connor seemed incredibly sad and desperate. She'd gotten to Frank in a way that most people didn't. His heart ached for her—and that puzzled him, compounding his sense of isolation. He was usually able to insulate himself from feelings like these. For some reason, he had not been able to do that today.

Get a grip, Frank, he thought. But he couldn't.

He had not felt this profoundly alone since Paulina died. His mind kept going back to that day (had it really been three years ago?), the scabbed-over wound in his soul ripped clean open by the tale of Diane's brutal rape.

Jesus Christ, he thought.

Frank's condo on White Bluff seemed cold and sterile as he opened the door. He hadn't been there much lately except to sleep, and even that had been fitful. The refrigerator was almost empty—leftover pizza, a few beers, a jar of Claussen pickles, a half-empty jar of Duke's mayo, an ancient, crusty bottle of Dijon mustard, and a package of Boar's Head sliced turkey past its sell-by date.

Maybe I need a dog, he thought.

He flipped through the mail, which he had picked up at the mailbox on the way in. It was mostly junk, as usual, but then he saw the envelope with blue fountain pen script on it and stopped cold.

"My God," he said out loud.

He recognized the loopy, calligraphic penmanship immediately. It was so much like Paulina's that it hurt his eyes. He picked up the letter opener from his desk, sat in his chair, turned on the green-shaded lamp on his desk, and carefully opened the envelope. His hands were trembling as he held the letter under the light.

Dear Frank, the letter began.

I'm sorry it's been so long since I've written. Time gets away from us and suddenly months have gone by, and we're left staring at the ceiling in the dark, wondering how we got so old. You'll see what I mean someday. It happens to all of us.

I've been thinking about you a lot lately. It's hard to believe that it's been three years since Paulina died. I still expect her voice when I answer the phone, and I sometimes think I see her car coming down my street. But it's always someone else, of course. She's gone, as much as my brain does not want to accept that.

I know you still blame yourself for what happened. Nothing I can say will change that, but I still want to say it: Paulina's death was not your fault. I loved my daughter, and I love you, too. What happened to Paulina was horrible, but it was something that no one could have predicted.

She was at her very best when she was with you. I had never seen her happier, not even as a child. You were so good to her,

Frank. And there is no one else I would have rather had as a son-in-law. You were her everything, and I know she was yours.

Please call me sometime. I know it may take some time, but I can wait until you're ready. At some point, I'd love to have dinner together and catch up. I truly miss you.

Love always,
Catherine

Gingerly, Frank put the letter down on the desktop and wiped tears from his eyes. "Dammit," he said. "I didn't need this today."

There was a bottle of vodka in the freezer. For a moment he thought about taking it out but decided against it. Too much potential for mayhem there.

Instead, he grabbed a cold Tropicália IPA from the fridge, opened the door to his balcony, and took a seat at the small table out there.

The lone potted cactus he kept on the table had shriveled up and turned a hideous gray. It was flopped over like a dead man's penis, albeit one spiked with tiny needles.

He lit a cigarette and watched as the smoke swirled about his head in the breeze. He tried to lose himself in the sonorous buzz of the cicadas as the sun settled in over the horizon, hoping to clear the cobwebs from his head and relax.

It wasn't happening.

He wasn't depressed, not really. Frank knew depression. For months after Paulina died, he'd languished in a dark and bottomless pit of misery. The world had become a bad joke to him, and the only way Frank muddled through it was by staying completely numb, anesthetizing himself to everything and everyone.

A car horn honked somewhere on Waters Avenue. A garbled exchange of curses ensued. Behind him, Frank heard the shrill *scree* of a raptor in a nearby tree, maybe a hawk.

He really needed a joint right now.

Frank still had nightmares about the day he'd come home and found her. Awakening in the middle of the night, his heart pounding and fingers clenched, he'd replay the whole scene in a continuous loop, like a clip from a bad horror movie.

The front door to their home had been left open. That had been the first clue.

Hernando Garcia had propped Paulina up against the island on the kitchen floor, legs splayed out, eyes wide open and unseeing. Her mouth was slightly agape, as if she was astonished. Blood covered her blouse and had spattered over the countertop, the oven, and the island as her dying heart had spurted her life away.

When Frank first saw her, he checked to see if she was still breathing. That was ridiculous, of course. The blade had sliced clean through her trachea and both carotids, cutting her neck all the way back to her spine.

Frank called 911 then, mainly because he didn't know what else to do. And then he called Pepper Stephens.

The five minutes or so that he sat there with her before the ambulance came were the worst of all. She was gone, and he knew it, and yet he was waiting with what was left of her. All he could do was cry and hold her hand, which was already cold and sticky with her blood.

Pep must have driven a hundred miles an hour. He arrived right after the ambulance.

The ambulance attendants checked her out and confirmed that she was dead, then called the cops. They did not move her. When Pep arrived, she was still sitting on the kitchen floor in a pool of dark blood.

"Jesus Christ," Pepper said as he glanced at Paulina's lifeless body.

He hugged Frank to his chest. Pep, as usual, smelled

vaguely of Old Spice, which Frank only recognized because it had been his dad's favorite aftershave.

"I'm sorry, Pep. I think I got some blood on you," Frank mumbled.

"Don't worry about it," Pep said.

The blood spatter analyst, an odd little gnomelike man who Frank was certain was an autistic genius, came next. The rest of the homicide team soon followed.

Pep took Frank into the living room while they picked Paulina's body up off the floor. "Let me have your gun, Frank," Pep said.

This was a good thing. Frank was insane with grief by that point. He had never understood suicide before, but he did that afternoon.

Frank handed Pepper his service Glock without saying another word.

They caught Garcia within a day's time. A convicted felon, his prints were all over the house, and he'd dropped the blood-covered murder weapon in an azalea bush in a neighbor's front yard as he left. That neighbor (good old Peggy Kravitz, God bless her) had seen Garcia leaving Frank's house covered in blood. She'd called 911 even before Frank did. Mrs. Kravitz was unflappable on the witness stand when she identified Garcia as the killer.

Garcia's motive was clear: Frank had busted up his Effingham County crystal meth operation a few years back. It had been the largest meth lab in South Georgia. After his conviction, Garcia had been sent to federal prison. But he still had lots of money, and he had used it to purchase the best hotshot defense lawyers money could buy. He had been released from his drug conviction after serving only seven years—and he desperately wanted revenge against the cop who put him away.

After Paulina's murder, Hernando Garcia was sent back to

prison, for life this time. He'd never get out again. But that was no consolation for Frank. A few months after Garcia returned to Reidsville State Prison for good, Frank had asked to meet with him. Surprisingly, Garcia agreed.

After he was seated in the prison's visitors' room, Frank said nothing at first. Instead, he just stared at Paulina's killer through the bulletproof glass.

Garcia was thinner. His hair had been cut short, and he had a new scar across his chin, but he still had that awful, flat, shark-eyed look. It was the look of all predators, simultaneously alert and cruel. His upper lip was curled into a perpetual sneer.

"I can't believe you agreed to meet with me," Frank said at last.

Garcia shrugged. "Got nothing better to do," he said.

Frank knew what he wanted to ask, but the words had lodged firmly in his throat and would not come out. His mouth was dry, his palms moist.

"Why did you kill Paulina?" Frank asked, at long last. He wasn't even certain he wanted to hear Garcia's answer.

"I went there to kill *you*," Garcia replied.

And there it was: What Frank had always thought had been confirmed.

Paulina had been collateral damage.

Frank felt sick. His eyes filled with tears. He wiped them away with his sleeve, but the nausea remained.

"How . . . how did it happen?" Frank said. His voice was hoarse.

"I jimmied the lock on your sliding glass door to get inside, but your lady saw me in the hall mirror. She picked up a knife from the kitchen and came after me. That woman fought me like a damned tiger. Sliced my forearms to ribbons. I've still got the scars," he said.

He held his arms up for Frank to see, but Frank shook his head, waving him off.

Garcia's voice cracked as he spoke. "I didn't really want to kill her, man. My beef was with you. But she fought me so hard that I thought for a minute that she was going to kill *me*. Eventually, I backed her up against the island in the kitchen and wrestled the knife away from her. I cut her throat so she couldn't come after me anymore. That was it." Garcia looked down for a second. When he looked back up, his eyes were bloodshot. "I should've just left, man," he said. "Can you forgive me?"

"You ruined my life," Frank said. Then he heard himself say something that surprised even him. "But I forgive you."

He meant it.

Frank simply couldn't carry the anger around anymore. Hatred and bitterness had leached out from the unplumbed depths of his soul like plutonium, killing him slowly from the inside, deadly and inexorable. He needed to be rid of it.

Still, Frank left the prison that day more depressed than ever.

Paulina would be alive today if she hadn't lived with me, he thought. *Garcia was coming after me, and Paulina died as a result.*

The hole Frank fell into after that was bottomless. For months, he barely existed. He sold the house the two of them had lived in because it was too full of memories, and he used the proceeds to pay for the nondescript condo he lived in now. He didn't really prefer living in cracker boxes like this, but after Paulina died, he simply didn't care anymore.

Before long, Frank had stopped caring about anything.

The depression was exhausting. It wore him out. But over time, it faded, too, like a flower pressed in wax paper between the pages of a book, leaving him with this soulless empty husk of a life.

Now, Frank just felt numb. A zombie stumbling through each day, he was anesthetized to the world. He supposed

that was better than the raw, searing pain he'd felt right after
Paulina died. Maybe.

Today had been a rough one. He'd been undeniably attracted to Diane O'Connor, which made him feel guilty because it felt like he was cheating on Paulina. He knew that was
irrational, but he couldn't help it. His attraction to Diane was
a problem in its own right; she'd been raped, and her sister
was missing. The whole thing felt completely unprofessional,
soaked with some intrinsic quasi-Biblical measure of unde-
fined sin. And then, when he got home, there was the letter
from Catherine. The beer wasn't helping one bit, and smoking
cigarettes did absolutely nothing.

And so, Frank gave in.

He hadn't smoked any pot in a while, but he kept a stash
of it just in case of moments like this. His buddy Cookie had
introduced him to it in Afghanistan. Pot seemed to calm his
jangled nerves when nothing else worked.

They might drug-test you, a little voice inside him said.

The voice was right, of course, but Frank was way beyond
caring.

He lit the joint and took a resounding hit, letting it fill his
lungs completely. He thought of Cookie, of Paulina, and everything else he had lost.

"Fuck it," he said out loud as he exhaled. And he meant it.

9

Frank had made another list of the critical people they needed to interview. He'd done this before, but he was a compulsive list-maker when he was in the middle of an investigation, deriving satisfaction from being able to list various things he had to do and then checking them off. This latest list read:

Phillip Carruthers
Diane O'Connor
Mary O'Connor
Richard O'Connor
Dave Wommack
Erika Carruthers
Janie's coworkers

Pepper had already questioned all of Janie's coworkers and her parents—Mary O'Connor, Janie's mother, and Richard O'Connor, Janie's father, who could not provide much history and then soon afterward had a heart attack and a stroke, never regaining consciousness. Interviewing Phillip and his sister, Erika, would require approval from Chief Brown since that would undoubtedly result in a visit from Morris Shefter. Frank was certain there would be others—there always were. But right now, Dave Wommack was Frank's only real remaining potentially accessible target.

Unfortunately, Dr. Wommack was a very busy man.

Frank called his orthopedic surgery office multiple times, leaving messages with the front office staff, but got nowhere. The staff stonewalled him, promising callbacks he never received and repeatedly assuring Frank that Dr. Wommack would call him "as soon as he can."

Apparently, he never could.

Frank went by the office in person but was told Dr. Wommack was not there. He went by Dr. Wommack's home, but no one answered the doorbell.

After a couple of days, Frank finally decided he would have to get creative.

Paulina had been a nurse anesthetist at Memorial, so Frank had some idea about how things worked there. He still had Paulina's hospital ID, as well as a couple of sets of Memorial scrubs that Paulina had taken for him to use as pajamas. He never used them, but since Paulina had given them to him, he couldn't bear to let them go. Frank also knew that doctors usually came to work very early, so he called the Memorial Hospital OR and pretended to be someone he was not.

"Hi, my name is Rich Cunningham, and I'm a third-year Mercer medical student who is supposed to be shadowing Dr. Wommack," Frank said. "I'm supposed to meet him tomorrow in the OR. Can you tell me when his first case starts?"

"Why, of course, dear," the receptionist said, in a honey-sweet drawl. "Let's see . . . Dr. Wommack is doing a total knee replacement starting at 7:30 a.m. tomorrow, followed by two arthroscopies, at 10:30 and 11:30, and then a left shoulder replacement at 1:00 p.m. After that, he's doing computer work in the office the rest of the afternoon. It's his admin day."

"Thank you so very much," Frank said, trying his best to sound like an overly eager medical student, the way Paulina had always described them to be. And then he hung up.

Frank rummaged through his bedroom closet, retrieving Paulina's old Littmann stethoscope. He purchased a white lab jacket at the uniform store, cut his hair, shaved his beard and mustache (which he had previously sworn he would never do), and dyed his hair back to the original shoe polish black shade of his youth.

Looking in the mirror, he was astonished.

"Not half bad for an old guy," he said to himself, rubbing his fingers across his newly clean-shaven chin. Frank had always stayed in decent physical condition. If he wore sunglasses to cover up his ancient eyes, he might even pass for someone twenty years younger. "Can't wear shades in the hospital, unfortunately," he said aloud.

By six the following morning, Frank Winger was stationed in the physicians' parking deck area at Memorial Health University Medical Center in his new identity as medical student Rich Cunningham. Fully decked out in scrubs, Paulina's stethoscope, and the med student lab coat, he looked the part, even down to the Memorial name tag (although his name tag, if anyone looked closely enough, said "Paulina").

Dave Wommack's massive black Denali SUV rumbled into the parking deck at 6:30 a.m. He had a red Georgia Bulldogs block *G* plate on the front, and his vanity license plate read "DAWG74," which represented Dave Wommack's jersey number as a Georgia offensive lineman.

Wommack parked the truck and locked it. Tall and broad shouldered, he was a much larger man than Frank had expected from his pictures. Dr. Wommack was carrying an overstuffed black backpack large enough for a weekend camping expedition.

"Dr. Wommack?" Frank asked, stepping into his role as shy medical student.

Wommack turned. "Can I help you?" he said.

"I'm . . . I'm . . . ," Frank stammered.

Wommack broke into a broad grin and clapped Frank on the back, almost knocking the wind out of him. "You must be the med student who called yesterday," he said. "Carrie said you'd be meeting me. Never had a student stake me out in the parking deck before, though. You must be really interested in orthopedics."

Frank nodded.

Dave grinned. "It's a competitive specialty, that's for sure, so you'll need every advantage you can get, and this is a good start."

He extended a meaty palm and shook Frank's hand.

"I'm Rich Cunningham," Frank said.

Dave stopped and stared at Frank. "Like the character from *Happy Days*?" Dave asked.

Frank blushed. *Busted.* "My parents loved that show," he improvised.

"You're a bit old for a med student," Dave said.

"About that . . . ," Frank began.

"You know, ortho is at least six years of residency after med school. I mean, I'm not trying to bust your bubble or anything, but if you're a third-year student, you've got eight more years to go, minimum, before you can even start practicing. Gotta think about that sort of thing, you know? Life moves fast. I mean, that's a cliché, but it's also true."

Frank decided it was time to come clean. "Listen, I'm not really a medical student," he said.

Wommack cocked his head to one side, a puzzled expression on his face. "You're not?"

Frank flashed his police badge. "I'm not. My name is Frank Winger. I'm a detective with the Savannah Police Department, and I've been investigating the disappearance of Janie O'Connor. I've been trying to talk to you all week, but your office has done a great job keeping me away from you. This was the only way I could speak to you."

"Well, it's about damned time," Dave said. "I've been wondering when you guys were going to call me. Let's go someplace we can talk in private."

—

Dave Wommack's office was utilitarian, almost spartan: a simple glass-top desk with a large double computer screen on top and a docking station for a tablet, a Bulldog paperweight, and a few neat stacks of papers. The usual diplomas were mounted neatly on the wall, along with a framed Georgia jersey and a picture of Dave shaking hands with former Georgia football coach Mark Richt. Twin bookshelves behind the desk contained a few awards and accolades—and at least four signed footballs.

"Getting to see you was difficult," Frank said. "Your staff kept stonewalling me."

Dave shrugged. "The office staff does that. They think they're protecting me. They once gave me a sign for my desk that said *Just say no* because I'm always overextending myself."

Frank nodded. He supposed that made sense.

The shelves also contained a photograph of Dave with an older couple. The man, rawboned and broad shouldered, wore a plaid red-and-black shirt, charcoal-gray overalls, and a battered baseball cap. His chestnut-colored skin was leathery and worn like an old saddle. He bore the hard expression of someone who had seen more than his share of heartache. The woman wore a simple cornflower-blue dress tied at the waist with a dark-blue belt. She was smiling. The edges of her eyes crinkled up so tightly that her green eyes were only slightly visible. Her faded blonde hair was pulled back in a ponytail, accentuating her high cheekbones. Frank could tell that she had once been beautiful—and still was, in the same way that the faded bloom of a daffodil still retained a vestige of its former glory.

"Your parents?" Frank asked, nodding at the photo.

Dave nodded. "They're good folks," he said. "I'm blessed."

On Dr. Wommack's desk was a framed photograph of Janie O'Connor. Janie was sitting on a dock, her face illuminated by the golden rays of a late afternoon sun. Her dark hair was swirling in a gentle breeze. She was staring straight at the camera with the same incredible sapphire eyes her sister had, head slightly cocked, her lips pursed in a bemused, playful smile.

"Gorgeous, isn't she?" Dave said.

"She really is," Frank said.

"I love that picture," Dave said. "It captures her well—her spirit, essence, whatever you want to call it. Janie has what the French call '*joie de vivre.*' Pardon my terrible pronunciation, but you get the idea. She's something."

"I understand," Frank said. *Paulina was like that,* he thought.

"I still can't believe she's gone. It's like a nightmare I can't wake up from."

Frank let that thought simmer for a moment. "Janie's sister, Diane, told me that you two were an item," Frank said.

Dave looked up at him sharply, his eyes red rimmed. "You say that like she was just somebody I used to date."

Frank shrugged. "That's precisely what Janie's sister said. That you dated."

"It's much more than that," Dave said. "I love her."

"How long did you and she date, the first time around?" Frank asked.

"From our sophomore year of undergrad until our senior year of medical school, right after match day. Seven years overall. I always assumed we'd get married. We were best friends before we started dating, but when we matched in different programs for residency, she decided that we needed to separate. It floored me. I never expected that."

"You weren't angry at her for breaking up with you like that?"

Dave shook his head. "Look, Janie has always been the ultimate pragmatist. When we were entering the residency matching program, UNC was her first choice and my second. I listed Johns Hopkins first, thinking there was no way I'd get in there. It's one of the top ortho programs in the world, and here I was, little ole Dave Wommack from Johnson County, hoping to match in Baltimore. I really figured Janie and I would both end up in Chapel Hill. It shocked me when I matched at Hopkins. When Janie realized that meant six years in different cities for both of us, she said, 'It makes absolutely no sense for us to try to maintain a long-distance relationship during the most important training period of our lives.' And that was how she ended it. There were no hard feelings between us, although I admit that it hurt me more than I let on."

"Diane told me you two had rekindled things recently."

"We had. We both ended up in Savannah after residency and stayed friends. After Janie broke up with Phillip, she called me a few times to talk, and we found ourselves back together. We had been dating again for a few months when she disappeared."

"So did you come to Savannah to practice because Janie was here?" Frank asked.

Dave smiled.

"Maybe," he said. "OK, probably. Coming out of Hopkins, I had lots of offers, but this one was near home, and Janie being here sort of clinched it. Like I said, I had always assumed we'd end up together."

Frank looked up at Dave, twiddling absently with the bell

of Paulina's stethoscope. "Dr. Wommack, did *you* kill Janie O'Connor?" he asked.

Dave sharply recoiled, as if a snake had struck at him. "What? You really mean that?"

Frank's stare remained steady. "The question has to be asked."

"Of course not! I told you—I love her."

"Most people who are murdered die at the hands of those who claim to love them. So where *were* you on the night of July 19, Dr. Wommack?"

"I was on ortho trauma call at Memorial. There were multiple trauma protocols that night. I was in the OR almost continuously until dawn. Dozens of people can back me up on that," Dave said.

"Let me get this straight, then: You say you knew her better than anyone, except maybe her parents and her sister. And yet you didn't seek us out to talk to us after she disappeared? Didn't volunteer *any* information?"

"I didn't really know anything, and I figured y'all would come to me, just like you have." Dave massaged his temples. "It's complicated."

"Try me."

"I'm not certain I should even tell you anything," Dave said. "I made a promise."

A chill trickled down Frank's back. *Is this it?* "We're trying to solve a possible murder case here, Dr. Wommack. A woman you love has vanished without a trace. So give it a shot."

Dave looked up. There were tears in his eyes. "OK. I suppose I should come clean with you," he said. Dave leaned back. His eyes were a thousand miles away. "After Janie broke it off with Phillip this past February, she called me. Our relationship picked right back up where it had left off years earlier. In some ways, it was even better. She seemed happy and content. She told me her time with Phillip had clarified exactly what she wanted in her life—and she wanted me. As spring drifted into early summer, we both realized that things might be evolving into something permanent."

Dave took a deep breath. "But in early summer, I began getting anonymous threats. At first, they were just emails and texts. I saved them all if you want to see them."

"What did they say?"

"Always the same thing: 'Leave the bitch alone.' I was sure they were about Janie."

Frank jotted that down. "Did you tell Janie about them?"

Dave nodded. "Of course. She was convinced it was Phillip feeling petty and jilted. She said to ignore them, that Phillip was childish but harmless. She thought he'd eventually give up."

"Did he?"

"He didn't. Things got worse. I found a dead rat in my mailbox one day, along with another note saying the same thing: 'Leave the bitch alone.' I took a picture."

Dave took out his phone and showed Frank a photo of a huge marsh rat. Its fur was matted with dark blood, the neck obviously broken. A bloodstained note accompanied it.

"Good Lord," Frank murmured.

"And then . . ." Dave cleared his throat. "Then came the fire."

PART TWO

THE FIRE

10

July 12

"You're getting too old for this," Janie said to Dave as she pulled off his jeans. They'd attended a welcome party for the new surgical interns thrown by the fifth-year surgery residents. Dave was off duty and had celebrated that fact with a few extra Jell-O shots. "You're barely able to stand. We're not undergrads anymore." She kissed him softly on the forehead.

"We're not?" Dave said, smiling at her warmly.

"No, you moron, we're not. As much as you'd rather believe otherwise."

She pulled the covers over him and kissed him again—on the lips this time.

"Get some sleep. I'm going over to my place," she said. "I have to feed Boodles, and I'm on call this coming weekend."

"I love you," Dave said, a crooked smile on his face.

"I know," Janie said, smiling back. "I love you, too."

She flicked off the light. "Sweet dreams," she said.

Janie plugged in his cell phone beside the bed and closed his bedroom door. Dave was asleep in seconds.

He was still fast asleep when his cell phone rang a few hours later, at 1:00 a.m.

"Hello?" Dave said, momentarily confused as he pushed back against the densely intertwined cobwebs of sleep and vodka shots.

"Dave, your front porch is on fire," his neighbor's voice said.

Suddenly wide awake, Dave leaped out of bed and sprinted to the front door. As he flung the door open, he was met by an orange wall of flames. He slammed the front door, called 911, then grabbed the fire extinguisher from the pantry and sprinted around to the front of the house.

The entire porch was ablaze. Flames licked the eaves and had even reached the margins of the roof, curling the edges of the shingles. A thick column of black smoke, swirling with embers that danced into the sky and winked out, billowed into the night, permeating the air with the oily aroma of burning tar.

Dave directed the fire extinguisher toward the center of the flames. White foam poured from the nozzle, but the flames just consumed it, getting hotter and hotter.

"Jesus Christ!" Dave shouted, staring at the fire extinguisher as if it were an alien artifact.

Screwing up his courage, Dave stepped closer so that he was almost in the flames. His face was burning; the aroma of singed hair filled his nostrils. Emptying the entire contents of the extinguisher into the center of the blaze, Dave saw the flames finally begin to die back, bit by bit, until they finally fizzled and sputtered out.

The entryway to Dave's porch was a smoking black hole. Despite the soot, he could still read the message someone had spray-painted in bright red on the tan-colored brick wall: *Leave the bitch alone!*

By the time the fire trucks arrived, there wasn't much left

to do. Neighbors had gathered on the sidewalk to gawk, but Dave ignored them. He wanted to speak to the firefighters first.

A stocky, muscular fortysomething man with close-cropped hair and a sunburn, still in full gear, was filling out paperwork on a clipboard when Dave approached him.

"I'm Dave Wommack. This is my place," he said.

"Bob Christian. I'm the crew chief," the man said, extending his hand. "Are you OK?"

"I'm fine, thanks," Dave said, shaking his hand.

"Mr. Wommack, as I'm certain you're already aware, it's pretty clear this was arson," Christian said.

"No shit," Dave said.

"You need to speak to the police. They'll send someone out here soon."

"I will, trust me."

"You know, you're very fortunate the whole house didn't go up. It was this close," Christian said, holding his index finger and thumb very close together. He closed the cover to the clipboard and put his pen behind his ear. "Stay safe," he said, walking away.

The police arrived in ten minutes or so. The officer, a ramrod-straight Black man who identified himself as Terrance McGillicuddy, had eyes so dark that Dave couldn't see the pupils. McGillicuddy immediately struck Dave as someone who wouldn't take shit from anyone.

"That looks personal," McGillicuddy said, pointing at the inscription on the wall.

"It is," Dave said.

"Do you have any idea who might have done this?"

"I have my suspicions," Dave said.

"Who might it be?"

"Phillip Carruthers."

McGillicuddy looked at Dave with a bemused expression,

his eyebrows raised. "Phillip Carruthers, the billionaire, set fire to your front porch?"

"Well, him or somebody working for him."

Officer McGillicuddy shook his head. "You sure it wasn't Bill Gates?" he said, a thin smile creasing his face.

"I have my reasons for suspecting Phillip Carruthers," Dave said. "I'm dating his ex-fiancée."

"Hey, I heard about all that! My wife is all into the Savannah gossip. She told me about the postponement of the Wedding of the Century. Wasn't Lionel Richie supposed to be performing?"

Dave shrugged. "I have no idea. I wasn't invited," he said. "And the Wedding of the Century wasn't just postponed. It's off for good. No matter what Playboy Phil tells people, Janie is with me now."

McGillicuddy chuckled. "Playboy Phil. That's what my wife calls him, too," he said. "Well, look, as of right now, all of this is just conjecture. We need proof—an eyewitness, camera footage, something tangible. The fact that you are dating Playboy Phil's ex isn't enough to bring him in for questioning."

"Wait a minute," Dave said. "I almost forgot. I have a Ring doorbell camera. Put it in a few years ago. All it had ever showed were deliveries from Amazon and UPS, plus an occasional Jehovah's Witness, so I haven't been paying it much attention. I haven't looked at the feed in over a year, but I'm sure I can access it."

"Can you pull it up on your phone?" McGillicuddy said.

"I can," Dave said. He logged into the Ring website and pulled up that morning's video feed.

The two men crowded around Dave's phone.

"And there he is," Dave said.

A heavyset man in a camo hoodie materialized on Dave's front porch, walking out of the darkness. He smashed the porch light with a pipe, causing the camera to flicker momentarily before it switched to infrared.

The man was a ghost in black and white, eyes glowing, as he spray-painted the inscription on the front porch wall. After dousing the entire porch with liquid from a two-gallon plastic gas can, he stepped back and lit a cylindrical wad of paper, then tossed the lit fuse onto the porch. The entire screen then filled up with flames. Nothing else was visible after that.

"Well, it's not Phillip Carruthers, but you've got the perp on film, all right. It's clearly arson, and you can see his face. Facial recognition software has come a long way these days. If this guy has any criminal record, we can nail him," McGillicuddy said.

"Can you call me if you find out anything?" Dave asked.

"I will," McGillicuddy said. "Here's my card. Send me that video as soon as you can. You can use the email on my card. And if you think of anything else, call me—day or night. I'll have the fire scene investigation team come out here in a bit, so don't clean up just yet. We can learn a lot from the site."

"Will do," Dave said.

After sunrise, Dave called Janie and told her about the fire.

"I think *the bitch* is referring to me," Janie said. "This has to be Phillip's doing."

"That's what I thought. But the guy on my Ring camera isn't Phillip. It's somebody else."

"Send me the picture," Janie said.

After looking at it, Janie gasped and said something that chilled Dave to the bone. "I recognize him," she said. "That's the same guy who broke into my garage last year."

"Good Lord," Dave said.

The fire scene investigators were meticulous, going over every bit of the scene in minute detail. Before the day was up, they'd know the accelerant (kerosene) and the paint type (Benjamin Moore Million Dollar Red, 2003-10).

More importantly, it took the police only one day to come up with a name. Officer McGillicuddy called Dave later that night to tell him the news. "Dr. Wommack, do you have any sort of beef with a guy named Trek Richards?"

"I don't know anyone by that name," Dave said.

"Well, that's who set your porch on fire. We have a positive ID on him. US Army vet dishonorably discharged. He has a criminal record a mile long, mostly minor stuff. There's no prior record of arson, though. He runs a company called SecuriCorp. Ever heard of them?"

"Nope," Dave said.

"They're local. Interestingly, they do all the security for the Carruthers organization. That's their only account. So in a way, you were right," McGillicuddy said.

"That explains a few things," Dave said.

"We can make an appointment for you to provide a formal statement tomorrow," Officer McGillicuddy said.

After the two of them hung up, Dave thought about the implications of all of this. It was more obvious than ever that Phillip Carruthers was not going away quietly.

I need to talk to Janie again, he thought.

Dave tried calling her several times but only got her voicemail. He figured she was probably in the OR.

He texted her instead: *Call me when you get a chance. It's not urgent, but there's something you need to know.*

Janie did not call him back until late morning on the following day. When they spoke, her voice seemed strained. Dave picked up on it immediately.

"You OK?" he asked.

"Never better. Just a long day in the OR. What's up?"

"The police were able to ID the guy who set fire to my front porch. His name is Trek Richards. And get this: He runs a company called SecuriCorp. Ever hear of them?"

Janie sighed. "I have. They're the security company for

Carruthers Enterprises. I've seen their logo on the trucks they use on the estate," she said. Janie paused a moment, then said, "Shit."

There was a hard edge to Janie's voice now. Dave could almost *feel* it, like a knife blade dangling in midair.

Dave knew what that meant. He'd seen it in action, in the OR and on the athletic field—the titanium core that had made Janie a great competitive athlete and a phenomenal surgeon.

The wheels are turning in there, Dave thought.

But he also knew better than to ask Janie what her plans were at this point. That would break her thought process up in its formative stages, during the time when she was putting all the pieces together. Janie's brain was off-limits to all outsiders when she was processing data and formulating a plan, so he gave her some space.

"Call me later, OK?" she said. "I've got to think."

"Deal. Love you."

"I love you, too," she said. And he could tell she meant it.

11

Present day

Frank was flummoxed.

"So a guy who works for Phillip Carruthers sets fire to your porch and spray-paints an insult on your house that specifically references your girlfriend, and then she goes missing a week later? And you somehow don't think this is important enough to go to the police?" he asked.

Dave shifted in his chair. "It's really complicated," he said.

"This whole damned *thing* is complicated, Dr. Wommack. Your girlfriend has vanished without a trace. We're trying to figure it all out, but when people know potentially relevant details and fail to report them, that gets in the way of our investigation. What if this Trek guy is responsible for Janie's disappearance?"

"Look, I promised a person I care about that I'd keep some things quiet. I'm a man of my word. I want to help you, but I don't want to violate anyone's trust."

"Who did you make a promise to?" Frank asked.

Dave sighed. "Diane O'Connor. Janie's younger sister."

Frank paused, blinking. Taking a deep breath, he decided

to go ahead and jump into the deep end. "Was it about her sexual assault just after the fire?"

Dave's eyes widened. "You know about that?"

Frank nodded.

"Well, that simplifies things," Dave said.

"Trek Richards is the man who raped her."

Dave's gaze was steady. "I know that now."

"That makes him a prime suspect in Janie's disappearance, don't you think?"

"It does."

"And you were just going to say nothing?"

Dave fidgeted in his chair. "I probably would have come forward sooner rather than later. But the rape freaked Diane out. When Janie told me about it, the day after it happened, she made me promise not to tell *anyone.* Diane was certain Trek would return and finish the job and that the Carruthers organization would cover their tracks. You don't cross the Carruthers family. You know that. *Everybody* knows that."

"They've got a lot of influence. . . ."

"It's more than influence. Bad things happen to people who cross them. Not just lawsuits. Surely you have heard those stories."

"That's just a lot of small-town gossip, Dr. Wommack. I've never seen anything credible to that effect."

"They cover it up. Too many people owe them too many things. I kept trying to tell Janie that while they were dating, but she said she was in love with Phillip, at least until she saw his true colors and broke up with him."

"Why did they break up? Do you know?"

Dave nodded. "Of course," he said. "Janie told me all about it."

—

February 17

Lauren Wycroffe, Phillip and Janie's wedding planner, was a bubbly little pixie who looked like Tinker Bell without wings. She had been given an unlimited budget for the Carruthers-O'Connor nuptials—not unexpected for an event the *Savannah Morning News* society page had deemed the Wedding of the Century. Various celebrities, from Elton John and Jennifer Aniston to Tom Hanks and Rita Wilson, were allegedly planning to attend. The governor would be there, of course, as would everyone and anyone who was socially prominent in Coastal Georgia. Money and power afforded one access to a rather exclusive circle, and Phillip had both. He'd forged many valuable connections during his lifetime, and people realized that wedding attendance was a reasonable and economical means of societal payback.

"We thought we'd have the cake done by Rodolfo. He's in New York, of course, but he's willing to fly down here to demo different types of cake and icing for us. He can show you all the designer cakes he's done for royalty and A-list celebrities. Rodolfo is the best in the world at what he does. We're so excited to have him!" Lauren exclaimed. Her green eyes sparkled.

Janie looked at a photograph of Rodolfo, the so-called cake designer to the stars, which Lauren displayed on her cell phone. He was a serious-looking, heavily tattooed mass of muscle and sinew dressed all in black. His charcoal eyes glowered beneath heavy eyebrows.

"Why can't we just have someone in Savannah do the cake?" Janie asked.

Lauren cackled, as though the suggestion was so absurd as to not even merit consideration. Patting Janie's arm, she shook her head and spoke to her in a soft Southern lilt. "Honey, there's *nobody* in this town who can do what Rodolfo does. And listen, I get it. I'm a Savannah girl, too. I use local talent whenever we can. But this wedding is just too big an event to leave to chance—and your Phillip has told me that he wants it to be the best of the best, no excuses." Lauren batted her impossibly long eyelashes and grinned a toothsome smile. "After all, that's what he's paying me for, darlin'. He wants it to be a night to remember!"

It should be a night to remember even without all this, Janie thought.

Janie had always imagined her wedding would be a simple, private affair—close friends and family, a priest, and perhaps a violinist or a soloist inside the Cathedral of St. John the Baptist. Her plans for a simple family wedding had now mutated beyond all recognition. It was still to take place at the cathedral, but Phillip's people had transformed the event into a hulking social Godzilla, trampling everything in its path.

We'll straighten this out over dinner tonight, Janie thought.

Janie had been looking forward to their upcoming dinner for one specific reason: Anna Brown, at Phillip's insistence, would be doing the cooking.

Anna had been with the Carruthers family for decades. A proud, no-nonsense African American woman in her seventies, she took proprietary ownership of everything that went on in the Carruthers family. When they had first met over a year earlier, Anna had not spoken much to Janie. Janie could feel herself being sized up under Anna's penetrating stare.

"How long has she worked here?" Janie whispered then, during an interlude when Anna had left the room.

"My whole life," Phillip had replied.

Phillip then told Janie about Anna's amazing backstory.

Cynthia Carruthers hired Anna as a cook and housekeeper in 1980, when Anna was about thirty. In those days, Anna had no car, so she rode the bus from her home in Coffee Bluff to the old Carruthers home every day.

It did not take long for Cynthia and Anderson to realize that Anna was smart and hardworking. She was also honest and fiercely loyal. With that realization, her duties (and compensation) rapidly expanded. She not only cleaned and cooked but, over time, assumed the day-to-day chores of running the entire Carruthers family household and the attached five hundred–acre estate. She managed the books, scheduled and supervised all repairs and maintenance, and even wrote checks to tradesmen for any jobs they had done. Anderson and Cynthia trusted her with everything—and she had never disappointed them, not once.

"You're the best employee I've ever had," Anderson was fond of saying.

"Thank you, Mr. Carruthers," Anna would reply, smiling briefly before going back to work.

After Anderson Carruthers died, Phillip decided to move out of his townhouse on Pulaski Square in downtown Savannah and build his own home elsewhere on the estate. Anna personally supervised the construction of Phillip's house from the foundation to the roof, staying on top of all the subcontractors until Phillip's sprawling mansion was completed. Even more than the Carruthers homeplace, where Cynthia now lived alone (with twenty-four-hour nursing care), Phillip's place truly *belonged* to Anna. She had built it, she ran it, and no one ever questioned that rigid, ironclad hierarchy.

Anderson Carruthers had been particularly fond of Anna. He appreciated Anna's uncompromising attention to order, a trait they shared. Moreover, he appreciated her role as a second mother to both of his children. More approachable than Anderson and wiser than Cynthia, Anna was the Carruthers family lodestone, a solid bastion of common sense, and Phillip and Erika invariably sought her counsel when it came to dealing with any "outsiders," which was Anna's term for anyone who was not a member of the immediate Carruthers family. If a friend or potential romantic interest did not pass muster with Anna, they would no longer be welcome on the property.

That was just the way things were. No one ever questioned her judgment.

In 2005, Anderson showed the depth of his appreciation for Anna by building her a very comfortable home on the Carruthers property. Perched on a tidal creek deep in the primeval maritime forest behind the old Carruthers place, the gift of Anna's home was a gesture of respect and admiration for which Anna was incredibly appreciative. It had only cemented her loyalty to the old man, a degree of loyalty that was already unquestioned.

While Erika and Phillip were children, Anna had cooked most of the meals for the Carruthers family. After Anderson Carruthers died, she limited her culinary efforts to the meals she prepared for Cynthia at the old family place each day, delegating food prep at Phillip's home to other hired help. Still, at Phillip's request, she'd occasionally prepare a special meal at his home.

Tonight was to be one of those nights.

After her initial cool reticence, Anna had warmed up to Janie. The two of them now got along quite well. There was a mutual respect between them, a respect that Janie greatly appreciated.

Janie parked her Volvo outside the house and was met by Alphonso Hernandez, Phillip's unfailingly pleasant parking attendant and groundskeeper. "Good evening, Dr. O'Connor," he said, grinning. "May I take your keys?"

"Can we leave the car close by the house this time, Al? I think I'm the only person here tonight, besides Phillip and Miss Anna."

"Of course, ma'am. Are you on call this evening?"

"No, that's not it. I just wanted to be able to get to my car if I needed to. I have a bunch of samples from the wedding planner that I might need access to, and I didn't want to have to walk all the way over to the garage to get them."

Alphonso saluted. "Roger that, ma'am. We'll leave it close by the front."

Janie was greeted at the door by Phillip's personal assistant, a muscular, broad-shouldered giant named Carmine Carpeggio.

"Good evening, Dr. O'Connor," Carmine said in his deep, mellifluous voice.

"Good evening, Carmine," Janie said, smiling.

Carmine, with close-cropped hair and an earpiece in place, was dressed all in black, as always. His posture was ramrod straight, his eyes dark and inscrutable. Carmine was polite and unfailingly professional, but Janie had never seen him smile, not once.

"Mr. Carruthers asked that I take you into the dining room. He'll be down directly."

"Thank you, Carmine," she said.

She followed Carmine through the foyer, with its vaulted marble ceiling and massive wrought-iron chandelier, and into the dining room. The room was traditional, with a large antique wooden Charleston-style table covered with a spotless white tablecloth. A massive fireplace, gas logs burning low, stood at one end of the room. Over the mantle hung a framed oil painting of a smiling Anderson and Cynthia, with a marsh background painted in the autumnal palette of the setting sun.

The door to the butler's pantry swung sharply open, and Anna came bustling through, arms extended wide. "Dr. O'Connor, so good to see you again!" Anna exclaimed, grinning from ear to ear.

"*Please* call me Janie, Miss Anna. I don't need to be called by my professional title among friends."

"Why, then, you can just call me Anna. Let's not stand on ceremony, seeing as you're going to be part of the family soon."

Anna hugged Janie so tightly that she could hardly breathe. During their embrace, she whispered, her voice barely audible as her lips softly brushed Janie's ear, "You're so good for my boy. God bless you, child."

That was all she said: an exchange among women, something private that was shared and understood. It was, however, a gift that also carried a certain expectation, the sort of thing one might find engraved in a locket, along with a tiny photograph or a lock of a loved one's hair.

Phillip swept into the room in grandiose fashion. He was dressed casually in a polo shirt, khaki pants, and docksiders without socks. He looked tanned and rested. "Two of my favorite women in the world!" he exclaimed. He kissed Anna on the cheek and then did the same to Janie. "What's for dinner, Anna?"

"You know the menu, young man. You picked it out yourself," Anna replied, a tight smile on her face.

Phillip, grinning, carefully lifted the lid of each of the chafing dishes and nodded his approval. "So I did," he said. "It all looks spectacular, as usual."

"It smells delicious!" Janie said.

"I fixed you grilled chicken and rice with collard greens, a salad, and homemade biscuits," Anna said.

"That sounds wonderful," Janie said.

Phillip pulled out a chair at the head of the dining room table and motioned for Janie to take a seat.

"Do you think we could just eat in the kitchen?" Janie asked. "This seems so formal."

"Of course, if you want," Phillip said.

They relocated the two plates, two napkins, and two sets of silverware onto the antique oak table in the kitchen, which had once belonged to Phillip's grandmother. It was simple and basic, like the meal Anna was serving them, but it was also beautiful. A vase sat in the center of the table, flanked by a pair of glass candlesticks.

Anna extinguished the candles in the dining room and

lit the candles on the kitchen table. She placed a bottle of red wine on the kitchen table and stashed another bottle of white into a silver ice-filled wine bucket, which she moved from the dining room into the kitchen.

The air in the kitchen was filled with the satisfying aroma of the food simmering in the buffet servers.

It smells like home in here, Janie thought. She felt warm and secure. All seemed right with the world.

"I can plate it for you if you like," Anna said.

"There's no need for that, Anna. We'll serve ourselves," Phillip said.

"Why don't you join us, Anna? There's plenty here for three," Janie said.

"That's very kind of you, but if it's OK with the two of y'all, I need to get back over to Ms. Cynthia's place. The nurses are there, of course, like always, but she always wants me to prepare her for bed. I'll come back over here after she goes to sleep and clean up. Y'all help yourselves and enjoy your privacy. I'm sure you two have lots to talk about, with the wedding coming up and all."

"Thank you so much for making us dinner. I'm sure it will be delicious," Janie said.

Anna smiled gently at her. "You're certainly welcome, child," she said.

The two women hugged once again—more briefly this time—and just like that, Anna was gone, disappearing abruptly into the South Georgia night. Janie could hear the electric whine of Anna's golf cart as she sped away into the darkness.

Phillip filled their plates and then sat down. They ate wordlessly for a moment, savoring the taste of the food.

"This is delicious," Janie said at last.

"It always is," Phillip said, nodding. "Personally, I like Anna's cooking better than most of the things Louis makes, although I would not tell him that. He's a very proud man."

"The coq au vin Louis made on the island was excellent," Janie said.

"I think Anna's chicken is better."

With a mouthful of Anna's chicken serving as evidence, Janie had to agree.

"So how is the wedding planning going? You like working with Lauren? She's supposed to be the best," Phillip said.

Janie put her fork down, sipped her wine, and cleared her throat. "I've been meaning to talk to you about that," she said.

"It's going to be grand, babe. At the cathedral, just like you wanted. The best floral designers on the East Coast, that Rodolfo guy from New York doing the cake, a reception catered by Bobby Flay, and Lionel Richie as the entertainment. They'll be talking about this wedding for years," Phillip said.

"Don't you think it's a bit much?" Janie said quietly.

Phillip straightened up, a perplexed look on his face. "Too much? What do you mean?"

She placed her hand on his arm. "It's just that . . . Well, it is true that I always wanted to be married in the cathedral. It feels like a holy place. I always felt that God was in there. But that place holds over a thousand people. I never thought we'd fill it up. And there's all this other stuff, all these details. It just seems so complex. Can't we scale it back a bit? Maybe make it a tad more intimate? It's just . . . It's a *lot*. And I know it's costing you a fortune."

Phillip grinned at her. "You're worried about the cost. I get it. Well, nothing's too good for my fiancée. I'd bring London Bridge here for you if that would make you happy."

"It's not the cost. That's not it at all. It's the *scale* of things. It almost seems like we're putting on a show for everyone else. I don't need that sort of extravaganza. I just need *you*."

Phillip fixed Janie with a slightly peeved expression, as if he'd bitten into something sour. "Let me get this straight: You're saying the wedding is too *big*?"

"That's exactly what I'm saying!" Janie said. "It's blown up into this huge deal that everyone in Savannah seems all excited about, but it's supposed to be *our* wedding, you know? Our families should be at the center of it all. Only we're not. It's like the ceremony is the sideshow, not the main act. Things have gotten a little out of control."

Phillip shook his head. "I don't think you understand all the implications here." His voice was measured but firm.

"I understand that Lauren has been planning our wedding with very little input from me, and she blows me off whenever I make any sort of suggestion."

Phillip put down his fork and wiped his lips with his napkin. "I get what you're saying. It's your big day. But since I'm paying for everything, I just thought you'd let me do a few things my way," he said.

A cold chill ran down Janie's back. She heard her mother's prophetic words echoing in her brain: *Men like Phillip are used to getting what they want.*

"Well, of course you're paying for everything, and I know it's going to be beautiful, but I just thought it would be a little less . . . grand, maybe?"

"I'm giving you a wedding that most women would be absolutely thrilled with, a wedding that people in this town will remember *forever*, and you don't want it?"

One of the candles was guttering now, its flame low and dim, the smoke from it drifting across the room like a wraith.

"I just thought it would be friends and family. Something more intimate," Janie said quietly.

Phillip chuckled, shaking his head. "That wouldn't be very many people at all," he said.

Janie put her hands in her lap and sat silently, her cheeks burning.

Phillip reached into Janie's lap and gently took her hand. "I know this is all weird to you, and I'm sorry that the wedding planner is so overbearing, but this is no ordinary wedding. My family's social obligations are extensive, our business relationships are complex, and this wedding needs to do more than just celebrate our union. It needs to be an *occasion*, an opportunity to solidify some important social and business connections. I know that all brides want to be the center of attention on their wedding day, but in this case, it's not just about you."

"I never thought that it was just about me. I just never understood that our wedding was expected to be a major networking event for Carruthers Enterprises," Janie said.

Phillip turned the wattage up on his most perfect grin and leaned forward, placing a hand on Janie's shoulder. "Hon, I'm sorry I didn't clarify that. Do you think Meghan Markle didn't understand that sort of thing when she agreed to marry Prince Harry? Being in a family like ours requires an understanding of the responsibilities that go with the territory. The Telfair Ball experience you had the other night? That was just the beginning. Being my wife will be a full-time job."

Janie stared at him. "What did you just say?" she asked.

"I'm only saying what should be obvious by now: As Mrs. Phillip Carruthers, certain things will be expected of you. That's all."

Janie was aghast. Phillip had never mentioned anything to this effect before. She couldn't believe what she was hearing. "I'm a *surgeon*, Phillip. *That's* my full-time job. Things are expected of me at work, too."

"You know, I know we haven't really talked about this, but I kinda figured after we were married, you might go part-time. I'll bet you'd enjoy being able to escape from the day-to-day stress of being a surgeon. Who wants that sort of hassle if they don't need it?"

Janie felt a volcanic anger boiling inside her. "Well, Phillip, this is certainly a new wrinkle. I'm a surgery attending, for

God's sake, a full professor at Mercer Medical School. I've dedicated myself to training young surgeons and teaching medical students, and I'm damned good at what I do. I never intended to go part-time or quit work after we are married!"

"You won't need the money, Janie."

"You're missing the point. I don't *care* about the money. I put my life on hold for ten years for my medical education and residency. I don't do surgery as a hobby. It's my *passion*. Don't you understand that?" She stood up. "I think I need to go now," she said, grabbing her purse.

Phillip's brow was furrowed, his eyes narrowing. "You're not done eating," he said coldly.

"I just need to leave," she said, shaking her head. "This is too much to process."

"Janie, wait . . ."

She whirled to face him. "I just don't get it. I really thought you knew me, but maybe you don't. Maybe we've rushed this too much." She turned again and walked toward the front door. Phillip sprinted ahead of her, meeting her just as she flung the door open.

"Janie, I'm sorry. You're right. It *was* presumptuous of me to expect all this without even discussing it with you. Let's go back inside and talk." His voice sounded desperate.

Janie stepped past him into the cool night air. She was grateful that Alphonso had left her Volvo in the driveway and had not taken it around to the garage area like he usually did. She used the remote to unlock it. The stars were out overhead, the Milky Way spangling the moonless sky with a scattering of tiny diamonds.

"Look, Phillip, we can talk some more tomorrow, OK? Right now, I just need to go home."

Phillip switched on the brilliant floodlights along the front driveway so that the two of them could see one another more clearly. The lights lit up Phillip's carefully landscaped front yard like a football stadium.

"Janie, why don't you just stay here tonight? It's late. You don't want to drive all the way back to your place at this hour. It might be dangerous."

Janie laughed, shaking her head in disbelief. "Phillip, I really don't know what sort of girl you think I am, but there's one thing I'm not: I'm no damsel in distress. I'm a *surgeon*. I get called into the hospital at all hours of the night. I can go from being sound asleep to wide awake in a matter of seconds. I walk into the Memorial ER all the time through a waiting room filled with all sorts of less-than-upstanding individuals and think nothing of it. I can take care of myself. I certainly don't have any issues with driving back to my house at, what, 8:40 p.m.? Come on!"

"Well, you might as well get used to living here, right? Once we're married and you sell your place, you'd go in from here anyway. So maybe you could do a dry run—you know, see what it's like to use this place as a home base. I don't know."

Janie drew back, eyes widening. "So now you're telling me you want me to sell my *house*?"

"No. I mean, not really. I just figured we'd be living here, and you don't need two houses. But if you want to keep it, sure. Whatever." Phillip's voice was unnaturally high-pitched, as if he'd been breathing helium. He was bailing furiously from a sinking ship, but he couldn't possibly bail fast enough. The ship was going down no matter what. "I mean, this place is ideal for raising kids. It's safe and secluded. There are lots of places for children to explore in the compound."

Janie put her hands on her hips, eyes blazing. "Don't go there again, Phillip," she said.

"But you want children, right? You said you did before."

"Oh, I want children, all right. I want lots of them. But that doesn't mean I'm just going to stay locked up like Rapunzel in an ivory tower, barefoot and pregnant, wasting all my years of training, when I could be out there helping people and teaching future doctors. Come on, Phillip, you should know me better than that. Have you ever thought I was the sort of person who could just sit at *home*?" She shook her head and began walking briskly toward her car.

Scowling, dark eyebrows creased, Phillip strode toward her, covering the ten feet between them in three strides. He reached her just as she opened her car door, grabbing Janie's left hand in his and gripping it tightly. "You see that ring? It's three carats, and it is flawless. It cost me over a hundred thousand dollars. It signifies a *commitment*, Janie. We're committed to each other."

"Dammit, Phillip, let go of me!" She pulled her hand away, glaring at him. "What the hell was *that*?" she asked, kneading her hand.

Phillip's face was flushed. He ran his fingers through his hair. "I'm sorry, Janie. I lost my temper."

"Jesus Christ, Phillip!"

"I'm *sorry*," he said again, with emphasis.

Janie twisted the engagement ring off her finger and handed it to Phillip. "I'll tell you what: You can have your hundred-thousand-dollar ring back. Go buy yourself a Porsche."

"Janie, come on."

"*No*. I mean it. Don't blame all this on simply being 'angry.' You can't tell me that there wasn't some shred of truth to what you said there. Otherwise, you wouldn't have said it."

Janie stared at Phillip, her eyes hard and cold. "You need to decide what sort of wife you want, then maybe we can talk. Or not. But for now, we're done here. I'm going home to Rose Dhu, back to the house that I transformed from a goddamned *wreck* with my own two hands. You're on your own this weekend."

Janie got into the Volvo and slammed the door. Cranking

the engine, she glanced in the rearview mirror. Phillip was silhouetted against the blazing floodlights, his arms open as if in supplication.

She turned a corner, and Phillip was gone.

12

Dave Wommack had to go to the OR for surgery, which was OK. Frank had more than enough to go on now. He left Dr. Wommack's office with renewed optimism about solving Janie O'Connor's disappearance.

Dr. O'Connor was gone, all right, and probably dead. No telling where or when they'd find her. But he had a hunch Diane was right: Janie's involvement with Phillip Carruthers was the linchpin of the situation. If Phillip was not directly involved, he was somehow in the mix.

He called Pepper Stephens to tell him what he'd found.

"What the fuck do you want now?" Pep said, answering the call.

"What kind of a salutation is that?" Frank asked.

"Frank? Oh, sorry. I thought you were somebody else. Did you get to speak with that doctor, the ex-boyfriend?" Pepper said.

"Well, first of all, he's the current boyfriend, which is a big part of everything I'm about to tell you. Anyway, I did speak to Dr. Wommack, and you won't believe this: That Trek guy, the one who raped Diane? He set fire to Dr. Wommack's house about a week before Janie O'Connor disappeared. They caught his image on a Ring doorbell cam. He even spray-painted 'Leave the bitch alone' on the wall of Wommack's house. And he works as a security guy for the Carruthers organization. The arson investigator confirmed it to Dave Wommack after he was identified as the guy who set his house on fire. If we find Trek Richards, we'll blow this case wide open."

"Well, there's a problem with that," Pepper said. "He's gone."

"Gone? What do you mean he's *gone*?"

"Outta here. Flown the coop. Vamoosed. He's been gone since right before Janie O'Connor's disappearance."

"Before?"

"Yep. I went by his apartment yesterday. It was messy, the bed unmade, dirty dishes in the sink, just lots of rubbish all over the place, roaches everywhere. It looked like he'd been gone for a while. It was as if he just vanished, leaving everything in its place. I spoke to his neighbors. They haven't seen him in over a week. The apartment manager who let me into Trek's place confirmed this. Trek usually paid his rent for up to a year in advance to get a discount, but he'd recently gotten behind on his payments. The manager tried calling him but got no answer, so he went by his place a week or so ago and found the same mess that I did. They were going to evict him if he didn't pay up soon."

"Is his vehicle still there?"

"Nope. The manager let me access the surveillance cameras from the complex. They showed him leaving in his truck in the early morning of July 14. He's never been back since."

Frank sat up, eyes wide. "July 14. That's the day after he set the fire at Dave Wommack's place—and the day he raped Diane O'Connor."

"Precisely. Trek is our prime suspect at this point, and he has a huge head start on us."

"What happened with that whole break-in story? Janie said that the person who raped Diane was the same person who broke into her garage last year. That would place Trek at Janie's house months before any of this took place. Did you look into that?"

"I reviewed the report. There's not much to it. Dr. O'Connor drove into her garage, and a guy was standing there who matched what we now know to be Trek Richards's description. He walked away without saying a word. It freaked her out, but that was about as far as it got."

"Janie's house at Rose Dhu has surveillance cameras all over the property. Was there any footage of the guy?"

"Nope. He somehow got into the garage without a single camera detecting him. From the officer's report, that was what rattled Dr. O'Connor the most. And get this: When the officer arrived, Phillip Carruthers was there with her."

"We really need to interview Phillip Carruthers," Frank said.

"Roger that. But you know how the chief feels about that. We'll need to clear it with him first."

Frank hung up feeling pretty good about how things were going.

Looking in the rearview mirror, he barely recognized himself. With his freshly shaven face and dyed hair, he looked like the version of Frank Winger from long ago—before Afghanistan, before Cookie. *Before Paulina.*

Frank suddenly felt tired. He thought he might stop by the condo before going into the station. Maybe he'd take a nap or smoke some weed. Or maybe both.

He looked at his reflection in the mirror again and smiled.

Pep's gonna give me a lot of shit about this, he thought.

He put on his blinker and set a course for home.

—

Frank stopped by Chief Brown's office the following morning with a plan in mind. He knew they had to speak with Phillip Carruthers. Phillip was indeed the linchpin, the key to everything else—and that linchpin had to be pulled, Morris Shefter be damned.

Only, the chief was not having anything to do with it.

"No, Frank—we're not hauling Phillip in here just yet. It's too early."

"Too *early*? He's the ex-boyfriend—and the victim just broke up with him a few months ago. He's a suspect, maybe even the number one suspect, and he has direct ties to Trek Richards, the guy who was threatening Janie O'Connor and Dave Wommack, her new boyfriend. We need to bring him in."

"Frank, this is a delicate situation. Phillip Carruthers is not just any suspect. He's got connections everywhere, and he has a killer legal team. We'll likely only get one shot with him, and we can't afford to blow it. We'll need to have all our ducks in a row when we bring him in. But we *will* bring him in, when the time is right. I promise."

"Unbelievable," Frank said, shaking his head.

The chief drained one last swig of Dasani water and tossed the empty bottle in the recycling bin behind him. His office was a shrine to his long, storied career in law enforcement. There were pictures of him with both Barack Obama and George W. Bush, an impressive gold-embossed diploma from the John Jay College of Criminal Justice at CUNY, and a framed FSU football jersey from his Seminole playing days.

Frank turned to go, but Chief Brown stopped him. "Mind if I ask you something, Frank?" he said.

"Go ahead."

"Are you dating someone?"

Frank hadn't been expecting that. "What?"

The chief's large hands fluttered up and down, sizing him up.

"You look . . . different. I mean, with the short hair and the dye job and all. Your clothes look more put together, not like your usual Jimmy Buffett beach bum ensemble. I barely recognized you. It's not a bad look. I mean, it's good. You look sharp. And after all this time, if you're seeing someone, I think that's a good thing." He paused for a moment, then added, in a softer voice, "You know Paulina would want you to be happy. And I do, too."

"I'm not dating anyone. I did this to try to question one of our suspects. I know it looks weird. But don't worry: I'll be reverting back to my usual middle-aged vagrant appearance before too long." Frank turned once again to leave.

"Frank," the chief said.

"Yeah, boss?"

"You've got to trust me on this. I know what I'm doing. We'll get Phillip Carruthers in here. But the timing has to be right. OK?"

"OK."

Frank left Chief Brown's office and softly closed the door behind him. He felt a bit queasy, as if he'd just eaten a bad burrito.

Something isn't right here, he thought, although he had no idea what it was.

13

August 10

Tina Baker had scooped the police again.

Frank had turned on the television to catch up on the world's events while he made his morning coffee when he saw the promo, along with headshots of Tina and Phillip Carruthers. The voiceover said, "Coming up: a doctor's disappearance and the grief of her billionaire fiancé. CBS correspondent Tina Baker brings you the latest on a Southern Gothic mystery."

"What the *hell?*" Frank said out loud.

He called Pep right away.

"I'm helping Candy get the kids ready for school, so I can't talk long," Pepper said. "What's up?"

"Tina Baker got an interview with Phillip Carruthers. It's airing nationally this morning."

"Are you shitting me? Please tell me you're shitting me."

"I am not shitting you. It's about to come on."

Frank could hear a child whining stridently in the background.

"Look, I'll have to look at it later. Becca wants to wear her new sparkly purple shoes with the school uniform, but they don't match. Plus, her hair is a tangled mess. I've got to go. The interview should be available online, right?" Pep said.

"Yeah, I guess so," Frank said, although he really had no idea.

"OK. See you in a bit."

Frank sat down in his old leather lounge chair with a cup of coffee and waited for the interview, which was being aired on *CBS This Morning.*

The interview took place in Phillip's home. Tina, as always, looked gorgeous, in an all-white dress that accentuated her flawless mahogany skin. Phillip, tan and relaxed in khakis and a polo shirt, was alternately charming and grief stricken as he answered the softball questions tossed at him by Savannah's best-known television celebrity.

"Good morning, Phillip. Thanks so much for agreeing to speak with us this morning. I know how difficult this must be for you."

"Thank you, Tina. And you're right: It's been hard."

"You and Dr. O'Connor were engaged to be married. Is that right?"

"That's right, Tina. We'd reserved the Cathedral of St. John the Baptist, which is the place Janie wanted. The date has been set for over a year."

"How did the two of you meet?"

"I was a patient," he said, smiling. "I agreed I'd find a new doctor after I asked her out."

"And how did you find out she was missing?"

"My sister, Erika, called and told me. I was in Atlanta on business."

Tina leaned forward, never taking her eyes off Phillip. "There were some rumors of premarital discord. Some have even said your wedding had been called off. Do you care to address those rumors?"

"Look, we had a disagreement," Phillip said, wiping tears from his eyes. "That sort of thing can happen to anyone. There were many wedding details to consider, tons of pressure from the media, and Janie felt like she needed a break. But we still loved each other. We were looking forward to starting our family."

"So the engagement was still on?" Tina asked.

"Oh, absolutely," Phillip said. "We're still very much in love. I've never met anybody like her." Phillip's handsome face crumpled in grief, his shoulders slumping as he sobbed.

"So what do you think happened to Janie, Phillip?"

"I don't know. What I do know is that I want her back, wherever she is. I miss her so much."

The interview ended there.

"Dammit!" Frank said, turning off the TV.

A few hours later, Frank fired up his laptop and clicked on YouTube. He watched the Phillip Carruthers interview again. It had already been viewed ten million times.

"This whole thing is starting to spin out of control," Frank said to himself.

By that evening, portions of Tina Baker's interview had aired on all the major news networks. The YouTube video of the interview had been viewed over thirty million times and was starting to metastasize onto various other social media platforms.

Women from coast to coast swooned.

—

Frank and Pepper took their seats in the twin wooden chairs in front of Savannah Police Chief Clarence "Gatehouse" Brown's massive desk the following morning. Pepper, disheveled as always, was a few minutes late. His chin was adorned with a small piece of blood-soaked toilet tissue.

"Cut myself shaving," Pepper said sheepishly.

The chief stood up and opened a small refrigerator on a shelf behind him. He pulled out a bottle of Dasani water and downed half before taking a single breath. "Either of you want some water?"

"Nah, I'm good," Frank replied, waving him off.

"Me too," said Pepper. "But thanks, Chief."

"Doc says I need to stay hydrated," the chief said, eyebrows raised. He took another deep swig and tossed the empty bottle into the half-filled recycling bin beside his desk. "Talk to me, gentlemen."

"Chief, like I said the other day, we need to get Phillip Carruthers in for questioning. Tina Baker is making us look bad."

"OK, I agree with you, Frank. Tina's interview has forced our hand. I'm OK with bringing him in. I've just been waiting for the right time."

"Chief, didn't you tell me once that you know Phillip Carruthers personally?" Pepper asked.

"We've met a few times. Savannah's a small town, and Phillip Carruthers is a big fish. So yeah, we know each other."

"Do you have his cell phone number?" Pepper asked.

"I do," Chief Brown said.

"Well, maybe you should make the first call. We could bring him into the station the back way to avoid the press. They always park out front."

"I like the way you're thinking, Detective. Let's try to avoid a circus here." He pulled another bottle of water from the refrigerator. "Are you sure y'all don't want a water? I've got plenty. And it's hot out there," the chief said. He cracked the cap and drank a huge gulp.

Frank waved him off. "You know, chief, if you keep drinking that much water, you might just float away," he said.

—

Frank looked out of the front door of Police Headquarters and whistled, shaking his head.

"Holy hell. Look at that," Frank said.

The street out in front of the building had been transformed into a media carnival. Reporters from Atlanta, Memphis, Charleston, and Jacksonville were all there. Fox News, CNN, and other national news organizations also appeared. News vans lined the streets and were logjammed at haphazard angles all over the sidewalks. Armies of camera-toting techs jockeyed for the best angles, banks of LED lights slung over their shoulders. One tech was draped over a tree branch.

"How the hell did they all find out he was coming in today?" Frank said.

"Must be a mole around here someplace," Pepper said.

"Glad he's coming in the back way," Frank said.

Morris Shefter's gleaming black Mercedes-Maybach sedan rolled up to the loading dock of Police Headquarters. Through the dark-tinted windows, nothing could be seen inside. It was not an inconspicuous vehicle but one that nevertheless allowed a certain degree of privacy.

Frank was standing on the loading dock as the car parked. He went down to meet them.

The driver got out and opened one of the rear doors of the Mercedes. Dressed in an expensive midnight-blue Savile Row suit, simple but clearly tailored, Shefter exited the car and walked around to the other side. The unruly Matterhorn of gray hair atop Shefter's head framed an angular, bony skull. A pair of bushy eyebrows arched over his slate-blue eyes, which darted back and forth as he surveyed the narrow alleyway they had pulled into.

"It's clear," Shefter said, opening the passenger side rear door.

Phillip stepped out. He blinked a couple of times, adjusting to the light. He wore khaki slacks, a long-sleeved green polo shirt, and docksiders without socks. Tan and trim, Phillip tried to flash a confident grin, but his shoulders were slumped.

Fresh off the yacht, Frank thought.

But Phillip's eyes were hollowed out and distant, an appearance Frank was familiar with. He'd seen it in Afghanistan after firefights, in people who'd lost loved ones, and in people who were completely confused about a sudden predicament they'd never imagined they'd face.

Frank had also seen that look among the guilty.

A skinny, scruffy-bearded cameraman suddenly materialized directly in front of Shefter and Carruthers. A bleached-blonde news correspondent accompanied him, flailing her microphone like a billy club.

Where the hell did she come from? Frank thought.

"Mr. Carruthers, are you a suspect in Dr. O'Connor's murder? Is this your attorney?" the blonde barked, shaking her microphone in Phillip's face.

Shefter pushed the microphone aside and moved past her without a word. His eyes were fixed on the metal loading dock door, and he homed in on it, his hand on Phillip's arm, as they strode forward.

"The public deserves answers, Mr. Carruthers. Did you kill Janie O'Connor?" the woman asked from behind them.

"Ignore her," Shefter muttered. "Let's get inside."

"Did you kill her, Phillip? DID YOU?" The blonde was almost screaming now. Frank could see the veins on her neck standing out. Frank heard a clattering noise behind him and was astonished to see a stampede of other members of the press swarming through the alley, like a horde of giant insects attracted by some unseen scent.

Phillip turned around. His eyes were bloodshot, his face crumpled.

"Phillip, *no*," Shefter said sharply.

Phillip yanked his arm away, defiant. "I love Janie. *Love* her. And no, I did not kill her. I miss her every day. Are you satisfied? Is that the sound bite you wanted?"

The reporter stood silent, her mouth agape. Her microphone seemed to wilt in her hand. She was at a complete loss for words.

"Let's go," Phillip said, turning away.

An officer opened the metal door, and they all moved inside the police station.

The interview room was stark and spare—a simple oak table, a few wooden chairs, a video camera with its unblinking ruby-colored eye gleaming in the shadows, a silvery one-way mirror on one wall. Pep and Frank took seats on one side of the table, while Shefter and Carruthers sat on the other side. Shefter glared at Pep and Frank like an eagle, sharp eyed and fierce, his bony fingers clutching the edge of the table like talons.

"First, let's set the ground rules: There will be no baiting of my client. I'll advise him not to answer any question I feel is inappropriate. If this gets confrontational, we're walking out, unless you want to arrest him—and you don't have nearly enough evidence to even consider that. This isn't the Spanish Inquisition, gentlemen. We're trying to be cooperative, but we won't be badgered. Understood?"

Everyone nodded, including Phillip.

"Either of you gentlemen want a drink? Coke, perhaps, or water?" Frank asked.

"No, thanks," Phillip said quietly. He was looking down at his hands folded on the table before him.

Shefter shuffled a stack of papers on the table but said nothing.

Frank ensured the camera was recording, then spoke: "Mr. Carruthers, can you tell me the nature of your relationship with Dr. Janie O'Connor?"

"We are engaged to be married."

"How long had you been engaged when she disappeared?"

"About a year."

"When was the last time you spoke to Dr. O'Connor?"

Phillip sighed. "March, I think," he said.

"March of this year, correct? For the record," Frank asked.

"That's right. I don't know the exact date."

"But you are engaged? How does that work?"

"We'd had a fight. We were on a break."

"But the engagement was still on?"

"I hadn't canceled the reservation at the cathedral, if that means anything."

"How can you be planning a wedding and not talking to one another?"

"Look, Janie and I had our problems. I'll admit that. After we married she wanted to continue to practice as a full-time surgeon. I wanted her to spend more time with me. I wanted to have lots of children, and she did, too, but the timing was up in the air. But I loved her. I took care of her. Ask anyone."

Frank nodded and made a note in his pad. "Where were you on July 19 and July 20?"

"I was in Atlanta on business. Greg Sullivan, my pilot, can confirm this, as can Carmine Carpeggio, my personal assistant and bodyguard. They were both with me the entire time. You can check the plane's flight log. It'll back me up. I did not return to Savannah until the morning of July 21."

"Who were you meeting with in Atlanta?"

"Contacts for our import-export business. We just built two new warehouses in Garden City, and I was trying to iron out the details on a trucking contract to transport goods from our warehouses to retailers in Atlanta."

"Can you provide those references?"

"Of course."

Frank fixed Phillip with a cold, hard stare. "Did you kill Janie O'Connor, Mr. Carruthers?"

Phillip looked up. His eyes were bloodshot. "No, I did not," he said defiantly.

"Did you have someone else kill her?"

"No! Like I said to that reporter outside, I love Janie with all my heart. Why would I have her killed?"

"Maybe you just got tired of her independent streak. She was a surgeon, after all, not some shrinking violet. Or perhaps you were jealous. Wasn't she seeing someone else after you and she separated?"

"Don't answer that," Shefter said.

Phillip quickly glanced at Shefter. There was a wounded look in his eyes.

Gotcha, Frank thought. "I'll ask again: Were you aware of Dr. O'Connor seeing anyone else while you two were estranged?"

"Don't answer," Shefter said, but Phillip waved him off.

"I wasn't aware of that, no."

"Do you know a Dr. Dave Wommack?"

"I've heard of him. He was Janie's ex-boyfriend. We've never met."

"Do you know that he's told us you sent threatening messages to him? That you had people from your organization come to his home and threaten him, vandalizing his home, telling him to leave Dr. O'Connor alone?"

"That's bullshit. I'd never do that," Phillip barked, shaking his head, his jaw muscles clenched tight.

Frank leaned forward, his forehead inches from Carruthers's own. "Dr. Wommack has given us a couple of emails, Phillip. They're anonymous, of course. I don't think you'd be so stupid as to send him this sort of thing from your personal email address. But who else would send Dr. Wommack emails telling him to 'leave the bitch alone'? Can you think of any more likely candidates than yourself?"

"Speculation," Morris Shefter said. "You have no proof my client had anything to do with that."

Frank pulled a somewhat pixilated image of a balding, overweight man in a camo hoodie from inside a manila folder and slapped it on the table in front of Carruthers.

"Do you know this man?" Frank said.

Phillip glanced at Shefter, who nodded. "I do," he said.

"Who is he?"

"That's Trek Richards. He used to work for me in security, but he quit recently. I don't even know where he is now. We haven't heard from him in weeks."

"This picture was taken by a Ring doorbell camera at Dr. Wommack's home several days before Dr. O'Connor disappeared. Mr. Richards set Dave Wommack's front porch on fire and spray-painted a threat on his wall. That message said 'Leave the bitch alone,' the same message as in the emails. Can you tell me why Mr. Richards, your head of security at the time, would have a reason to visit Dr. Wommack's residence and set fire to his porch? And why he would spray-paint such a threat on the wall?"

"I have no idea. Like I said, Trek used to work for me, but he sometimes freelanced if he perceived a threat to the organization."

"He freelanced?"

"Took matters into his own hands. Improvised. He was valuable to us, but he could be hard to control. That's one of the reasons we decided to let him go."

"I thought you said he quit," Frank said.

"His departure was a mutually acceptable solution to an untenable situation. He resigned, and we were happy to accept it."

Shefter glared at Phillip, his eyes like rapiers, but said nothing.

"Sounds like you had a loose cannon there, Mr. Carruthers," Frank said.

"We recognized that. At first, his positive attributes seemed to outweigh his negative ones. He was always very loyal to the organization. We started to see his shortcomings only after he'd been employed with us for a while."

"When did you let Mr. Richards go, Mr. Carruthers?"

"As I said, I misspoke earlier. He resigned. We had thought about firing him, but he resigned before we could terminate him."

"And what date was that?"

"I think it was around the middle of July."

"Could it have been July 14?"

"Maybe. I don't have his employment record in front of me."

"The fire on Dr. Wommack's front porch was set in the early morning hours of July 13. That was just a few days before Dr. O'Connor disappeared, right?" Frank said.

"If it was that week, it could be that date. I remember Trek resigned a few days before Janie disappeared."

"But you didn't fire him?"

"No."

"Did you know that Trek Richards physically and sexually assaulted Janie's sister, Diane O'Connor, in Janie's home at Rose Dhu on the morning of July 14?"

Phillip reared back in his chair, an astonished look on his face. "What?"

"The attack apparently went unreported because Trek told the victim he worked for the Carruthers family, alluding that he would make Janie's and Diane's lives a living hell."

Phillip's shoulders slumped. "I had no idea," he said quietly.

"No one has been able to locate Trek Richards. He's

vanished. Shortly after that, Dr. O'Connor vanished, too. Why do people around you keep vanishing, Mr. Carruthers?"

Phillip's face was an expressionless mask. "I don't know," he said flatly.

Frank glanced over at Pepper, who was twirling a pen between his fingers but had been strangely silent.

"Did you kill Janie O'Connor?" Frank asked.

"You asked me that already. The reporter outside asked me the same question just before we came in here. You heard my answer both times. It hasn't changed."

Phillip's response was quiet and measured. Far from the confident, relaxed man who had entered the interview room a few minutes earlier, he now appeared spent, hollowed out, his eyes staring off into forever.

"State it, then, for the record."

Phillip sighed and rolled his eyes. Shefter touched his arm, almost imperceptibly. "No, I did not kill Janie. I'll swear it on a stack of Bibles," Phillip replied.

"We may be able to oblige you in that request, Mr. Carruthers. Give us a little time," Frank said.

Shefter abruptly stood and picked up his briefcase.

"Phillip, we're leaving," he said, his hoarse voice dripping with venom.

The two of them hustled through the doorway of the cramped interview room and slammed the heavy steel behind them, stirring up a sparkling swirl of dust motes that danced lazily in the flickering light before disappearing into oblivion.

"What a prince of a guy," Frank muttered, shaking his head.

By the time Shefter and Carruthers left, the news crews had all dissipated. It was as though someone had generously sprayed the entire block with reporter repellent.

"Ain't that some shit?" Pepper asked. He whistled, low and long, as he rolled his bulging eyes skyward.

"How much you wanna bet the Carruthers people paid them all off?" Frank said.

Pep waved his hands in front of him, shaking his head. "Ain't touchin' that one," he said. "Those people scare me."

"So what do you think, Pep?"

"Well, if he's guilty, he's doing a good job of hiding it. He's appropriately concerned about Janie and is consistently sticking to his alibi. And he seemed genuinely surprised by the revelation of Trek's assault on Diane."

Frank nodded. "It's curious, all right. Maybe Trek was freelancing again and took Janie out or even kidnapped her. But where is he?"

"That's the million-dollar question," Pep said. "But I have another question, maybe worth about ten bucks."

"What's that?"

He pointed to Frank's hair. "What's with the do? You seeing somebody? Because that would be OK," Pep said.

Frank rolled his eyes. "That's what the chief said. And no, for the record, I'm not dating. This was an undercover disguise."

"Hey, man, I'd stick with it. You might actually get a date like that."

Frank playfully socked Pepper in the arm. "Shut up, you idiot," he said.

14

Frank's gut was rarely wrong.

He knew this was unscientific. A gut feeling would never be admissible in court. Still, Frank's gut had saved his life innumerable times, both as a soldier in Afghanistan and as a cop. The analytical part of his mind realized that what he termed a "gut feeling" was probably the amalgamation of direct sensory input coupled with years of observation and experience.

Frank's gut knew that finding Trek Richards was the key to this case. He didn't know if Trek was the actual murderer, but all roads of inquiry led to him.

Frank had to find him.

Trek Richards drove a white 2012 Ford F-150 pickup, Georgia license plate RRX3983. Traffic cameras in Chatham County were becoming more plentiful, but they weren't ubiquitous. There was a precocious kid in the IT department (he was actually an adult, but Frank increasingly thought of anyone under thirty as a "kid") who had a rare set of computer skills and, in particular, a crazy genius for tracking cars on street cams. His name was Jonathan Kramer but everyone called him the Kid, likely for the same reasons Frank did (and maybe *because* Frank called him that).

The Kid was a nice enough young man—and he could be extraordinarily helpful at times. He liked Snickers bars, too, and could be bribed with them on occasion, particularly the special edition ones.

"Hey, Kid," Frank said. "Would you mind helping me with something?" He waggled a dark chocolate Snickers between his index finger and his thumb.

The Kid looked up from his computer and grinned. His round, rimless John Lennon glasses had slid down to the end of his nose. "Of course, Detective. How can I help?"

"There's this guy, Trek Richards, who is involved with a disappearance I'm investigating. He's a key player, maybe even a suspect. The odd thing is, *he's* disappeared, as well. Can you find him if I give you his vehicle description and license plate number?"

"The guy you suspect in a disappearance has disappeared himself?"

Frank nodded.

"Is this the O'Connor case?"

"Of course," Frank said.

The Kid took the proffered Snickers bar, unwrapped it, and took a bite. "Do you have a picture of the missing guy's driver's license? Having his credit card and bank account numbers would help, too."

"I have all that," Frank said.

"If I combine his facial images and account numbers, that may help me find him, too. He'll leave a digital signature wherever he goes. I have some proprietary large language model AI software in beta testing that I can use here, but it's top secret, and it'll cost you." The Kid grinned again. Chocolate was smeared on his teeth.

"Cost me?" Frank asked.

"Yep. A six pack of Red Bull. But you can get it to me later," the Kid said.

Frank opened a folder and removed a few sheets of paper. "Here's a copy of his DL, the description of his vehicle with the license plate number, and his bank account and credit card numbers. Also his home address and social."

The Kid's fingers flew over the keyboard so fast that Frank could barely see them. He used a handheld scanner to scan in the driver's license, then hit enter.

"Is there any specific geographic location where I should focus my search?" the Kid said.

"Try his apartment, of course. And the victim's home on Rose Dhu Road." Frank recalled what Diane had said about Trek needing to catch a flight. "Look at the Savannah airport, too," he said.

"What dates?"

"July 12 through 20."

The Kid entered more data and leaned back in his chair. "Here we go," he said.

"He bought gasoline at the Enmark on Waters on the evening of July 12," the Kid said. "Then he bought some food at the McDonald's on Waters and took it home. Very ordinary." The Kid looked at the screen again, then ran his fingers through the thick, unruly dark mass of his hair. "Wait," he said. "He left the apartment again at midnight. There's a camera across the street from his apartment complex, and I can track him from there."

He typed in other camera locations, trying to follow the truck.

"I've lost him," the Kid said. "No, wait, I've got him again. Ardsley Park. He was driving down Forty-Fourth Street around 1:00 a.m. on the thirteenth."

"That's Dave Wommack's street," Frank murmured.

"Lost him again," the Kid said. "But there were lots of

emergency vehicles in that area shortly after that. Fire trucks and police. Goes on for hours."

The Kid was typing furiously.

"He went home after that, and his truck didn't budge from the apartment parking lot for a day or so. I've got him moving again on the morning of July 14, at around 6:00 a.m. He heads out to Wilmington Island, drives down Bradley Point Road, and turns into some big gated compound. Can't access any images beyond that."

"Let me see that," Frank said.

The Kid swung the screen around so Frank could see.

"Sonofabitch. That's the Carruthers family compound," Frank said. His throat muscles were tight, and a trickle of sweat tingled his armpits.

"Here he is, less than an hour later, leaving the compound. He's driving fast, maybe seventy-five or eighty miles an hour. Goes down Victory, then the southbound Truman Parkway. Gets off at White Bluff."

"He's headed toward Rose Dhu," Frank said. "Is he by himself?"

"It looks like it," the Kid said. "Only one person visible in the car." He typed in some other data. "I lose him after that. There are no publicly accessible cameras beyond the entrance to Windsor Forest." He looked up, a puzzled expression on his face. "And that's it," he said.

Frank blinked. "That's it?"

"That's the last of him. He went down White Bluff and never left. And this is weird: There's not a single digital signature of him after that. No charges, no bank account activity, nothing. I can't find the truck anywhere. Not at the airport, not on the interstate, nowhere. It's gone. He's vanished."

"I don't understand," Frank said.

The Kid shrugged. "On July 14, Trek Richards drove into Rose Dhu, all right. But as far as I can tell, he never came back out."

—

Pepper sounded almost excited when he called Frank the following morning.

"They found it!" he said.

"Found what?"

"Trek's truck. It's in Rose Dhu, and we're headed out there. I'll pick you up in ten minutes."

Half an hour later, for the third time in a week, Frank found himself in the sleepy marshside community of Rose Dhu. Trek's battered white F-150, marked with the SecuriCorp insignia, was mired up to its wheel wells in the marsh near Houston Creek. The vehicle was unlocked, but its contents were essentially untouched, as far as anyone could tell. Dried blood was smeared across the door handle, the steering wheel, the seat, and the dashboard.

"We're certain the truck is his?" Frank asked.

"It is," Pepper said. "The license plate checks out, and the truck's VIN number is consistent with Trek's vehicle registration. Some insurance cards, a few napkins from McDonald's, and a bunch of fast-food receipts were in the glove compartment. He left a half-empty can of Pepsi in the cupholder. It's like he drove the damned thing out into the marsh and left it. It's weird."

"No gun?"

"No gun."

"Bizarre," Frank said.

The truck was mired so deeply that it took a tow truck equipped with a heavy-duty winch to drag it out of the marsh. A gaggle of onlookers gathered to watch as the tow truck backed up, beeping loudly, its rear wheels digging into the dark marsh mud.

A bespectacled redheaded kid on a battered twelve-speed bike pedaled up and stood next to Frank, who was standing by

Pepper, taking pictures of the scene with his iPhone.

"That thing's been out there for weeks," the kid said, vigorously chewing a mouthful of gum, his glasses half fogged.

"It has?" Frank said, looking up.

"Yup," the kid replied. "I told my parents about it, but they told me they weren't getting involved. Not this time, anyway."

"What did they mean by that?"

The kid popped a bubble and shook his head. "Beats me," he said, wheeling away among the moss-draped live oaks.

"How does a truck sit out here in the marsh for weeks and not get reported?" Pepper said.

"It's Rose Dhu," a withered-looking old woman nearby said. She wore a shapeless pastel purple housedress and sensible black shoes. Her face looked like a dried apricot.

"What do you mean?" Frank asked.

"You ever hear the phrase 'Don't ask, don't tell'?"

"I have, but what does that have to do with Rose Dhu?"

"Folks in Rose Dhu tend to mind their own business. There are some families who have lived in this neck of the woods for decades. It's a matter of pride that they sort of stick to themselves. We had people bowhunting deer in the neighborhood a few years back. Someone even gutted one and strung it up in his yard. Nobody said anything. Some other folks were growing weed in their home back here and we only found out about it because Georgia Power noted a spike in their power bill and told the cops, who busted the place early one morning. Turns out lots of the people in the neighborhood knew about it already but figured it was not their problem. Heck, back in the eighties, the mob took drug deliveries by shrimp boat right off the Vernon River near here. A truck stuck in the marsh? That's nothing. Worse shit than that washes up here during hurricane season every year."

Frank shielded his eyes and peered across the marsh. In the distance, he could see the distinctive red metal roof of Twin Oaks.

"See that, Pep? It's Janie's house," Frank said, pointing. "This spot is within easy walking distance from there, either by the road or along the marsh's edge. And it's in a tidal zone. Trek could have parked the truck here at low tide and gotten stuck as the tide came in."

"I'll look it up," Pepper said, glancing at his phone. "Bingo," he said. "On July 14, it was dead low tide here at 7:00 a.m. It was a full moon, and tide was an eight-footer that day. It would have come in fast."

After the truck was loaded up, Pep and Frank went back by the police station, then stopped at the Breakfast Place for a late breakfast. Frank deviated from his usual fare and ordered oatmeal with fruit, which prompted Pepper to razz him unmercifully for being a "health nut."

"I eat one thing that's supposed to be good for me, and you give me shit?" Frank asked.

"It's just so unlike you," Pepper responded. "First the haircut, then the dye job, you shave your beard, you start dressing like you give a shit, and now you're eating oatmeal with *fruit*? What have you done with my partner?"

Pep sipped his coffee (black and hot, like always), and steam fogged his glasses, curling around his ears.

Frank grinned, shaking his head.

"I knew you'd give me crap about this, but let's get on to the actual important stuff. What are you thinking?" Frank asked.

"Trek's truck, stuck in the marsh, with blood all over the door handle and the steering wheel. I'll bet the blood is his. That goes along with Diane's story of Trek being attacked by the family dog and escaping. It all fits. I think Trek inadvertently parked his truck in a tidal area. After the rape, he came back and found the truck stuck in the mud. What happened after that is anyone's guess," Pepper said.

"But where's Trek?"

Pepper shrugged. "Beats me," he said. "We need to look in

the woods near the Girl Scout camp. He could be hiding out there."

"For *weeks*? That seems unlikely," Frank said.

Pepper shrugged again. "Maybe died of blood loss, or maybe he killed himself. Who knows?"

"Maybe there was a killer clown hiding out in the sewer system," Frank said.

"I seriously doubt that," Pepper said, a confused look on his face.

"What is the deal with that Rose Dhu place?" Frank said.

Pepper shook his head. "That whole place seems chock full of nutjobs."

He popped the last piece of biscuit into his mouth and finished his coffee just as Lurlene brought the check over and slapped it on the table.

"See y'all tomorrow, boys. And good choice with the oatmeal, Frank. I like it when a man knows what's good for him," Lurlene said, winking at him.

"Like I said before, she's sweet on you, Frankie," Pepper said.

"Shut up, Pep," Frank replied, taking out his wallet.

—

Frank couldn't sleep.

Insomnia had been a persistent problem for him ever since Paulina died. He still dreamed about her sometimes. In his dreams, she was always alive. It was only after awakening that he realized she was gone. It was almost like the universe was taunting him, goading him, making him feel guilty for being the cause of her death.

Which he was, of course.

Frank's dreams were routinely haunted by memories of Afghanistan, as well.

Cookie Alvarez had been his best friend in the platoon. A veteran soldier, battle hardened and resilient, Cookie was a rock, keeping everyone in the platoon grounded—and alive. He could adapt to any environment and had always been a survivor, at least until that awful day he wasn't.

Frank had been a typical greenie when he arrived in Afghanistan: cautious, tentative, always second-guessing himself. As he did with all the greenies, Cookie had taken him under his wing, teaching Frank who he could trust and who he could not.

Frank saw a great deal of evil in Afghanistan: men vaporized by IEDs that leveled entire buildings; old men with rusty, curved wood-handled knives hidden beneath their robes; veiled women, steps small and eyes downcast, wearing bomb vests laced with ball bearings beneath their chadors; bands of children roving the streets with automatic weapons and soccer balls, everything a game to them, life and death having no currency in a world where either could come and go in the blink of an eye. He'd been shot at by friends and aided by enemies so many times that he trusted no one, believed nothing, and suspected everything.

Cookie taught him that.

One night, their platoon was overrun by a band of crazed jihadists who had somehow made it inside the wire while they were sleeping. Cookie, trying to direct the firefight, took a round in the groin, right above the femur. The bullet shattered his femoral artery. Frank tried to put a tourniquet on Cookie's leg, but the wound was too high and blood pulsed around it, despite Frank's efforts to hold pressure on it.

Frank stayed with Cookie while they waited for a Black Hawk medevac chopper to pick him up. He could only watch, tears streaming down his face, as he begged his friend to hold on.

"Come on, Cook, don't die on me, man. Think of your son!

Think of your baby daughter! Hang in there; they're almost here; we've got you, bro."

It was pointless. Cookie died in his arms before the Black Hawk arrived.

"I love you, man" was the last thing Cookie said before his eyes closed.

They captured one of the Taliban fighters that night. He was wiry and rail thin, with a scraggly black beard. They nicknamed him Abdul. Abdul wouldn't talk to them, not even in Pashto. They kept him trussed up in a tent, a blindfold on, arms behind his back. Frank was assigned to guard him, but the only thing Frank could see when he looked at Abdul was Cookie, his color an unnatural, bloodless gray, eyes rolled back in his head. Whenever he thought about Cookie, he wanted to clock Abdul in the teeth with the butt of his M16. Hell, he wanted to *kill* him, just put a round in the back of the SOB's head and be done with it.

Fuck him. Fuck him and the camel he rode in on.

Fighting off his worst impulses, Frank squatted and pulled the blindfold down. He took a long, hard look into Abdul's dark, implacable eyes, not speaking at first. Eventually, Frank cleared his throat and asked Abdul one simple question: "Why?"

Abdul answered, in perfect Oxford-accented English, "Because you came here, an infidel, to a place you do not belong. That is why."

Frank was stunned.

Staring at Abdul, Frank realized something profound: To Abdul, life meant nothing. Death was merely a means to an end, a doorway to a promised paradise in the afterlife, an acceptable outcome. Worse still, there were thousands upon thousands more like him, men for whom devotion to Allah meant more than family, more than love, even more than life itself.

That realization changed Frank forever.

Abdul was taken away to prison the next day. Frank never saw him again—but he never forgot him, either.

After Frank returned home a few months later, he had the word *Infidel* tattooed across the center of his chest, along with Cookie's name and the date of his death. Cookie's essence, burned into Frank's skin, would be with him until his last day on earth.

Cookie had been gone fifteen years now. His wife remarried, his son dropped out of school, and his daughter was now a rebellious teenager who'd never really known her father.

That hurt Frank to the core.

Frank's entire life had been shaped by tragedy. Almost everyone he had ever loved or cared about was gone. The losses had contracted his soul, making his heart small and hard, like a walnut. Paulina's death, so painful, had been the final straw. As a result, Frank no longer strove for love, happiness, or spiritual fulfillment. He didn't go to church anymore. He hadn't even uttered a prayer in years.

Justice was now his only deity.

Frank looked at the digital clock beside his bed. It was a little after 3:00 a.m.

He walked over to the desk where his laptop sat and clicked it on. The screen's dim glow bathed his face as he did a Google search for "Carruthers Enterprises."

The breadth of the company's reach surprised him.

Carruthers Enterprises had started over two centuries ago as a simple shipping company. As the port of Savannah grew, its presence expanded. It was now the leading import-export company in all of Georgia, its tentacles extending southward into northern and central Florida, northward past Atlanta toward Charlotte and Raleigh-Durham, and westward toward Birmingham. The company had branched into commercial construction, real estate, auto retailing, and petroleum and natural gas sales, among other things. Carruthers Enterprises was privately held by the Carruthers family and was valued at several billion dollars.

Phillip Carruthers was CEO, and his sister, Erika, was COO. The corporate website did not list any other executives or board members.

Frank clicked on Phillip Carruthers's corporate bio. Phillip was thirty-eight and in excellent shape, having run a competitive triathlon in Hawaii as recently as a year ago (which was something the Carruthers website bragged about). Erika was thirty-five and was an even better athlete, a former track star at the University of Oregon, now nationally ranked in her age group in women's tennis. Both were single and strikingly attractive, somewhat resembling George Clooney and Nicole Kidman.

Anderson Carruthers, their father, had been killed ten years earlier in a tragic hunting accident in Screven County. Phillip, who was with him on that day, had called 911 on his satellite phone to summon the EMS, but after being life-flighted back to Savannah, Anderson had died in the Memorial Hospital ER. Phillip had assumed the role of Carruthers Enterprises CEO at the tender age of twenty-eight.

Frank googled other things relevant to Carruthers Enterprises and mainly found older references to Anderson and Cynthia Carruthers's involvement with local charities, like the Telfair Museum or the Savannah Music Festival—banal stuff punctuated by the typical group photos of smiling people in evening wear taken at charity events.

"Boring as shit," Frank said out loud.

However, there was one hit, a single random Carruthers reference, that caught his eye.

A man named John Straub had been hospitalized a month earlier with what appeared to be a self-inflicted gunshot wound. The mention was a mere blurb in the *Savannah*

Morning News, not particularly newsworthy were it not for a tiny detail: Straub, a longtime employee of Carruthers Enterprises, had shot himself in the head in a scrub pine forest behind his home in the Southbridge subdivision. Neighbors found him after seeing a huddled wake of vultures scrabbling in the trees overhead, waiting for him to die.

But John Straub had not died.

Somehow, by the grace of God, Straub made it to Memorial alive.

The date John Straub was found was particularly interesting to Frank: July 19. The day before Janie O'Connor disappeared.

Frank wrote Straub's name in his case notebook, which he always kept in his pocket. Then he closed the laptop and lay on the bed, hoping for a few moments' sleep before sunrise.

15

The following morning, Frank stopped by Memorial during visiting hours and checked to see if John Straub was still an inpatient there. After he discovered that Straub was still in the ICU, he made his way over to the ICU bed tower.

Flashing his police badge, he asked to speak to Straub's nurse.

The ICU nurse was a young, coltish twentysomething whose name tag said "Molly." Her brown eyes were flecked with gold, her skin smooth. Molly had the casual insouciance of the young, that supremely self-confident attitude that comes naturally to young people who still believe they are immortal.

I was like that once, Frank thought, a slight smile creasing his lips.

"What is your name again?" Molly asked.

"Frank Winger. I'm a detective with the SPD. We're investigating the nature of Mr. Straub's injury."

She typed Frank's name into the computer.

"So how is he doing?" Frank asked.

"Better, finally. He was really bad off when he got here. ENT, Neurosurgery, Trauma—they were all over him when he first hit the door. He'd shot himself through the mouth, and the bullet tore through his face and jaw, but he got lucky. The neurosurgeon said the bullet ricocheted off the bottom of his skull, if you can believe that. The projectile never actually hit his brain. Instead, it fragmented, scattering pieces throughout the rest of his skull. He had some god-awful facial swelling early on, but that's much better now."

"Has he been able to talk?"

"Oh God, no. His jaw was shattered. They wired it shut. He nearly died a few times after that—line sepsis, ARDS, a collapsed lung that resulted in a chest tube, C. diff colitis, the usual trauma service stuff. He's got a PEG tube in for feeding and a Foley draining his urine, but the pressors are off, and we're finally taking out some of his lines. The pulmonary guys are even talking about extubating him in the next few days, which I never would have believed possible just a few weeks ago."

"How long has he been here?" Frank asked.

"A few weeks. He was admitted on July 19," she said, consulting the computer terminal.

Frank glanced into the ICU room. John Straub lay immobile and supine on the bed, his arms and legs splayed apart. He was intubated via a tracheostomy. His face was still very swollen; his eyes were taped shut. The wild tangle of reddish hair atop his head and his expansive copper-colored beard made him look vaguely like an out-of-context character from *Game of Thrones.*

The ventilator hissed and sighed. Bedside monitors beeped and squawked as they traced squiggly red, green, blue, and yellow lines across a broad flat-screen high-res display that Frank was certain cost thousands of dollars.

"This is him doing *better*?" Frank asked.

Molly nodded. "Much better," she said, smiling.

Frank shook his head. "He still looks pretty damned sick to me."

"That's why he's in the ICU," Molly said, a smidgen of condescension in her voice.

"Does his family ever come visit?" Frank asked.

"Sometimes. Mainly his wife. Their kids are little, and they were pretty torn up seeing their dad like this early on, especially when they thought he might die. Now that it looks like he's gonna make it, his wife is waiting until after he is extubated to bring the kids back." She cocked her head. "You don't think somebody shot him, do you? His wife said he left a suicide note. Have you seen it?"

"I haven't, not yet. But this is my first day checking into this." Frank thought for a minute. "Did anyone else ever come to visit him here? Besides his family, I mean."

"I'm not here every day, but I can only remember one other visitor—a tall, striking-looking blonde woman. She came by only once, right after he was hospitalized. She didn't ask many questions. She just wanted to know if we expected him to survive. We didn't know at that point, so that's what I told her. I've not seen her since."

Frank thought for a moment, then pulled out his cell phone and did a quick search. "Was this her?" Frank asked Molly, showing her his screen.

Molly looked at the image and nodded. "That's her, all right," she said. "How did you know?"

Frank looked at his phone once again.

A picture of Erika Carruthers, Phillip's sister, stared back at him.

"Just a hunch," Frank said.

—

Erika Carruthers lived in a two-hundred-year-old, four-story restored townhouse on fashionable Jones Street in Savannah's historic district. The home was once featured in *Garden and*

Gun. The photo spread in the magazine article revealed an opulent home furnished with expensive handwoven drapes and thick Persian rugs covering its wide-planked heart pine floors. Every single room was filled with imported English antiques. The Christ Church Tour of Homes had used a single word to describe the eight-thousand-square-foot townhouse in its brochure the previous year: *"glorious."*

Frank and Pepper pulled the generic SPD squad car, which Chief Brown had insisted that they use, adjacent to the Jones Street curb beneath a moss-draped live oak.

"Is this it?" Pepper asked.

"That's what it says. 120 West Jones Street. She's supposed to be expecting us," Frank replied.

"Well, let's go," Pepper said.

Frank rang the doorbell. When the door opened, a statuesque green-eyed blonde who looked like she spent most of each day in the gym stood before them. Barefoot and dressed only in a white bathrobe, she wore no makeup but was strikingly beautiful nonetheless. With high cheekbones, flawless skin, and cascades of blonde hair tumbling down to her shoulders, she looked like a supermodel.

The men just stared at her, struck dumb.

"Can I help you gentlemen?" the woman said.

"I'm Detective Stephens and this is Detective Winger. We're here to bring Erika Carruthers in for questioning," Pepper said, flashing his badge.

"Excuse me for a moment," the woman said, closing the door gently.

"I think that was her," Frank said. "I've only seen her in pictures, though."

"Do you think she's making a run for it?" Pepper asked.

"I doubt that. She's too easy to find. Probably just getting dressed."

A few moments later, the same blonde woman reappeared.

Now dressed in a fitted black T-shirt and tight designer jeans accented by an oversized bejeweled belt buckle shaped like a blue crab, she clutched a small sequined purse, also in the shape of a crab.

"You're Erika Carruthers?" Pepper asked.

"In the flesh," Erika replied.

"We need to escort you downtown, ma'am," Pepper said.

"Is all this really necessary? I mean, you could question me right here. Why do we need to go downtown?"

"We have our orders, ma'am," Frank said.

Erika shook her head. "Fucking ridiculous. Can I at least call my attorney?"

"Of course," Frank said.

Erika made the call and then went with the officers. The short ride to the police station was quiet. Pepper, who was driving, glanced at Erika in the rearview mirror. She was looking out the window. Sunlight dappled her impassive face as the trees flashed by. When Pepper looked back again, Erika was staring straight at him. Her emerald eyes were brilliant and piercing. She licked her lips, a sly grin on her face. "What are you looking at, Detective?" she said.

"Just checking on you," he replied.

"If I were you, I'd keep my eyes forward. You're supposed to be driving. I won't bite."

Pepper did exactly that for the rest of their journey.

They arrived at SPD Headquarters on Habersham Street in ten minutes. Frank opened the squad car door for Erika, who got out and walked inside the police station without a word.

After Erika was checked in, Frank returned to the vehicle. Glancing into the back seat, he saw something wedged between the seat cushions. Cocking his head, he opened the back door to the squad car and squatted to get a better look.

A bit of black lace was protruding from the seat. It was

wrapped around something else, something gleaming and metallic.

What the hell?

Tugging at the lace, Frank dislodged the object, which was heavier than he had expected. Unwrapping it carefully, he dropped it like it was radioactive when he recognized what it was.

The silver object was the bejeweled blue crab belt buckle Erika had been wearing.

It had been wrapped tightly in a sheer pair of black lace panties and was accompanied by a short message, written in black ink on a small piece of paper in a bold, jagged script.

Fuck you, the note said.

16

Morris Shefter was in a foul mood.

He was standing, absently twirling the ruby ring on his pinkie, his piercing blue-gray eyes cold as a glacier. Erika, seated at the table in the interview room, her carefully manicured hands folded in front of her, was the picture of contrition.

"This is harassment, pure and simple," Morris huffed. "My clients have done nothing wrong, and you're treating them like common criminals. Hauling Erika into the police station for questioning on a *weekend*? Where is your sense of decency?"

Frank sat down, smiling. "Criminal investigations don't take time off, Mr. Shefter. You know that."

Erika turned and glanced at Shefter, touching him gently on the hand. "It's OK, Morris," she said. "Sit down and let's get this over with."

Frank and Pepper were seated opposite Shefter and Erika. Frank positioned a unidirectional microphone in the center of the table and turned on the cameras. The fluorescent light overhead flickered a bit.

"You still haven't fixed that light?" Shefter said.

Frank shrugged. "The government," he said.

Frank opened a leather binder before him and took out a folder. "Ms. Carruthers, Detective Stephens and I are the lead investigators in the disappearance of Dr. Janie O'Connor. Are you familiar with Dr. O'Connor?"

"She was my brother's fiancée, so yes."

"This interview is being recorded, both on audio and video. Would you please state your name?" he said.

"Erika Carruthers."

"And where do you live?"

"Right here in Savannah. 120 West Jones Street."

"Are you married or single?"

"Single."

"Any children?"

"Of course not."

"And what is your occupation?"

"I'm the chief operating officer for Carruthers Enterprises, a private family-owned business based here in Savannah. My brother, Phillip, is the CEO."

"What exactly does Carruthers Enterprises do?"

"We primarily specialize in the import and export business, operating out of the ports of Brunswick and Savannah. We own several warehouses here, operate more distribution warehouses in Atlanta and Charlotte, and have a trucking company that transports goods between the port and our distribution centers in the big cities. We also own a fuel distributorship with gas stations all over Georgia, mainly to ensure our trucking operations don't run out of fuel during a crisis. We have other side businesses—payday lenders, auto dealerships, a couple of TV stations, that sort of thing. We own some business real estate investments in downtown Savannah and a few investment properties in Atlanta. The import-export business is our core, though."

"Ms. Carruthers, is your company publicly traded?" Pepper asked.

"It's not. Like I said, it's a family-owned business."

"Who are the shareholders?"

"Me, my brother, and my mother. That's it."

"Your family's been at this for over two hundred years, and there are only three shareholders?" Pepper asked.

Erika nodded. "Our family company has always been passed down to the oldest male heir. That's the way it has always been done. My father broke with that tradition a little, leaving half of the company to our mother and dividing the other half equally between me and my brother. When my mom dies, her shares will go equally to Phillip and me. If I died, my shares would go to Phillip, since I'm not married and don't have any children. If Phillip died, his shares would go to me."

"If Phillip marries, what happens to his shares?" Frank asked.

"We haven't spoken about it, but I'd expect they'd go to his wife—and any children, once he has them."

"So is it safe to say you have a vested financial interest in keeping Phillip single and childless?" said Frank.

"Hold on there, Detective. That's speculative," Shefter interjected.

"We're not in a courtroom, counselor. She doesn't have to answer if she doesn't want to," Frank replied, frowning at Shefter, who glowered back at him from beneath a pair of bushy eyebrows. Frank turned back to Erika.

"I'll answer. It's true that I would benefit if Phillip stays single and childless, but I really don't care if Phillip marries or has kids. If he does, I do want him to marry the right person, of course."

"Did you ever meet Dr. Janie O'Connor?"

"Casually, a few times. We've never been friends, but my brother wanted to marry her, so I have seen her around."

"What do you think of her?"

Erika thought for a moment. "Smart, for sure. Straightforward, no-nonsense, like you'd expect a surgeon to be."

"Do you like her?"

"I respect her, but we have never had enough interaction for me to form an opinion of her as a person. We aren't friends."

"Were you in favor of them getting married?"

"Honestly, I never thought she and Phillip were a good match. In my opinion, Janie is too independent and too career focused. Phillip needs someone more willing to stay home. But he's never cared much for my opinion about his love life."

Frank tapped his pen on the legal pad in front of him, shaking his head slowly. *They really don't want any potential spouse for Phillip to have a brain,* he thought.

He cleared his throat and started again. "I understand that issue is part of what led to their breakup."

"You'll have to ask Phillip about that."

"But you didn't approve of her as a potential spouse for him."

Erika sighed, shaking her head. "Look, Phillip has always dated bimbos, OK? Gorgeous, vapid girls from socially connected families. Dr. O'Connor was against type for him. I just didn't think he was going to be happy with her. That's all. Ultimately, what Phillip does in his personal life is his business."

Frank looked up at Erika and cleared his throat. "I'm going to be very direct here: Did you kill Janie O'Connor?" he asked her.

"Of course not."

"Did you order anyone to kill her?"

Erika laughed. "How could I order anyone to be killed? Do I look like some sort of mafia boss?"

"I'll ask the questions here, thank you," Frank said. "Where were you on the night of July 19?"

"In fact, I had a minor procedure that day. My plastic

surgeon will vouch for me. I was at his office until 9:00 p.m. that evening, and a friend drove me home. I can give you her name, too."

"You do that," he said, handing her a pen and paper. "Write your surgeon's name and your friend's name down and we'll give them a call."

As Erika wrote, Frank shuffled his papers. After she handed the sheet back to him, Frank looked at it, placed the sheet in his notebook, then pulled out a glossy photograph of a smiling, heavyset man with a rusty beard and spun it across the table. "Do you recognize this person?"

Erika nodded. "He works for us. John something. I call him Fat John, because a skinny man named John who is about the same age works in the same department."

"Does the name *John Straub* sound familiar?"

Erika nodded. "I think that's right."

"It's right, because this photo is from his Carruthers Enterprises employee ID. Were you aware that Mr. Straub is currently hospitalized in the Memorial ICU with an apparent self-inflicted gunshot wound to the head?"

"Really? That's horrible!" she exclaimed.

Frank smiled, tight lipped. Erika was not a good liar. Her eyes were open too wide, and her exclamation seemed forced, like an actress exaggeratedly flailing along in a middle school play.

"You didn't know he was hospitalized?"

"I had no idea," she said, her well-manicured hands flopping about like wounded birds.

"That's funny. One of the ICU nurses identified you as having visited him. Straub has been there since July 19. I'm sure the hospital surveillance cameras will corroborate what she says."

Erika sat back in her chair, eyebrows arched high, her arms folded across her chest.

"I try to go see any of our employees who are hospitalized. What's wrong with that?"

"Well, if it was simply a routine employee visit, why did you lie about knowing he was in the hospital?"

Erika's eyes flashed at him, but she said nothing.

"How many employees do you have, Ms. Carruthers?" Frank asked.

"Over a thousand."

Frank leaned forward, his eyes boring into Erika's. "And how many of those employees are in the ICU at any given time?" he asked.

Erika glanced briefly at Shefter. He stared back at her, his slate eyes as bottomless as the sea, and shook his head slowly. Erika, her face flushed, broke her gaze with him and slammed her fist on the table.

"Look, the guy tried to kill himself. It's a tragedy. I tried to do the right thing for him, showing respect for him and his family, and you're trying to make me out to be some crook. This is harassment, and it's uncalled for. I mean, for God's sake, the guy left a friggin' *note*," Erika barked.

Frank glanced over at Pepper. He was smiling, thin lipped, looking down at his folded hands.

"Nobody said anything about a suicide note. How did you know that, Ms. Carruthers?" Frank said quietly.

Morris Shefter, his brow furrowed, cleared his throat. "I think it's time we ended this," he said, standing.

"No, wait," Erika said, holding up an index finger. "Are you saying I'm a suspect?"

"I'm not saying anything of the sort. I just don't understand why you lied to me. In my experience, people who lie are usually hiding something. What are *you* hiding, Ms. Carruthers?" Frank asked.

"Erika, let's go," Shefter said, his jaw set.

Frank slid an image from the Ring camera surveillance of

Trek Richards across the table. Erika, standing, glanced down at it and recoiled.

"Do you know this man, Ms. Carruthers?" he asked.

"I *told* you we were done!" Shefter exclaimed, standing up abruptly.

Erika's eyes narrowed into slits, the muscles in her temples working. She shook her head slowly. "Fuck you, Detective," she said.

Shefter grabbed Erika by the arm and escorted her out of the room, slamming the door behind them. Overhead, the fluorescent light flickered, as always.

"That was interesting," Pepper said.

"It was indeed," Frank replied. "I think we got to her."

"She's known to have anger management issues. Do you know what they call her in Savannah's social circles?" Pepper asked.

"Nope," Frank said.

"Her nickname is 'the Wasp.' Everyone's afraid of her. Phillip is supposed to be the nice one. Erika has a reputation for being mean as hell."

Frank looked at Pepper, eyebrows arched slightly.

"How do you know that? I mean, it's not like you're some paragon of social connection," Frank said.

"Candy knows her. They met at some Country Day charity function a few years back. She can't stand her."

Frank grinned. "Just when I think I know everything about you, you come at me with some curveball like that," he said.

Pepper glanced up at the stuttering light overhead. "I suppose we should get that fixed," he said.

"I don't know. I kind of like it. It makes bad people nervous," Frank said.

As they left, Frank turned the lights off, plunging the cramped interrogation room into utter darkness.

17

"OK, gentlemen, what do we have?" Chief Brown said.

The chief was nursing his omnipresent bottle of Dasani and munching on cashews, which he kept in a stash in his drawer.

Frank stood up and went to the whiteboard, drawing a line from left to right. He then drew a series of short vertical marks along the line and marked them with dates.

"Here's what we know: Janie O'Connor broke off her engagement with Phillip Carruthers in mid-February. Shortly after that, she hooked back up with Dr. Dave Wommack, an orthopedic surgeon who was her old boyfriend from college and med school, and they began dating. After they began dating again, Dr. Wommack began receiving anonymous threatening emails and other messages. At one point, a dead rat was left in his mailbox. In the wee morning hours of July 13, a Carruthers employee named Trek Richards set fire to Dave Wommack's porch. Around that same time, Richards was either fired or resigned from the Carruthers organization. At approximately 7:00 a.m. on July 14, he raped Diane O'Connor, Janie's sister, at Janie's home in Rose Dhu. Janie came home from being on call at the hospital that morning, interrupted the rape, and beat Trek up with a crowbar. Her dog attacked Trek, injuring him in the process, and Janie chased Trek away from her home. Trek's bloodstained truck was later discovered stuck in the marsh in Rose Dhu, near Dr. O'Connor's house. The bloodstains on it have been confirmed as Richards's, so he made it back to the truck at one point, but there is no evidence he ever left Rose Dhu. The plantation property is on a peninsula, with only one way in and one way out."

"So Trek Richards has been missing since July 14?" Chief Brown asked.

"That's right."

"And Diane O'Connor's rape was never reported?"

"It was not."

"Was she seriously injured?"

Frank nodded. "He beat the hell out of her. Diane is convinced he would have killed her if Janie had not returned home. Janie O'Connor was able to dress Diane's wounds, gave her a morning-after pill, and treated her prophylactically for STDs. Afterward, Diane stayed at Janie's home at Rose Dhu as she recovered. She'd been staying there a lot lately after Janie and Phillip broke up."

Chief Brown took a few notes and a big swig of water. "What about the night Janie disappeared?"

"Janie left work around 7:30 p.m. on July 19, arriving home around 7:45, and spoke to Diane. Diane took a sleeping pill and went to bed, waking up around 7:00 a.m. on July 20, to find Janie gone. Diane assumed that Janie had simply gone to work, but Janie was supposed to be at the hospital at 6:00 a.m. on July 20 for a series of operations due to start at 7:00 a.m. and did not show up. That set the alarm bells off."

"And no evidence of foul play?" Chief Brown asked.

"None. Janie's bed was made, and the lights were on in her

bedroom. It looked as though she had never gone to bed. Her car was gone, but none of her other things were missing. She hasn't been seen or heard from since."

"Her car is gone? But nobody saw it leaving?"

Frank nodded.

"So Janie O'Connor and Trek Richards have both disappeared, and we have no information about the whereabouts of either?"

Frank shook his head. "None," he said.

"What about Phillip Carruthers?"

"He was in Atlanta on business on the nineteenth. He stayed at the St. Regis in Buckhead. The hotel has confirmed it. We have video from the lobby cameras showing him checking in earlier in the week and checking out on July 21, the day after Janie went missing. Phillip flew into Dekalb-Peachtree Airport on his private jet on July 16. The flight logs were filed appropriately. We've interviewed Phillip's pilot, Greg Sullivan, and Carmine Carpeggio, Phillip's personal assistant and bodyguard, who were both in Atlanta with him. Both men confirmed their location and itinerary. We also spoke to his business associates in Atlanta, who confirmed that he met with them and provided minutes of the meetings. Phillip's alibi is airtight, just like he said it would be."

"Remember that break-in at Dr. O'Connor's place last year?" Pepper asked. "Nothing really came of it, but the assailant left by boat. According to Diane, Janie identified Trek as the guy who broke into her house. Could Trek have kidnapped Dr. O'Connor and left Rose Dhu by boat once again?"

Frank slammed his palm on the table, grabbed Pepper by the sides of his face, and kissed the top of his balding head. "Pepper Stephens, you crazy genius! That might be it! Do you have a copy of that break-in report?" Frank asked.

"I can get it," Pepper said.

"Gentlemen, this gives us a game plan," Chief Brown said.

"Let's pull the report of the break-in and see if we find any reports of stolen boats at Rose Dhu between July 14 and July 20. And let's do that pronto. If Trek Richards has kidnapped Janie O'Connor, every minute we waste could be the difference between her life and her death."

Frank and Pepper got up to leave. Chief Brown mopped his forehead with a handkerchief. "Does it seem too hot in here to you guys?"

Frank and Pepper glanced at each other and shook their heads. "Feels all right to me, boss," Pepper said.

Chief Brown shook his head. "I swear it must be these blood pressure pills I'm taking. I feel like I've been running wind sprints," he said.

He took a big swig of Dasani, crumpled the plastic bottle in his massive fist, and tossed it into the recycling bin. "Well, don't just stand there staring at me, gentlemen. Hop to it!"

Frank and Pepper left Chief Brown's office, closing the door behind them.

—

Chief Brown settled back in his leather desk chair and pulled another bottle of Dasani from the refrigerator. He sat the bottle on a coaster and watched as it beaded up with sweat.

He knew who he had to call. He'd been hesitant before, fearing it might place her in conflict somehow. But he had to know something about Phillip Carruthers that could only be answered by someone who saw him on an everyday basis, someone beyond reproach, a person who he knew was a good judge of character.

The phone rang only twice before it was answered.

"Hey, Mama," Chief Brown said.

"Hey, yourself," Anna Brown replied.

18

Anna Brown had been raised as Anna Butler, the oldest of three siblings. The Butler family, poor but proud, had lived in a little wooden shack just off Coffee Bluff Road. Though small and nondescript, their home was always clean and tidy, with rows of paperwhites and clusters of purple hydrangeas planted out front. The house had no electricity or running water when Anna was a child. Lucius Butler, her father, had dug a well out back during the 1940s, but that was it. The bathroom was a ramshackle wooden outhouse with a rusty corrugated metal roof discreetly hidden among flanking azalea hedges.

Like many poor Black families in the pre–Civil Rights era in the South, the Butlers made do with what they could. Lucius worked at a seafood plant in Sandfly during the week and did weekend carpentry work. Mattie Butler, his wife, worked as a domestic for a wealthy family in nearby Vernonburg. The Butlers raised chickens, grew some vegetables, and did odd jobs. Their needs were not great, and they got by this way for years until disaster struck.

When Anna was sixteen, Lucius was killed in a boiler room accident at the seafood plant. A scant two years later, after being sick for nearly a year, Mattie died of metastatic breast cancer at the Georgia Infirmary.

Anna Butler, who had just graduated from Alfred E. Beach High School, was suddenly forced to raise her younger siblings alone. Anna's younger siblings, the twins Violet and Albert, were only thirteen when their mother died. Anna soon became their rock and their salvation.

Smart, hardworking, and principled, Anna had been an excellent student. She dreamed of going away to college and escaping Coffee Bluff once and for all. Her teachers at Beach had thought she would make an excellent nurse. But her parents' deaths ended those dreams abruptly. Anna had to go to work.

As a Black woman, eighteen years old and with no experience, Anna faced limited employment opportunities. Using the client contacts established by her mother, Anna eventually found a job as a domestic. Over time, she built up a sterling reputation for being efficient and honest. Her clients loved her, and word of mouth kept her in high demand.

Raising her younger siblings meant that Anna never had much time for love. Her personal life always took a back seat to her responsibility. She eventually did marry, when she was twenty-three, after the twins graduated from high school and went away to college, achieving the dream that Anna had once had for herself.

John Brown, Anna's husband, was a big, gregarious man who everyone called Pops. He had steady work as a mechanic at J. C. Lewis Ford. They met at a Sunday church picnic, having been introduced by mutual friends. Anna had never been prouder than when she stood at the altar at First Mount Pleasant Baptist Church on Coffee Bluff Road, the church she'd grown up in, and became Mrs. Anna Brown. But the marriage did not last.

Pops had always wanted to make lots of money. That desire

caused him to develop friendships with some unsavory folks. These men had hard eyes and mean dispositions, and they smoked, drank, and cursed too much, activities Anna disapproved of. They also involved Pops in myriad shady deals and marginal enterprises, many of which kept Pops out late at night. When Anna asked where her husband was going, he always had the same cryptic response: "Out."

Anna would not let Pops bring those people into the house. As a result of the explicit banishment of his new acquaintances, Pops spent more and more time away from home.

One day, a shrimp trawler filled with marijuana was raided by federal agents as it unloaded its cargo onto the earthwork shrimp boat dock at Rose Dhu. *The Savannah Morning News* printed the names of the folks who were arrested. Anna recognized a few of them as some of her husband's "friends."

"Were you involved in that?" Anna asked.

Pops shook his head but said nothing.

For a little while after the shrimp boat raid, he stuck closer to home, right up until the night he disappeared.

"I'm going out for a bit," Pops had muttered, his hot breath smelling of whiskey and stale cigarettes. "Be back before daybreak."

He kissed her on the cheek before he left. Anna rolled over in bed, turning away from him as he left, her eyes filled with tears.

She never saw Pops again after that.

Anna lived alone for years after her husband vanished. She immersed herself in her work and the church, where she eventually became the only female deacon. Despite her youth, people in First Mount Pleasant Baptist looked up to her, implicitly trusting her honesty, sagacity, and godliness. She lived in her parents' old home off Coffee Bluff Road, which she had gradually modernized over the years, installing indoor plumbing, electricity, and the like. Her younger siblings, both professionals, had permanently relocated to Atlanta after graduating from Morehouse and only rarely made it back home.

As a result, Anna mostly spent her days alone.

A few years after Pops left, when she was thirty-one, Anna became pregnant with Clarence because of a brief fling. Clarence Brown never knew who his father was. Anna never spoke of him. After he grew older, realizing that having a baby took two people, he asked his mother about his father's identity. Anna's response was characteristically cryptic: "Your daddy's gone, Clarence. That's all you need to know."

Anna was a tough, relentless taskmaster. She pushed Clarence in football, academics, and as a person, holding him accountable for every action. The steel and grit others attributed to Chief Brown had come directly from his mother, the toughest person Clarence had ever known. Clarence "Gatehouse" Brown was an All-American football player for Bobby Bowden at FSU, but Anna was most proud of him when he graduated with honors from college, and she told him so.

If Chief Brown knew any single truth, it was this one: It was Anna Brown who had made him a man.

Anna's job with the Carruthers family was the best she'd ever had, the culmination of years of hard work. She now had her own beautiful home on the Carruthers property, plenty of food, a retirement package, full health and disability benefits, and a very nice income. There were only a couple of stipulations: perpetual availability and unequivocal discretion.

Which is why Anna was wary of the out-of-the-blue phone call from her only son.

"It's about time you called. You too busy to call your mama these days, Mr. Big Shot Chief of Police?"

"Mama, you know how it is. Things happen, and yes, I get busy sometimes. I'm never too busy to call you, but this investigation I'm working on potentially involves you. I can't just call you and ask you stuff about your employer during an active investigation. That's police business. I've got to make sure I'm not violating protocol—or putting your job at risk."

"I presume this is about the disappearance of Dr. O'Connor?" she asked.

"It is."

"She was a fine woman. It was a shame she and Phillip broke up. She might have been the one to set him right."

"Set him right? What do you mean by that?"

"Phillip has had to deal with a lot since his father died. He needs people in his life who challenge him to be a better person. Dr. O'Connor did that. The other women he has dated did not. I had high hopes for that relationship."

Clarence sighed. "He's not your son, Mama. You aren't responsible for him."

"Clarence, I've raised that boy since he was a baby. Whether you like it or not, I have an interest in how Phillip turns out. His daddy's gone, and poor Miz Cynthia's mind is fading. She's barely hanging on. The young man needs all the positive influences he can get."

Clarence was used to this sort of talk. He'd heard it forever. Still, it always irritated him, like a burr in his saddle, for reasons he could never quite put a finger on.

I'm your son, Clarence thought. *Not him.*

But he didn't say it.

"I want to warn you, Ma: You'll probably be formally questioned about this. It's just a matter of time."

"Questions don't bother me. You know that. I just always tell the truth. That keeps things simple."

"I know you'll tell the truth, Ma. That's not why I'm calling."

"So what exactly do you need, son?"

Clarence sighed. *Always right to the point,* he thought. "Mama, I just need to know something about the Carruthers family."

"I can't talk about them off the record, Clarence. That might get me fired."

"I'm not going to ask you to do that, Mama. No specifics. I just need to know one simple thing, because I trust your opinions about people."

Pausing, Clarence took a deep breath, then asked, "Mama, do you think Phillip Carruthers is a killer?"

Anna was silent at first. He could almost hear her thinking.

"No," she said at last. "No, I don't think he is. But I'm not so sure about Erika."

Then, without saying another word, Anna hung up.

19

Pepper and Frank had an uncanny knack for calling each other at the most inconvenient times. It had become an inside joke between the two men, happening so frequently that they seemed to enjoy the inappropriateness of each episode.

So when the phone rang while Frank was in the bathroom, he had to grin.

"Are you on the john?" Pepper asked, as he often did.

"Yes," Frank said.

"For real?"

"For real."

"Why did you answer the phone, then?"

"Because it was you," Frank said.

"How sweet."

Frank flushed the toilet and washed his hands. "So what have you got?" he asked.

"I pulled the police report for the break-in at Dr. O'Connor's house, like we talked about. It happened in the fall of last year. She came home to find a strange man standing in her garage. He didn't say a word to her. He walked right past her out of the garage and left by boat. Took advantage of a dead spot in her surveillance cameras so that there was no record of his coming or going. There wasn't much to it, except that the guy who did it met the description of Trek Richards. One interesting tidbit: When the investigating patrolman showed up, Phillip was there with Janie, and they seemed tight. Their relationship at that point was still pretty solid."

"Anything else?"

"I investigated any missing or stolen boat reports near Rose Dhu during the week of the fire and Janie's disappearance, and there *was* one—only, it was for July 14, the day of Diane's rape. No stolen boat was reported after that, and certainly nothing for July 19 or 20, when Janie O'Connor went missing."

"I'll need to talk to Diane O'Connor again," Frank said. "Perhaps there's a clue about the break-in that we're missing."

"I think you're sweet on that woman, compadre," Pepper said.

"It's strictly professional," Frank said.

"Right. Either way, good for you."

"So is that all you have for me right now?" Frank asked.

"For now. We did get a strange call from somebody in the Rose Dhu area. Some kids were on the property and said they saw bloodstains on the door of an abandoned house near Houston Creek. I'm going to check that out."

"Fine. I'll go talk to Diane O'Connor," Frank said.

"Keep it professional, Detective."

"Shut up already," Frank said. He hung up.

Frank usually dressed casually. It was his nature, but it was also one of the few perks of being a detective. The more generic his appearance, the more he blended in with his surroundings. He was a chameleon, always part of the background. No one would ever mistake him for a cop. He usually looked more like a roadie for an '80s hair metal band.

But today, he found himself looking in the bathroom mirror.

He *did* look younger after the makeover he underwent for his interview with Dave Wommack. His hair was darker and close cropped. Although he had some lines on his face, they seemed less pronounced. His eyes, which had always looked haunted, had a spark again, rekindling some of the youthful devil-may-care glint that he'd had before Paulina died.

He washed his face and changed into a tight-fitting black T-shirt and gray slacks, a nice pair Paulina had bought for him shortly before she died. *You need some clothes,* she'd said—but he had only worn them once, because they reminded him of her, and that was too painful to bear.

He had to admit it: He looked forward to seeing Diane O'Connor again.

Frank knew his little crush on Janie O'Connor's sister was not exactly kosher. He'd hide it, of course. But Diane had been through a lot of pain lately, and Frank felt a desire to protect her from all of this, to keep her safe.

Get over it, Frankie boy, Cookie admonished him from inside his head.

But Frank couldn't.

At least, not yet.

—

Once again, Diane O'Connor sat across from Frank in the den at Twin Oaks. Dressed in white slacks and a pastel violet-and-pink top, she looked stunning. The bruises were gone, her face was more relaxed, and she looked better rested, as though the nightmare of her assault was finally fading a bit as well.

"Thanks for meeting with me again on such short notice," Frank said.

"I'm glad to give you any help I can in finding my sister," Diane replied.

Diane sat in a leather wingback chair near the fireplace,

legs crossed, her eyes gleaming an impossible cerulean blue. Her posture was perfect. "Have you lost weight, Detective? You look thinner."

"It's the clothes, I'm sure," Frank said, his cheeks burning.

"Any new developments? It seems like you guys have been working hard on the case."

Frank cocked his head slightly. "We have, but how would you know that?"

Diane smiled. "Word gets around. There were some police officers down the street earlier, milling around the abandoned house on the marsh. Old Mrs. Purdy's place. I haven't seen anyone go down there in years, ever since she went to a nursing home."

"Whose house was that again?" Frank asked.

"Agnes Purdy. She's dead now. A little over ten years ago, Agnes got old and feeble and went into the Summer Breeze nursing home. She faded away quickly, like they often do in those places, and was gone inside a year. Her house was supposed to go to her children after she died, but her kids were always a sorry bunch. After she passed, her kids took whatever they wanted out of the house, leaving some rickety pieces of brown furniture, some old pictures on the walls, and that sort of thing, but they could never agree on a price for the house, so it was never listed. Two of her sons are dead now, leaving their part of the house to *their* children, who don't care about it, either. The house has been falling apart for years. It's an eyesore. The paint is peeling, the English Ivy has grown up over the walls to the eaves, and the wooden trim is rotting away. There's no telling what it looks like inside. It's probably an unholy mess, like this place was before Janie fixed it up. Nobody ever goes in it, though, because of the ghosts."

Frank looked up. "Ghosts?"

Diane nodded. "For years, people have said that house is haunted. Some folks claim they've heard strange noises coming out of the house—moans, screams, rattling chains, that sort of thing. And there have been reports of flickering lights inside the house at times. The door is padlocked, but the rumors about the ghosts keep mischievous kids out. It's probably for the best. I'm sure they would be in there getting into all kinds of trouble, and the place is probably full of rats and snakes." Diane shook her head slowly. "Agnes would be mortified if she knew, God bless her," Diane said, crossing herself. She stood up. "Would you like some iced tea?"

"I'd love some," Frank replied.

Diane briefly stepped out of the den and into the kitchen. She brought him a tall glass of iced tea a moment later and placed it on a coaster on the end table, then settled back into the wingback chair and leaned forward intently. "So what brings you out here, Detective? New leads? New questions?" she asked, smiling broadly.

"Both," Frank said. He pulled out a picture of Trek Richards. Diane's smile vanished instantly. "This is the man who raped you, is it not?"

"It is," she said, her lips tight.

"Didn't you say that Janie was certain this was also the man who broke into her garage in the fall?"

Diane nodded. "She recognized him, all right. And not just his look. She knew his *smell*. She said he smelled rotten. It was the smell that tipped her off initially."

"And he left the scene by boat?" Frank asked.

"That's what Janie said." Diane brushed a tear from her eye. "She told me the whole story."

—

October, last year
"Hey," Janie said over the phone.

"Hey," Phillip said back.

The hands-free connection wasn't perfect. She'd hit the dead zone as the on-ramp led onto the Truman Parkway where the phone signal frequently dropped out. Still, she could hear him well enough.

"You're done?" he said.

She nodded reflexively, knowing he could not see her. "I'm headed home," she said. "Just finished up at the office."

The sun was just settling into the horizon as she crossed the Vernon River. The tidal marsh, aglow with shades of orange and red, reflected the sky above. A few wispy cirrus clouds overhead caught the last golden rays of the sun and held them aloft, their edges gilded for a precious few seconds before they drifted into night.

"You work too hard," Phillip said. "I'd take more time off if I were you."

"Says the man who is *always* available for his business," Janie said. "I've seen you answer calls in the shower. Or on the boat, with a fish on the line. You handed me the rod and reel."

"That's different. Like you've always said, it's a *family* business, Janie, and I'm the CEO. I'm expected to handle the details 24/7. It's what they pay me for."

"Well, don't lecture me about taking more time off, then. I have expectations the same as you. I train young doctors. Don't you think there's an analogy there someplace?"

"Can't argue that logic," he said. "What do you want to do about dinner? You wanna eat out? Or should I have Anna fix us something?"

"Let Anna go home. We'll go out, maybe someplace in Sandfly," she said. "I do want to go on a run first. I'll call you after I shower."

"Deal," he said. "See you in a bit."

Janie took the White Bluff exit off the Truman, turning left onto the ancient road leading to her Rose Dhu home. The waning late afternoon sunlight trickled through the arching canopy of live oaks draped with Spanish moss. Most of those oaks had been there for well over a century. A few had been there far longer.

Janie felt her shoulders relax as she drove. She cracked her window slightly so that she could inhale the rich organic tang of the marsh. She was almost home.

A couple of deer—a doe and a muscular eight-point buck— glanced up at her as she passed the gate. The buck flicked its ears, defiant, staring her down. The doe lowered her head and ate some grass from the marsh's edge.

Janie pulled into her driveway, stopping briefly to retrieve the newspaper. It had been delivered after she'd left home that morning.

Her garage lights were still on. A moth fluttered around one of them in erratic circles. As the garage opened, she noted that the overhead light didn't come on again. She'd called the garage door repair people about the same problem the week before, but it had started working again before they came out to check on it.

"Probably a short," the garage door company receptionist had said. "It'll probably go out again."

"Well, I don't see any sense in fixing something that isn't broken right now," Janie had replied. And she hung up. But now the short was back, as promised. A nuisance. She'd have to get the repair folks out here after all.

Janie got out of the car and caught her breath.

A man was standing in her garage.

He was silhouetted against the window. Heavyset, wearing a gray hoodie, he was just standing there, his hands loose and unclenched by his side. His features, hidden in the half-light, were molded in shadow.

Janie heard him breathing.

"I've got a gun," she said, mustering up her most commanding operating room voice.

"No, you don't," he replied, his voice as rough as sandpaper.

She closed her eyes, as if to wish him away. But when she opened them, he was five feet away and moving closer.

Janie backed up, arms raised and ready to fight, but the shadow-faced man strode right by her, his head down. The admixed aromas of cheap aftershave, BO, and mildew swirled around her as he passed.

"How did you get in here?" she asked.

The man continued past her, saying nothing, fists jammed into the pockets of his hoodie. He strode briskly toward the river, his silhouette melting into the pooling shadows along a clump of river oaks just before the marsh.

Moments later, out of sight, an outboard boat motor cranked just beyond the trees—and then Janie heard the boat pulling away, its engine noise dropping an octave as it left the shoreline and vanished into the night.

Janie stared hard and long into the darkness at the river's edge. A ragged breeze rustled the vast expanse of marsh stretching out before her. A few stars winked into view overhead, but Janie focused on the waterline, wanting to be certain that the man was truly gone.

Keith Ellis's ancient basset hound next door began baying, hoarse and low. An evening fog began drifting in. Thick, moist air filled her lungs. Her heart was pounding, her hands trembling, her mouth dry. Janie felt isolated, alone, and off kilter. It was a sensation she wasn't used to, and it pissed her off.

Get a grip, she said to herself.

Janie began walking briskly toward her back door, glancing over her shoulder as she did so. She was hyperaware, sensing everything. She could hear the palmetto fronds rattling in the breeze. Gray strands of Spanish moss undulated in the dark, like ghosts.

Janie unlocked the back door, turned off the alarm, and flicked on the backyard floodlights. Scanning the marsh line one last time, she locked the deadbolt, which closed with a solid *click*, and then leaned against the wall in the entranceway.

She pulled out her iPhone and called Phillip. The phone rang twice before he picked up.

"You're done running already?" he asked.

"No," she said. "I never went."

"You sound weird. What's wrong?" Phillip said.

"A man was standing in my garage when I got home. I have no idea how he got in there."

"Jesus, are you OK?"

"I'm fine. I'm in the house now, and the alarm was still on, so I don't think he ever got in here. It was so strange—he walked right past me, went down toward the river, and was gone. I think he left by boat."

"What was he doing there?"

"I don't know. He was just standing inside the garage when I opened the door. I've barely had time to process the situation. I haven't even gone through the house."

"I'll stay on the phone and drive over. Is the dog OK?"

"Let me check," she said. "Boodles?" she called.

The black Labrador ambled into the kitchen, his thick tail wagging lazily, tongue lolling out of the side of his mouth.

"There you are, buddy," she said. She knelt and scratched the old dog between his ears. Boodles grunted happily.

"He's fine," Janie said. "I'm going to take a walk through the house, but like I said, the alarm was still on, and Boodles seems as calm as ever—and you know how he gets with strangers. Anyway, I don't think the guy got in the house."

With Phillip still on the line, Janie flicked on the additional floodlights around the garage and on the breezeway that connected the garage to the house, then walked all through the house. Nothing was disturbed. Everything was exactly as she had left it.

Boodles followed her as she toured the house, dutifully walking close by her side, glancing up at her occasionally to ensure she was still there. His drool spattered all over the hardwood floor.

"You're hungry, aren't you? I'm sorry, buddy," Janie said, patting his broad head. She poured him a bowl full of kibble and refilled his water bowl.

"I'm here," Phillip said. "Just pulling in."

A flash of light panned across the house from the driveway. Janie recognized the distinctive bluish tint of Phillip's BMW headlights.

Phillip pulled to the back of the house near the garage and locked his car. Janie met him at the back door. He kissed her gently, razor stubble brushing her chin, then took her into his arms and held her. "Are you OK?" Phillip asked.

"I am now," she said.

"Have you ever had this kind of problem before?" he asked.

"Never! What really makes me mad is that I got no alerts on the surveillance cameras. Nothing! I paid a lot for that system, and it failed me. I've got to check the recorded video, but he never should have been able to approach the house without being seen."

"You must have been scared to death," Phillip said.

"I was, at first. Now I'm just pissed off."

Phillip chuckled. "There's my girl," he said, patting her on the back.

"Did you get a good look at his face? Could you identify him?" Phillip asked.

Janie shook her head. "He was wearing a hoodie, so I really couldn't see his face at all. I just can't figure out how he got into the garage. The doors were all locked from the inside, and nothing was broken—not a door or a window. Nothing was missing, either. It's just weird."

Phillip held her out at arm's length. "We need to call the police," he said.

"Of course," she replied, nodding.

But deep down inside, she knew there was little point to it.

—

As Janie had expected, the police investigation revealed nothing of substance. There were no signs of forced entry. No fingerprints left behind. No physical evidence at all. The officer, a serious, soft-spoken young man named Lieutenant Chu, reviewed the video surveillance footage with Janie and Phillip and confirmed that there was not a single image of the intruder anywhere.

"You were right, Dr. O'Connor. The intruder didn't break into the garage; he had access. Perhaps a door was left open, or he had some other mode of entry. Does anyone else have a key to this place? Or a remote for the garage door?" Lieutenant Chu asked.

"My sister and my parents," Janie said. "Nobody else."

"I have a key, too," Phillip said.

"Of course," Janie said.

"How long have you two lived here?" Lieutenant Chu asked.

"Oh, we're not married. This is my place. Phillip's my . . ." She glanced up at him. "Boyfriend?" she said.

"Passionate lover," Phillip said, grinning. "We're engaged."

Janie blushed.

Lieutenant Chu looked vaguely uncomfortable. "Well, anyway, I'm pretty much done here. Do you have any questions?" he said.

"No," Phillip said. "And thanks."

"You're welcome, Mr. Carruthers. Glad to help. I'll let you know if we get any leads," Chu said.

As the squad car drove away, taillights briefly flashing red at the bend in Rose Dhu Road, Janie looked up at Phillip and shook her head. "He knew who you were," she said.

"It goes with the territory," Phillip said with a slight shrug. "Savannah is a small town. You know that."

Later that night, after returning from dinner, Janie turned on the alarm and then settled into the desk in her home office to review the surveillance footage once more. The alarm system she had put into the house was state of the art. Surveillance cameras were positioned by each door, on the front and back porches, and next to the mailbox on the driveway. She pulled up the camera website on the computer.

"All right, you sonofabitch. Where are you?" she muttered.

But when Janie scrolled through the images, once again, there was nothing.

She realized the flaw in her camera layout. There was no camera near the garage, nor was there one on her dock. An intruder could enter her property from the river and approach her garage without being picked up on video at all.

She needed to fix that.

—

"Was there any further investigation of that incident?" Frank asked.

"Nothing ever came of it," Diane said.

"Phillip was there for Janie that day. Isn't that a little different from the way you described him before?"

"Phillip has no problem being the hero. Galloping in on a white horse is something he's comfortable with. But he likes to be in control. That was the root of their problem. He always told Janie how to act and how to behave. He tried to run her life for her. And Janie has never needed guidance from anyone. She's always been her own woman."

Frank took a sip of iced tea. "This is really good," he said, holding up his glass.

"Family recipe," Diane said, smiling. "So where are we with the investigation? Have you found Trek Richards yet?"

"We haven't. It's weird—after he came in here on July 14, the day . . ."

"I know what day that was," Diane said.

Frank nodded. "Well, there's no evidence that he ever left Rose Dhu. His truck was found stuck in the marsh near here. His apartment was untouched, as if he'd never returned home. There has been no sighting of him anywhere since. He came in here and vanished. That's why I'm here talking to you today. Since he left here by boat once before, perhaps he did that again," Frank said.

Diane tapped her index finger to her temple. "Good thinking," she said.

Frank stood up. "I suppose I'd better go now. Thanks for seeing me again," he said.

"Always glad to help. I hope you catch that bastard. Pardon my French," Diane said.

As Frank drove away from Rose Dhu, a murder of crows suddenly took flight from the marsh. Wheeling overhead, calling hoarsely to one another, they flew across the river, their obsidian wings gleaming in the afternoon sun.

Frank recalled a Native American legend he'd once read about crows being the guardians of the underworld. "That figures," he said out loud, turning onto White Bluff as he headed home.

20

September

Pepper called Frank just after sunrise.

Once again, Frank could not sleep. The O'Connor case was dredging up all the old ghosts. Their spirits haunted his dreams, stalking him in that shadowy twilight between daylight and death.

So he was sitting on his balcony in the darkness, smoking more weed to try to soothe his jangled nerves, just as the first rays of the morning sun began filtering through the trees.

When his phone rang, it startled him.

"Mornin', Pep. You're up early," Frank said.

"Frank, we've got something," Pepper said.

"What do you mean?"

"I've got to show you. You won't believe it. Meet me at the station and we'll drive out to Rose Dhu together."

"Now?"

"Yes, *now.*"

Pep was rarely that insistent, so Frank got dressed quickly and drove to the police station.

Pepper was waiting outside his truck, which was parked

at the curb. He looked rumpled and disheveled, as always. His combover was particularly atrocious. "You drive," he said. "My truck is hawkin' loogies."

"What the hell does that mean?" Frank asked.

"It's making weird noises, like it has something stuck in its tailpipe," Pepper said, opening the passenger door to Frank's car.

"I think *you* have something stuck in your tailpipe," Frank said.

"I probably do."

Frank turned down White Bluff once again and headed back into the tunnel of trees that led to Rose Dhu. "This drive is becoming too familiar," he said.

"It's about to get worse," Pepper said.

"What did they find out here?"

Pepper waggled his eyebrows like Groucho Marx and leered at Frank. "Bodies," Pepper said.

Frank turned to him. *"Bodies?* As in more than one? Is it Trek and Janie?"

"Nope. I mean, yes, there are several, but none of them are our mysterious missing people."

"Well, who are they, then?"

Pepper spat into his palm and smoothed down a few stray hairs.

"That's just gross," Frank said.

"Do you remember those murders a few years back? The ones where the killer bit his victims multiple times before killing them?"

"You mean the Piranha?"

"Yep. That guy."

"He was never caught."

"I know. You may also recall several people during that time just disappeared and were never heard from again. At least one of them, Vanita Casagrande, was clearly linked to the Piranha. He sent the police a taunting letter about her, but they never found her body. And after she disappeared, there were no more Piranha murders. He just faded away."

"I do remember that. It was eight or so years ago."

"Well, hold on to your britches, compadre. I think we've found where he was working from," Pepper said.

They were turning down Rose Dhu Road.

Once again, crows filled the ancient oak trees that bordered the marsh next to Rose Dhu Road, squawking and scrabbling among themselves. They flapped noisily between the trees, calling hoarsely to one another. Several gangly vultures circled lazily overhead, as well, their bald heads turning this way and that with the wind.

"What's going on with all the birds?" Pepper asked.

"Hell if I know," Frank said.

"Anyway, the Kid was poking around in the backyard of that abandoned house at Rose Dhu with the bloodstains on it, and they found Vanita Casagrande's remains, along with those of at least three other people. And guess what."

"I give up."

"Trek Richards *was* there, as least at some point. We've got DNA evidence showing that. But he's not there now—and there's no evidence of Janie, either."

Frank pieced together what Pep was saying. "Do you think *Trek* could be the Piranha?"

Pepper shrugged. "Who knows?" he said. "This whole case just gets weirder and weirder."

Agnes Purdy's 1950s ranch-style home, crouching amid a brace of ugly old pines, was just as Diane had described it: a crumbling ruin, boarded up and overgrown with a wild tangle of ivy. The brick chimney was cracked, listing to one side. Waist-high weeds filled the yard.

The home was now sealed off with yellow police tape. A small army of young men in white hazmat outfits scrambled about like termites in the nest, planting tiny red evidence flags around the yard as they dug, sifted, and tried to make order out of chaos.

Despite the constraints of the hazmat suits, Frank recognized the stance of Jonathan Kramer and walked over to him. "What is the deal here, Kid?" he asked.

The Kid pulled off his hazmat hood and spoke to Frank. "We looked at the bloodstains on the door first. They were from Trek Richards. It's a one hundred percent match. The same with a bloodstained shirt we found in the kitchen sink. There's no running water here, so he couldn't clean it, but he ditched the shirt in the house—probably so he wouldn't draw attention to himself. None of Trek's other stuff is here," he said.

"No gun?"

"No gun."

"How did you find these other bodies?"

"I saw some people-shaped depressions in the dirt out back, so I got the ground-penetrating radar out here and bingo! We found four bodies. All were dismembered, but the skeletons are complete, just in disarray. Dental records for one of the bodies matched Vanita Casagrande. We're still looking up the others, but all were females, most likely all under forty."

Frank glanced at Pepper, who nodded.

"There's one more thing," the Kid said. "These women were *butchered*, Detective. No doubt about it. And we are pretty certain that there was cannibalism involved, because some of the bones had human bite marks on them. But these skeletons have all been in the ground for at least eight or nine years. There are no fresh bodies. So this doesn't help us much with Janie O'Connor's disappearance, except to place Trek Richards at the house and at his truck at some point after the rape."

"So we are no closer to solving the O'Connor case than we were yesterday. We just have more dead bodies in Rose Dhu, from an unsolved serial killer case several years ago," Frank said, shaking his head.

Pepper grinned broadly at Frank, his Billy Joel eyes bulging even more than usual. "I *told* you it was weird."

—

After all the excitement of the discovery of the bodies at the abandoned Purdy house, the trail leading to Janie O'Connor went cold.

Both Phillip and Erika Carruthers could account for their whereabouts, as could Diane O'Connor (although Frank had to admit that he did not aggressively pursue her as a suspect, perhaps because his all-knowing gut told him she wasn't one). Trek Richards, the prime suspect, had vanished from the face of the earth. Janie's car had never been found, despite the Kid's best efforts with his fancy surveillance software. The police had no new leads and no new direction to go in. Over time, the easily distractable news media moved on to other things.

In October, the O'Connor family was temporarily thrust back into the spotlight by yet another tragedy. Rick O'Connor, Janie and Diane's father, had finally died of complications of the heart attack and subsequent stroke he had suffered shortly after Janie disappeared, never having fully regained consciousness. Rick had been a ruddy-faced giant of a man, very active in the local community. His death was another shock to a family battered by recent events.

But after that, the world moved on.

In early December, someone made an anonymous call to a Savannah Police Department tip line. The caller's voice, which was male, was mechanically distorted and sounded like he was speaking through a rusty pair of tin cans connected by a wire.

"Dr. O'Connor is dead. I know where she's buried," the robot-voiced caller said. "The grave's in the marsh near Rose

Dhu Road, right beside the approach road to the Girl Scout camp. There is a clump of twisted-up cedar trees there, and a historical marker for a Civil War ironclad." He gave exact coordinates, the longitude and latitude precise down to a fraction of a degree. The description was perfect. He paused as if catching his breath. "They say that place is haunted."

He was silent for a moment. An electric hum was in the background, an undercurrent punctuated by a static crackle of interference.

"They're right," the man with the robotic voice croaked, his voice barely a whisper. And then he hung up.

PART THREE

THE DISCOVERY

21

December 5

They found Janie's body, or what was left of it, on a frigid afternoon when the sun loitered behind a lead-gray shroud that stretched from horizon to horizon.

Janie's remains were unearthed exactly at the spot the caller had said: in a shallow, unmarked grave in the dense tidal marsh that bearded the mercury ribbon of the Vernon River near the meandering course of its tributary, Houston Creek.

The Kid, who'd had a hunch about the site, had been right after all.

The police surrounded the area with yellow crime scene tape and called in the excavation team. Clad in full hazmat gear, complete with goggles, air-filtration masks, and Day-Glo orange suits, the team attracted a curious crowd of onlookers as they began digging through the thick mud with hand tools and brushes. Working impassively and methodically, water vapor billowing about their heads as they breathed in the chill December air, the excavators washed the stubborn muck from their gloved hands through sieves, plucking random slivers of bone from the aggregated detritus of waterlogged reeds and oyster shell fragments. The marsh grass rattled cold and dry as armies of fiddler crabs scurried about in ragged platoons.

In the end, there wasn't much to the grave itself. It was an afterthought, a hollowed-out bit of tidal zone no-man's land. The final recovered booty was a meager ruin: a few loose finger bones, some scattered teeth, the splintered greenstick remains of what might have been ribs, and part of a single shoulder blade, partly exposed, standing straight up above the waterline like an angel's wing. Janie's mud-encrusted 10-karat gold medical school ring was buried deep, at the bottom of everything, as if it were ashamed of its final resting place. Once they had cleaned it, they saw her name, in cursive, inscribed along the inside. A swatch of blue plaid fabric that matched one of Janie's shirts was discovered tangled among the deep roots of the woody marsh grass.

The brittle shards of bone had been scattered randomly about in the mud, likely the work of buzzards or raccoons. Nevertheless, the recovered teeth—a couple of molars—were surprisingly intact, gleaming pearl white against the rich, dark mud.

"Bingo," Frank Winger muttered quietly when he saw the teeth.

Frank lit a cigarette as he watched the team drop the teeth into plastic evidence bags. Blue smoke curled wraithlike about his head. He knew what the teeth meant.

Teeth were like little DNA time capsules. The hardest things in the human body, made of a calcium hydroxyapatite matrix virtually impervious to degradation, the molars had sealed Janie's precious DNA inside for all eternity. With a little biochemical coaxing, the teeth would ultimately yield their precious nucleic acid cargo. The police then recovered DNA from Dr. O'Connor's electric toothbrush and hairbrush, cross-referenced it with DNA taken from Janie's sister and mother, and compared those specimens to the DNA isolated from the molars the forensics team had found. Janie had also submitted DNA for genealogy research purposes in the past that could be accessed through GEDMatch, a national public DNA database, providing an additional source of confirmation. It was through the DNA contained in the few teeth found in the Rose Dhu gravesite that the police were able to definitively establish that the mysterious disappearance of Janie O'Connor, MD, was the result of her murder.

Police Chief Clarence "Gatehouse" Brown held a press conference the day after her identity was confirmed.

Frank Winger sat in a folding chair at the very back of the room, his eyes shaded by a battered pair of Ray-Bans, which dated back to his Army days.

"The remains discovered off Rose Dhu Road last week were indeed the remains of Dr. Jane Dillon O'Connor, who had been missing since this past July," Chief Brown said, pushing his reading glasses up his nose as he spoke. The press room lights gleamed silver off his wire-rimmed spectacles.

"We believe that her body had been there for several months, most likely ever since she disappeared. The remains are substantially degraded, but we have a positive ID through DNA testing, and we are now reclassifying this as a homicide," he said.

"Do you have any leads?" asked Tina Baker, holding her ungainly parabolic microphone aloft. Tina's teeth were impossibly white, and her makeup was somewhat exaggerated for the camera's benefit, but her hair was perfect, as always.

"We have some leads, but I'm not at liberty to comment about the status of an ongoing criminal investigation until an arrest has been made."

Frank glanced around the room at the pack of news reporters. Ravenous, their eyes hungry and gleaming, they seemed like wolves in expensive suits and designer dresses. He thought of the original Brothers Grimm story of Little Red

Riding Hood—not the sanitized cartoon version, but the more sinister one, where the wolf who had just eaten Red's grandmother lay in bed dressed in the dead grandmother's nightgown, patiently waiting for the little girl to show up.

"My, Grandma, what big teeth you have!" Red Riding Hood had exclaimed.

"The better to *eat* you with, my dear," the wolf had replied, saliva dripping from his fangs.

What a friggin' circus, Frank thought, shaking his head as he got up to leave.

—

Frank Winger held what was left of Janie O'Connor sealed in a nondescript dark-green plastic box, the sort one might see used for storage of duct tape or other mundane household items.

Carrying Janie's remains this way made Frank sad. Everything Frank had learned about Dr. O'Connor was a testament to what a fundamentally decent person she had been. Now, she was reduced to a random collection of teeth, fragments of bone, and a few shreds of clothing, all neatly sealed in plastic.

With the forensic investigation of her remains complete, Frank was tasked with turning over what little was left of Janie to her sister, Diane.

Diane stood up when Frank entered the room. Illuminated by the brilliant afternoon sun, Diane seemed luminous, almost transparent.

Frank felt a strange clutching sensation in his chest. *I hate this,* he thought.

"Ms. O'Connor," Frank said, extending his hand.

"Detective Winger," Diane said, taking it loosely. Unsmiling, she was stiff, too formal, her sadness draped across her like a shroud. "It's been a while since we last spoke. I was beginning to think we'd reached a dead end."

"We had," Frank said. "I wanted to be the one to do this, although I'm sorry this is why we are meeting today. As you know, we got a break from an anonymous tip that led us to Janie's remains. We put the remains through all the testing you and I talked about earlier, but we're done now, so I can hand them over to you for burial."

Diane took her sunglasses off. Her brilliant cobalt-blue eyes were reddened and tear-filled. When Frank held the box out to her, Diane appeared stunned. "That's all there is?" she asked.

Frank nodded. "That's all," he replied.

Diane's shoulders slumped, as though the gravity in the room had suddenly doubled. "How is that possible?"

Frank swallowed, feeling a distinct lump in his throat. "Diane, this isn't going to be easy," he began.

"Tell me. I'm a big girl."

"She may have been dismembered. She was in a tidal area frequented by scavengers like raccoons, vultures, and fiddler crabs, so the water and the marsh animals probably got to the body after she died. We searched the whole area and didn't find any more of her, so there's at least a chance the killer may have disposed of other body parts elsewhere."

Diane's face crumpled up in grief, and she shook her head slowly. "So there's nothing else left of Janie?" Her voice was nearly a whisper.

Frank shook his head. "You already have her class ring, but otherwise, this was all we found. I'll keep you posted if anything else turns up."

"What happened with Trek Richards?" she asked.

"He's vanished. No one has seen him since . . ." Frank looked down.

"Since he raped me."

"Yes," Frank said. "Since that day. They found his blood-stained truck in the marsh near your home, but he's never resurfaced."

"I'll bet Phillip and Erika killed him," Diane said, her jaw set. "Some part of me *hopes* they killed him." She dabbed away a few tears. "I keep going back to the last time I saw Janie, the night before she went missing. I told her I loved her and went right to bed. The sleeping pills knocked me out. And the next day, she was gone forever. Just like that. I never got to say goodbye."

Frank felt he should hug her, but he held back, sensing it would be inappropriate, an invisible line he shouldn't cross.

"You know, when Janie first went missing, I had this recurring fantasy that she was away somewhere, maybe traveling overseas. But deep down inside, I knew better. Janie has never been the sort of person who bails on folks. It's not like her at all."

She glanced sidelong at the plastic box, as if she were afraid to look at it directly. "There's no coming back from this. It's permanent," she said.

"As permanent as it gets," Frank said.

Without warning, Diane threw her arms around Frank and buried her head in his shoulder, sobbing. Her vaguely floral scent filled Frank's nostrils.

"It's not fair!" she said in a muffled voice.

"I know," Frank said.

Clutching the container in one hand, Frank gingerly wrapped his arms around Diane's shoulders. He was struck by how fragile she seemed, as though she had been constructed from scraps of straw wrapped in baling wire.

"Janie was a good person. She deserved better than this," Diane said. Abruptly, she pulled away from him, smoothing her hair. "I'm sorry," she said. "That was uncalled for."

"It's OK," Frank said, faking a smile. He'd never been good

at false platitudes, and the smile came out crooked and stillborn, his expression as lifeless as a doll's.

"We're planning her funeral," Diane said. She dabbed a few more tears from her eyes. "You can come if you like."

"I might, at that," Frank said. *Her killer might be there,* he thought. *Sometimes the bastards just can't help themselves.*

Diane held the plastic box at arm's length and stared at it, like it was somehow toxic.

"Either Phillip or Erika Carruthers, and possibly both of them, murdered my sister. Promise me you'll get them, Detective. Promise me!"

The container Diane was holding shook in her hands as she spoke, rattling the meager collection of her sister's bones inside. Her eyes bored into him like lasers.

"We'll do our best," Frank said. "I can promise you that."

22

Frank got up early on the day of Janie O'Connor's funeral and drove downtown at 7:00 a.m., even though the service was not scheduled until noon. After parking his car near the Sorrel-Weed House a few blocks away, he walked toward the cathedral.

The day was gorgeous for mid-December—in the low 50s, the air crisp and clean, the brilliant sun rising into a clear blue sky with a few wispy strands of cirrus clouds high overhead. The leaves had not yet fully turned. Instead, they hung on, confused by the unseasonal warmth that was the norm these days, creating a strange mélange of green, yellow, and ocher, as though the seasons had simply stopped trying to define themselves. Overall, the palette was unbelievably beautiful.

Frank smoked a cigarette as he walked. He hated to defile the pristine atmosphere, but smoking, a habit he'd picked up in Afghanistan, always helped calm his jangled nerves. Besides the occasional joint and a deep-seated affection for high-quality craft beer, it was his only remaining vice.

The detective stood across the street from the sanctuary,

slouching against a weathered wall made of Savannah Grey brick, his cigarette dangling loosely from his mouth.

Frank had not dyed his hair again and had allowed himself to gradually go back to his old look over the last few months. Bearded, with tufts of salt-and-pepper hair peeking out from beneath a gray knitted cap, he was dressed as usual in old blue jeans and his leather bomber jacket, along with a vintage Led Zeppelin *Physical Graffiti* T-shirt, a relic he'd salvaged from a downtown thrift shop. The vagrant look was exactly the look he wanted; people wouldn't usually even look directly at him when he dressed this way. It was perfect because Frank wanted to flatten out and disappear, to bleed into the ancient brick like old paint, a mirage shimmering at the edge of reality, a nondescript spirit that no one wanted to be haunted by. There was absolutely nothing memorable about Frank Winger.

His inherent capacity for anonymity had helped make him a damned good detective.

The local news channels showed up at the funeral early. Tina Baker, her voice low and respectful, broadcast live and in person from the sidewalk outside the cathedral, her breath curling about her perfectly coiffed head as she spoke. Many other correspondents from the major network affiliates did, too. CNN, MSNBC, and Fox News all showed up, their antenna-festooned trucks parked obscenely close to the twin towering church spires, which pointed straight to heaven.

The cathedral started filling up three hours before the service. Diane O'Connor, accompanied by her mother, Mary, and Dave Wommack, arrived over two hours early. The three of them emerged slowly from a black Lincoln Town Car, courtesy of Brown Brothers Funeral Home.

Frank was shocked when he saw Mary O'Connor.

He'd only seen photographs of her before, but even accounting for that variable, Janie and Diane's mother seemed to have aged dramatically in the months since her daughter's death. Thin and pale, she was dressed in a shapeless black dress with no makeup and a wild, windblown corona of graying hair. Deep lines crisscrossed her face. Mary was withering away like an unwatered houseplant, her life force slowed to a mere trickle. Dave Wommack, his face pale, was dressed in a charcoal-gray suit with a red tie emblazoned with the block *G* of the University of Georgia. He held tightly to Mary's arm, catching her once as she stumbled over a curb.

Mary will be joining Janie and Rick soon, Frank thought, shaking his head.

Diane wore a midnight-blue dress and a black wool overcoat, her platinum hair a shimmering halo around her face. Her attire only accentuated her thinness. Oversized Jackie Onassis–style sunglasses covered her incredible sapphire-colored eyes. Sunlight gleamed from a simple gold pendant, an ankh, draped around her neck.

As she exited the limo, Diane looked directly at Frank and nodded. Her acknowledgment was almost imperceptible, but just enough.

The Carruthers family arrived shortly after the O'Connors, pulling up to the curb in a gleaming black BMW Alpina limousine. A muscular, broad-shouldered gentleman with close-cropped hair and sunglasses exited the front seat from the passenger side and opened the passenger side rear door. Tall and erect in a fitted black suit, Phillip helped Cynthia, his white-haired mother, from the car. Anna Brown was also with them, dressed in black, standing close by Cynthia's side and gently holding the old woman's elbow.

Erika Carruthers was conspicuously absent.

Frank stubbed out his cigarette as he watched more throngs of people arrive.

The Catholics came dressed in their best funeral attire, with knots of old women fingering rosaries and praying softly to themselves, their withered lips moving in whispered reverence for the dead. Janie's hospital colleagues had gathered there, too. Surveying the crowd, Frank realized he did not know what he was looking for. Criminals looked just like everybody else. Whoever had killed Janie woke up that morning, took a leak, brushed their teeth, and took a shower. They didn't pin a scarlet letter *M* to their clothing or affix a flickering neon sign to their heads that said "Murderer!" Still, sometimes if you watch hard enough, you'll see something—an aberration, some little detail that just seems *wrong*. Tiny details like that can often become clues that might unlock the entire mystery.

If fifteen-plus years of detective work had taught him anything, it was that.

Stubbing his last cigarette on the sidewalk, Frank crossed the street to enter the sanctuary. There was a weight pressing down on him that he could not fully explain. The funeral had become a macabre celebrity event, a metamorphosis that seemed wrong to Frank. But it also had something else: an air of finality, snuffing out any remaining traces of hope for Janie's survival that might have lingered over the past several months.

Janie O'Connor was dead, and nothing in this world was going to change that.

23

March 1

Frank was dreaming of Paulina when his phone began ringing.

He awoke with a start, his heart racing and palms sweaty. His iPhone was ringing, dancing atop the bedside table. He picked it up and saw that he'd missed two calls from Pepper.

"Yeah, Pep, what is it?"

"I'm sorry to bother you in the middle of the night like this, Frankie, but the media's going to get wind of this by morning, and I thought you needed to be aware of it in advance. Whole thing's crazy, how the stuff about that O'Connor girl just came out of nowhere, and now the press is all over this case again like flies on shit."

"Pep, what the hell are you talking about?"

"Tina Baker got a call from someone on her cell phone early this morning. She said the caller's voice was like the voice of that robot on *Lost in Space* or something. Sound familiar?"

"Uh-huh. Just like that initial call on the tip line that told us where the body was."

"Bingo. Sounds like the same guy, all right. Well, get this: The voice gave her a name."

"The voice called Tina a name?" Winger was confused.

"He *didn't call* her a name, you idiot. He *gave* her a name. The name of a suspect. And it'll shock you who it is."

"Spill it, Pep."

"Phillip Carruthers."

Frank smiled. "This is why you called me at three o'clock in the morning? Because some anonymous caller implicated the victim's ex-boyfriend, who was originally our prime suspect in this case? A man we've already questioned, who had an airtight alibi? Come on, Pep, you've got to do better than that."

"Well, the caller sent Tina an anonymous email with an attachment. The attachment contained a snippet of time- and date-stamped video from Janie O'Connor's home surveillance video cameras. And that video showed Phillip Carruthers at her house in Rose Dhu on July 19. The night she went missing. When he was supposedly in Atlanta."

Frank sucked in a breath. "But we checked all the footage from that night."

"Turns out not *all* the footage. We looked at the web-based archives of all her cameras, but this feed was from another separate camera system, which she had apparently added on the garage, from a different vendor. It might have been something she did in response to the home invasion incident last fall. These new cameras weren't connected to the old account, and the images were stored in a different place on the cloud. We weren't even aware they were different from her other cameras, so we missed them the first time around."

Frank's mouth suddenly went dry. He swallowed a tenacious lump of early morning phlegm. "It's Phillip Carruthers? For sure?"

"Unmistakable. He looks right at the camera. Can't be anybody else."

"Well, can't we just find out who sent the email? That

should nail down the source pretty quickly. And the phone, too."

"The phone was a burner, as you might suspect. And the Kid is already working on the email thing," Pepper said.

"Any way you slice it, we'll need to bring Phillip back in for further questioning. And we need to get a search warrant for his place," Frank said.

"For sure. But we need to think this through a bit first. We don't want to cross swords with the Carruthers organization unless we know we've got all our ducks in a row. Morris Shefter will be up our asses inside an hour," Pepper said.

"Pep, listen. It was friggin' *Tina Baker* who got the call. She's not going to let this go. It'll be all over the news. This is the story of the spring. Heck, if it turns out Phillip Carruthers killed Janie, it'll be the story of the *year.*"

"So what do you suggest we do?" Pepper said.

Frank thought momentarily, trying to clear the early morning cobwebs from his head.

"OK, I have an idea. Let's call Tina back first thing this morning, once the sun comes up. Bring her into the loop. Ask her to hold off on announcing this until we get more information—and in exchange, we'll give her an exclusive on the investigation. She'll get the inside scoop before any of the big news networks. She's talented and ambitious, and it would be her big chance at an exclusive national story. That might buy us a little time," Frank said.

"We'd need to run all this by the chief first," Pepper replied.

"Of course."

"You know this may all be a setup. There are lots of people out there who would like to see Phillip Carruthers fall," Pepper said.

"That's true. We've got to let the evidence speak for itself," Frank said.

Now that the cobwebs were fully cleared, an idea popped into Frank's head, like one of those idea light bulbs in a cartoon.

"Look, Pep, go ahead and get that search warrant. We'll visit Phillip today, out at his place, with the video. We can go out there with the idea that we're warning him about a possible blackmail attempt instead of being confrontational. Then we'll see what shakes out. But right now, I'm going to try to go back to sleep for at least two more hours."

"OK, Frank. I'll see you when you get in. Sleep tight."

"Yeah, yeah, I know. Don't let the bedbugs bite," Frank said.

—

"Oh, *hell* no, Frank. You can't just show up at the Carruthers compound with a search warrant."

Chief Clarence Brown leaned back in his desk chair so far that it cracked, sounding as though the wood might simply splinter.

"Look, Boss, Pep and I understand the difficult politics of simply showing up at Carruthersland with a search warrant," Frank said. "But we've got an idea about how to approach this."

"Fire away," Chief Brown said.

"The thing is, the video was sent to Tina Baker. She's going to be all over this. I offered her an exclusive if she'd hold off a bit and she agreed, but she won't hold off for long. If we don't address it somehow, it'll look like we're covering up for the Carruthers organization."

"You realize that this could be a frame-up. The Carruthers family has rubbed a lot of folks the wrong way over the years. The video could be from anybody: some angry ex-employee, a business associate who felt wronged, you name it. And it's easy to fake a video these days. People do it all the time. We've got to be damned careful here," Chief Brown said.

Frank was absolutely gobsmacked by Chief Brown's reticence. This was so unlike the principled, hard-charging, no-nonsense man he had grown to respect over the years.

What the hell is he afraid of? Frank thought.

"Pep and I had an idea about that, too. We figured we could tell Phillip that we're looking out for his interests and are concerned that someone is trying to set him up. We can just say we need to talk to him. The warrant could come later," Frank said.

Chief Brown nodded. "I like that plan. It buys us a little time while we sort this out. Let's get moving, gentlemen."

Frank and Pepper left the chief's office and entered the battleship-gray hallway. Standing next to the bulletin board, out of earshot of anyone else, Frank looked both ways before talking further to Pep. "Anything we do here has to be kept between you, me, and the chief. You know that, right?" Frank said.

"Why is that?"

"Because there's probably some truth to what Trek told Diane. I'm pretty sure there are some people on the police force who are informants for the Carruthers organization. We need to keep everything in our investigation on a 'need to know' basis. Only the people directly involved in the investigation need access to any details. I don't want them to know what we've got, or what we don't have. Until we sort this out, keep all the investigation details on the down-low."

Pepper cocked his head like a curious dog. "What does 'on the down-low' mean?"

Frank shook his head. "Seriously? You've never heard that expression?"

"Never in my life."

"You're a friggin' Philistine, Pep. Honestly," Frank said.

Pepper arched his eyebrows.

"You don't know what a Philistine is, do you?" Frank asked.

"Is that like in the Bible?" Pep asked.

"Yes, like in the Bible," Frank said, shaking his head.

Frank and Pepper rode out to the Carruthers compound on Wilmington Island in Frank's battered Hyundai. Pepper was sporting an oversized pair of black-framed Ray-Bans and reeked of cigar smoke. He was dressed in a drab gray suit, which he had inexplicably paired with a garish canary-yellow tie. His gut strained mightily against the pair of dark-red suspenders holding up his pants.

Frank glanced over at Pepper and shook his head. "Who dresses you, Pep?" Frank asked.

"I dress myself. Why?"

"Just a word of advice: You might want to ask Candy's opinion about your outfits every once in a while."

"You ain't exactly a fashion plate over there, especially now that you've gone back to your old appearance."

"Nobody cares how I look. I would think your wife cares how you look."

Pepper shook his head. "Everybody's a critic."

The Carruthers family owned a huge five-hundred-plus-acre estate tract off Morningside Drive. The land had been in their family dating back to a colonial-era King's Grant, long before Savannah's waterfront property became outrageously expensive. Most of it was an undeveloped, pristine maritime forest thick with live oaks and cedars—the exact sort of semi-tropical vegetation that Oglethorpe had encountered when he first landed in 1733.

The two detectives pulled up to the massive stone-gated archway near dusk. A pair of three-foot-tall gaslights cast long, flickering shadows that danced around them like ghosts. The double gate itself was made of black heavy-gauge wrought iron. Each gate had a huge capital letter *C* mounted on it in Gothic script.

"Good Lord," Pep said, taking off his Ray-Bans. "Have you ever been out here before?"

Frank shook his head. "That gate looks like something out of *Jurassic Park*," he said.

"Maybe this *is* Jurassic Park," Pep said. His voice was hoarse. He cleared his throat before coughing deeply. "You know, Frank, if we drive in there and actually do get chased by a T. rex, I'm going to just outrun your slow ass." He coughed again, spitting a greenish wad of phlegm into his handkerchief. Folding it neatly, Pep placed the soiled handkerchief in his front pocket.

Frank shot a quick glance at his partner and smiled. "*You're* going to outrun *me*?"

"That's the plan, Stan."

"Pep, if I can't outrun you, I don't deserve to live anyway."

There was an intercom button with a speaker, a keypad, and a glowing ruby-colored button next to the gate. A domed video camera winked its all-seeing tiny blue eye at them.

Frank pushed the intercom button and spoke hesitatingly. "Detectives Frank Winger and Pepper Stephens from the SPD, here to speak with Phillip Carruthers. We have an appointment."

There was no reply at first. They sat there in silence, the car idling. Somewhere in the distance, a pair of loons called to one another.

"Well, what do we do now?" Pepper said.

Suddenly, the intercom button light turned green. Frank and Pep heard a deep metallic *clank*, and the gates slowly began to swing open, creaking on their gargantuan iron hinges. The gaslights flickered a little more. Frank half expected them to shoot columns of flame high into the night sky.

All part of the show, he thought.

He'd seen this sort of thing before. It was an old power play; judges did it all the time. So did elected officials. It was a way to make a statement, setting expectations from the outset. And those expectations relayed certain unspoken truths loud and clear: *I'm important. Fear me.*

But Frank was not afraid.

He knew what fear looked like.

Frank and Pepper kept driving. The winding driveway meandered past cypress swamps filled with roosting waterfowl and past bamboo thickets packed so tight that a child could not walk through them. The arching live oaks with their long, moss-draped arms framed the entire driveway and stole any glimmer of remaining sunlight, hastening a night that was at once oppressive and foreboding.

The house finally came into view after the driveway's fourth turn.

"Holy hell," Pep said when he saw it.

The Carruthers mansion was massive—and made entirely of stone.

It's one thing to build a stone house where stones are lying around. England, Scotland, Scandinavia, and the higher latitudes of North America had plenty of stones left over from the retreat of ancient glaciers, piles of rock fragments carved from the sides of mountains as the great rivers of ice had flowed past thousands of years earlier. Hilly areas like North Georgia had places underground, the residua of ancient lava flows and tectonic plate collisions, where rock could be quarried. But there were no such rock deposits near Savannah, a coastal city that had been beneath the ocean's surface as recently as eleven thousand years earlier. Rock like this had to be imported—and the Carruthers mansion was constructed from a very large rock pile.

Frank parked his Hyundai directly in front of the house. As he switched off the engine, a small man impeccably attired in a black suit appeared out of the darkness. He extended a white-gloved hand, palm up. Frank tried to shake it, but the man looked appalled.

"Your keys," the man said.

"I'm keeping them," said Frank.

"Forgive my rudeness in not introducing myself first," the man said. "I'm Alphonso Hernandez, Mr. Carruthers's valet and groundskeeper. Mr. Carruthers does not like vehicles parked directly in front of the house. It's the bomb threat, you understand. A well-placed ammonium nitrate car bomb could take down the entire building. Your vehicle will be parked a safe distance away near our garage area. I will retrieve it for you when you depart."

"Don't you guys know everyone who comes in here?" Pep asked.

"You can't be too careful," the valet said. "We don't *really* know you."

Frank, eyebrows raised, glanced at Pep as he handed Hernandez the keys.

"Thank you, Detective. Carmine will escort the two of you to Mr. Carruthers," he said as he took the wheel of Frank's battered Hyundai.

He's probably never had to park a Hyundai here, Frank thought.

"Who's Carmine?" Pep asked.

"That's me," a deep voice behind them said.

The voice had come from another impeccably dressed man in a black suit—but this man was a giant, broad shouldered and muscular, at about six feet five and 260 pounds, with a close-cropped hairstyle and an earpiece in place. His posture was ramrod straight, and Frank noticed something else: Carmine was packing. There was a leather shoulder holster beneath his jacket.

The man looked like a professional soldier, a look Frank knew all too well.

Frank extended his hand. "Detective Frank Winger," he said, shaking Carmine's big mitt.

"Carmine Carpeggio," the big man said.

"Ex-military?" Frank asked.

Carmine nodded. "Army, 75th Ranger Regiment, 1st Battalion. I was stationed at Hunter for a bit. I got a job with Mr. Carruthers after I left the service. He needed a personal assistant who could double as a bodyguard, and Mr. Carruthers likes to hire veterans," Carmine said, stone faced. "Did you serve?"

Frank nodded. "Army, too. I did a couple of tours in Afghanistan. Nothing special, though—just an everyday grunt. I was stationed at Hunter after returning stateside as an MP, so the transition to police work was easy after I got out."

Carmine opened the six-inch-thick oak front door and ushered them into the expansive foyer. The floor was polished Carrara marble in a checkerboard pattern of black and white squares. Colorful Persian rugs covered most of the foyer's surface. The Gothic-style arched ceiling vaulted three stories high. Overhead, a chandelier as large as a wagon wheel was suspended from a trio of heavy iron chains. The marble double staircase on the foyer's opposite side curved around a burbling fountain. Alcoves along the staircase were adorned with statues of Georgia luminaries, and a panoramic stained-glass window in the stairwell depicted General Oglethorpe's 1733 disembarkation onto the Savannah River bluff.

"This is some place," Pep said.

"It's Mr. Carruthers's sanctuary," Carmine said. "He built it himself. He can relax here without any worries or regrets and with all the privacy he needs." Carmine turned on his heel, then turned back. "If you gentlemen will wait here, I'll bring Mr. Carruthers to you straightaway."

Carmine left the room quickly. *He's like the Flash,* Frank thought. *Only quieter. And likely more deadly.*

"I can see why he calls this place a sanctuary," Pep said. "It looks like a friggin' cathedral." Pep had stuffed his hands in his pockets, as he always did when he was uncomfortable. He had a guilty look about him as if he'd stolen something.

"Gentlemen," a voice said behind them.

Pep jumped.

A grinning Phillip Carruthers was striding toward them with his arms outstretched, as if he were greeting old friends. Carmine trailed him by a step, ever vigilant, as though he expected an ambush at any moment.

"Mr. Carruthers, as you probably remember, I'm Detective Frank Winger, and this is Detective Pepper Stephens. We're with the Savannah Police Department," Frank said.

"Yes, I remember. Sorry our last interaction was so confrontational. Morris can be very protective of me at times," Phillip said.

"Don't sweat it. It's all good," Pepper said.

"I do want to thank you for all your hard work investigating Janie's disappearance. I know it's been a bit of a slog. Chief Brown says you have something new you wanted to share with me?"

Frank nodded. "It's sensitive new information and confidential, of course, but the chief felt like you ought to be brought into the loop early. Unfortunately, it was sent to a member of the news media first, so we're a little behind the eight ball."

Phillip looked up at Carmine, looming behind Pepper and Frank, and dismissed him with a hand wave. "Carmine, you can go. We're fine," he said.

After Carmine departed, Phillip motioned for them to move to a small study just off the foyer. He ignited the gas logs in a wood-and-marble fireplace against the study's back wall and closed the sliding wooden door.

The study had oak library shelves from its floor to its ceiling, with a rolling ladder in place to access the books. A large wooden Jefferson-style desk was in the middle of the room, facing the fireplace. A pair of massive leather wingback chairs crouched in front of the desk. A life-size oil painting of Anderson Carruthers, Phillip's father, hung over the fireplace.

The old man's image stood tall and erect, a gold-embossed shotgun cradled in his hand and a pair of faithful pointers at his feet. His ice-blue eyes blazed with a cruel intensity.

Frank and Pep sat in the wingbacks, which carried the pervasive scent of old leather and tobacco. The heat from the fireplace licked feverishly at the back of Frank's elbows.

"Brandy?" Phillip asked, picking up a crystal decanter from a small table between the two chairs.

Frank put a hand up, shaking his head. "We're on duty, Mr. Carruthers," he said.

"Of course. My apologies."

Phillip poured himself a glass and sat in the large leather chair behind the desk. "It's been a really tough few months. Being back at the church Janie and I were to be married in, but for her *funeral*, was . . . not easy." Phillip's lower lip trembled a bit, and he paused for a moment but then continued. "You know, when Janie first disappeared, I imagined all sorts of things. She often went into the hospital in the middle of the night, so I figured maybe she fell asleep, and her car went into the river. They never found her car, right?"

Pep shot a sidelong glance at Frank, but Frank ignored him.

Phillip's shoulders slumped. He buried his face in his hands. "I never thought about *murder* at all until they—you—found her remains."

Now Frank glanced back over at Pep, who raised his eyebrows and cocked his head. *If he's guilty and faking it, he's a pretty good actor,* Frank thought.

Phillip sniffled, his eyes bloodshot, then looked up. "Have you found Trek Richards? Any more leads there?"

"None. He's vanished. Nobody has seen or heard anything from him since July 14. Have *you* heard from him, Mr. Carruthers?"

"I have not," Phillip said.

Pepper nodded and spoke up at last. "Mr. Carruthers, a

local news reporter received a time- and date-stamped video from Dr. O'Connor's home the night before she went missing."

"Can I see the video?" Carruthers said.

"That's why we brought it," Frank said. He opened a laptop and clicked on the video icon.

Carruthers watched, eyes wide. He swallowed, hard.

"Recognize him?" Frank said.

"That's me," Phillip said.

"Are you sure?" Frank asked.

Phillip nodded.

"Do you see the date stamp? That's from the night of July 19—the night before Dr. O'Connor went missing. You were supposed to be in Atlanta that day."

"I *was* in Atlanta that day."

Frank leveled a stare at him. "Then how do you explain this?"

"Well, it's . . . complicated. And I . . ." Phillip's voice trailed off, and he glanced up at them. He was red faced and flustered, clearly surprised by what he'd seen. "I want to make one thing clear: I didn't kill Janie. You must know that. I *loved* her." Phillip stood up. His hands were trembling. "Before I say anything else, I'll need to speak to my lawyer." He reached beneath the edge of his desk, and Carmine Carpeggio suddenly reappeared out of nowhere.

"Gentlemen, I'll show you out now," Carmine said.

They walked in silence to the mansion's front door. Frank's Hyundai, with its engine running, was waiting for them outside. Alphonso stood by it, holding the door open.

"Good day," Carmine said, nodding almost imperceptibly. He closed the front door to the Carruthers mansion with a solid *kerchunk*. The deadbolt clicked immediately behind them.

"Follow the estate road out," Alphonso said. "It leads directly to the gate. There are surveillance cameras all along the route. Please stay on the main estate road and do not deviate. Security will be dispatched to find you if you have not reached the exit within ten minutes."

Frank and Pepper got into the Hyundai and drove away.

"Well, that was weird," Frank said as he drove down the access road. "He seemed genuinely upset about Janie's death. But then he admitted that it was him in the video and didn't even try to deny that he was there."

"Maybe he *was* there but had a legitimate reason for it," Pep replied.

"Maybe. But that would blow his entire alibi if he was. He was supposed to be in Atlanta. That's what he told us the first time. And if he's lying about that . . ."

"He could be lying about all of it," Pep said.

"Looks like we'll be getting a search warrant after all," Frank said.

24

Frank got up before dawn the following day, as always.

He'd always liked the predawn hours. The air was cool, and the world still slept. It afforded him a respite from the world's chaos and helped him think.

Frank got a blank piece of paper from his printer and opened the O'Connor case file. He knew something was missing here. The pieces didn't fit just right.

He drew a square in the middle of the page and labeled it "Janie." He then drew a circle to the square's right and wrote "Phillip" on it. Another circle, drawn next to Phillip's, he labeled "Erika."

To the left of the Janie square, he drew another circle he labeled "Diane." He then placed the names of Janie and Diane's parents in a circle above the two of them.

He'd spoken to Diane at length, of course. Phillip would be brought in for additional questioning any day now. He couldn't question Janie unless he held a séance—and he doubted that would be admissible in court. Frank and Pep had interviewed Janie's parents, coworkers, neighbors, and friends, all to no avail. Every single person expressed absolute consternation about Janie's disappearance. Nobody provided any earth-shattering revelations.

But something here bugged him.

Frank read through Pepper's interview transcripts, which were largely unrevealing. Pep's interviews with Janie's parents were almost cryptic, containing no helpful information. He noted that Janie's now-deceased father was "very emotional" but offered no relevant details about Janie's potential whereabouts or state of mind, saying simply over and over that she was "such a good girl." He'd had a stroke just a day or two after that interview and had never awakened. Pep's interview with Janie's mother, Mary, was almost as useless. Her comments were rambling and disjointed, corroborating Pep's analysis that Mary's mind had been scrambled by the disappearance of her daughter.

But, by all accounts, Janie and her mother had a good relationship, so it stood to reason Mary knew something about Janie's relationship with Phillip. *She's got to know something,* Frank thought. *Even if it's buried deep down in some cortical borrow pit.*

Frank decided to stop by Azalealand nursing home, where Mary was now a resident, on his way home from work that day. Azalealand was a low-slung cinderblock-and-brick edifice just off Skidaway Road. Surrounded by moss-draped live oaks and banks of the namesake azaleas, the place stank of stale urine and antiseptic, the sort of aroma you hoped you'd never have yourself but knew you probably would someday.

Mary O'Connor was seated in a wheelchair in her tiny room, gazing out of an unadorned square window at the setting sun. Gaunt and hollow cheeked, her formerly coal-black hair now wispy and gray, she looked like the killer's dead mother in *Psycho.*

"Mrs. O'Connor?"

The old woman turned and looked at him. "Yes?" she asked.

Her eyes were the same striking sapphire blue as both of her daughters'.

"I'm Frank Winger. I'm the lead investigator on your daughter's murder case. Do you have a minute to talk?"

"Why, of course, Detective. I know who you are. I last saw you standing on the sidewalk outside the cathedral at Janie's funeral back in December. You looked a bit out of sorts that day."

Frank was taken aback, shocked at her lucidity. "Funerals aren't my thing," he mumbled. "Never have been."

He pulled up a sturdy wooden chair and sat so that they could see each other. He had never been this close to her before. Her eyes were not only a brilliant blue, but it was clear from how radiant they were that she was much less debilitated than he had been led to believe.

"Mrs. O'Connor, a suspect has emerged in your daughter's murder."

She nodded, her blue eyes narrowing to mere slits. "It's Phillip Carruthers, isn't it?" she asked.

"Why do you say that?"

"Who else could it be? Janie didn't have an enemy in the world. Everybody loved her. Phillip and Janie had recently broken up when she disappeared. Phillip is the sort of man used to having things his own way. My mother would have said he was 'spoiled rotten,' and he was. He also had a horrible temper. When Janie broke up with him, he threw her diamond engagement ring into the marsh. Can you imagine? Such a waste. But I wouldn't have expected anything else from someone like him." She sighed. "When Janie vanished, I knew she was dead. That girl was born responsible. She never would have left town without talking to us. She cared about everybody, especially her family."

Mary looked up at Frank. She shook her head slowly. Tears filled her red-rimmed eyes. "When Janie was seven, she found a wounded pigeon flopping around in our yard. Someone had shot it with a BB gun. She kept the poor thing in an abandoned garage apartment behind our house in Ardsley Park and fed it with an eyedropper until it was better. I didn't even know that bird was out there until she was ready to let it go. After it had healed, she took the wounded pigeon out into the backyard, and it took wing and flew away. That was my Janie. She was always doing whatever was necessary to make others better. That's just part of who she is. Or was."

Mary's hands were shaking. She dabbed at her eyes with her fingers.

"Mary, what else about your daughter's relationship with Phillip made you suspect him?"

"Phillip never cared enough about Janie to try to understand her *soul*. He'd take her to fancy restaurants in New York, or they'd fly on his private jet to the various Carruthers properties around the world, but he never understood what made Janie tick. She loved helping others with a passion that exceeded everything else." Mary was clenching her fists now, nails digging into her palms. "Phillip wanted her to give up everything she loved. He was poison to her. I wish they'd never met."

"Phillip told us that they were still engaged and that their wedding was still technically on the books when she disappeared," Frank said.

Mary glanced up at him, her tear-filled blue eyes blazing. "That's a bald-faced lie," she said. "They were long since done. When Janie went missing, she was already back with Dave. He even went with us to Janie's funeral. Phillip was insanely jealous of Dave even before the engagement was broken off." Mary leaned forward, eyes narrowed, her jaw set. "Frankly, I'm a little surprised Phillip hasn't made Dave disappear, too."

"Mrs. O'Connor, if you felt this way, why didn't you tell us about this earlier? Why wait until now?"

"Oh, I did! I spoke to another detective at length about my concerns with Phillip. We talked well over an hour. I remember it distinctly. It was in early September, right before Georgia played South Carolina. I told him everything I just told you. Nothing's changed since then, except now we know for certain that Janie's dead." She dabbed at the corner of one eye, wiping away a tear.

"Who did you speak to back then?"

"Detective Stephens. He gave me his card."

She opened a drawer in her bedside table and found Pepper Stephens's card, slightly smudged, with his cell number scrawled across the obverse in his easily recognizable handwriting.

"He said to be sure to call him personally, day or night, if I came across any other information I thought might be useful regarding Janie's disappearance. Such a nice man," she said, smiling.

Frank, staring intently at his partner's card, felt a wave of nausea sweep over him. He could feel his pulse throbbing away in his temples. His palms were sweaty.

Jesus Christ, he thought.

—

Frank got into his car outside Azalealand and ran trembling fingers through his hair.

Maybe she's just better now, he thought.

That could happen, couldn't it? With all the stress she'd been through, Mary's brain could have just decamped for a while and come back, right?

But Frank now suspected that she'd never left.

Mary remembered every detail of her prior conversation with Pep and found his card in the bedside table drawer without any hesitation. She was lucid and coherent and had excellent recall, all of which raised other considerations about Pep's previous interview with her.

At that moment, a crack opened in Frank's mind, a crack that insidiously spiderwebbed across his consciousness, allowing a smidgen of doubt to seep in.

Did Pep downplay what she had said? Why would he do that?

Frank then thought about Pep's disengagement during their recent interview with Phillip, only speaking up to say that the video may have been faked.

Pep was more than Frank's partner. He was also Frank's best friend. They had eaten many meals and downed many (perhaps too many) brews with one another. Although Frank was an Orioles and Ravens guy and Pep was a dyed-in-the-wool Braves and Falcons man, they had watched innumerable baseball and football games together. Moreover, they had shared more than a few long sleepless nights on stakeouts, simply talking shit. Frank had become a regular visitor to the Stephens household, known as "Uncle Frank" to Pep's kids, and he attended their school plays and ball games regularly.

In many respects, Pep was the brother Frank had never had.

But that was not all.

When Paulina died, Pep had been Frank's rock. Pep was the first person Frank called when he found Paulina on the kitchen floor, glassy eyed, with her mouth half open, lying in a sticky pool of her own blood. Pep had even taken Frank's gun that day, talking him down when all Frank wanted to do was end it all.

Pep was likely the sole reason Frank was alive.

So was Pep just lazy? Or what?

Pep could be ethically challenged sometimes when it didn't matter. He'd cheat at Monopoly, taking extra money from the till when he was the banker. Pep never had a problem accepting free food and booze in bars, which was something Frank would never do.

But lots of cops do that, right? Frank thought.

Besides, it was harmless. There was no quid pro quo, just a pat on the back, a tacit acknowledgment of the good work the police were doing to keep the community safe.

No harm, no foul, as far as Frank was concerned.

But Pep was *never* lazy when it came to work. Meticulous and detail oriented, his documentation was always impeccable. The two of them would never have gotten along if Pep had been careless about his work—because after Paulina died, work was all Frank had.

For now, Frank had no concrete reason to suspect anything about Pep. He'd give his old friend the benefit of the doubt. Pep had earned that.

But the crack in Frank's mind, tiny as it was, remained nonetheless.

25

The following evening, Morris Shefter and Phillip Carruthers arrived at the police station at 10:00 p.m. in Shefter's black Mercedes sedan, taking advantage of the darkness to avoid the omnipresent news crews, who had returned with a vengeance.

Frank interviewed Phillip by himself this time.

Turning on the audio and video equipment, Frank took a seat at the interview room table across from Shefter and Carruthers.

"We're recording this interview as per usual protocol."

"We are aware of standard police protocol, Detective," Shefter said.

"I just wanted to ensure you knew everything you say is on the record."

"Where's your sidekick?" Carruthers asked.

"He had something going on with his kids tonight, so you're stuck with me," Frank said.

That's what I'm telling you, *anyway,* Frank thought.

The fluorescent light overhead began flickering again.

Morris Shefter glanced up at it briefly and shook his head. "Good God," he muttered.

"Mr. Carruthers, did we recently bring a video to your attention during a meeting at your home?" Frank asked.

"You did."

"And what was on that video?"

"Footage of a man at Janie O'Connor's home, date- and time-stamped on the evening of July 19."

"And what is the significance of that date?"

Phillip cleared his throat. "That's the day before my fiancée was reported missing," he said hoarsely.

"And yet when we showed you this video, you identified the man on the video as yourself, did you not?"

"It is me. I admit that."

"When we first questioned you about this several months ago, you informed us that you were in Atlanta that night, did you not? You'd flown there on your private jet on business on July 16 and flew back to Savannah on July 21. Isn't that what you said?"

"It is. And I *was* in Atlanta that night. Greg Sullivan, my pilot, has confirmed this, as did Carmine Carpeggio, my personal assistant and bodyguard. They were both with me the entire time. The plane's flight log also backs up my story, as do the testimonies of my business associates in Atlanta. But you guys knew all that already."

"So how do you reconcile your version of events with what we've seen on the video?"

Phillip leaned toward the table. He was self-assured and confident, not anxious at all. "The video is a fake," he said.

Frank threw up his hands. "It's a *fake*? You previously admitted that it was you on the video. Do you now contend that's not the case?"

"It's me, all right, but somebody must have altered the time and date stamp, or maybe the camera dates are wrong. Perhaps someone fabricated the whole thing. All I know is that I was in Atlanta that night."

"Did you step in something on the way in here, Mr. Carruthers? Because this sounds like a load of bullshit to me."

"It's not bullshit," Phillip said. His face was flushed, neck veins bulging. "I didn't kill Janie. I told you that already!"

"So instead, you contend some mysterious, unknown person altered the time and date stamp on a video, which you admit shows you coming up to Janie O'Connor's garage on the night she disappeared, and then kept it for several months before sending it to a news reporter to frame you for a crime you did not commit?"

Phillip shrugged. "Video can be altered, you know. People do it all the time. Fake news is everywhere."

Frank shook his head. "Who would try to frame you for a murder you did not commit?"

"Lots of people. I run a large, multifaceted corporation. We've made more than a few enemies along the way. It's part of the collateral damage of doing lots of business in a small town like this one."

"Did you murder Janie O'Connor?"

Phillip sighed, shaking his head. "No, I did not. How many times are you going to ask me that?"

"As many times as it takes to get at the truth," Frank said.

Shefter stood up, eyes ablaze. He picked up his briefcase, white knuckled, his jaw set defiantly. "That's it. We're done here."

"We'll be getting a warrant to search your home. Are you going to give us any trouble with that?" Frank said.

"Get your warrant. My client has nothing to hide," Shefter replied.

And then they were gone.

—

Frank was eating a deliciously greasy hamburger from Five Guys at his desk when his cell phone rang.

He stared at the phone, read the name of the person calling, and shook his head in disbelief. "Unreal," he said out loud. Swallowing the mouthful of ground beef he was chewing, he answered the call. "Tina. How can I help you?"

"This may be about how *I* can help *you*," Tina said.

"With all due respect, I doubt that, Ms. Baker, but go ahead."

"You remember that anonymous email account? The one that sent me the video?"

"That was that Proton Mail service, right? Our IT guys told me about it. I didn't even know that sort of thing existed."

"I didn't, either, but I just got another one from them."

"From who?"

"I think it's from the same person who sent me the video. It's anonymous, so I can't be sure, but it *seems* the same. You're getting a warrant to search Phillip Carruthers's place, right?"

"How did you know that?" Frank asked.

"Give me some credit, Detective. I have my sources. You need to see this email before you do the Carruthers search. I've printed you a copy. Is there someplace we could meet?"

"Why don't you just forward the email to me?" Frank said.

"Apparently it's encrypted. You can't just forward it."

"Can't you just take a picture and send it?"

"Frank, look. Anything I take a picture of with my phone is in the cloud. That means someone could access it. I don't know who these people are, but they clearly have some sort of agenda. Hell, it could be the Russians."

Frank grinned. "I don't think the Russians are sending you emails, Tina," he said.

"Well, *something* is going on. I've had threatening messages left on my voicemail, telling me to back off the O'Connor story. People have been following me. I've even seen shady-looking folks standing on the sidewalk outside my condo, just watching. And my office email was hacked recently. I've changed my password three times in the past two weeks. Don't blame me if I'm just a little paranoid," Tina said.

Frank swallowed and then asked the most relevant question he could think of. "How do you know you can trust me? Maybe I'm one of them, too."

"Look, I've been a reporter quite a long time and can tell when someone isn't genuine a mile away. You seem like a man with integrity."

"So you're trusting me based on gut instinct?"

"I guess I am," Baker admitted. "But my gut has served me well so far. I've built my whole career on it."

"I can respect that," Frank said. "I trust my gut, too."

"So where can we meet?" Tina asked.

"I'm at the station downtown. Can you take a walk in Colonial Park Cemetery? We could meet at the Button Gwinnett gravesite."

"That's fine. I'll be there in fifteen minutes."

She hung up.

Frank wolfed down the rest of his burger, crammed a handful of fries into his mouth, and wiped his mouth and fingers with his napkin.

—

Tina Baker was standing beside the four-columned marble Gwinnett gravesite, located roughly in the center of the cemetery. She was dressed casually, in jeans and a simple light-blue blouse, and her hair was pulled back into a ponytail. Her locally famous eyes were invisible beneath a pair of oversized, dark designer sunglasses.

"Thanks for meeting me on such short notice," she said, flashing a brilliant smile.

"Thanks for reaching out," he replied.

"I'm just trying to do whatever I can to help the investigation," she said.

Frank looked at her, one eyebrow raised skeptically.

"Look, Frank, I'm being honest here. I knew Janie O'Connor. I first interviewed her during the sugar refinery explosion a few years back. She was only a surgical resident then, but she was impressive. Even then, I knew that she was going places. We ran into each other on several occasions since and got to know each other socially. She'd built a great reputation in the local medical community and was a role model for many young women. She was always willing to give back to her hometown. For me, Janie's death goes way beyond the news story. It's personal. I counted her as a friend. I was shocked when she went missing. I want to help catch her killer any way I can."

"I didn't know her," Frank said. "The only time we ever met, she was a pile of bones and a few teeth buried in a shallow grave."

Tina handed a piece of paper to Frank. "Here's the email. There was no attached file this time, so this is all I got."

Frank glanced down at the piece of paper. "Our IT guy tells me that the encryption on this Proton Mail service is incredible. The friggin' Homeland Security Office couldn't breach it. Whoever sent it doesn't want anything sourced back to them."

Evidence for the dead doctor is hidden at the Carruthers mansion. Look in the crawl space beneath the garage. It's locked with a padlock. Inside, you'll find a bag with the murder weapon—and some other things.

Frank read it twice, then glanced up at Tina. She seemed to be looking over Frank's shoulder at something. Her mouth opened briefly—and then she suddenly turned and began walking briskly toward the cemetery's iron gates without saying another word, as if she had seen a ghost.

"Tina?" Frank called after her.

Tina shook her head and kept walking, waving him off without turning back around.

Frank turned, looking behind him. Two men in dark suits, sunglasses, and overcoats stood at the cemetery's edge in the shade of a large cedar tree. They were both wearing earpieces. The men might as well have had *Federal Agent* tattooed on their foreheads. When they noticed Frank was staring at them, they quickly left the graveyard.

Frank started jogging after them. "Gentlemen? Can I help you?" Frank called.

This is stupid, he thought. *You don't know what you're getting into.*

The men turned the corner at Oglethorpe Avenue and moved out of sight. Frank, slightly out of breath, thought he might catch them after he rounded the corner. By the time he got there, the men had vanished.

An elderly gentleman in a cherry-red windbreaker was standing on the corner, waiting for the light to change. Otherwise, there wasn't another pedestrian in sight.

"Did you just see two men in dark suits come through here?" Frank asked the old man, gazing down the street.

"Pardon?" said the old man, tapping the hearing aid in his right ear. "Hearing's not what it used to be." He grinned kindly at Frank with yellow, worn teeth.

"Two men in black suits. Like in that movie," Frank said.

The old man seemed to ignore him.

When the light changed, the old man ambled slowly across Oglethorpe in his comfortable shoes, mumbling incoherently to himself.

As the man neared the other side of the street, Frank noticed something else: the outline of a handgun in a shoulder holster beneath the old codger's jacket.

That's ridiculous. You're letting your imagination get the best of you, Frankie boy.

But when the old man reached the far side of Oglethorpe, he turned, and Frank saw that his lips were still moving, and he was wearing a black earpiece in his left ear, the same sort the other two men had been wearing.

"Hey!" Frank shouted after him. But the light changed once again, and a surge of cars, trucks, and buses flew past.

By the time the street finally cleared, the old man was gone.

26

March 12

Chief Brown called Arnold Boynton, the Chatham County DA. The call was routine procedural stuff, the kind of thing the two of them dealt with every day. "Arnie, I need some help getting a search warrant for the Carruthers compound on Wilmington Island."

"What for?"

"We've had a few new leads emerge in the O'Connor case. The leads potentially implicate Phillip Carruthers as a suspect. We need to go over his place with a fine-tooth comb. I can't seem to get any of the judges around town to grant us a search warrant even though we have probable cause. However, Judge Mitchell says he'd sign off on it if you agree to it. I know you guys are tight. Can you help me out here?"

"Didn't we go over this seven months ago?"

"We did, but Phillip had a pretty good alibi then. The new evidence blows a few holes in his story."

"So you're telling me that you did a shitty job last summer, but now that you have new evidence you're going to do a better one? What kind of statement does that make about the SPD?"

"Come on, Arnie, give me a break. I'm just asking for some help getting a search warrant. I'm not asking for your firstborn son."

"You can have my firstborn son. He's more trouble than he's worth—and if I give him away, I don't have to deal with Morris Shefter. If I help you get a search warrant for the Carruthers place, I will."

"You're telling me that you're busting my balls about helping with a search warrant for Phillip Carruthers's place because you're scared of his *lawyer*?"

Although I do get it, Chief Brown thought. *I don't like dealing with Morris Shefter any more than you do.*

"I'm telling you that we'd better have a damned good reason for going back out there or Shefter will be up my ass sideways with a crowbar. You know the deal as well as I do. So what is this new evidence?"

"A video, time- and date-stamped, that places Phillip Carruthers at Janie O'Connor's home the night before she went missing, during a time he claimed he was in Atlanta on business."

"Videos can be faked," Boynton said.

"So can anything, Arnie. That doesn't mean we should turn a blind eye to new evidence just because you're a chicken-shit DA who is afraid of a hotshot corporate attorney."

Chief Brown then played his trump card. "Do you want my support in the next election, Arnie?"

"Come on, man. That's dirty pool," Boynton said indignantly.

"It's not. You barely beat Mike Devereaux last time. What was it, two percentage points? My endorsement swung the Black vote your way. You lose me, and you lose the election. So what's it gonna be, Arnie? Am I going to get my search warrant?"

"Shit," Boynton said.

"That's a good lad," Chief Brown replied.

Boynton sighed. "I'll speak to Judge Mitchell in support of the warrant, but you're gonna have to be done before nightfall. I don't want you disturbing the Carruthers family after business hours."

Chief Brown rolled his eyes. "Business hours for a cop are 24/7, Arnie. You know that."

"Take it or leave it, Clarence. That's all I'm going to authorize."

"I'll take it," Chief Brown said.

"I'll be counting on your support next fall," Boynton said.

"Thanks for your help as always, Arnie," Chief Brown said.

And then he hung up.

—

Frank and Pepper drove out to Wilmington Island, this time in Pep's battered white Dodge Ram pickup, the sort of truck favored by construction workers and government agencies.

"This piece of crap makes my Hyundai look fancy," Frank said.

"I love this truck. Why do you feel compelled to harass me about it?" Pep asked.

"I'm just amazed at you. You live in this big-ass house, your wife drives a brand-new Lexus, you have three kids at Country Day, and you sputter around town in this rolling junkpile."

The ancient truck backfired, belching out a cloud of black smoke.

"Ah, now you've done it. You've made Mabel mad," Pepper said.

"You call this old clunker *Mabel*?" Frank said, grinning.

Pep's lower lip poked out as if he were offended. "Mabel was my grandmother's name," he mumbled.

The Wilmington River bridge flung itself across a watery

tableau of verdant marshland. The river's meandering tributaries gleamed in the midmorning sun like ribbons of quicksilver among a broad savanna dotted with random hammocks filled with scrub cedars and palmettos.

Frank had fallen in love with Savannah while he was stationed at Hunter. The city's marshlands and estuaries reminded him of the coastal area of Maryland—and Savannah was warmer and less expensive than Baltimore.

With his parents gone and no remaining ties to his old hometown, Frank had decided to find a job in Savannah as soon as he left the Army. Just as Frank's Army commission expired, fate intervened: An opioid epidemic–induced crime wave led to an immediate need for more law enforcement agents in Savannah. Frank had the sort of training and experience the Savannah Police Department sought, and he was hired immediately. Frank left Charm City for the Georgia coast and never looked back.

On days like these, he fell in love with his adopted home all over again.

Chief Brown had gone to great lengths to keep the formal search of the Carruthers compound discreet. The police cars were all unmarked. There was no police tape and no crime scene marking. When Pepper and Frank pulled up to the front of the mansion, it looked like a bunch of folks had just parked their cars for an oyster roast.

Of course, the cars were all parked off to the side, behind the garage.

Alphonso has been busy, Frank thought.

The craziest thing of all was that Chief Brown was there himself.

"Gentlemen, gentlemen, glad to see you," the chief said heartily as he approached the two men. "We're coordinating our search through Carmine over here, who works with Mr. Carruthers."

Frank looked at Carmine, who nodded impassively. "We know each other," Frank said.

"Of *course* you do! I forgot that you two had already been out here!" Chief Brown said.

The chief was decidedly not himself. Clarence Brown usually cracked crises open with his bare hands and sucked out the marrow. The chief was a gamer, the sort of man Frank would want next to him in a foxhole. But today? Clarence "Gatehouse" Brown, Mr. Gameday himself, seemed as anxious as a chicken in the fox's den.

Carmine Carpeggio stood defiantly in front of the house, hands on his hips. He was scowling, perturbed that the order he meticulously maintained on the estate had been temporarily upended. Police investigators were swarming like flies, crawling into every nook and cranny.

So far, they'd found nothing.

Frank had decided that he was not going to tell anyone, not even Pep, about the tip he'd gotten from Tina Baker. The search warrant for the Carruthers compound had been served even without knowledge of that most recent anonymous email. With the possibility of informants within the police force, the fewer people who knew about Tina's tip, the better. If the information was accurate and if there were Carruthers insiders lurking about, Frank didn't want the evidence to disappear. He waited for the right moment to play his hand.

As the day wound to a close and the five o'clock deadline approached, that moment finally presented itself.

"I think it's time we wrapped this up. We've found nothing of substance here," Chief Brown said, clapping Carmine on the back.

Caught off guard, Carmine shot the chief a sharp glance, but then he relaxed and even registered an almost imperceptible grin.

The massive ten-car garage was a tabby building roughly

half a football field away from one side of the estate house. All the police cars had been parked behind it in an orderly fashion, including Pepper's truck.

It's now or never, Frank thought.

Glancing over at Pepper, who was standing with his hands in his pockets, Frank said softly, "Walk with me."

Pep raised an eyebrow, and the two men walked across the carefully manicured front lawn toward the garage. They were met halfway there by Alphonso, who appeared out of nowhere.

"Can I help you, gentlemen? If you're leaving, I'd be glad to retrieve your vehicle," he said.

Frank pointed to a small, padlocked door at the base of the garage, almost hidden between a pair of camellia bushes. "What's that?" he asked.

"The door to the crawl space," said Alphonso.

"Why is it padlocked?"

"We don't want people to have free access. You never know who might end up in there. This is a big property. We've had all sorts of folks just show up on the premises—hunters, hikers, homeless people, you name it. Mr. Carruthers is very careful with his privacy. He likes to keep things tidy."

"With good reason," Frank said, nodding. "Could you unlock that crawl space for us?"

Alphonso hesitated, but only for a moment. "Why, certainly," he said, smiling.

He walked with them into the garage, leading them into a small, cluttered office with a tiny window. The office had a functional-looking gray Steelcase desk in its center. A glowing battery of surveillance camera monitors covered one wall. On the opposite wall, there was a framed photograph of an attractive dark-haired woman and two smiling young children sitting in white wicker chairs on a very green lawn. Another photo, of a cheerful-looking black Airedale, was mounted beside it. A wooden hat rack stood guard in the corner of the room. On it was a large keychain with dozens of color-coded keys.

Alphonso picked up the keychain.

Frank glanced at the picture of the young woman and children and smiled. "Is this your family?" he asked.

Alphonso grinned back at him, nodding. "My wife, Teresita; son, Miguel; and my daughter, Mary Elva. And the dog's name is Sparky. That dog is my biggest baby," he said.

"They're all beautiful," Frank said.

"Thank you," said Alphonso. He walked them around to the small, padlocked door. "We usually don't have to go in here for anything, although we had to a few years back."

"Why did you have to go in at that time?"

Alphonso raised one eyebrow. "Rats," he said. "Marsh rats, in fact. Really huge ones, almost as big as cats. Mr. Carruthers wasn't too pleased about it. That's one reason the door stays padlocked."

A heavy-duty Schlage padlock was affixed to a large steel hasp. Like everything else on the estate, it looked brand-new.

The key Alphonso tried did not fit.

"That's strange," he said. "This is definitely the right one."

He tried two or three others. None worked.

"If you can't open it with a key, I'll need you to break the lock," Frank said.

"I'll have to get Mr. Carruthers for that."

Frank shook his head. "We have a search warrant, Mr. Hernandez, so the lock comes off. Either you unlock it or we cut it."

"I don't know where the right key is," he said, shaking his head.

"Pep, get the irons. And a couple of flashlights," Frank said.

Pepper came back from his truck with a Halligan bar and a

flathead axe. He jammed the pick end of the Halligan into the eye of the padlock and broke the lock off cleanly with a single swing of the axe.

"You've done this before," Alphonso said.

Pep shrugged. "I'm a cop," he said, grinning. "And a crook."

The crawl space reeked of rot and mildew. Frank flicked on his flashlight and immediately saw dozens of rat traps all along the walls. Some had the fur-shrouded skeletal remains of large rodents still trapped in them.

There were a couple of old beer bottles on a ledge across the way. A broken light bulb rested on the floor.

And then Frank saw it.

The flashlight illuminated a small bundle up against the wall support between two rat traps. It looked like someone had wrapped something in a towel and stuffed the towel into an open-handled leather tote.

"What's that?" Frank said.

"I don't know," Alphonso replied. "I don't remember seeing that before."

Frank went over to look at it.

The towel had something encrusted on it.

That's blood, Frank thought. The hairs on the back of his neck stood up. "Everybody out! And get the forensics team in here. We've got something."

27

March 14

Morris Shefter stood in Chief Brown's office, his briefcase clutched in a clawlike hand.

"Once again, this is total bullshit, Clarence! Illegal search and seizure, trespassing, you name it. Total and complete *bullshit*!"

"Mr. Shefter, we had a warrant, and I can assure you that proper police protocols were followed—"

Shefter slammed his hand down on the chief's desk so forcefully that dust motes were jolted loose and sent wafting randomly into the air. His pinkie ring glittered crimson and gold in the waning sunlight.

"God *damn* it, Clarence! You know as well as I do that this was a setup! My client is being framed!" The lawyer leaned forward on the desk, his elbows crooked. He looked like a huge, flightless bird of prey. Morris Shefter was universally feared because he was smart and ruthless, and he had a Sherman-like scorched-earth policy toward anyone who opposed his clients.

And the Carruthers family was his most important client of all.

Spittle flew from his mouth as he spoke. "A media personality gets an anonymous email with a faked video and you bring my client in for questioning. Another anonymous email is sent, and you search my client's home and property, conveniently discovering a hammer wrapped in a blood-soaked towel that links him to that O'Connor girl's death. Do you have my client's fingerprints on the murder weapon? His DNA?"

"The evidence is being processed, Mr. Shefter. You know that as well as anybody. But the blood type on the hammer is the same as Janie O'Connor's, and I would not be shocked one bit if the DNA evidence confirmed that it was her blood. We should have those results in a day or so," Chief Brown said.

"You're trying to railroad my client into a guilty verdict!"

Chief Brown's eyes narrowed. "Mr. Shefter, we don't fabricate evidence here. We collect it so that a jury can reach the appropriate opinion. We have zero interest in railroading anybody. What we are after is justice for Dr. O'Connor. If your client has any evidence to help us arrive at that truth, I suggest he provide it. In the meantime, we found a bloody claw hammer wrapped in a blood-soaked towel behind a padlocked door on your client's property, and the blood on both items matches the blood type of the murder victim, who just happens to be his ex-girlfriend. That ex-girlfriend, the murder victim, had broken up with Mr. Carruthers a few months before she disappeared and had recently started dating another man. That man, Dr. Dave Wommack, was harassed by a former employee of Mr. Carruthers, Mr. Trek Richards, who set fire to Dr. Wommack's front porch and left a threatening message on said porch before raping Dr. O'Connor's sister. Trek Richards has since also conveniently disappeared. All of this makes your client a prime suspect in her murder. Are we clear, sir?"

Shefter pulled back and brushed a speck of lint from his five-thousand-dollar suit. "Crystal," he said, turning on his heel and leaving the chief's office without another word, still gripping his briefcase tightly in a white-knuckled fist.

"Jesus," Chief Brown muttered.

—

March 15

The next evening, Frank was nursing a Tropicália on his balcony, cigarette smoke drifting around his head, when his phone rang.

"Hello?" Frank asked, not recognizing the number on the caller ID.

"Detective? This is Molly Sims, the ICU nurse who was taking care of John Straub at Memorial. We spoke last summer. I just wanted to let you know that since we last talked, Mr. Straub was extubated, completed his facial reconstruction surgery, has been going through rehab, and is doing pretty well now. I've become friends with his family. When I told him you visited him in the ICU last summer, he said he wanted to talk to you when he was strong enough. He just called me and said that he feels he has reached that point now. He's in rehab, but they're thinking about discharging him home in the next few days."

"What does he want to talk about?"

"He won't tell me anything beyond that. He will only talk to you. In private," Molly said.

"Where is he now?"

"Seven Gables Rehab, on Seawright Road. Room 347."

Frank wrote it down. "Can I come see him tomorrow?"

"That would be fine. John usually has a break around noon," Molly said.

Frank hung up the phone, finished drinking his Tropicália, and then put out his cigarette.

He wasn't sure what John Straub wanted to tell him. Frank was not the sort of person who liked secrets. He liked his facts the way he liked his bourbon: straight, with no garnish and no chaser.

Off in the distance, he could hear a crow cawing. Frank smiled to himself. *Only one crow this time.*

—

Frank parked his Hyundai in the Seven Gables Rehab guest parking lot and walked into the lobby. A pink-haired twenty-something woman dressed in powder-blue scrubs manned the front desk. She had multiple earrings piercing her left ear and a single pink feather dangling from her right. She wore a name tag that said "Cherie."

"Good morning. I'm Detective Frank Winger, here to see John Straub. He's in room 347," Frank said.

"Sign in here," Cherie said, handing Frank a pen.

Frank signed his name.

"You're a real detective?" Cherie asked.

"Some folks say that," Frank replied.

"Cool," she said, smiling. Cherie took the pen back and put it in a drawer. "Mr. Straub is on the third floor, at the end of the hall on the left. He should be in his room right now, getting ready for lunch."

Frank took the elevator to the third floor. The small nursing station just beyond the elevator was almost deserted, occupied only by a single middle-aged man, also in powder-blue scrubs, staring intently at a computer monitor.

Frank walked down the empty hallway to room 347 and knocked on the door, which was partly open.

"Come in," a voice from inside said.

A hospital bed sat in the center of the room, and John

Straub was seated on it, his head bowed. A halo of shaggy reddish-brown hair surrounded his face.

"Mr. Straub? I'm Detective Frank Winger. I came to visit you when you were in the ICU. Molly Sims said you wanted to talk to me?"

Straub looked up.

A scraggly beard covered what was left of John Straub's face. His skull, pitted with innumerable scars and indentations, looked like the surface of an asteroid. His right eye was missing, its eyelid sewn shut. Straub's reconstructed jaw gaped, misshapen and asymmetrical, with only a handful of teeth remaining. But his left eye, a glittering aquamarine, stared intensely at Frank, sizing him up.

"Sorry about the way I look," Straub said in a ragged voice. "It's taken a bit of work to even get this far."

"I've seen worse," Frank said.

"You're ex-Army, right? Served in Afghanistan?"

Frank nodded, surprised this man knew about his past.

"And I think I read you moved here from Baltimore."

"Where'd you read that?"

"There's this thing called the internet. Ever hear of it?" Straub shifted his weight on the bed so that he faced Frank directly. "Sorry to be a smart-ass," he said. "I just need to be careful who I talk to. I wrestled for months about talking to *anyone* about the things I'm about to tell you today. There were days when I simply wanted to keep my head down and not make waves—just get better and move on, you know? Take my family and relocate someplace far away from here. But then I thought of the way my folks raised me, how they stressed being honorable and decent, and I realized that I couldn't hide from my past anymore. I had to come clean. When I heard from Nurse Molly that you'd come to see me while I was in the hospital, I figured it was a sign from God. And the fact that you're not from Savannah, and are ex-Army, like me? Even better." Straub straightened himself on the bed, squaring his shoulders. He was thin now, but his frame was that of a much larger man, with broad shoulders and large hands. In his erect posture and jutting chin, Frank could see the soldier Straub had once been.

"So you checked me out so you could be sure you could trust me?" Frank asked.

Straub nodded. "Being a fellow vet hopefully means you have your own sense of honor and decency. Can you promise you won't rat me out to the bad guys, soldier?"

Frank raised his right hand. "Loyalty, duty, respect, service, honor, integrity, and personal courage, soldier. You know the deal."

Straub grinned. His smile was crooked and out of kilter, but it radiated a fundamental honesty that managed to break through the jumble of his surgically reconstructed face.

"Well then," he said. "We have a lot to talk about."

28

The meal the orderly set before Straub was simple: pureed carrots, mashed potatoes, shredded chicken, a soft dinner roll, and a small pudding container for dessert. A plastic cup containing sweetened iced tea, beading with sweat, sat on one corner of the tray.

"Mind if I eat while we talk?" he asked.

"Not a bit," Frank said.

Straub took a sip of iced tea. "So I guess you're wondering what happened to me."

"I was wondering that, yes," Frank said.

Staring off into space, Straub shook his head slowly. "Coming out of the Army, I had more than a few regrets. I'd seen enough death to last a lifetime, so I wanted nothing to do with the military. I stayed here in Savannah and bounced around from job to job, working at fast-food places and the like, really getting nowhere. And then I met Marina."

"That's your wife?"

John nodded. "Marina came into the store I was working in one day. She was gorgeous. Do you believe in love at first sight? I didn't back then, but I do now. Marina and I dated for six months before we got married. My daughter, Alison, was born about a year later. After Alison was born, I realized I needed a better job—something stable, with health insurance and a retirement plan, so I started looking around. One day, I ran into a guy named Carmine Carpeggio at the gym. I had known Carmine when I was in the Army. Carmine said the Carruthers organization liked hiring people who were ex-military because they would follow orders. One thing led to another, and the next thing I knew, I was in an interview with Erika Carruthers. She hired me as soon as the interview was over."

Tears filled Straub's eye. He wiped them away. "Taking that job was the worst decision I ever made in my life," he said, shaking his head.

"What sort of work did you do for them?"

"The job was advertised as a simple warehouse job. You know what I mean? I thought it would be dry goods or routine container work—unloading trucks with a forklift, electronic inventory, that sort of thing. I'd done some of that in the Army. But it wasn't that, not at all. I had no idea what I was getting myself into. I'd swear to that on a stack of Bibles."

"What sort of thing was it?"

John looked up at Frank. His misshapen face was a jumbled mess, his cyclopean eye now red and swollen. "Human trafficking," he said. "And once I was in it, I could not find a way out."

—

July 18

Erika Carruthers hated dealing with people in general.

Truth be told, she preferred animals. Most of them could be trained, and they lacked the capacity for duplicity. They didn't try to think for themselves, never caused trouble, and didn't generally get in the way. In the rare instances that they did, you could simply put them down. It simplified things.

Human beings were more complicated to deal with. Even the stupid ones could get you in trouble.

Especially the stupid ones, she thought.

She had just finished an intense session on her Peloton and was headed to the shower when the phone rang. At first, when she saw the number, she almost didn't answer it. If a call was from someone she did not have in her address book, she usually assumed it was spam. But then she saw the prefix and realized that it was one of the burner phones she'd given the smugglers to use in case of an emergency.

"Oh shit," she said out loud, stripping out of her exercise clothes. She dropped them into the hamper, turned on the shower, and then answered the call.

"This had better be good," Erika said.

"We've got a problem, ma'am," the voice on the other end of the line said.

"Who is this?"

"John Straub, ma'am. I'm one of the runners."

"Are you Fat John or Skinny John?"

The man hesitated for a moment. "Fat," he said with a sigh.

"OK, Fat John, spill it. What's going on?"

"We had a problem with one of the containers. It was compromised."

"Speak English. What exactly do you mean by *compromised*?"

Steam was filling the bathroom now, fogging the mirror. Erika stared at her reflection, looking at her flat belly and perfect tits, and smiled.

"When we opened the container, we discovered some of the cargo didn't make it."

Erika shut off the shower. "What the fuck are you talking about, John?"

"The shipment had eighteen subjects this time. There were four men, eight women, and six children. One of the kids died. We don't know how. When we opened the container, he was just dead. The kid was cold, and his face was all blue and mottled. His mama was holding him and crying her eyes out. She kept calling out 'el médico, el médico,' wanting us to get a doctor, but there was nothing we could do for him. She doesn't seem to understand that he's gone."

"How the hell did this happen? Was the kid sick when they loaded him?"

"The coyotes said everyone was healthy. They had plenty of food and water, too—some was even left over in the container when we opened it. But they were out in the Caribbean for a few days, and it can get hot sometimes on the boat. Maybe he had some illness we didn't know about."

"Well, that sucks," Erika said. She thought for a moment. This sort of thing had to be dealt with swiftly and decisively, or it could spiral out of hand.

"Is anyone else with them?" she asked.

"I told you, there were eighteen in the container—"

"Not with them in the container, you idiot. I mean *with* them. Any other relatives besides the kid's mother? Other kids?"

"Nope. Just the two of them."

Well, that makes it a little easier, Erika thought. "Where are they from?"

"El Salvador."

"And we've been paid?"

"Affirmative."

"OK, here's what we do: Give the other sixteen their papers and let them go, as usual. Wrap up the dead child in a sheet and bring him and his mother to our family's compound on Wilmington Island."

John was silent for a moment. "You want me to bring them out *there*? For real?"

"Are you stupid, or are you just deaf? Yes, bring them to the compound. Put the body in the trunk of your car and tell his mother that you're going to find him a doctor."

"Where are we going to find a doctor to look at a kid who is dead?"

"We're *not,* Fat John. That's the lie you're telling her to get her to go with you."

"I'm not sure I feel good about doing that, ma'am," John said.

"Listen to me, you moron," Erika said, jabbing her finger into the air like a stiletto. "You either bring the boy and his mother to me, or you're fired—and once you're fired, you're of no use to us anymore, which makes you expendable. Do you understand what that means?"

"Yes, ma'am," Fat John said quietly.

"So bring them to the compound, and I mean pronto. We'll meet you at the gate."

After she hung up, Erika turned the shower back on, stepped inside, and lathered up. The Jerusalem tile of the shower floor, slightly uneven beneath her feet, was arranged in a meticulous pattern in the shape of a dolphin, and she watched the sudsy water lazily circle the drain next to the dolphin's midsection.

After she dried off, Erika called Carmine.

"Go to the compound's front gate in twenty minutes," she told him. "Fat John from the smuggling operation will be coming with some compromised cargo. We have some business to attend to."

—

When Fat John drove up to the massive stone front gate of the Carruthers compound, Carmine Carpeggio was waiting for him. Dressed in black khakis, a skin-tight black polo shirt, and wraparound sunglasses, muscular arms folded across his chest, Carmine was leaning against a black Range Rover. He looked impatient.

"El médico?" the woman in the back seat asked hoarsely.

John glanced at the woman in the rearview mirror. She was thin and disheveled, her face lined and drawn, her bloodshot eyes swollen with tears. Her clothes were threadbare and mismatched, and they hung loosely on her spare frame. Gazing at her made John's chest ache.

"Sí," John said quietly. He didn't really know what else to say.

She trusts you, John, he thought.

That notion made the ache in his chest a little worse.

Carmine entered a code into the keypad, and the gate clanked slowly open. John rolled down the car window. "Good morning, Carmine. Where are we going?"

"Just pull over when you get inside. You'll be following us," he said, getting into the driver's side of the Range Rover and cranking the engine.

A sick feeling settled into the pit of John's stomach.

I should run, John thought. But he was trapped. There was no way out.

No, he would follow orders. He'd be a good soldier, keep his head down, and do what he was told.

A voice somewhere inside him whispered, *You're not a bad person. You're just doing as you're told.*

But he knew that voice all too well. It was the voice of the snake, the greedy little viper that had convinced him to keep this job even after he realized what it involved.

The money is too good to pass up, the viper had said then.

Think of your family. You can do it for a few years and then quit with no regrets.

The viper was always seductive and convincing, and John had buried his concerns deep in concentric layers of onion-skinned rationalization.

They drove along the winding road, which twisted deep into the moss-draped maritime forest. The woman seated behind John blinked her tear-filled eyes, bony hands clasped in front of her narrow chest in prayer. Once or twice, she looked behind her as if she wanted to crawl right into the trunk with her son's cold and lifeless body.

"El médico?" she asked again, her voice tremulous.

"Sí, sí," John said, nodding.

It's OK, the viper whispered reassuringly.

But John knew the viper always lied.

The Range Rover took a left-hand turn onto a narrow dirt road John had never even noticed before, a claustrophobic trail that snaked through the deep woods around tidal ponds and long-forgotten rice paddies. Palm fronds and dangling vines slapped his car as the wheels jounced along an ancient, root-studded levee.

And then they stopped.

They had parked at a small clearing. A brackish pond, its edges lined with cattails, cedars, and massive oaks, spread out before them. A thin haze drifted across the pond's surface. Like a stubby fishing pier, a rude wooden platform stood at the pond's edge.

Where are we? John wondered.

Carmine and Erika got out of the Range Rover. Carmine looked at John and nodded. John turned off his car's ignition and glanced at the distraught woman in his back seat.

"Sal del auto," John said to the woman in a soft voice. He averted his eyes so that she could not see them and pocketed his keys as he exited the car.

The woman left the car slowly, her dark-brown eyes wide and uncertain.

Carmine and Erika walked up. Erika was dressed in blue jeans and a tight-fitting olive drab T-shirt. Her long legs, accentuated by her knee-high leather boots, moved with a slow and deliberate precision, like the limbs of a praying mantis.

"Where's the kid?" Carmine said gruffly.

"In the trunk," John replied.

"Open it."

John popped the trunk and Carmine picked up the boy's shrouded form. A mottled hand dropped out, lifeless. The boy's mother scrambled to his side, crying hysterically.

"Médico! Médico!" she wailed.

Carmine casually tossed the boy's inert body onto the ground. His mother ran to him and dropped to her knees beside his body. Her desperate fingers pulled back the layers of the shroud from her son's pale face. The boy's sunken, lifeless eyes stared into an empty sky.

"Enough of this shit," Carmine said. He pulled a silenced .22 handgun out of his jacket and fired a couple of quick rounds into the back of the woman's skull. She shuddered and fell face down into the leaves, her right arm draped protectively across her son's body. A crimson rivulet of blood streamed from the back of her head, matting her hair.

Tears filled John's eyes. He blinked them back, but they returned, relentless, so he wiped them away.

When he glanced up, he saw Erika staring at him, her brilliant emerald eyes filled with venom. "Don't you start getting all sentimental on us, Fat John," Erika said. "There's no room for that in this business. You're a soldier. Follow orders."

"Pick up the kid and follow me," Carmine barked.

"What are we doing with him?" John asked.

"We're disposing of the evidence," Carmine said.

They walked over to the wooden platform. It had been

constructed off the levee, and the ground sloped away sharply from the shoreline, making the water beneath the platform quite a bit deeper than John had initially surmised. The pond's surface was dotted with lily pads, and its dark waters were choked with algae. John couldn't even see through the tannin-stained water to the bottom. For all he knew, the pond was bottomless.

A dense fog over the pond's surface obscured the opposite shoreline, but John heard a heavy splash in the distance.

A couple of green slider turtles, perched on a nearby log, suddenly dropped into the water next to the platform—*plop! plop!*—but John sensed that there was something else out there. He could feel it in his bones.

The dark water below the platform eddied lazily around the pilings. For an instant, John thought he saw something dark moving in the swirling current, something massive and ominous.

Could it be?

"Throw the kid's body in," Carmine said.

John did as he was told. When the boy hit the water, the sheet wrapped around him spread like a pair of gossamer wings. And then he rolled over, his mouth open but his dead eyes wide and unseeing, before he began to sink beneath the water.

Suddenly, the sinking stopped.

The boy's body lurched suddenly upward out of the water as if shot out of some unseen cannon. His arms flailed limply upward, as if pulled by a crazed puppet master, before flopping back to his sides. It was only as the boy's body toppled back into the water that John saw the shadowy bulk looming below.

Burt, John thought. *The damned thing is* real.

He'd heard stories of this creature, but it was the first time he'd ever glimpsed it with his own eyes.

Burt was a sixteen-foot-long bull gator with a taste for

human flesh. Rumors of the monster's existence had percolated among those involved with the shadier nether regions of the Carruthers organization for years. John had heard that the creature lurked in one of the murky ponds somewhere near the shorebird rookery. Phillip, who had first discovered it, reportedly nicknamed the animal after the quintessential Southern boy, Burt Reynolds.

For Carruthers Enterprises employees, this was their Loch Ness Monster. "We'll take you to see Burt" was the ultimate threat for anyone who dared betray the company.

The gigantic gator had clamped its huge jaws around the boy's torso. Its obsidian tail slashed back and forth, churning the water into a yellowish froth. One of the gator's eyes was sealed permanently shut, and a pale, jagged scar tore across it. The other eye gleamed a dull topaz, its cruel light glimmering like a dim beacon lighting the way into the depths of hell.

"Good God," John murmured.

"Impressive, isn't it?" Erika said, a thin-lipped smile on her face.

Carmine picked up the dead woman's limp body like a sack of potatoes, walked back over to the platform, and tossed her remains into the pond. An awful thrashing sound followed, the intermittent slap of leather against wood and the occasional grunt punctuating the air as the gator feasted yet again.

John didn't look. Hell, he *couldn't* look.

He'd seen enough of Burt to last a lifetime.

"Let's get the fuck out of here," Erika said, turning to walk back toward her Range Rover. But then she stopped and turned her laser beam eyes back to John. "I saw you wiping those tears from your eyes back there. Remember: We pay you very well for doing what you do. Those people are cargo, nothing more. Forget everything you saw here today. Go home, kiss your wife, hug your kids, have a few beers, and be *grateful*. Do we understand each other?"

"Yes, ma'am."

"Very well, then. Go home."

John followed the Range Rover through the dense forest, focusing on the taillights as they flashed crimson streaks across his retinas. The woman's screams burned inside his brain like battery acid.

I never even knew their names, he thought.

The Range Rover pulled over at the gate to the compound. Carmine got out and clambered into a camouflage-painted four-wheeled ATV, briefly waving to John before driving back into the woods.

He looks so casual, John thought. *All of that was nothing to him.*

John thought he knew Carmine. As it turned out, he really did not know him at all.

As he drove home to Southbridge in a daze, his mind was in a fog bank. He didn't even remember the drive. At some point, he pulled into the garage and switched off the car's engine, then went into the house like he always did. Dropping his keys and his wallet into the basket by the front door, he gave Marina a peck on the cheek.

"How was work?" Marina asked, her voice light and airy.

"Fine," John lied. "Just another day."

Alison and Mikey were watching cartoons on TV and eating apple slices from a yellow plastic bowl. John sat down between them for a moment, hugging them both as their eyes stayed glued to a giant white rabbit that was bouncing crazily on the screen.

Kiss your wife, hug your kids, have a few beers, and be grateful.

He was trapped. If he tried to quit, the Carruthers organization would come after him—or, worse still, they would come after his family. Carmine Carpeggio and Erika Carruthers were ruthless. They might try to hurt Marina, Alison, or even little Mikey. That thought was almost incomprehensible to him, but it was the truth, and he knew it.

It'll be OK by morning, the viper hissed. *You'll forget it and move on, like before.*

But the viper lied. The viper always lied.

And so, at 5:00 a.m., while his wife and children slept, John wrote his wife a letter she would never understand. The note said simply: *Marina, I'm sorry. I love you. Please take care of the kids and let them know I love them, too. I had to do this. I had no choice. Love, John.*

Tiptoeing quietly into their bedroom in the dark, John kissed his sleeping children in their beds and closed the door to their bedroom. He retrieved the 9 mm Browning Parabellum from the glove compartment of his car. He then walked into the woods behind his home and placed the muzzle of the gun inside his mouth. He could feel the cold steel on his teeth, along with the curious saltpeter taste of gunpowder.

As he stood in the predawn mist, John thought he heard a dog howling plaintively in the distance. He imagined the poor mutt, all skin and bones, chained to a post in the yard of a double-wide someplace. But the din inside his head grew progressively louder, drowning out everything else.

With a single gunshot, Fat John silenced all the voices once and for all.

29

March 15

Frank stared at Straub, stunned.

"The Carrutherses are engaging in human trafficking?" he said.

"Among other things."

Frank swallowed. His mouth was parched, as if all the saliva had dried up. "What 'other things'?"

Straub sighed. "Look, I don't know all of it. Like I said, I generally kept my head down and worked in my area. I didn't interact with anyone else except Carmine and Erika—mostly Carmine. I rarely saw Erika. However, South American drug cartels fund most of the human trafficking, primarily because it's very lucrative, so I wouldn't be surprised if the Carruthers organization is dealing with them in other transactions, too."

"Erika Carruthers visited you in the ICU while you were intubated and unconscious," Frank said.

"I know. Molly told me. Thankfully, I haven't seen her. She's not one of my favorite people."

"Did Carmine ever visit you?" Frank asked.

"Not that I know of. That surprised me. At one point, we were friends. I thought we were, at least."

"Did Phillip Carruthers come see you?"

"I've never even met him," Straub said.

Frank stepped forward, placing a hand on Straub's shoulder. "So you'd be willing to testify in court about all you've seen?"

Straub, who was looking at his feet, nodded. "I'd need to make sure my family is safe. Witness protection, relocation, a new life, a different job, all of it. Someplace far from here, where they can't find us."

"The FBI does that sort of thing with mob cases, but the SPD isn't that big an organization. Our funds are more limited."

Straub looked up at Frank through his one remaining eye.

"These are *evil* people we are dealing with, Detective. They've corrupted everything from the city administration to the police force. They have operatives in the DA's office and others embedded in the local news outlets. Every one of those organizations has people on the Carruthers payroll. That's why I tried to kill myself. I could not keep doing what I was doing and live with the guilt—but they'd have come after my family if I simply quit. I did not see a way out." He shook his head. "Until now."

—

Frank spread the Janie O'Connor case files out on his kitchen table and reviewed them all one more time.

He could not believe what he was seeing.

Pepper Stephens's name was all over the file, just like Frank's was. That was expected, as they were the lead investigators, but Frank was perplexed. Every interview Pep had conducted led to a dead end. The information he had obtained led nowhere or, in some cases, was frankly contradictory to what Frank knew to be true. He described Mary, Janie's mother, as "incoherent" when she clearly was not. He'd blown off the break-in at Janie's house as "irrelevant," stating that it seemed a "random event."

Frank could not find the DNA report from the blood-soaked hammer and towel they had discovered at the Carruthers estate. He'd seen it, so he knew it existed—but the report was not in the physical file nor the electronic one. The file on the break-in at Janie O'Connor's home at Rose Dhu was limited to Lieutenant Chu's one-page police report. There were no leads chased down, as Pep had once said. There had been no investigation at all.

"What the hell is going on here?" Frank asked out loud.

On a whim, Frank looked at the online police records of Phillip Carruthers. They were clean as a whistle, despite the fact that Frank knew Phillip had gotten a DUI when he was a teenager.

Frank knew one other place he could look.

Frank remembered that Anderson Carruthers had died in Memorial Hospital after a hunting accident shortly after Frank had started the SPD job. Locating Anderson's obituary online was easy enough. Anderson Carruthers died ten years earlier. He was lionized in the press and lauded for all he had done for Savannah's charities and for its business community. The online pictures showed a youthful-looking Phillip, age twenty-eight, a spiky-haired Erika, age twenty-five, and a regal-appearing Cynthia Carruthers, who had rarely been seen in public since.

Frank located the case files. There had been an autopsy, as is required in any accidental death, and the report was un-equivocal about Anderson Carruthers's cause of death. He had sustained a penetrating right thoracic chest wound inflicted by a high-powered rifle bullet. The 30.06 projectile had entered the right side of his chest from the rear, collapsing the right lung and resulting in a tension pneumothorax, which had been treated with the insertion of a chest tube in the Memorial ER. That alone might have been fatal. But the bullet had also snapped one of Anderson's ribs, severing the intercostal artery, resulting in massive blood loss. The combination of the pneumothorax and the blood loss had resulted in a myocardial infarction—a heart attack.

The police report was more telling.

Anderson and Phillip Carruthers had been deer hunting on some isolated family property in Screven County, about sixty miles north of Savannah. They were there alone. Phillip's statement seemed straightforward: They'd seen an eight-point buck, Phillip lined up the shot, and his father had stepped into the line of sight just as Phillip pulled the trigger. Anderson was conscious immediately afterward, and Phillip called 911 immediately, but by the time the EMTs arrived, Anderson was unconscious and in shock. He never regained consciousness.

The report concluded that there was no evidence of wrongdoing and evaluated Anderson Carruthers's death as accidental. No charges were ever filed.

The officer who filed the report was Pepper Stephens.

Frank felt a cold chill drift over him. He was nauseous, the room spinning around him, darkness closing in around his shoulders like a funeral shroud.

When Chief Brown had first paired Frank Winger with Pepper Stephens, Frank could not figure out why their lifestyles differed so much. Frank could barely afford to purchase a new washing machine when his old Whirlpool went on the fritz, but Pepper lived at an entirely different financial level— not at all consistent with a detective's salary. His wife, Candy, didn't work. She was a full-time mom who hailed from a normal middle-class family in rural Georgia.

What was once a distasteful possibility began to germinate into a nasty, full-blown probability. The pieces of the puzzle were all clicking into place.

"Pep's on the take," Frank whispered aloud.

Corruption in the Savannah Police Department wasn't unheard of. But the people Frank worked with had his back, and he trusted them. They were his friends.

Weren't they?

His thoughts turned to Pep once again. The idea of Pep being a crooked cop made him sick, but all the missing elements in the Janie O'Connor case seemed to be things Pep had touched.

When Frank looked at the big picture, the conclusion was obvious: Pep had been bought. There was no other logical explanation.

Frank's first instinct was to address this man-to-man. That seemed like the honorable thing to do. He owed Pep that courtesy.

But then he thought about the far-reaching influence of the Carruthers family. Would they come after Frank if he spoke to Pep first? And if Pep was guilty, wouldn't speaking to him first give him a chance to remove the evidence?

Frank was sitting on a granite bench in Rousakis Plaza on River Street. The early evening sun was burning its way into the river. Some school-age children were playing in a sandbox nearby. Frank lit a cigarette and took a deep drag on it, listening to the gentle *flap flap* of the waves against the seawall as a noisy flock of seagulls wheeled randomly overhead.

If Paulina had lived, they'd probably have had kids by now. She'd always wanted them. It was Frank who'd been resistant.

Time had moved on since then. These days, with the right woman, he could see himself as a dad. The fact that he would never see Paulina's look of astonishment as he told her that fact was just one of his many regrets.

In the end, Frank decided he'd have to go straight to the one person he was sure was incorruptible: Clarence Brown.

—

Frank hesitated for a moment outside Chief Brown's office.

He'd put his cigarette out even before he entered Police Headquarters because there was almost no smoking here anymore, dammit. His hands were trembling, but it was probably just his nerves, which were raw in a way that reminded him of how he'd always felt on guard duty in Afghanistan.

Spidey senses on alert, he thought.

He heard the chief's muffled laughter as he talked on the phone with someone—a deep ursine chuckle that was at once amusing and terrifying.

Frank's head swam. He'd be turning in his partner, exposing him to accusations that might ruin his career—and for what? Was this really his fight?

And then he thought of the forlorn pile of bones and teeth encased in a sealed box, the last earthly remnants of Janie O'Connor, who by all accounts had been a wonderful human being. He recalled the profound hurt in Diane's luminous sapphire eyes and the heat of their mother's righteous anger as she spoke about Phillip Carruthers.

"Fuck it," Frank said out loud. His gut was seldom wrong about things—and in his gut, he knew that Pepper Stephens was a crooked cop.

He knocked on the door.

"Come in," the chief called.

Chief Brown was eating a huge chocolate chip cookie, with a whole plate of them sitting in front of him. "Earline did some baking," he explained. "Want one?"

"No, thanks."

"Suit yourself, but you're missing out." He took a swig from his water bottle. "Have a seat. How can I help you?"

Frank ran his fingers through his hair and cleared his throat. "Can I close the door?" he asked.

"Of course."

Frank did so and sat back down. "This is going to sound weird, and there may be nothing to it, but please hear me out before you say anything. I've been investigating the O'Connor murder ever since she went missing. From the anonymous phone call that was the first break in the case to the videos that were sent to Tina Baker, this whole thing has been weird."

"That's the understatement of the year," Chief Brown said, picking up another cookie.

"Recently, with all the new developments, I decided to review all the case files one more time. When I dug into them this second time, I found a few things missing. For example, there were no reports of some interviews I knew had been done. Other interviews contained information at odds with what I knew to be true. There had allegedly been an investigation of a break-in at Dr. O'Connor's home in the year before she disappeared, but I can't find any record of it. All I can find is the police report of the break-in itself."

Chief Brown put down the cookie. "What?" he said, suddenly serious.

"You may recall Dr. O'Connor reported encountering a strange man in her garage. Pep said they had investigated the break-in and that it was pretty much a dead end. But there's no record in the case file of any investigation. We now know that the man who broke into Janie's garage was Trek Richards—the same guy who attacked Diane right before her sister disappeared. He worked for the Carruthers family, and he's now gone, too. Things just don't add up in this case. When I found out that Pep was the lead investigator in

Anderson Carruthers's shooting death, things just started to fall into place."

"What are you saying here, Frank?"

Frank looked down at his hands, which were folded in his lap, before looking back up at Chief Brown. "I think Pep may be working for the Carruthers organization."

The chief straightened up in his chair, which creaked a bit, and shuffled some of the papers on his desk. "That's a serious allegation. Do you have any proof?"

"No direct proof," Frank said, shaking his head. "But there are other things about Pep that don't add up. Have you ever seen his house at the Landings?"

"Nope."

"It's huge. His wife drives a brand-new Lexus. All three of his kids are in private school at Savannah Country Day, and the tuition there is crazy expensive—like twenty thousand dollars apiece per year. And do you remember that two-week Alaskan cruise he took his whole family on last year? I've always wanted to go to Alaska, so I priced it and realized that I couldn't even come close to affording it. I can't see how he does all that on a cop's salary."

"Is his wife rich?"

"I thought of that, but unless she won the lottery recently, she's not. And you know Pep. Is he the sort of guy who'd keep working if he had access to money from some other source?"

Chief Brown chuckled. "Nope. He'd be sippin' piña coladas on a beach someplace."

"Exactly."

"Would you excuse me for a minute?" Chief Brown said.

"Sure. You want me to wait here?" said Frank.

"If you don't mind." Chief Brown got up, deftly maneuvered his massive bulk around the desk, and left the office without another word.

Shit, Frank thought.

His palms were sweaty again, and he suddenly realized that he had no idea how pervasive the corruption could be in the department. A horrible thought crept into his brain: *What if the* chief *is involved?*

If that were the case, Frank decided he would turn in his badge and move on, like he had with the Army after Afghanistan. Hell, he'd been running all his adult life. Grass never grew under Frank Winger's feet. Paulina had said as much years ago.

"You're rootless, Frank," she'd said. *"No ties anywhere. Why is that?"*

He'd wanted to answer her. He really had. But to do so would have called up all those chattering skeletons from his closet. Frank had not wanted to face them. So he'd just shrugged and changed the subject, blowing her off like he always did when anyone tried to talk about his past.

And now Paulina was just another skeleton herself. *E pluribus unum.*

There were days when Frank wondered if she might be alive today if he'd been more open with her. He'd always tried to shield her from the uglier side of his work, the seamy underbelly of humanity that he encountered every single goddamned day. Would Paulina have been prepared for Garcia if she'd known he was a potential threat? Would she have taken additional steps to defend herself? There was no way he'd ever know that, of course. But he could not help wondering.

"Frank?"

Frank looked up to see Chief Brown standing with two other men, who were dressed in identical dark, neatly pressed suits.

He knew them instantly. "You're the two guys I saw in the cemetery," Frank said.

"Meet Special Agents Smythe and Weston. They're with

the FBI," the chief said. "And I think they'd be very interested in some of the things you've brought to my attention today."

Agent Smythe wore a pair of dark-tinted Ray-Bans indoors, so Frank could not see his eyes. His face was severe, hatchet-like, and he did not smile. He looked a lot like the character of a similar name from *The Matrix*. Agent Weston was a tall, thin African American man, also unsmiling, with close-cropped hair and dark eyes that seemed bottomless.

"The men in black," Frank said.

"Don't call us that," Smythe said.

"How did you guys get involved in a local murder case?" Frank asked.

"I asked for the Bureau's help," Chief Brown said. He cleared his throat. "Early on in this investigation, I also noticed that some of the evidence we gathered was disappearing. Judges dragged their feet granting us search warrants. The DA's office didn't want to pursue any arrests. Even the newspaper seemed to be involved. References to the Carruthers family were buried or excised, and there were several editorials in the *Savannah Morning News* implying that the police investigation of the case was either biased or grossly incompetent. I became convinced that there were individuals inside our department, in the DA's office, and at the newspaper feeding information to the Carruthers organization. We even wondered about you, Frank," Chief Brown said.

That surprised him. "About me?"

"Well, you and Pep were the lead investigators on the case—and that investigation was going nowhere fast. Eventually, I decided we needed outside help. It seemed like the whole town was on the take. We needed people who had no local influence."

"So it's a good thing you came forward, Detective," Agent Smythe said.

"I don't know anything for certain," Frank said.

"But you do know your partner better than just about any-body. You guys are tight. And the fact that you are suspicious of him helps us nail down where to go next in this investiga-tion," Smythe said. At long last, Smythe grinned. "Welcome to the good guys, Detective Winger. We're damned glad to have you."

30

Pepper Stephens was anxious as hell.

Chief Brown was leading Pep to the small station conference room they called the Pillbox. It was a nondescript oblong matchbox with claustrophobically low tiled ceilings and unadorned battleship gray walls, and it stank of sweat, mildew, and cigarettes. The Pillbox was the only room in the entire main police station where smoking was still allowed (a fact that many of the officers took advantage of, especially when it was cold outside).

Pepper's heart was hammering away in his chest, and his left eye was twitching like a motherfucker. A few wispy strands of hair stuck to his temples like weeds. He felt sweat dribbling down the small of his back. As he passed Frank, Pep shot him a worried glance, but Frank dodged it, averting his eyes so they could not make eye contact.

Frank knows, he thought. At that precise moment, Pepper understood that no matter what happened, it was over between them.

Pepper hadn't originally set out to deviate from the straight and narrow. He wasn't a bad guy at heart. He was just a man caught up in the broad gap between a detective's pedestrian salary and the overwhelming need to keep his wife happy.

Candy Stephens was a petite blonde with a cute figure from rural Glennville, in Evans County. She first came to Savannah twenty years ago to attend Armstrong State College, dreaming of bigger things.

Pepper had met Candy during a freshman English class at Armstrong. They dated all through college and got engaged shortly after graduation. Pep's grandmama took an instant liking to Candy, calling her a "firecracker," which was about the biggest compliment Grandma Stephens ever gave anyone. Candy loved her God, her country, and her family, in that order—and Pep loved her, unconditionally and wholeheartedly.

Pepper felt like he had hit the jackpot when Candy agreed to marry him. Even at twenty-three, he had been prematurely rumpled, balding, and overweight. Candy, who was beautiful and vivacious, was the former head cheerleader at Pinewood Christian Academy. Pepper had unequivocally "married up," as his aunt had once said. Consequently, he had spent a lifetime trying to compensate for what he perceived to be the vast social gulf between them. Money was a tangible metric, something quantifiable that he could bring into their relationship.

Phillip Carruthers first approached him about being an informant for the Carruthers family after Anderson Carruthers died. At the time, Pep really hadn't seen the harm in it. Why not take some off-the-books cash in exchange for a little inside baseball? Especially when that cash came from the most powerful and wealthy family in Coastal Georgia. Sometimes, Pep might give Phillip dirt on people Phillip was doing business with that might provide him with leverage in his dealings. At other times, a Carruthers employee might need an untimely arrest to go away. Inconvenient documents, like the record of Phillip's teenage DUI, were routinely expunged from the official police files. In essence, Pep was on retainer to be Phillip's fixer with the police, but it was almost always little things, minor transgressions in life's gray zones that Pep could rationalize as wholly innocuous. It wasn't like anybody had *died* (well, nobody except Anderson Carruthers, but that was an entirely different story).

But then Janie O'Connor disappeared.

That was when the shit hit the fan.

Suddenly, Pepper felt like one of those awful, crooked policemen in the movies, the corrupt backstabbers who undermine their colleagues and redirect investigations on behalf of the bad guys. Pepper didn't know if Phillip Carruthers was truly a bad guy, but he now saw their arrangement for what it was. Good guys generally did not pay detectives to feed them inside information.

Pepper realized that he had become something he had never wanted to be: a dirty cop.

When Pep and Chief Brown entered the conference room, two men in dark suits were there to greet them.

"Pep, Special Agents Smythe and Weston here are with the FBI. They'd like to talk to you about a few things," Chief Brown said.

The men, unsmiling, stood ramrod straight. Pepper shook the hand of each. There were no salutations. On an ordinary day, Pepper would have cracked wise on the absurd coincidence of a couple of federal agents named Smythe and Weston. But this was no ordinary day—and so Pepper, queasy, his hands trembling ever so slightly, said nothing.

"Sit down," said Agent Smythe.

Pepper sat down. So did Agent Smythe. Agent Weston remained standing, arms akimbo, his obsidian eyes seeming to bore a hole right through Pepper's skull.

The fluorescent light overhead flickered.

"Can you fix that?" Smythe said.

"Nope," said Chief Brown. "It's been that way for years.

We've changed the bulb and the entire fixture, and the damned thing keeps doing that. We think it's in the wiring."

"Jesus," Smythe said. "If this keeps up, somebody's going to have a seizure."

Special Agent Smythe took off his sunglasses and leaned on the conference table, palms down, his cold gray eyes only a few inches from Pepper's own.

"I'm going to cut to the chase here, Detective Stephens. We have evidence that you have been taking money from the Carruthers organization in exchange for providing them with certain assistance with police matters. Is that true?"

Pepper did not meet the agent's gaze. Instead, he looked down at his hands, which were folded on the table in front of him.

I could lawyer up, he thought. *That's what Morris Shefter would tell me to do.*

But Pepper was tired. He'd felt the noose tightening around his neck ever since the O'Connor disappearance. The whole escapade was wearing him down. Sneaking around behind his partner's back made him feel like a two-faced sleazebag. He was nauseous all day, every single day.

And then he thought of the way Frank had looked away from him, like he was *ashamed* of him. That made him feel like shit. Frank was a decent guy and deserved better.

Then there was Candy, who somehow loved him. Their home was covered with flags and bunting every Fourth of July, the Christmas decorations were increasingly lavish every year, and the light on their side porch was perpetually lit up in squad-car blue, in support of law enforcement. She was proud to be married to an honest-to-God detective, a man who made the world safer for everyone else. A public trial would destroy that illusion—and maybe their marriage.

Pepper knew he had one chance here to set things right.

He sighed, then looked up at the FBI agents. Both were

glaring at him, stone faced. "Gentlemen, before we start this whole discussion, may I suggest we cut a deal?" he asked. "Because I know some things."

Smythe and Weston glanced at one another.

"You want a lawyer, Pep?" Chief Brown said.

"Nah," Pepper said. "I'm good. I know my rights."

"I think we might be able to work something out," Special Agent Smythe said.

At that exact moment, Pepper Stephens felt his perilously off-kilter world right itself just a little bit.

—

Frank sat at his desk while the FBI agents and Chief Brown interviewed Pepper. He tried to do some work, but he could not concentrate. He cracked his knuckles, got up to pee once, made a cup of coffee and drank it, read some stuff online about the Baltimore Ravens and their abysmal offense, and ate one of the nasty-tasting protein bars he had stashed in his desk. (He'd bought a crate of them on sale at Sam's Club and was determined to get his money's worth, but they were dense as hell and tasted like they were made from cardboard and glue.)

Eventually, he just stared out the window, lost in his thoughts. He was imagining Pepper sitting in the Pillbox, sweaty and anxious, spilling his guts to the feds—and hating Frank, his "brother from another mother," for turning him in.

Reading people was one of Frank's gifts—and he knew what made Pep tick.

Pep's wife, Candy, had pushed him hard to be a better provider—and Pep loved Candy desperately. He was selflessly dedicated to her and their kids and wanted to make them happy. Pepper was also one of those guys whose ethical compass could waver a bit, the needle occasionally nudged away from true north by the false gravity of rationalization. Pep could always justify a little bit of ethical compromise by saying to himself, *I deserve this.*

All of that didn't make Pep a bad man. It just made him a weak one.

And Frank truly, genuinely loved the guy, which made all this infinitely worse.

Over an hour passed before the door to the Pillbox opened. One of the guards who worked in the holding cells met the two agents. The guard led Pepper away into the bowels of the police station. Pep was slump shouldered, his eyes downcast, his pale hands clasped in front of him like the choirboy he wasn't. He looked broken and ashamed.

Jesus, what have I done? Frank thought.

Chief Brown went into his office and closed the door.

Frank got up, walked to the chief's door, and knocked.

"Come in," Chief Brown said.

Frank stepped in and closed the door.

"How can I help you, Frank?" the chief said.

"How did it go?"

"It went fine."

Frank said nothing for a moment.

Chief Brown fixed him with a glance. "You did the right thing, Frank. There's no need to second-guess yourself."

"I know. It's just . . . Pep's my best friend. I haven't had many people like him in my life. And now I've destroyed that relationship."

"You didn't destroy the relationship. He compromised it by selling his soul to the Devil. That's not your fault."

"Does he seem OK?" Frank asked.

"He's doing surprisingly well. I think the whole situation has been eating at him for a while. He's told us some things about the Carruthers organization we never realized. Pep's level of cooperation will help us a great deal—and it will help him, too. He's busted the whole thing wide open."

Frank paused, then cleared his throat. "Chief, do you think I could speak to him for a moment? In private?"

Chief Brown glared at him. "You're not involved in this, are you?"

"No, sir," Frank said. "Scout's honor."

The chief stared at him for a moment before nodding. "I believe you." He got up from behind the desk and came over to Frank, putting one massive hand on Frank's shoulder. "Pep's being held in one of the basement solitary cells in cellblock A. The solitary confinement is for his own protection. The Carruthers family's claims to having people everywhere are no joke. I'll have the guards take you to him. Let's do it tomorrow, though, after he has a chance to get settled in."

"Thanks, boss," Frank said.

"Close the door on your way out," the chief said.

—

When Pepper first saw Candy standing outside his jail cell, dressed in the pink floral Lilly Pulitzer dress he had bought her in that little boutique on Nantucket last year, he started crying.

Pep was not an emotional sort of guy. He usually kept his feelings bottled up inside, the cap screwed on tight no matter how much pressure there was. But this whole situation had blown a head gasket somewhere in his brain, and the waterworks were flowing.

"Pepper?" Candy said, a note of hesitation in her voice.

"Hey, babe," he said, his husky voice barely above a whisper—and then the tears blurred his vision once again.

"I'll give you two some privacy," the guard said, unlocking the jail cell door. "Just call me when you're ready to go. I'll be right down the hall."

"Thank you, Officer," Candy said, managing a faint smile.

She sat down in the lone spare metal chair in his cell. Pepper took a seat on the bunk.

"When Chief Brown said you needed to speak to me, I didn't think I'd be meeting you in a jail cell," she said.

"They have me here for my own protection," Pep said.

"Protection from who?"

"The Carruthers organization."

"Why would the Carruthers organization be out to get you?" she asked.

He leaned forward. "Candy, I've done some things I'm not proud of. If I could go back in time, I'd undo it all, but it's too late for that. I'm trying to make things right, though. I really am. I want you to be proud of me."

"What exactly have you done?" Candy asked. She had clasped her thin, well-manicured hands in her lap, but he could see they were trembling.

"For the last ten years or so, Phillip Carruthers has paid me to help him out with police matters. I'd give him inside access to things going on here at the station, sometimes fixing things he needed fixed."

"Did you break the law?"

Pep broke Candy's gaze and stared at the floor, shaking his head. "Sometimes."

"So you were on the take this whole time?"

Pep glanced back up at her.

"I did it for you, and for the kids. I wanted you to have a better life, you know? Cops don't make the kind of money I needed to give you what you deserve, not even detectives— and you deserve the *best*, Candy. I've never thought I was good enough for you, and I was afraid if I could not provide you a good life, you'd leave and find somebody else, someone who could give you the things I couldn't. I just kept getting in deeper and deeper, and there seemed to be no way out, and . . ."

The words left him then. Tears cascaded down Pep's ruined

face. His shoulders were slumped, his thinning hair a tousled mess.

"So that's what you think of me? That I'm so shallow and materialistic that I'd just leave you if we weren't rich?" Candy asked.

Pep, blinded by tears, could not see her, but her voice had a serrated edge to it that stung him.

"I'm sorry. I'm so sorry," he blubbered. "It's not that. It's just . . . It's just that I love you so much. I couldn't stand to see you go."

Suddenly, Candy's arms were around him, and she drew him into her so close that he could smell the faint scent of jasmine in her hair. He wrapped his arms around her shoulders and clenched her petite Pilates-toned body tightly to himself.

"I love you, you big idiot. Did you know that? *For better or for worse.* Isn't that what we said when we were married? You aren't going to lose me over money, Pep. I don't need all that stuff. I just need *you,*" she said.

Pepper felt something unclench in his gut. For one brief, horrifying moment, he thought he might puke—but that passed quickly, and he could look at her. "You mean that?"

Candy nodded. "Every last bit of it."

Pepper sighed.

"So how's Frank taking this?" Candy asked.

"We haven't talked, but I think he's pissed."

"He should be. You lied to him."

"I've been lying to everybody, and it's been eating me alive. But that's over. I'm coming clean now, turning over a new leaf."

Candy pulled away from him. Inexplicably, she was smiling. It was just about the best thing Pepper had ever seen in his life, apart from the look she had given him at the altar at First Baptist on the day they were married, nearly fifteen years ago.

"You've made things right with me. Now, you've got to make things right with Frank," Candy said.

Pep nodded. "I will," he said—and he meant it.

—

In exchange for a promise of immunity from prosecution, Pepper Stephens told the FBI agents all he knew about the entire Carruthers organization, which was involved with everything from drug smuggling to weapons sales. They had legitimate businesses, too, but the biggest moneymakers were the off-the-books enterprises—things that the FBI and the DOJ could sink their teeth into. Armed with that information, Agents Smythe and Weston turned their attention to the other members of the Carruthers family supporting cast. News of his arrest had not yet hit the papers—Smythe and Weston didn't want to spook Phillip or Erika—but the Savannah rumor mill was already churning, and it was just a matter of time before the rest of the dominoes began to fall.

The next domino to fall was jet pilot Greg Sullivan. He was brought in for questioning the following morning.

Sullivan was an ex-fighter jock, and he looked the part: He was a compact, ripped, clean-shaven guy with close-cropped hair, wearing a tight V-neck T-shirt and reflective aviator sunglasses. When Sullivan was brought in for questioning, he greeted Frank with a grin and a firm handshake as if they were old college pals who hadn't seen each other in a while.

"Good to meet you, Detective," he said, pumping Frank's hand like a politician.

As he entered the interrogation room, Sullivan removed his sunglasses to reveal piercing green eyes. After stuffing his shades into his pants pocket, Sullivan folded his muscular arms in front of himself. An exquisitely detailed tattoo of the red, black, and gold Marine Corps insignia adorned his right bicep.

Frank Winger and Agent Smythe sat facing Sullivan across the crudely rendered plain wooden interview table. A dim, flickering fluorescent light dangled crookedly overhead. Agent Weston loomed in the corner, at the edge of the shadows, positioned as though he would be ready to tag in and join the fray immediately. A mirrored observation window on the wall opposite the door was the only thing that broke up the monotonous gray wall space. Two video cameras, their tiny red eyes unblinking, stared at the men from opposite corners of the room.

Agent Smythe folded up his own Ray-Bans and put them into the inside pocket of his suit jacket, then fixed Sullivan with a steely glance. He was silent, almost taciturn, his jaw set.

"Water?" Frank asked.

Sullivan nodded. Smythe uncapped the water bottle and handed it to him.

"Smoke?"

Sullivan grinned. "I'm a pilot. We don't do that," he said. "Jet fuel, you know? It blows up sometimes."

Smart-ass, Frank thought, but he held his tongue and leaned toward the small microphone on the desk. "State your name, for the record," he said.

"Greg Sullivan."

"And what is your position in the Carruthers organization?"

"I'm the lead pilot for the Carruthers family's private jet. They have other jet jockeys they occasionally use on a contract basis, but I'm the only pilot the Carruthers family employs full-time."

"And why have you come forward today?"

"Because I was asked to. You guys called me," he said, smirking.

Frank did not like this man.

Agent Smythe shuffled through a stack of papers before him, then looked up. "I'm Special Agent Smythe of the FBI. You were interviewed about this situation before, this past summer, were you not?" Smythe asked.

"I was."

"Do you remember who conducted that interview?"

"I believe it was a Detective Pepper Stephens."

Frank's eyes flicked briefly over to Smythe, who was impassive.

"And what did he ask you?" Smythe queried.

"It was a short discussion. He just asked me about what I did, same as you, and then questioned me about what happened between July 16 and 21 of last year. He wanted to know if I was with Mr. Carruthers in Atlanta during that time, which I was, and asked if what I had filed in my flight log was accurate."

"And what did you tell him at that time?"

"I told him that it was."

"Was it?"

Sullivan shot a glance at a shadow-draped Agent Weston, who was as impassive as the Sphinx. "No," Sullivan said.

Bingo, Frank thought.

"So you lied?" Smythe said.

"I did."

"And just so we're clear, you know that altering a flight log is against FAA regulations."

Sullivan nodded once. "I do."

"So what really happened, then? For the record."

Sullivan leaned forward, took a sip of water, and leaned back in his chair, folding his arms again. "On the evening of July 19, shortly after dinnertime, Phillip got a text from Dr. O'Connor saying that she wanted to talk to him, and that it was urgent. He told me they had been arguing lately but were trying to patch things up. Phillip was hooked on her big time, really obsessed with her. As soon as he got the text, I knew we would be headed back. Sure enough, he told me to fire up the jet, and we headed back to Savannah immediately."

"Who was with you?"

"It was just me, Mr. Carruthers, and Carmine Carpeggio. Carmine always travels with Mr. Carruthers when he has business meetings. He's Mr. Carruthers's right-hand man and bodyguard. I think you know him."

Smythe nodded. "So what happened?"

"We flew back to Savannah, arriving at the Signature Aviation terminal at the Savannah airport a little before 10:00 p.m. on July 19. Phillip—Mr. Carruthers—took his own vehicle, a black 7 Series BMW, from the terminal after we landed, intending to drive to Dr. O'Connor's house with plans to meet her there. About an hour later, I got a call from Mr. Carruthers telling me he was done and we would head back to Atlanta that night. He wanted me to meet him on the tarmac by about 11:45 p.m. We were wheels up by 11:55 p.m. and landed back at PDK in Atlanta a little after 12:40 a.m."

Agent Smythe scribbled something onto the yellow legal pad in front of him. "You returned to Atlanta a little after midnight on the morning of July 20, right?"

"Correct."

"When you saw Mr. Carruthers after he returned to the airport on the night of July 19, did he appear disheveled in any way? Any bloodstains? Anything else amiss?"

"No."

"Was he dressed the same as when he left?"

Sullivan nodded. "He was, exactly."

"What did he say happened?"

"He said he went by Dr. O'Connor's place, and no one was there. Her car was missing, too. He called her cell, and she didn't answer. He still had a key to her place and thought about going in, but eventually he decided not to and just left. He texted her after that several times but got no response. At that point, he called me saying he wanted to return immediately to Atlanta."

"That's it? He offered no other details?"

"We didn't talk about it again until it became apparent the following day that Dr. O'Connor was missing. It was after that when he asked me to change the flight logs to eliminate any record of the short trip back to Savannah on the night of July 19 to 20. After that change, the flight logs reflected only the trip we made back to Savannah on the morning of Saturday, July 21, which was the date we had originally planned to return to Savannah anyway."

"And you changed the flight log without questioning him?" Smythe said.

"He was my boss. I wanted to keep my job. What exactly was I supposed to do?"

"Why didn't you come forward with this information before?"

"I didn't think it was that big a deal," Sullivan said.

Frank Winger was seething and could not contain his anger any longer. He slammed his fist on the table. "You didn't think a *murder investigation* was a big deal?"

Sullivan bowed up, his neck muscles taut, as if he was gearing up for a fight. "Well, first of all, I didn't think Mr. Carruthers killed her. He can be a dick, like most of the business execs I've worked with, but he's no murderer. And you've got to remember that part of our job as private pilots is predicated upon discretion. We don't talk about who we fly, where we fly them, or why we are flying them there. I've been paid very, very well by the Carruthers family. I would have been fired if I ever blabbed about what I was doing. Worse than that, Phillip would have blackballed me and seen to it that no one in the industry ever hired me again. The private jet pilot community is relatively small." He shrugged, palms up. "Besides that, no one ever actually charged Mr. Carruthers with murder. When Dr. O'Connor first disappeared, for all we knew, she could have just left town. Had there been an actual murder investigation, I might have come forward sooner. But that did not happen until recently."

Frank cracked his knuckles but said nothing.

Sullivan took another sip from the bottle of water in front of him. "I knew Mr. Carruthers and Dr. O'Connor had been fighting," he said. "I figured maybe they had another big argument, and she decided to get out of town. The Carruthers family can make it awfully hard on someone living in Savannah when they want to."

"Jesus Christ. From how you're talking, you'd think they were the mob or something," Smythe said.

Sullivan blinked. "You think they're *not*?"

"What exactly do you mean by that?" Smythe asked.

"You guys really don't get it, do you?" Sullivan said.

"I guess we don't," said Smythe. "Enlighten us."

Greg Sullivan shook his head slowly. "You obviously aren't from around here, Agent Weston. Well, I'm not, either. I grew up in Des Moines, Iowa. I first came to this area while stationed at MCAS Beaufort as an F/A-18 pilot with the Marines. I liked Savannah, so when I got out of the Corps a decade ago, I called in a few favors and got hired by Gulfstream as a test pilot. You wanna hear a weird story?"

"I'm all ears," Smythe said.

"After I'd been at Gulfstream a while, I got a phone call out of the blue from Carmine Carpeggio. Carmine was an ex–Special Forces guy. I knew plenty of guys like him during my time in the Marines, all super gung-ho about the job. When he called me, he told me that Mr. Carruthers had heard through the grapevine that I was a top-notch pilot. 'What grapevine is that?' I said. 'Let's just say we have our sources,' he said. 'That's how I got your phone number.' Carmine then proceeded to tell me everything about myself—how much I made, where I lived, how many kids I had, my wife's name, and where she worked, all of it. It was very creepy."

"I can imagine," Smythe said.

"And then he made me this absurd offer—high salary, full health benefits, private school tuition for both of my kids, a one hundred percent match on a 401(k), everything. All I had to do was be available to fly whenever the Carruthers family wanted me to. It was truly an offer I couldn't refuse."

"So you took it," Smythe said.

"How could I not?" Sullivan replied.

"So how are they like the mob?" Smythe asked.

Sullivan scoffed. "They're actually worse, at least around here."

"Worse? How do you get that?" Smythe asked.

"First of all, there's no competition. They don't have to worry about some rival gang or organization knocking them off. Second, they're billionaires. They've got more money than they know what to do with. Third, they're very, very connected. They've managed to infiltrate almost everyone and everything in Savannah—people around here owe them. I'm pretty sure there are multiple snitches on the police force." Sullivan shot a momentary glance at Frank. "Maybe even you, Detective Winger."

"I'm not that kind of person," Frank said.

"I didn't think I was, either. But after a while, you realize that every man has his price."

Frank felt like he was going to be sick. He took a brisk swig of Diet Cherry Coke and belched once. That settled his stomach—for now.

"So what made you decide to tell the truth now?" Agent Smythe asked.

Sullivan shrugged again. "I can see the handwriting on

the wall. Dominoes seem to be falling. You guys will bring Carmine Carpeggio in sooner or later, and Carmine knows *everything*. Once he talks, all hell's gonna break loose. From where I'm sitting, the Carruthers empire is about to collapse. You don't need to be a genius to see that. I figured I'd cooperate now and get on the right side of things early on. No reason to go down with the ship, you know what I'm saying?"

Frank stood up, running his fingers through his hair, and turned away from Sullivan, shaking his head.

Agent Weston took Frank's seat. "One last question," he asked. He held up a picture of Trek Richards. "Have you seen this man?" he asked.

Sullivan nodded. "Sure."

"Can you identify him?"

"That's Trek Richards. He was head of security for the Carruthers organization."

"When did you last see him?"

Sullivan thought for a moment. "Last summer, when I flew him out to Montana."

Agent Weston glanced up at Frank and Smythe. "Why did you fly him out to Montana?"

"Because Erika and Phillip Carruthers wanted me to. As usual, I did as I was told."

"And was that before or after Dr. O'Connor disappeared?"

"A few days before. I can't recall exactly. That was eight months ago."

"Where exactly did you take him in Montana?"

"The Carruthers compound near Kalispell. Phillip's father bought that property years ago."

"Can you give us the address?"

"Of course. I can do even better than that: I can drop a pin on Google Maps that will take you right to the gate."

Weston folded up his legal pad and stood. "That'll be all for now, Mr. Sullivan. We'll be in touch," he said.

"So I'm free to go?"

"Yes, sir. Thank you for your cooperation."

Weston opened the door to the Pillbox and let Sullivan out. The three men looked at one another.

"Who's next?" Frank asked.

"Carmine Carpeggio. We're bringing him in tomorrow," Smythe said.

31

Before going home for the day, Frank stopped by Chief Brown's office. "Do you think I could talk to Pep now?" he asked.

"Of course," Chief Brown said.

The chief called someone on his phone, and a pair of curiously mismatched guards appeared shortly thereafter. The younger guard was short and rail thin, with a long, sad face and droopy eyes. The second one was balding, portly, and middle-aged, with a bowling ball head and greasy horn-rimmed glasses that had slid down to the end of his nose. They reminded Frank of Laurel and Hardy in uniform. *Savannah's finest,* he thought.

Laurel and Hardy took Frank to the restricted-use elevator that went to the holding area down below. The three of them rode the elevator to the lower level in silence, each of them avoiding eye contact. The skinny guard absently picked at his nose, apparently not caring that he had company.

When the door opened, the two guards escorted Frank down a long, dimly lit hallway toward cellblock A.

Frank had visited cellblock A many times. It was a depressing place in the bowels of the station, where the SPD usually stashed the most violent offenders—murderers, rapists, and gangbangers, the folks most likely to be hurt by others or to hurt someone else. The place always seemed humid—Frank supposed it was below the water table, although he wasn't certain—and it was permeated by a peculiar, pervasive aroma of decay, as though a legion of rats had died somewhere inside its walls.

Frank could feel a distinct pressure building up inside his skull, like storm clouds gathering. He could almost see it: towering bruise-colored thunderheads climbing up into the high stratosphere of his mind.

Frank had always felt like this in Afghanistan whenever a firefight was imminent—jangly nerves, heartbeat too rapid, palms sweaty, eyes darting this way and that, like everything in the world had been sped up a notch. He supposed it was adrenaline, or cortisol, the sort of fight-or-flight response he'd read about in those dark years afterward, when he was trying to understand everything he'd been through.

Cookie used to call this feeling "the willies."

I've got the willies, he'd say—and Frank knew exactly what Cookie meant because he had the willies, too.

The fat guard unlocked the cell to let Frank in. His key-chain rattled against his belt. "Call us when you want out, Detective. We'll be right down the hall," he said.

"Roger that," Frank said.

Laurel and Hardy jangled off down the hallway in tandem, the dim fluorescent lights blinking intermittently overhead.

As jail cells go, Pep's was decent enough. The sturdy basement walls were made of large blocks of rough-hewn stone, enclosing a cell about the size of a small bedroom. There was a single bunk built into the wall, a sink with a metal mirror, and a stainless-steel toilet. A short privacy wall by the toilet was a small luxury. A slit-like horizontal window cut high into one wall allowed Pep to see the sun, the branches of a few trees, and the occasional bird. A single LED light burned from a recessed canister in the ceiling overhead.

Pepper was already dressed in a too-large Day-Glo orange prison jumper. He looked thinner in the oversized prison garb, and the salt-and-pepper scruff of his beard looked oddly out of place on his usually clean-shaven face. Still, he seemed calm and unbothered.

The two men stood there silently for a moment, sizing one another up.

"You OK?" Frank asked at long last.

"Yeah," Pep said. "You?"

"I'm fine."

"Have a seat." Pepper motioned to the narrow bunk.

Frank sat on the bunk, which creaked under his weight.

"I'd hug you, but I don't think they want us to do that. They're watching," Pep said, nodding to a camera mounted on the wall opposite the cell.

Pepper leaned against the short privacy wall beside the toilet. He didn't seem anxious at all. Frank could feel the pressure inside his brain begin to dissipate. A few stray beams of light shone through. The willies were gone.

"You're not pissed at me?" Frank asked.

Pep laughed. "Hell, no. You did me a favor. I was trapped in an impossibly bad situation, and you blew that entire situation up. You may have saved my life."

Frank had not thought of it that way, but the idea gave him some measure of relief. "Have you talked to Candy?" he asked.

Pep nodded.

"How's she taking all of this?"

"She's OK. I told her I did it for her and the kids, and she believes me. She's hanging in there. The hardest part for her will be telling the kids why I'm not at home. Saying Daddy is in jail will raise a lot of questions, even if I eventually get out of this."

Frank leaned forward. "Pep, I came here for a reason. I need to ask you something. I've always trusted your instincts about people."

"Shoot."

"Given your understanding of the Carruthers organization, do you think Phillip killed Janie O'Connor?"

Pepper looked around, shot a glance at the camera, then leaned forward. He spoke sotto voce, barely above a whisper. "I'll tell you what I told the FBI guys. Phillip's a self-righteous asshole, and he can be a prick at times, but he's not violent—and he does *not* like to get his hands dirty. As much as people want to make Phillip out to be the bad guy here, he's not a natural-born killer like Carmine Carpeggio. He'd have to be pushed, and pushed hard, to do something like that. I do believe he loved Dr. O'Connor, or at least he loved the *idea* of her. The only way I could see him killing her would have been as a crime of passion, not something premeditated. Now, his sister, Erika? She's mean as hell—and she thinks she's untouchable. They don't call her the Wasp for nothing. She did *not* like the idea of Janie O'Connor being part of the family. Erika would have killed Janie with her bare hands if she thought she could get away with it."

A shadow began flickering about in the room. Frank and Pep both jumped as if an electric current had passed through the two of them. Frank looked up. A pale moth was circling the overhead light, casting shadows against the stone walls of the jail cell.

"Jesus, I'm jittery," Frank said.

"You and me both," Pep said.

Frank thought for a moment.

"Here's something else I've been wondering. What about Anderson Carruthers's death? Was that really an accident? Or was it murder? Because if Phillip shot his dad in cold blood, maybe you might need to reconsider your assessment of what he's capable of. It was just the two of them there that day, after all—and you did bury that investigation, too," Frank said.

Pep nodded in contrition. "I buried the investigation, but I looked at the facts of the case. I interviewed Phillip, read the autopsy report, and even visited the site in Screven County where the shooting occurred to get an idea about what happened. I think it was really an accident. I have no reason to believe otherwise."

"But *why* did you bury the investigation?"

Pepper shrugged. "Anderson Carruthers was dead and was not coming back. Per explicit stipulations in Anderson's will, Phillip and Erika were set to take over the company. There was no need to drag the family into a protracted trial. Nobody wanted Phillip to go through that, especially not Mrs. Cynthia. So we took Phillip at his word, listed it as the accidental shooting death I truly thought it was, and moved on without pressing any charges. It was ultimately in everyone's best interest."

Frank decided to let it go. "So who do you think killed Dr. O'Connor? Do you have any idea?"

"I think there's something else at work here, likely driven by the family's power dynamics. The Carruthers organization values loyalty, but it's a species of loyalty largely driven by fear. It reminds me of *The Sopranos*," he said.

"I thought you hadn't watched *The Sopranos*."

"I started watching it after you called me a Philistine," Pepper said. "I watched *Game of Thrones*, too. That's also about power. So I'm learning."

"Good for you, Pep. Maybe you're not a Philistine after all."

"I'm working on it," Pepper said, grinning.

"So what's your gut feeling here?" Frank asked.

Pepper leaned forward. "My gut feeling is that Erika is at the root of all this. She likely wouldn't do it herself, but I wouldn't put it past her to have ordered someone to kill Janie and then set Phillip up for the murder. My money would be on

Carmine, because he is loyal to the organization as a whole, the sort of person who would do anything necessary to keep the team's goals intact. Trek was Phillip's pet monster, and sort of a loose cannon. Erika and Trek never got along. She didn't trust him one bit."

"Speaking of Trek Richards, he disappeared right before Dr. O'Connor did. What do you know about that?"

"When I found out that Trek had been implicated in the fire on Dave Wommack's front porch, I called Phillip and told him he needed to cut ties with Trek. Phillip called Trek in that morning, brought him into his office, and fired him immediately. I really don't know what happened to him after that. My consternation over his disappearance was genuine, same as yours."

So Phillip was lying about Trek quitting, Frank thought. *What was up with that?* But he said nothing.

"So what was the deal about Diane's rape? How do you think that came about? Was that a failed murder attempt on Janie?"

"I don't know anything about all that, but I do know Trek Richards. He's an impulsive, vengeful, paranoid little weirdo, always talking to himself—and he's got a mean streak a mile wide. Personally, I think Trek blamed Janie for being fired and showed up at Janie's house that morning planning to take revenge on her. Janie was not there, but Diane was, so he attacked Diane instead. Diane became a victim that day simply because she was in the wrong place at the wrong time."

"Greg Sullivan, Phillip's pilot, said he took Trek to Montana right before Janie went missing. Were you aware of that?"

Pep shook his head. "I was not."

"So you truly had no idea what happened to Trek after Diane's rape?"

"Nope. But if the pilot says he took him to Montana, I'd look there first. The Carruthers organization owns a large plot of woodland near Kalispell."

Frank thought for a moment. "Do you think someone else in the Carruthers organization may have killed Trek?"

"I guess it's possible, but I honestly don't know. They didn't ever share that sort of detail with me."

Frank stood up to leave. Pepper's eyes were once again filled with tears, and his lower lip was quivering. "Look, Frank, there's one thing I want to say here."

"Go ahead."

"I screwed up. I know that. I doctored reports, covered things up, and did a lot of other things I'm ashamed of. It was unequivocal obstruction of justice, but I didn't really think I was hurting anyone."

"Until Janie O'Connor disappeared."

Pep's shoulders slumped. "Well, yeah," he said. "I guess that investigation going nowhere was partly my fault."

"It was *mostly* your fault, Pep," Frank said.

"Fair enough. But I'm trying to make it right, you know?" Pepper said, wiping tears from his eyes with an orange sleeve.

Spurning Pep's concerns over camera surveillance, Frank hugged Pepper, patting him on the back. "They're bringing Carmine Carpeggio in for questioning in the morning," Frank said.

"Well, that'll be interesting," Pepper said. "Carmine is the consummate insider in the Carruthers organization. He knows where all the bodies are buried." He raised his eyebrows knowingly. "In some cases, maybe even literally," Pepper said. "But I doubt Carmine will talk."

—

As it turned out, Carmine Carpeggio, who had always seemed as taciturn as an old oak, was quite the talker.

He told the investigators everything he knew in exchange

for a lighter sentence. Before too long, Agents Smythe and Weston had learned all about the Carruthers family's extensive involvement in human trafficking, arms sales to developing countries, drug deals with Mexican cartels, the giant alligator named Burt Reynolds used to dispose of unwanted individuals, and a host of other scurrilous details that had been hidden in darkness for so long.

One line of questioning was of interest to both the agents and to Frank.

The fluorescent light overhead in the interview room was still flickering, as it always did, but Carpeggio did not seem to notice it at all. His face was impassive, almost stony, as he answered every question the agents asked him, concisely and without a trace of emotion.

"Did you kill Dr. Janie O'Connor?" Agent Weston asked him.

"I did not."

"Do you know who killed Dr. O'Connor?"

"I don't."

"Do you know what happened to Trek Richards?"

"He was fired. After that, I have no idea. I was only concerned about what happened to the Carruthers organization. Once Trek was out, I had nothing to do with him."

"So just to be clear, no one ordered you to eliminate him?"

"You mean, nobody ordered me to *kill* him?"

"That's right."

"No. I always thought Trek was an idiot, and I told Mr. Carruthers so on several occasions, but once he was gone, he was no longer my concern. I was not asked to kill him, I did not kill him, and I have no idea where he is today."

Carmine did confess to murdering the woman whose child had died and admitted to feeding the bodies to Burt.

As the long, rambling interview wound to a close,

Carpeggio put up one meaty palm, as if he were raising his hand in an elementary school class to ask a question. "I only have one request."

"What's that?" Agent Weston asked.

"I want to be in solitary confinement," he said.

Weston arched his eyebrows. "You *want* solitary? For real?"

Carpeggio nodded. "I don't need anybody else's company. If I'm around other people, the folks I used to work for will find somebody who can get to me, and they'll eventually kill me. I certainly don't want that."

And that was it.

After over two hundred years, the walls of the vast Carruthers empire finally began to crumble and fall.

—

After the Carpeggio interview was finished, Agent Smythe looked up at Frank and Agent Weston. His jaw was set, his eyes cold and hard.

"There's more than enough here to arrest Phillip and Erika Carruthers, and we need to move fast. If Phillip and Erika get word that Carpeggio has talked—and they will, trust me— they'll bolt. They're both significant flight risks. Extraditing them from overseas might be difficult."

"What are the charges?" Frank asked.

"I think we can arrest them both for the criminal activities we now know the Carruthers organization has been involved in. And we have enough evidence to arrest Phillip for murder. The pilot's testimony shows that Phillip lied about his whereabouts on the night Janie O'Connor disappeared, and the video corroborates that."

"We still don't know who sent the video," Frank said.

"Does it really matter? We have a motive, we have human remains with an ID confirmed by DNA evidence, we

discovered a potential murder weapon with the victim's blood
on it, confirmed by DNA as well, on the suspect's property, we
can place him at her home on the night before she went missing. Now we know he lied to cover up his whereabouts that
evening. Trek Richards, the other potential suspect, was flown
out to Montana right before Dr. O'Connor disappeared—and
now he's off the radar screen, too. We don't have all the pieces
together yet, but at this point, we have more than sufficient
grounds to arrest Phillip Carruthers on suspicion of murder.
It's time we brought him in," Smythe said.

32

Anna Brown was used to hardship.

The South had not been a kind place for poor, uneducated Black girls in the 1960s. Opportunities were few and far between. But she had learned early on the value of honesty and hard work, which ultimately had given her a productive, rewarding life.

Anna's job with the Carruthers family was the culmination of her lifetime of service to others. She had her own home, an excellent salary, and job security. But she was also a realist, and she understood that anything she had could be taken away at a moment's notice. Stuff fell apart. People died. Even the most fervently whispered prayers sometimes went unanswered.

God knows it had all happened before.

Which was why she was not surprised at all when Clarence called.

"Mama, I'm coming to get you," he said.

"Why?" she asked.

"Phillip Carruthers is about to be arrested for murder, and Erika Carruthers is going to be arrested as well, for other reasons. When all of this goes down, I don't want you on the Carruthers property. I need to get you out of there."

Anna chuckled softly to herself. "Why are you worried about that, Clarence? Phillip's so busy these days that I hardly ever see him. And Erika lives downtown and only comes here when she needs to. On the other hand, Miz Cynthia's got dementia, and she needs me. She's got around-the-clock nurses, but I'm the only friend she has in the world, and she trusts me. I can't just leave her. Erika and Phillip don't know my connection to you, anyway," she said.

Clarence was silent for a moment. Anna could almost hear the gears turning in his brain.

"Mama, do you mean to tell me that after all this time, they don't know I'm your son?" he said at last.

"I'm pretty sure they don't."

"I find that hard to believe."

Anna gazed out of the bay window in her kitchen as she talked to her son. Outside, it was a moonless night. The sky was pitch black. A gentle wind rustled in the trees. Someplace, far away, an owl hooted softly in the woods.

"Look, Mama, like it or not, I'm coming to get you. I need to make sure you're safe," Clarence said.

Anna sighed. She'd known she wouldn't be able to talk him out of it. After all, that was how she'd raised him. "Well, you'll need a code to enter the estate's front gate. Mine is 0616. Just punch it in the keypad as you come in."

"See you soon." Clarence hung up without another word.

Anna looked around her place and stuffed some clothes, her toothbrush, and a few toiletries in an overnight bag. *I can come back later for the rest,* she thought.

The problem was, she didn't know if that was true. Life didn't always work that way. The Bible said it best: *The Lord giveth and the Lord taketh away.*

Before too long, she heard the distinctive throaty rumble

of Clarence's truck engine in the distance. She glanced around her beloved bungalow one last time, taking it all in and committing it to memory. It was, without question, the nicest place she had ever lived. For many reasons, she would be very sad to leave it.

Anna recalled the first time she ever saw the house. Anderson Carruthers had driven the two of them over from the main compound in his golf cart all those years ago. A wide, semicircular crushed-shell drive wound between huge live oaks and banks of blooming pink and fuchsia azaleas.

"Well, what do you think?" Anderson had asked.

The tabby Low Country–style home, with a large front porch and twin gaslights on either side of the front door, sat on two acres of landscaped grounds in the middle of the maritime forest. A tidal creek wound its way through the verdant marsh out back. The trees had been pruned back to yield an expansive view stretching to the horizon.

"It's beautiful," she said.

"It's yours."

Anna, shocked, had looked over at him. "Andy, I can't accept this," she said.

"Why not? You've certainly earned it."

"I have a home. And besides, this is too much. People will talk."

Anderson shook his head. "Let them talk, then," he said, taking Anna's hand in his own.

Anna had accepted his gift in the end. She loved the huge kitchen, with its double Thermador ovens and a bay window overlooking the marsh. Every evening, she watched the sunset through that window as the shorebirds came winging in for the evening. Deer roamed freely through the yard, and terrapins nested in her flower beds. It was clear that Andy Carruthers had been paying attention when Anna had told him about her dream home, for he had spared nothing in re-creating even the smallest details.

It was perfect.

Anna truly loved this place, as she had loved the man who gave it to her. But her lover was long gone now, his ashes scattered among the cypress trees in his beloved Darkwater Swamp.

Now, she supposed she'd have to leave this last little bit of him behind, as well.

Anna briefly considered Cynthia Carruthers, but she realized she'd be OK. With 24/7 nursing care, her old friend might miss her, but she did not *need* her.

I'll check on her when all of this is over.

Anna picked up her bag and opened the front door. As they drove away, Anna looked over her shoulder to catch one final glimpse of the home that Anderson Carruthers had built for her. It felt as if something vital was being torn away.

She dared not mention her pain to Clarence. If she'd learned anything in her long and difficult life, it was that certain things were better left unsaid.

Goodbye, Andy, she thought. *I love you.*

—

"What do you mean, Phillip Carruthers is *gone*?" Chief Brown exclaimed. He drained the last of his water and slammed the bottle down hard on his desk, crushing it like an eggshell. He'd dropped his mother off at his home with Earline and come back to the station right after.

"He's gone. We were able to bring Erika in, but Phillip took off in his private jet to parts unknown," Frank said.

"I thought we had his jet pilot on our side. Hell, the pilot has been *cooperating* with us," Chief Brown said.

"Sullivan is his main pilot, but he's not the only one," Frank replied. "Sullivan told us that Carruthers has other pilots he uses as backups."

"Do we know where he went?" Chief Brown said.

"Phillip's *plane* is in Jackson Hole, Wyoming, right now, but we can't be certain he's on it," Frank said.

"Get the FBI guys to impound it," Chief Brown said. "Phillip Carruthers is now the main suspect in an active murder investigation."

"Already done," Frank said. He turned to leave but stopped himself. "Chief?"

"Yes, Frank?"

"Thank you for believing in me. I know I haven't been at my best since Paulina died, but you didn't give up on me. I just wanted to let you know that I appreciate that. It means a lot."

"I never doubted you for a moment. You're a great detective, Frank." He looked Frank in the eye. His gaze was direct and unwavering. "Let's finish this," he said. "Find those assholes and bring them in."

"Yes, sir," Frank said.

33

Frank awoke in the middle of the night to his cell phone buzzing with an incoming call.

He had fallen asleep on the sofa while watching a dull thriller on HBO, so when he first woke up, he was disoriented. The television was still on, but it had gone back to the menu screen, which was silent.

"Frank?" an unfamiliar voice asked.

Frank looked at his phone. It was a little after 2:00 a.m. "Yes? Who is this?"

"Ben Smythe, FBI. Sorry to call you so late, but I thought you might want to know about a few developments in the Carruthers situation. We got a ping on a credit card for Phillip Carruthers at a gas station in Kalispell, Montana. The surveillance video is grainy, but it looks like him. You may remember that that's where Greg Sullivan said he took Trek right before Dr. O'Connor went missing. We finally tracked down the pilot of the Carruthers jet that we impounded in Jackson Hole, the guy who was filling in for Sullivan, and he confirmed that he'd made a stop in Kalispell to drop Carruthers off before leaving to go to Jackson Hole. The Carruthers family owns a thousand-acre piece of backwoods property near Kalispell, with one big house and another smaller cabin onsite. The pilot told us exactly where the property was and described where the houses were. It matches the location Sullivan gave us. The odds are high that Phillip Carruthers is on that property right now. We're headed to Montana this morning to check things out and make an arrest, maybe even two. You want to go?"

"Hell, yes. When is the flight? Nothing commercial leaves the Savannah airport this early."

"Detective Winger, we aren't flying commercial. That's why I'm calling you. We're taking one of the Bureau's planes. We're leaving in about an hour from the Savannah airport. We can send someone over to pick you up if you like," Smythe said.

"No, that's OK. I can drive myself to the airport. I'll be there by three."

After Frank hung up, he felt the gloom that had clung to him for so long begin to lift. He'd been feeling sorry for himself for far too long. Having the chance to take down Phillip Carruthers was just the tonic he needed to move on with his life.

He went into the bathroom to take a quick shower. Afterward, as he toweled off, he gazed at himself in the mirror. "You're not getting any younger, Frankie boy," he said to himself.

The wrinkles on his face and neck were deeper, his lips thinner, and his eyebrows had sprouted a crop of stray hairs resembling antennae. His hair, jet black after he had dyed it months earlier, was once again intermingled with strands of gray. The crucifix tattoo on his chest was sagging and faded, its black lines now darker blue, along with the inscription below it in Gothic script: *Infidel.*

He gazed at the increasingly flaccid tattoo. Its appearance would require a little explanation when he drifted into the nursing home phase of his life, which suddenly didn't seem so far away anymore.

As he left the condo, Frank gazed at a framed picture of Paulina that he had propped up on his desk. She was on the beach at Tybee, wearing a white sundress, her hair swirling about her head like a halo as the sun settled into the ocean behind her.

God, I miss her, he thought. But for the first time in nearly four years now, he could at least *see* the future. And that was something, wasn't it?

Maybe he could move on after all. Maybe he would finally get past the nightmares and the loneliness and start to live again. Frank felt something shifting in the universe, something vital and real, although he was not entirely sure what that something was.

Hope, perhaps?

Indeed, there was hope, at long last: hope that the end of the darkness of the Janie O'Connor saga might represent a new beginning for Detective Franklin Williamson Winger, SPD.

As he walked to his car, a small black cat crossed his path, its topaz eyes glancing up at him.

"Here, kitty," Frank said, reaching out to it—but the cat ran away from him, disappearing beneath a nearby VW.

Frank grinned. A part of him, long ago, would have viewed this event as a bad omen, a sign that luck was not going to favor him. But Frank had learned in Afghanistan that there was no such thing as luck. There was no fate, no destiny, no karma. That was all fantasy. Things simply were as they were.

You make your own luck, Cookie used to say. It was his favorite saying, something he uttered at least two or three times a week, and it had stuck with Frank ever since Afghanistan. He regularly heard it inside his head, in Cookie's distinctive Louisiana drawl, just as plain and as clear as he'd heard it the last time the man himself uttered the phrase, right before he died.

You're damned right, Cook, Frank thought as he cranked

the balky engine of the battered Hyundai and pulled out of the parking lot onto a completely empty Waters Avenue.

—

As Smythe had predicted, it was still dark when the FBI's Gulfstream IV touched down in Montana. Frank was jolted awake as the G4's wheels hit the tarmac. He looked outside and was surprised to see a large, well-lit aircraft facility with several large jets on the ground.

"Isn't this place sort of out of the way?" Frank asked.

"It is," Smythe said.

"Why are all these big planes here, then?"

"Glacier," Agent Weston said, taking off his headphones. He folded the headphones up, put them in his backpack, and zipped it up tight.

"What?"

"This is the main airport for Glacier National Park. Lots of summer tourist traffic. In winter, this place is dead, but it picks up again in the spring, and the tourist industry runs heavy from May through August, until school starts. The snow comes back in soon after that, and things die down," Weston said.

"How do you know so much about the airport in Kalispell, Montana?" Frank asked.

Weston shrugged. "My parents were national park geeks. We went to a different one every summer. Glacier is one of my favorites. Haven't been back here since I was fifteen, though."

"Don't believe that. He downplays it, but Weston's brain is like Google. He remembers everything. He kills everybody in *Jeopardy!* and Trivial Pursuit. He's the only Harvard grad I've ever actually worked with," Smythe said.

"That's not true," Weston said. "Director Simmons went to Harvard, too."

"I haven't worked with him," Smythe said. "Hell, I've only met him twice."

"How did you end up working for the FBI?" Frank asked.

Agent Weston was checking his sidearm. He slid a fully loaded clip into place, checked the slide, and clicked on the safety before holstering it once again.

"My dad was a beat cop," Weston said. His steely gaze softened. "He was shot and killed during my freshman year in college, breaking up a fight at a family reunion, of all things. Dad always said that his dream job was to work for the FBI. When I was a junior, the FBI sent people to Cambridge to recruit candidates for Quantico. I joined the Bureau to honor him."

"Ask him to say something for you in Russian," Smythe said.

Frank looked at Weston. "You speak Russian?"

"The Bureau likes you to speak a foreign language. I know Russian and Arabic. Smythe speaks Spanish. It helps with what we do."

"I can curse in Turkish, too," Smythe said.

"You learned that in a bar," Weston said, grinning.

The pilots had taxied to the terminal and parked the plane on the tarmac. The copilot opened the aircraft door.

"Well, Detective Winger, welcome to Montana!" Agent Smythe said.

Frank took a deep breath of the cool, crisp air and smiled.

Frank had never been to this part of the country, not even once. Still, the feeling he had was very familiar. He was on a mission, fighting for a just cause. He was locked and loaded, and it suited him, sealing over the cracks in his fractured soul.

Godspeed, Frankie boy, Cookie's rich, warm voice said inside him. *Bring it all home.*

34

The rental vehicle the FBI had arranged for Agents Smythe and Weston was a mammoth Dodge Ram 3500 pickup truck—a special edition with a front-mounted winch and a 6.7-liter Cummins turbo diesel engine.

"Guess they're expecting us to engage in a little off-roading," Frank said.

"I asked for this," Agent Smythe said. "You never know what the roads will be like around here, or if there will even be roads. A truck like this is our best bet."

"I don't know a damned thing about trucks, so I'll take your word for it," Frank said.

Frank took a seat in the crew cab. Smythe and Weston sat in the front. All three were dressed in black body armor with "FBI" spelled out across the front and back in gold letters.

"Just in case they doubt us," Smythe had said as they suited up.

"Carpeggio said that the estate was just outside of town, north of Kalispell, just off US 2 on the way into Glacier," Weston said. "He gave us a map, some directions, and the address. Greg Sullivan gave us the same coordinates. I'm entering them into Google Maps right now."

"We're not checking into our hotel first?" Frank asked.

Smythe laughed. "This is a grab-and-go operation, Frank, not a vacation. We aren't spending the night. We're here just to arrest Phillip Carruthers, and maybe Trek Richards, and hightail it back to Savannah. Our pilots will be waiting."

Frank looked out the window into the early morning darkness. They were in a desolate, flat generic everyland that could have been plucked from any rural area in the country. He had always thought of Montana as mountainous and rugged, but what he could see from the truck's window was anything but that.

They passed a collection of low-slung buildings—auto body shops and storage facilities and a tiny church with a metal roof and a white cross out front with a simple inscription that said *Jesus Loves Me*. Only one gas station was open, a sprawling one with an attached convenience store. Its brilliant searchlights arced skyward as though it were announcing a movie premiere. As they passed, Frank saw a flickering neon sign out front proclaiming *Showers for a Dollar! Clean Bunks for Ten Bucks!* as if those things were novelties.

After they passed through Columbia Falls and Hungry Horse, Frank could finally see mountains looming up around them, their flanks randomly spangled with lights that looked like earthbound stars.

"The turn is up ahead," Agent Weston said. "It's on the left."

The road to the Carruthers estate was paved but unmarked. It wound uphill through an increasingly thick forest until they arrived at a simple metal gate. Surveillance cameras were pointed at them from all sides. A box with a touchpad sat right outside the gate. Agent Smythe pulled the truck up close.

"This is private property," a man's voice crackled over the loudspeaker. "You need to turn your truck around and leave the way you came."

"We're with the FBI. We're here to see Phillip Carruthers," Smythe said.

"There is no one here by that name," the box replied.

"Look, sir, we know this address is correct. Carmine Carpeggio gave it to us. We have a warrant for Mr. Carruthers's arrest. He can either come with us peacefully or we will come in and get him. Either way, he's coming with us today. We aren't leaving without him," Smythe said.

The box was silent for a moment.

"I need to see some ID," it said at last.

Smythe took Weston's FBI identification badge and his own and held them up to the camera mounted over the keypad.

"Your names are Smythe and Weston?" the box asked.

"Yes, sir, they are," Smythe replied.

"Mr. Carruthers is not here," the box said. "And if you're going to keep using fake government identification, you might want to get a more believable set of names. Smith and Wesson? Really? This is one of the more elaborate tricks you reporters have devised. One tip: Even if Mr. Carruthers were here, he wouldn't be talking to you. He doesn't do interviews."

Weston looked at Smythe, palms raised, a perplexed look on his face. "Sir, we are not reporters. We are agents of the Federal Bureau of Investigation. We are here to arrest Mr. Carruthers for murder."

"I've had just about enough," the box said. "You need to get out of here right now. Otherwise, I will send a security team to escort you out."

Smythe rolled the window up and threw the truck into reverse, scowling.

"We're leaving?" Frank asked.

"Hell, no," Smythe said.

After putting the truck in park, Smythe got out and hooked the winch on to the gate. He then got back into the cab, looked behind him, and threw the engine into reverse. "Hang on!" he shouted.

The wheels were grinding on the asphalt driveway for a moment as the gate bent slightly. Smythe started fishtailing the truck back and forth, and the gate bent even more. As the engine growled, its transmission grinding, Frank heard squawks of protest from the call box next to the gate.

Suddenly, the truck lurched backward as the gate gave way, flinging wide open with a metallic *clank!* Smythe put the vehicle back in park and unhooked the winch.

"We've got to move. Carruthers's security people will be here soon," he said.

He put the truck back into drive and smashed right through the twisted remains of the battered gate. Weston unholstered his sidearm and turned around to Frank.

"Get ready, Frank," he said. "We're headed into the hot zone. There's no telling what might happen."

The gravel driveway wound through the forest through a dense tunnel of trees. Smythe barreled through the next two turns in the driveway without incident, but on the third switchback they heard gunshots coming from someplace.

Frank could tell that the gunfire was coming from in front of them. The reports sounded like they came from an assault weapon, possibly an AK-47. One round struck the vehicle in the back, near the truck bed, with a dull *thwonk!*

"Thank God they can't shoot straight, or that round might have pierced the gas tank," Smythe muttered, rounding another curve.

A pair of forest-green pickups blocked the road ahead. Several men crouched behind the trucks, firing random bursts of gunfire as the FBI agents' vehicle hurtled forward.

"Hold on!" Smythe barked.

He jerked the wheel to the right, plunging through a shallow ditch on the side of the road. The truck's wheels spun and then dug in, sending gobbets of earth and loam flying. Smythe maneuvered the Ram between a pair of giant western hemlock trees and bounced it across the grasping arm-thick roots of a towering Douglas fir. They caromed right past a mammoth lichen-encrusted boulder, scraping the passenger side a bit, before Smythe jerked the truck back toward the roadway.

"Now!" Smythe shouted.

Weston took aim and fired four quick shots.

"Did you get 'em?"

"I hit the front and back tires on the first one. I think I got only the front tire on the second, but I did get a parting shot in on the radiator. That puppy won't last long," Weston said.

"I told you he was a badass," Smythe said, grinning at Frank in the mirror.

The Ram jounced back through the ditch beyond the roadblock, and the tires bit into the gravel once again. The green-truck boys scrambled to get back into their vehicles.

"Fucking amateurs," Smythe muttered.

The house stood in the middle of a large clearing. It was grand: a huge log-cabin-style edifice with a stacked stone foundation, stone chimneys, and a cedar-shingled roof. The front porch was broad, its roof held up by mortared columns of stacked stone. A bluish wisp of smoke curled up from one of the chimneys in the early morning light.

Smythe parked the Ram right in front of the door to the house and killed the engine. "They'll call for backup, so we'll have to move fast. Frank, get behind that stone pillar and watch for the trucks. Lay down some gunfire if you have to, but try not to hit anyone. Weston and I are going to try to make the arrest."

Smythe rapped on the large oak door. "FBI! Open up!"

A petite elderly woman with a rumpled face opened the

door. Her scraggly gray hair was pulled into a tight bun. She wore a simple gray maid's outfit and sensible white leather shoes.

"Can I help you?" she asked.

"We're with the FBI. We're looking for Phillip Carruthers."

The woman smiled at them sweetly. "Mr. Carruthers has not been here for two days. He's staying at the cabin. He said he wanted some privacy," she said.

A gunshot whizzed overhead and struck one of the pillars.

"Hands up!" one of the Carruthers guards said through a megaphone.

"Gentlemen, we are FBI agents, here to arrest Phillip Carruthers for murder!" Smythe shouted. "There will be hell to pay if you shoot us!"

The man with the megaphone was quiet for a moment. "You're really FBI agents?" he asked at last, his voice subdued.

Frank stepped out from behind the pillar, his arms raised. "Look at my vest," he said. "We just came here to do a job. I'm going to put my weapon down now. There's no reason for this to get ugly. We could rain holy hell down on this place if you guys want us to, but if that happens, you may all end up dead."

Megaphone Man—a short-statured, pear-shaped guy who looked like he spent far more time watching TV and drinking beer than engaging in any actual physical activity—glanced anxiously at his fellow security detail members.

Frank carefully placed his handgun on the porch in front of him, keeping his hands up. Megaphone Man nodded and motioned to his colleagues in the trucks, who lowered their weapons.

Smythe, Weston, and Frank approached Megaphone Man. He was dressed in khaki slacks and a dark-green polo shirt with the Carruthers logo on it. The man looked dressed for a day on the golf course.

"Bill Acker," the man said, extending his hand. "I'm chief of security here."

"I'm Special Agent Ben Smythe, this is Special Agent Caleb Weston, and this is Officer Frank Winger," Smythe said, shaking Acker's hand.

"Look, we don't want any trouble with you people," Acker said. "We're just here to provide security for the estate. There are rarely any visitors to this property, although we've had a few reporters sniffing around lately. Mr. Carruthers left the big house two days ago to go to the cabin back in the deep woods. I haven't heard a peep from him since he went there. He values his privacy, so we only go out there if he calls us."

"Could he have left the compound?" Smythe asked.

"I suppose it's possible. There's a back road out, an old dirt logging trail, but a landslide a couple of years ago partially blocked it, making it hard to get through. This is the only other road. If he came out the front way, which is what he'd normally do, he'd have to drive past this house to get out, and we'd have seen him. Normally, if he's ready to leave Kalispell, he'd have me call the pilot in advance to have the plane ready to pick him up. As far as I know, he's still at the cabin."

"Can you show me where this cabin is?" Smythe said.

"I can take you right to it," Acker said. He glanced at the bullet hole in the truck bed. "Sorry about your truck."

"It's a rental. Sorry about your gate," Smythe said.

Acker shrugged. "It ain't really my gate, anyway."

The cabin was hidden deep in the Montana forest, in a place so remote that an ATV would have had a difficult time getting there in winter. It was not nearly as tough now, although the ruddy, rock-strewn road was rutted and overgrown in spots.

For at least the second time that day, Frank was glad they were in a huge truck.

"It's just around the curve up here," Bill Acker said.

The log cabin, with a squat stone chimney, was nestled in a dense thicket of firs. Two gargantuan boulders, deposited by retreating glaciers eons ago, stood next to it like a pair of stone sentinels. The property ran down past a small thicket of aspen and birch trees to a nearby creek, which wound its way through the forest among more large moss-covered boulders.

"The Range Rover there belongs to the estate. That's what Mr. Carruthers was driving when he left the main house, which tells me he's still here. But I don't know that car," Acker said, pointing to a battered forest-green Jeep Wrangler parked next to the cabin. "Never seen it, in fact. And look at that—it's been set on fire."

He pointed to the left side of the Jeep. The gas cap was missing and the area around it was burned, the paint having blistered up all over the blackened left rear quarter-panel and across the vehicle's top.

The four men got out of the truck. The wind whispered in the branches overhead and the creek burbled away nearby, but otherwise everything around them was deathly quiet.

"Mr. Carruthers?" Acker called out.

There was no answer.

Acker drew his sidearm. "I've got a bad feeling about this," he said.

Frank and Agents Smythe and Weston drew their weapons, too.

The sun was climbing higher in the sky now, dappling the forest floor with tiny replicas of itself. Frank heard a crow cawing someplace in the distance.

Acker walked up the front stairs. They creaked with each step.

"Mr. Carruthers?" Acker called out again. "It's Bill. Just coming out to check on you." As he reached the front porch, Acker shook his head and turned around. "Front door's open."

Acker pushed the door open with the barrel of his gun,

keeping it level as he did so. The lights inside the cabin were all ablaze, as if it were still night.

Frank heard a faint humming sound as they walked inside, but he'd only taken a couple of steps before the stench hit him.

"Good God!" Acker exclaimed. He stumbled back past Frank, Weston, and Smythe before he spilled his guts, puking over the front porch railing into the bushes.

Frank slowly walked the rest of the way into the cabin.

The room was filled with the unmistakable stench of rotten flesh. Frank knew it well, having filled his lungs with it all too often in Afghanistan. He thought of Cookie and all the others he'd known who had gone too soon, the piles of black rubber body bags pregnant with the dead, their mortal remains airlifted out of the desolate backcountry for the long journey back home.

A man's body was propped up against one wall, his eyes open. Flies were all around him, crawling in and out of his nose and mouth. He was wearing a blood-soaked white Oxford dress shirt. Each side of his chest was pierced by a single gunshot wound. He was still holding a gun in his right hand. The man's face was gray and blotchy, but Frank would know it anywhere.

"That's Phillip Carruthers," he said.

Across the room, in an expansive leather chair behind a broad wooden desk, sat another man, also very dead. A blood-spattered bear pelt was nailed to the wall behind him. The dead man was facing Carruthers, and in fact would have been looking straight at him if he could still see. Heavyset, balding, dressed in camouflage fatigues, he was missing the entire left half of his skull. A dense cloud of flies swarmed around him. There was a pistol lying on the floor below his right hand.

"And that's Trek Richards," Frank said.

Frank glanced around the room. The stench of decay was so pervasive he could taste it. Trek's collapsed eyeball crawled with flies, and maggots wriggled in his mouth like tiny grains of rice. He could see the rotting gyre of Trek's brain.

"I think I'm gonna be sick again," Acker said, gagging.

Frank realized that none of it shocked him. He really didn't care about anything he saw in that death-filled cabin deep in the Montana woods. He had seen the nondescript box holding the remains of Janie O'Connor and he was certain that one, or maybe both, of these men were responsible for that injustice.

And now, justice had been served.

"Well, I don't think we'll be making any arrests today," Agent Weston said, holstering his sidearm.

"Copy that," Smythe said, shaking his head.

All Frank cared about was that it was over.

<h1 style="text-align:center">35</h1>

Anna came downstairs just before dawn, rubbing the sleep from her eyes. "Have you been up all night?"

Clarence nodded. "I couldn't sleep."

"I couldn't, either," Anna said. "I tossed and turned all night."

Anna took a seat at the kitchen table. An antique wooden cuckoo clock on the wall, purchased by Clarence and Earline years ago during a vacation in Germany, was ticking like a metronome.

Anna shook her head and sighed. "Clarence, there's something I need to tell you."

"What?" he asked.

"Come over here to the table and sit down, son," Anna said, patting the seat next to her.

Clarence sat next to her warily. "What is it, Mama? Are you OK?"

"I'm fine. We just need to talk. Just the two of us."

The cuckoo clock chimed seven times.

Anna took his hand in hers. "With all that has been

happening, I think you need to know the truth." She dabbed at her eyes with a napkin.

As far as he could remember, Clarence had never seen his mother cry. Her rawhide exterior was held together with roofing nails. Nothing ever fazed her.

Until *this*, whatever *this* was.

"*What* truth?" Clarence asked.

Anna stared straight at her son, dark eyes boring into him—but her lower lip quivered just a bit, breaking the impenetrable, stoic mask she usually wore.

"Anderson Carruthers is your father," she said.

Clarence stood up suddenly, breathing hard. Sweat beaded across his forehead. "Mama, what the *hell* are you talking about?"

"Anderson and I had a very close relationship for years."

"That can't be true."

Anna nodded. "It is."

Clarence felt lightheaded. He sat back down, shaking his head slowly. "All these years of not knowing who my dad is. All the unanswered questions. I met that man over a dozen times and he never said *anything*. Neither of you did! Why?"

"Andy and I were close friends who had a moment of weakness. The affair didn't last. When I found out I was pregnant, we decided we would keep the whole thing quiet. He was never going to leave his wife for me, and I did not want him to. I wanted to keep working for the family. It was the best job I'd ever had. He appreciated what I brought to his life and to his household. Plus, I never wanted to hurt Miz Cynthia. She's a sweet woman, and she had always trusted me." Anna broke down, her tears torrential now.

Clarence stared at her, dumbfounded.

"That's probably the biggest burden I've had with all of this—knowing that I betrayed Miz Cynthia's trust. Andy and

I were just two people who enjoyed each other's company, you know? And then things got physical, just once, when they shouldn't have. We both knew better—but like the Bible says, the flesh is weak." Anna grasped her son's hand. "My pregnancy made Andy reevaluate what was important in his life. It set him back on the straight and narrow, making him get out of some of the less scrupulous business enterprises the family had been involved in for years."

"So he just kept you around—the mother of his bastard child—right under his wife's nose?"

"He never thought of you that way. He thought of you as his *son*," she said. "Andy did offer to let me go someplace else, someplace where he could support me, but I didn't want that, and he didn't really, either. One secret was bad enough. Maintaining a second family in another location would have been too much deception for him."

"So your relationship with him ended after you became pregnant?"

"We never had physical relations again, but we remained close friends until he died. He was able to see you grow up. You got where you are through hard work and self-sacrifice. Andy respected that a great deal—and he respected *you*."

Clarence shook his head slowly in disbelief. He thought about his life, which had all seemed relatively straightforward before. The biggest void in his entire existence had always been the profound mystery about his missing father. As a child, he had harbored fantasies about finding out that his father was a sports hero, somebody like Michael Jordan or Herschel Walker, and that his superstar parent would come back and claim him after he grew up. As he grew older and began to understand the arcane ways of men and women, Clarence had eventually resigned himself to the idea that he had been the accidental by-product of an anonymous one-night stand. That was why he had stopped asking his mother questions about the situation. He had wrongly surmised that his mother simply did not know the answer.

The whole superstructure of Clarence "Gatehouse" Brown's life had been built upon the foundation of an illicit tryst. He'd been spawned by a lie.

"Clarence?" Anna asked quietly.

"Yes, Mama?"

"Are you disappointed in me?"

He looked at her and smiled. "I could never be disappointed in you, Mama. I'm just a little confused, that's all. This was not anything I expected."

Anna got up and put her arms around her only son's massive shoulders. "I want you to know this in case somebody in the Carruthers organization figures out the truth about us and tries to use it against you. Otherwise, I would have taken this secret to my grave." Anna kissed Clarence on the top of his head. "I love you, boy."

"I love you, too, Mama," Clarence said, patting her hand.

The sun was up now. Clarence stood and walked to the window over the kitchen sink. Pulling back the curtains, he peered outside. "I'm going to go wake Earline."

"Are you going to tell her?" Anna asked.

"Mama, I have to. Earline and I have no secrets," Clarence said.

Seeing the pain in his mother's eyes, he instantly regretted saying that.

36

Morris Shefter arrived at the police station before daybreak the following morning. He was in a foul mood by the time Frank and the FBI agents entered the Pillbox. Leaning over the spare wooden table like a vulture, the ruby ring on his pinkie gleaming like the eye of some pagan god, he glared at them with absolute disdain. "Where have you been?" Shefter said. "I've been here for an hour."

"The interview was scheduled for 7:00 a.m., Mr. Shefter. You were early."

Shefter shook his head in disgust. "Such a complete waste of my time."

Agents Weston and Smythe sat on either side of Frank Winger. Shefter sat opposite them. A laptop was sitting on the table between them. Weston was staring intently at the laptop's screen. Its blue light reflected softly on his face.

"Let's get on with this charade," Shefter said. "My client has a plane to catch."

"Your client is under arrest and is a flight risk. She's not going anywhere."

"We can make any bail amount."

"There will be no bail," Smythe said.

"We'll see about that," Shefter replied, his perfectly capped teeth exposed in a sharklike grin.

The guards brought Erika into the interrogation room in handcuffs. She was dressed in an orange prison jumpsuit and wore no makeup. She still looked stunning, her blonde hair cascading down to her shoulders. An unopened bottle of water sat in front of her. She took a seat and the guards unlocked her handcuffs.

"Detective Winger," Erika said, fixing Frank in a sultry gaze as she rubbed her wrists. "So good to see you again."

Frank nodded. "Ms. Carruthers."

"Call me Erika, please," she said. "Or you can call me 'that bitch,' like I'm sure you do in private."

Frank scribbled something on his notepad, ignoring her.

"We're here to talk to you about a few things," Weston said. "I'm Agent Weston and this is Agent Smythe. We're with the FBI and we've been assisting Chief Brown with his investigation. We need to ask you a few questions."

"Fire away," Erika said.

"I want you to know that this conversation is being recorded on video. Do you understand this?"

"I do," Erika said.

"We would appreciate it if you would answer questions clearly, as in *yes, no, or maybe* format, and refrain from using phrases such as *uh-huh* or simply nodding your head. Is that understood?"

"Uh-huh," Erika said, grinning.

Weston was stone faced. "State your name, please."

"Erika Carruthers."

"What is your principal place of residence?"

"120 West Jones Street in Savannah."

"Are you married, single, or divorced?"

"Single. Interested?"

Weston ignored her. "What sort of work do you do?"

"I'm an investor, a shareholder in the family business. You might call me an *active* shareholder."

"What is the name of that business?"

"Carruthers Enterprises."

"And what sort of work does Carruthers Enterprises engage in?"

"We have multiple interests. Real estate is one—we own lots of that. We have a chain of payday lending sites, a company called Cash Back. You've probably seen our ads on TV."

"I haven't," Weston said. "I'm not from around here."

"You know I told all of this to Detective Winger earlier. I'm sure there's a transcript somewhere."

Weston nodded. "Humor me," he said.

Erika sighed. "We also have an import-export business, based in the ports of Savannah and Brunswick, and a heavy-equipment leasing company based in Jacksonville. We have a trucking company, an oil distribution business, and we develop commercial property, mainly warehouses and office buildings. We don't build houses anymore, although we used to when my father was alive. Phillip got us out of that after he took over because the margins weren't high enough."

"Is that all?" Weston asked.

"That's pretty much it."

"Are you aware of any illicit activities your company has been involved in?"

"No," Erika said. "We always play by the rules."

Special Agent Weston leaned forward slightly. "So you don't view smuggling synthetic narcotics from China and crystal methamphetamine from Mexico as illegal? Or selling military-grade weapons to known terrorist organizations?"

"We don't do that."

Weston flipped the laptop around so that she could see it.

"The data on this spreadsheet would disagree with you, Ms. Carruthers."

"Where did you get that?" she asked, flushing red.

Weston ignored her. He spun the laptop back around so that he could see it again and tapped away on the keyboard. "Do you think of human trafficking as illegal? Smuggling people into this country in shipping containers for money? Or selling some of them into sexual slavery?"

"Of course. Anybody would."

"So why did Carruthers Enterprises engage in that sort of business?"

"We . . ."

"Don't answer him, Erika," Shefter said.

Weston spun the laptop back around so that she could see it again. "So here we have a record of the names and dates of shipments, which ports they came into, and where the containers were stored. And what do you think was in those shipments?"

"I have no idea," Erika said.

"*People*, Ms. Carruthers. Your company was trafficking human beings. Narcotics and weapons, too. Again, you know that all of this is illegal, don't you? That's what you just said a moment ago."

"Don't answer him," Shefter said, his voice raised.

"Is murder illegal?" Frank said.

Erika stared at him. "Of course," she said.

"What's the name of the big bull alligator on your property that you sometimes fed people to if they got in your way? You guys called him Burt, right? After Burt Reynolds?"

The fluorescent light overhead began to flicker. To Frank, it seemed more intense, more urgent than usual, the pace increasing.

"I . . . I don't know what you're talking about," Erika said.

"Yes, you do," Smythe said. "Carmine Carpeggio told us all about it."

"Carmine . . . ," Erika said, a stunned expression on her face.

"We got a gator handler to take that old one-eyed monster out of his swimming hole. He's a massive creature, for sure, and is being relocated to the Okefenokee Swamp as we speak. We have divers looking for the human remains that we know are there, since Carmine told us about at least five people who you trussed up and fed to that thing. And Trek Richards, who you paid to leave town when he was about to be arrested? I'm sure you thought he was a dumbass. Turns out he wasn't quite so stupid after all—because we got all the spreadsheet data you were just looking at from *him*. This is a laptop we retrieved from your family's cabin in Kalispell, where Trek was staying. It's got lots of information about all the illegitimate businesses you were running. I suppose Trek looked at it as insurance. To add insult to injury, I've got a cop who will testify that you guys bribed him to feed you inside information about the police force. You remember Pepper Stephens, Detective Winger's partner?"

Erika nodded slowly.

"He's confessed. He's going to testify against you, too—and bribing a cop is another felony. You remember John Straub, who you visited in the hospital? You called him Fat John, I think. He tried to kill himself a while back after he watched you guys feed a young immigrant woman and her son to that damned gator. Poor John spent about a month on a ventilator, but he's recovered, he's in rehab—and he's talking. We've got Trek, we've got Carmine, we've got Detective Stephens, we've got John Straub, we have Greg Sullivan, and they're all going to testify against you. We have the laptop, and if Carmine is telling the truth, we'll soon have the remains of a few dead bodies extracted from the gator pond on your family's property. So basically, Erika, you're fucked."

"We're done here," Shefter said, standing up. "My client won't just sit here and let you harass her."

"Shut up and sit down, Morris," Erika snapped.

"Erika, I'd strongly—"

She turned to him, glaring. The veins in her neck stood out like ropes. "Morris, let me talk, OK? I pay you quite well to do what I ask, so just be quiet for a moment. I have something I want to say."

Shefter sat back down and sighed, glancing up at the ceiling, and drummed his thin fingers on the table as he slowly shook his head.

Erika leaned forward across the table, her eyes narrowing. "I know what's going on here. Phillip's trying to set me up. My weasel of a brother wants me to take the fall for all of this. I recognize that laptop—you got it from Phillip, not from that idiot Trek, who is too stupid to tie his own shoelaces. Well, let me tell you something: Everything you are talking about was Phillip's idea, every bit of it. My father wanted *me* to run the company. I would have done it the right way, the way he did. Daddy couldn't stand Phillip. He thought Phillip was a spineless piece of shit and was planning to leave *me* in charge, at least until Daddy's unfortunate 'hunting accident,' when my brother murdered my father by shooting him in the back. Morris here told me to play along, to be quiet and not disrupt things, and as usual, I did as I was told. But after Phillip took over, it became all about the margins—and the margins were a lot higher doing the things that weren't legal. It was *Phillip* who got Carruthers Enterprises into the drugs, the human trafficking, the weapons trading. Everything. All of that was *his* idea. He was the CEO, and that meant he was in *charge*, OK? I'm not letting him pin the blame for all of this on me—"

"Erika, my God, will you please *shut up*?" Shefter said.

Frank was incredulous at what he was hearing.

She cracked, he thought. He could scarcely believe it. "Was your brother involved in the murder of Dr. Janie O'Connor?" he asked.

She rolled her eyes. "What do you think? She was his fiancée, then she broke up with him. She disappeared right after that. Coincidence? I don't think so."

"But he never admitted to you that he killed her?"

"No, but I'm sure he did. Either him or that lunatic Trek Richards. Trek was always the one Phillip used to deal with the stuff that might get my brother's dainty little hands dirty, at least until we relocated that stupid shithead to Montana."

"We?" Frank asked.

Morris Shefter slammed his hand on the table and shook his head. "God *damn* it, Erika!" Shefter exclaimed.

"And when, exactly, did you relocate Trek to Montana?" Frank asked.

Shefter stood up again, briefcase in hand. "Erika, as your attorney, I'm advising you not to answer that question. It's past time we ended this."

"Hold on, Morris," Erika hissed. "I'm not finished, and I'm not ready to return to my cell just yet. Detective Winger, who oversees this investigation locally?"

"I do," Frank said.

"And who is your boss?"

"Chief Clarence Brown," Frank said.

"Precisely. You might want to ask Chief Brown what *he* expects to gain from all of this."

"What do you mean by that?" Frank said.

"Well, he is my half brother, after all, so if Phillip does a plea bargain and I go down in flames, Chief Brown might just get everything. Or didn't you know that?" she said.

Agents Weston and Smythe both looked at Frank, who shrugged. Frank then stood up, leaned forward over Erika, and looked her straight in the eye. "I don't know anything about that, Erika. I do know that Clarence Brown is the most ethical man I've ever met, so if there's truly that sort of angle there, it won't influence his judgment. Here's something *you* didn't know: Phillip and Trek are both dead. It looks like they shot each other in your family's cabin in Montana. *That's* how we got the laptop. It was sitting right on the desk in front of Trek's dead body. So you just confessed to knowing about all this shit on your own, and we didn't have to do a goddamned thing."

Erika lunged across the table at Frank, knocking over her water bottle like a bowling pin. The two lumpish guards sprang to restrain her, but not before she had managed to scratch Frank's face with the nails of her right hand. "You asshole! Don't you realize that we *own* this town? We will *destroy* you, Detective Winger! You don't cross the Carruthers family. That's what that bitch Janie O'Connor found out, and you will, too. You'll see! You're *done*!" she screamed.

The guards forced Erika down onto the cold, hard floor, cuffing her hands behind her back. Her beautiful face, pressed to the floor, was now purple with rage.

Frank leaned down, putting his lips close to Erika's ear. "There's nothing you can take from me, Erika. But I can take *everything* from you," he whispered.

Frank stood up. He wiped a rivulet of blood from his face with a paper towel, then tossed the crumpled-up towel into the trash can. "It's *you* who should be afraid, Erika. Not me." Turning to Morris Shefter, Frank raised one eyebrow and said, "I know a few judges too, Mr. Shefter. There will be no bail. I guarantee it."

Shefter shook his head sheepishly and followed his handcuffed client out through the interrogation room door without saying a word.

PART FOUR

VERITAS ET CONSEQUENTIAE

37

October, five months later

Frank smelled the rich aroma of coffee.

It awakened him from a deep and dreamless sleep, a sleep no longer tormented by ghosts. Sunlight streamed in from the river through the half-parted curtains, and he looked at his watch, which lay beside him on the bedside table.

"Jesus," he said. "I never sleep this late."

Frank got out of bed, still naked, and draped the bathrobe he'd hung over the four-poster bed over his shoulders, tying the sash around his waist. He heard the raucous crows squabbling loudly outside, just like he did every morning, but they didn't bother him anymore.

He supposed that was because he was happy.

Dishes were clattering downstairs. Diane was making breakfast. This was a weekend routine they had settled into over the past few months: pancakes or waffles with cups of fruit and crispy strips of bacon, on the back porch if the weather was nice, reading the print version of the *Savannah Morning News* over coffee, making small talk. He knew that reading a newspaper was increasingly considered old school, but it was a luxury he'd sorely missed in Afghanistan, like good barbecue and craft beer, and he was not about to give it up now.

Diane stood at the kitchen island in her nightgown—a clingy, lace-trimmed silk number with gold piping, which draped perfectly over her shoulders and hips. Boodles's tail thumped rhythmically against the floor as Frank entered the kitchen.

She turned to him, smiling, sapphire eyes bright and cheerful, blonde hair shimmering. "Glad you could join us, sleepyhead," she said, her arms pulling Frank in and kissing him long and slow on the lips, eyes closed.

"I was so tired last night," he said.

"You could have fooled me," she replied.

"Well, I'm never too tired for *that*," he said, raising his eyebrows ever so slightly as he grinned at her.

"You bad boy," she responded, patting him smartly on the ass.

She whirled away from him, picking up two plates from the granite island. She'd made him buttered grits this time, along with waffles piled high with blueberries, strawberries, and whipped cream, and she had garnished each plate with a delicate violet-colored orchid.

"You had this ready to go. How did you know when I'd wake up?" he asked.

"I've got this whole ESP thing with you. Plus, if you hadn't gotten up, I was just going to go upstairs and get you."

It was fall, but still warm enough in Savannah for them to enjoy the view of the marsh and the Vernon River from the back porch of Twin Oaks as they ate. Boodles joined them, taking his place close by their feet so that he could beg table scraps with only a modicum of effort.

Frank took a sip of coffee and scanned the front page of the newspaper. "Clarence is leading big in the polls," he said. "Everyone is saying he's a shoo-in."

"He deserves to win," Diane said, taking a seat beside him. "He's a good man. He'll be the best mayor this city has had in years."

Frank thought about how all this had happened. After the horrors of Afghanistan and the unspeakable nightmare of Paulina's death, to have a murder investigation into a tragic and senseless death somehow morph into him having breakfast on the river porch of the murder victim's home with the victim's sister seemed more than just an improbable twist of fate. It seemed like the universe had conspired, at long last, to give him a well-deserved break.

Frank's mind was hardwired to survive and advance. He was a cultural troglodyte, not geared toward aesthetics. He had never noticed architecture, only listened to classic rock and roll, and ate food only to survive. Nevertheless, he had developed a genuine appreciation for the old house that Janie had so lovingly restored. Everything at Twin Oaks was done perfectly, from the crown molding to the wide-planked antique heart pine flooring. Even the river porch, where they now sat, was a marvel, with its wrought-iron railings, flickering gas lamps beside the back door, and lazily turning ceiling fans. An array of hanging baskets filled with huge Boston ferns was strung across the porch, the fronds undulating in the steady breeze that blew in across the marsh from the river.

Frank supposed his appreciation stemmed from Janie's meticulous attention to detail, a quality he appreciated professionally.

He had never met Janie, but he thought he would have liked her.

Frank and Diane sat together quietly for a few moments. A pair of snowy egrets sailed across the marsh, one of them crying out with a guttural *gronk!*

Diane sipped her coffee as steam swirled gently around her

head. "You know, I still pray every night for Janie, even though I know she's in heaven. She didn't deserve to die."

"No, she didn't," Frank said.

"You know what's weird to me? The thing about all this that never made any sense?"

"What's that?"

"Erika and Phillip sent Trek away to Montana so that he would be out of the equation. Why would Phillip go up there to see him in person?"

"I told you that, remember? He had stolen Phillip's laptop. Trek texted Phillip to come see him. We think he was trying to blackmail Phillip, and they ended up shooting each other."

"But there's no definite proof of that. The Carruthers family clearly had no issues with murdering others. So why wouldn't they just send someone to kill Trek? Why would Phillip go up there himself?"

Frank shrugged. "I guess we'll never really know," he said.

But Diane had a point. It made no sense at all.

38

Frank almost threw the bill away.

He was going through the mail, sorting the junk from the invoices, when he saw the plain white envelope addressed to Janie O'Connor.

Well, at least I won't need to save this for her, he thought.

But then he saw the return address. It was from a company called Proton Mail. That jogged his memory a bit. So he opened it, reading the generic wording half-heartedly.

> *Dear Client:*
>
> *We have been attempting to bill your credit card for the services rendered, but it has been declined. In addition, the email address you supplied us as a backup is no longer active. Would you be so kind as to log back into your account to change the payer source? Alternatively, you could remit the full amount of the attached invoice by check or by transfer of bank funds.*
>
> *Sincerely yours, Proton Mail Customer Service*

It was simple and to the point. He'd have to let them know that they would never be getting their money. But where had he heard of Proton Mail?

He googled the company on his iPhone. When he read the company profile, he felt a sudden shock of recognition.

"It's that anonymous email service," he whispered in realization.

The emails sent to Tina Baker with the incriminating videos had all been sent through Proton Mail. Likewise, the emails that had told him where to look for the evidence on Phillip's estate and that, quite literally, had told him where Janie's body was buried had all been sent through the same service. He'd never heard of it before then, but the Kid had said that emails sent through Proton Mail were untraceable.

"Shit," he said out loud.

He folded the bill up and stuffed it into his pocket.

"Anything important?" Diane said.

"Just a bunch of crap," Frank said, instantly feeling guilty for lying to her. "I'm putting it in recycling."

An ugly, dark thought began bubbling up just beneath the surface, something his cop brain forced him to think about, even as his lover's brain tried to submerge it, attempting to drown it in the swamp waters of blissful oblivion.

Could Diane have been involved in her sister's disappearance?

Maybe the whole thing was nothing—a mere coincidence, a twisted joke by the cosmic powers that be. After all, the Proton Mail bill was addressed to Janie, not Diane, and Janie was dead. That ended it, right?

But it was weird that the only two times he'd ever heard of Proton Mail had to do with Janie's disappearance—and anonymous clues that led the police straight to Phillip Carruthers, whom Diane despised.

Part of him wanted to forget he'd ever seen the Proton

Mail bill. He thought about burning it or tearing it into tiny pieces. But Frank was a bloodhound by nature—and bloodhounds don't give up the scent when they are on the hunt, not ever.

In the end, Frank decided he had to do a little snooping around. He hated the fact that he wasn't being candid with Diane, but he had to know the truth. He had some ideas about how he would go about it. But he wanted to do it in a way that wouldn't mess things up with her.

Because I love her, he realized.

It was the first time he'd felt that way about anyone in a very long time.

—

Frank had been increasingly involved with SPD administrative duties as Clarence Brown's mayoral campaign hit the final stretch, leaving him less time for actual police work. He missed the investigative stuff, though. He enjoyed being a detective. It made him feel as though he was doing something constructive, something useful to society—and it exercised those brain cells, which he had read was increasingly important as one got older.

In late October, Frank decided to take on a particularly challenging case involving a murder that had taken place on a houseboat at Isle of Hope. Ultimately, the pivotal evidence that clinched the case was video taken from several dock cameras in the area, which showed the actual murder from several different angles. The killer had approached the victim's houseboat in his own watercraft, which was clearly marked with state registration numbers, committed the crime, and then left by water, in the same way he came. The murderer had thought he'd get away with it because he had approached the victim's boat from the river, leaving little evidence—but the dock video cameras, which he had not known about, had nailed him. Faced with that evidence, the accused had agreed to a plea bargain, admitting his guilt in the murder to avoid the death penalty without even darkening the courtroom door. The conclusion of that case in such an open-and-shut fashion was a particularly satisfying outcome for Frank.

Jonathan Kramer, the SPD forensics expert and computer wiz who Frank called the Kid, had obtained and analyzed the critical videos. Frank asked him why the docks at Isle of Hope all happened to have video cameras on them.

"Everybody does that these days, Detective," the Kid said, adjusting his funky horn-rimmed glasses. "These cameras are cheap, they're easy to set up, and they're everywhere. And since people are always stealing things off docks, a dock-mounted motion-activated wireless camera can be a real deterrent. They're often high-resolution jobs with infrared capability so that they can see in the dark. They can pick up all sorts of stuff."

As Frank drove back to the home at Rose Dhu, he passed the place where Janie's body had been found. It was a nondescript shallow depression at the edge of the marsh now, barely recognizable as something of any consequence.

But there were a pair of docks within plain view.

"Sonofabitch," Frank said, chastising himself for not realizing this sooner.

That evening, Frank asked the neighbors who owned the two docks in question if they had surveillance cameras. He struck out with the first one, which was not surprising. That dock had been damaged during Hurricane Matthew and was a dilapidated wreck, with missing boards and rotting pilings. Having a surveillance camera on that relic would have been pointless. But the second dock owner responded in the affirmative and was happy to let Frank review his surveillance video data.

"Is this video archived anywhere?" Frank asked.

"Sure. It's all online, but you can look at any footage you want. I'll give you the link and the log-in," the man said.

Which is how Frank ended up spending the wee hours of the following morning in Dr. Janie O'Connor's old study at Twin Oaks, looking at video footage of the darkened marsh from that fateful July 19 night.

The video interface was easy to use online. Frank was able to type in the date and scroll through the images in real time, slow motion or fast forward.

Most of the video from the night of July 19 was boring. He saw several deer, a fox, a couple walking their dog, and several golf carts making the early evening rounds. And then . . . nothing, really. For hours.

A dense fog had rolled in from the river around 9:00 p.m., its tendrils curling among the undulating marsh grass and making it look like the moors in *The Hound of the Baskervilles*. Frank thought he saw someone moving in the fog once, but he soon realized it was another deer.

And then, he saw it, at 9:36 p.m.: a shadowy human figure moving through the shadows of Rose Dhu Road. It was walking down the half-lit ribbon of asphalt that split the marsh in two. The person was wearing a Braves baseball cap and was carrying something long and straight, like a pole, in his right hand. Drifting through the swirling mists like a wraith, indistinct and yet substantial, the figure made its way toward the marsh. For a brief instant, the lone streetlight on that stretch of road gave Frank a better view, and he realized that the "pole" was really a shovel. There was a bag dangling from the man's left hand, as well.

Abruptly, the figure stopped, turned, and walked straight into the marsh, stopping about ten feet in from the edge, right near the Water Witch historical marker, where a Civil War ironclad of the same name had been run aground during the siege of Savannah over 150 years earlier.

The hair on the back of Frank's neck stood up. The person on the video was standing at the exact spot where Janie's body had been found.

Abruptly, the figure dropped the bag he was holding in his left hand and began digging.

It's him, Frank thought.

He was almost certainly staring right at the man who had murdered Janie O'Connor.

He didn't have an entire body. That explained why the remains they had found were so scant. The bag might have contained a head, maybe the hands, but the rest of the body had to be someplace else. Perhaps the torso had been dumped in the ocean, stripped of all identifying features, although its DNA could not tell a lie.

But it's been well over a year, Frank thought. *Not likely to be much left now.*

The digging went slowly at first, but the killer soon found a rhythm and picked up the pace. Marsh mud, choked with interlaced Spartina roots and the razor-sharp shells of long-dead oysters, could be deceptively hard to dig through. To make matters worse, if the tide wasn't right, the hole could fill up with water, making the digging frustratingly tricky. But the killer was methodical, his shoulders hunched over the shovel as he worked, without a break, until 10:17 p.m. At that moment, a Jeep moved past, and the man dropped the shovel, knelt in the marsh grass, and seemed to disappear, his figure wholly consumed by the marsh grass and the thickening fog.

Where is he? Frank thought.

At 10:25 p.m., a second pair of headlights rounded the corner on Rose Dhu Road. This vehicle was moving at a high rate of speed. As the car flashed past, Frank could see that it was a black BMW 750.

Although the BMW sported a Georgia tag, Frank could not make out the numbers on the license plate. Still, there couldn't be too many late-model black BMW 7 Series cars in Chatham County—and Phillip Carruthers owned one of them. This timing would jibe with the pilot's story that he flew with Phillip to Savannah on the evening of July 19, landing a little before 10:00 p.m., but was in the air on the way back to Atlanta with Phillip by 11:55 p.m. that same night. Suddenly, Frank was struck by a stark realization: *If I am looking at the killer digging Janie's grave, and that's Phillip driving toward Twin Oaks, this video exonerates him.*

At 10:49 p.m., the black BMW sped by again, this time traveling in the other direction. Its blue headlights threw out twin cones of light as they cut their way through the increasingly foggy night.

After the BMW passed, the digging man stood back up from his hiding place in the marsh, finished digging the grave, and dropped the bag's contents into the hole. He then filled the hole, tamped it down with the shovel, and walked back down Rose Dhu Road. This time, he headed in the opposite direction from Twin Oaks, shovel still in hand. As he approached the lone streetlight on the narrow stretch of marsh-bound road, the man turned briefly toward the camera, and Frank almost got a look at his face.

Almost, but not quite. The baseball cap kept his face hidden in the shadows.

Still, the illumination from the streetlight silhouetted the digging man. A breeze from the marsh parted the fog for a brief instant, and the man's silhouette made one thing plainly evident, providing Frank with his second shock of the night.

The digging man wasn't a man at all.

It was a woman.

39

Diane was kneeling in the yard, weeding a flower bed, when Frank turned into the Twin Oaks driveway. She wore a short denim skirt with a simple white blouse tied at the waist. Her hair, pulled back in a ponytail, poked out from beneath her broad-brimmed hat, and a pair of dark, oversized sunglasses hid her eyes. She beamed and vigorously waved a gloved hand at him, as if he'd been away at sea for a year. Frank waved back, smiling.

But his heart ached. The person who'd buried Janie's remains in the marsh at Rose Dhu was unmistakably female.

Frank felt sick.

All the seemingly logical assumptions the police investigation had previously made about the Janie O'Connor case had been wrong. Frank now knew Janie's killer was not Phillip, whose decomposing body now lay beneath an ornate marble mausoleum in Bonaventure Cemetery. He likewise knew that it was not Trek, who had been cremated, his ashes scattered someplace known only to his estranged sister and to God.

A woman.

Frank thought about turning the video over to Chief

Brown but knew he couldn't. There were only two women who had a motive to kill Janie. One of them was Erika Carruthers, of course.

But the other one was Diane.

Frank's mind was twisted up in torment. Diane was a gentle, sweet soul who loved animals and sappy romances on the Hallmark Channel. She listened to Joni Mitchell and James Taylor, dancing slowly to their gentle acoustic rhythms in her white apron as she made dinner. And she was utterly devoted to Frank in a way that eclipsed any relationship he'd ever had—even with Paulina. Diane's love for Frank had brought him back from the dead, something he'd once thought impossible.

Still, Diane was Janie's only heir, and Janie's death had made her a rich woman. She was now a millionaire several times over, having inherited Twin Oaks and all of Janie's investment accounts after her sister's death. A few months ago, she had moved into Twin Oaks permanently, selling her home in Isle of Hope for a substantial profit. As a direct result of her sister's generosity, Diane would never have to work again. And she had tried to cast anyone and everyone else as likely suspects, from Trek Richards to Phillip Carruthers.

The motive was real, all right.

Still, Diane and Janie had loved each other. There had rarely been a cross word between them. Diane spoke of Janie with a reverence that bordered on worship. She'd even had a large oil painting done of Janie after her death, a painting that now hung in the hallway of the foyer at Twin Oaks.

"Now she will always be a part of this house," Diane had said, smiling, after the painting was hung.

Although Frank's instincts told him that nothing could ever make Diane into a killer, he also knew that he could not exclude her. He would have to do the investigation himself, keeping it a secret from her, at least until he was confident of the truth. That fact lodged in his heart like a spiny sea urchin, cutting and stabbing his soul every time he saw her.

As Frank left the garage, Diane scurried up to him. Shucking off her yard gloves, she threw her arms around him and kissed him full on the lips. "Hello, lover," she said with a grin as she pulled back from him. But then her face clouded. "What's wrong?"

"I'm just tired," he said. "It's been a long day, and I've been having trouble sleeping."

"I noticed you got up pretty early this morning," she said.

Frank nodded. "Tough case. A murder. I'm trying to put the pieces together," he said.

"Well, if anyone can figure it out, you can. I have absolute faith in you," she said. She took off her sunglasses, clipping them into her blouse between her breasts, and stared at him with her amazing sapphire eyes. "I love you, Frank. You know that, right?"

"I do."

"Well, just remember this: I've got your back. I know you'll do the right thing because that's the sort of man you are. I trust you implicitly. Apart from my father, I've never been able to say that about a single man in my life. That's a fact." She took his hand in hers as they went into the house together. "I'll wash up and start making dinner."

"We'll do it together," he replied and kissed her on the cheek.

He already knew what he had to do.

—

November

Frank left Savannah shortly after daybreak. He could have set the cruise control and driven straight on to Macon on I-16, then north on I-75 toward the burgeoning megalopolis of Atlanta. That would be easier, and he'd have cell service the entire time—but Frank didn't want that. He wanted silence. He wanted solitude.

He needed time to think.

He'd asked Chief Brown for a day off and had gotten it, no questions asked. Clarence had won the mayoral election in a landslide. Frank had been his right-hand man ever since. The chief had even hinted that he'd support having Frank named as his replacement, as interim chief of police, although nothing had been set in stone just yet.

"I have some family business to attend to. I'll probably be back by nightfall," Frank had said before kissing Diane softly on the lips and walking out the door.

"Drive safe," she said. "And hurry back to me."

"I promise," he said.

The "family business" part was only partly a lie. Diane did not know that it was *her* family's business, and more specifically Janie's, that he was attending to.

The Hyundai was humming along in the early morning light with hardly a sputter, which was surprising. Frank could never understand the quirky nature of his vehicle. It was a temperamental little sedan, but at least today looked like it would be a good day.

He tried to find something on satellite radio, settling on the '80s-on-8 station at long last, listening to some of the more banal tunes from Huey Lewis and better songs by Michael Jackson from the *Thriller* album as he headed down I-16.

He'd stopped smoking since he'd moved in with Diane, but he'd kept an emergency pack of Camels and a lighter hidden in the Hyundai's center console and lit one up now, cracking the window as he exhaled, the thin stream of blue-gray smoke wisping outside into the thin air of the early morning like a ghost.

As he passed the Metter exit, he watched as the ocher sunlight broke through the tree line over the sandhills, relics from some ancient shoreline. As his cell service disappeared, Frank was now truly alone. Nobody could get to him.

He was headed to Lee Arrendale State Prison in Alto, a place he had only been to once before.

It wasn't a trip he wanted. The prison, a collection of stark, functional-appearing buildings sprawled out behind a towering razor-wire fence, housed over fourteen hundred female inmates. All of Georgia's female death row prisoners were kept there—including one Erika Leigh Carruthers, GDC inmate number 0014300643.

Frank got to Arrendale by 11:00 a.m. After the initial promise of daybreak, the sky had slipped back into an oppressive gray. The cold weather and leaden sky overhead only deepened Frank's dour mood.

Frank was escorted by a burly, grim-faced guard with close-cropped hair. She led him into a private meeting room. There was a plexiglass barrier between him and an identical chamber on the other side. An old-style black Bakelite telephone receiver sat in a cradle on each side of the plexiglass.

"Sit here," the guard barked.

Frank did as he was told.

The door on the opposite side opened, and Erika Carruthers walked in, followed by another muscular guard at least six feet tall.

Erika was dressed in a shapeless orange prison jumpsuit with her inmate number stenciled on the back. She had transformed her body since Frank last saw her at her trial. She was larger now, with broad, muscular shoulders and a neck so thick that it seemed to blend in with her occiput, which only accentuated the sharp bony contour of her skull. Erika's laser-like eyes fixed upon Frank when she entered the room and did not let him go.

Jesus, she looks just like her old man, Frank thought.

He picked up the receiver, which crackled a bit. "You shaved your head," Frank said.

Erika shrugged. "Having hair is pointless in here." She leaned forward and bared her teeth as she talked. "Let's cut through the bullshit, Detective Winger. I know you didn't drive all the way up to Arrendale to talk about my hair."

"I did not."

"So why are you here?"

"I needed to ask you a question, and I wanted to do it in person."

"Will my answer get me out of here?"

"It depends. I might be able to get you into a cell by yourself. Nothing you say can reverse your conviction, though."

Erika stood up. "Don't waste my time, then," she said.

"It may exonerate your brother, though."

Erika hesitated. "Phillip's dead," she said. "How does that help *me*?"

"If you help me find Janie O'Connor's true killer, that may get you some favors from the state," he said.

Erika laughed, a low chuckle which sounded like boiling mud. "Whoever killed Dr. O'Connor is dead. It was almost certainly either Trek or my brother, wasn't it?"

Frank was silent.

"Wasn't it?" Erika asked again, sitting back down.

Frank sighed. "I have some evidence that the killer may have been a woman. Or, at the very least, a woman may have helped dispose of Janie's remains. You wouldn't happen to know anything about that, would you?"

Erika threw her head back and laughed out loud. "You're asking me again if I killed that bitch?"

"You had a motive."

"You're damned straight I had a motive. I *told* Phillip she was trouble. I warned him that he did not want a smart person around, that she'd eventually see through all his bullshit. But he didn't listen to me and look what happened: He's dead, I'm on death row, our family company is in shambles, and generally everything has gone to hell. So yeah, I had a motive. I would have killed her with my bare hands if I'd had the opportunity."

Frank leaned forward, running his fingers through his salt-and-pepper hair, which had gotten too long and was beginning to curl.

"But *did* you?"

"Did I what? Kill her?"

Frank nodded.

Erika's eyes narrowed. "Look, I've got nothing to lose, OK? I'm in here for the rest of my life, however long that may be. Morris Shefter is appealing my conviction and my death sentence, and he is a fucking legal genius, so we'll have to see how that goes. Anyway, I'm going to be straight up with you: I had nothing to do with Janie O'Connor's death, although in retrospect I wish I had. She ruined everything for us."

Frank felt his heart sinking in his chest. "You're not lying," he said.

"I'm not."

Frank stood up to go.

"That's it? That's all you came to ask me?" Erika asked.

Frank nodded. "That's it," he said.

Erika shook her head. "I don't get it," she said. "How does that help . . ."

At that moment, a broad smile slowly broke out across Erika's face. "You're dating the *sister*," she said.

Frank's head jerked toward Erika in a single convulsive motion, as if he'd been tasered.

"You *are!* I'd heard that through the grapevine—the walls have ears in this place, you know—but now I know for sure. *That's* why you drove up here. If it was a woman who killed Dr. O'Connor, and if it wasn't me, then your new girlfriend is the most likely culprit!" Erika stood up then and slammed her palms against the plexiglass.

"Hey! That's enough of that shit!" the guard said, pulling Erika back.

"The plot just got exponentially thicker, didn't it? What's the term for that? Sororicide? How does *that* spice up your relationship?" Erika screamed.

Frank turned to the guard on his side of the plexiglass. "I'm done here," he said.

The guard opened the door to let Frank out. By this point, Erika was screaming herself hoarse. Her shackled arms had been twisted behind her back by the prison guard who accompanied her, but she did not even seem to feel it.

"It's karma, baby—and it's beautiful!" Erika croaked before spitting a gelatinous wad of phlegm on the floor.

Then the heavy metal door closed, and she was gone.

The drive back to Savannah was as depressing as Frank could ever remember taking. Halfway back home, angry dark clouds clumped overhead, and it started to drizzle. Rain was soon falling in torrents, lightning stabbing down out of the pitch-black sky. Gusts of wind buffeted him, pushing his hydroplaning car crossways on the interstate, and Frank had to concentrate just to keep the struggling Hyundai on the road. Inside his head, a hurricane of emotion raged as well.

Was he sleeping with a murderer?

Trust your gut, Cookie had always said. *It will tell you the truth.*

Diane is no killer, he decided. *There's got to be another explanation.*

—

In the end, Frank knew that he would have to go back to Kalispell.

The double murder of Phillip Carruthers and Trek Richards had seemed like the most open-and-shut case of all time. It was clear that Richards was trying to blackmail Carruthers by using the information on the stolen laptop they had recovered at the scene. Trek had prompted their face-to-face meeting by text-messaging Phillip. The ballistics from each man's weapon matched the projectiles found in each victim. The respective shooters had purchased both guns, and gunshot residue was found on each of them. There were no other suspects, nor was there any evidence that anyone else was involved.

But Frank knew something wasn't right.

He'd reviewed all the evidence in Janie's murder again and again but had seen nothing to dissuade him from his original hypothesis that Phillip and Trek, who both bore some complicity in Janie's death, had shot and killed one another.

The dock video had changed his view on that. A woman was involved. That brought both Diane and Erika back into the picture. And Frank was *certain* that what happened in the cabin in Montana was somehow related to Janie's death.

If there were any answers out there, they were going to be in Kalispell.

—

Frank and Diane were walking Boodles around Rose Dhu when he first told her he would be taking a trip to Montana. It was near sunset, and the shorebirds were winging their way in from the river to roost.

"Why are you going back out there?" she asked.

"I just want to make sure we have all the relevant details about Trek Richards and Phillip Carruthers before we close the case for good," he replied.

Boodles was straining at the leash, his nose to the ground in fruitless pursuit of some unseen prey.

Diane was quiet for a moment, eyes downcast. "I'm not the sort of person who ever wishes ill for anyone, but I have to say this: I was happy when those two were found dead. I know that sounds awfully un-Christian, but I can't help it. I thought Trek Richards was going to kill me—and I think he would have, had it not been for Janie and Boodles."

She scratched the old dog, who looked up at her lovingly with his chocolate eyes and wagged his bushy tail.

"Well, you're safe now," Frank said, taking her hand. "I'm not going to let anything happen to you."

He had planned to be in Montana a couple of days at the most, so he packed as lightly as possible, putting everything in his carry-on bag. He had to be prepared for cold weather, though. Even though it was only November, it had already snowed there, and the average high was around 35 degrees these days.

Definitely not Savannah, he thought.

It was nearing sunset and snowing in Kalispell when Frank's flight landed at Glacier Park International Airport. He'd flown United, connecting through O'Hare, and the layover was so tight that he'd had to run between gates just to make his connection. He remembered the first time he had flown out here, on the FBI's private jet. That had been an entirely different experience.

In advance, Frank had touched base with Bill Acker, the head of security at the Carruthers property in Montana, and Acker had agreed to let Frank look around the property as much as he needed to the following day.

"I thought you guys thought this case was airtight," he said.

"We do. Just tying up some loose ends before we put it to bed," Frank replied.

"The property's for sale, you know. No buyers yet, but there have been some nibbles from a couple of dotcom billionaires out of Seattle and a Saudi prince. Can you imagine a Saudi prince in Kalispell?"

"I can't," Frank said, although he really had no perspective on the issue.

Frank got a rental car (learning from his prior experience in the town, he leased a truck with four-wheel drive), grabbed a tasty burger and fries at a place called MudMan Burgers, and checked into the Holiday Inn Express near the airport. He was exhausted, but he did call Diane to let her know that he had safely arrived.

"How is it?" she asked.

"Cold as hell," Frank replied.

"Hurry home, then. It's going to be 70 degrees here tomorrow."

The sky was crystal clear the following morning. The sun was so brilliant that it hurt. Frank had to put on his sunglasses to drive due to the sunlight's snow-amplified glare. He had the address but could drive to the Carruthers property from memory. Bill Acker met him at the gate.

"Beautiful day, eh?" Acker said as he unlatched the gate.

"It's certainly picturesque, with the snow and all. I've never been a fan of cold weather, though. Snow's just not my thing."

Frank thought of the winter he spent in Afghanistan. It had been incredibly cold, the coldest weather he'd ever experienced, and there was very little sunlight. He had hated it, and he vowed that when he returned home, he'd live someplace warm.

I could not live here, he thought.

They drove past the main house straight back to the cabin. Almost buried in snow, it looked smaller now, like the house of some Tolkienesque snow hobbit, and it was clear that no one had been there in some time. The stubby stone chimney stuck up from the roof like a hitchhiker's thumb.

Acker pointed to an oblong lump of snow near the front door.

"That burned-up Jeep is still here," he said. "The inside of the cabin is exactly the way the feds left it after cleanup. Nobody else has been back here since."

Acker rattled a set of keys and unlocked a padlock on the door.

"Can't leave these things unlocked around here," he said almost sheepishly. "Squatters will move in, and they're hell to root out. Bears, too, sometimes."

Acker cut his eyes over to glance at Frank, who wasn't certain if he was kidding or not.

As the cabin door opened, Frank had a flashback to the last time he walked through that doorway. The stench of death and decay that had hung in the air that day was long gone. The blood, the bodies, and the flies were gone, too. The cabin had reverted to what it always was: a simple log-and-stone structure in the woods with various expertly preserved specimens of taxidermy and prints of mountain scenes on the walls, a bearskin rug on the floor by the large wood-framed bed in front of the now-dead fireplace, a primitive kitchen area with a range and an ancient, rust-pocked Frigidaire refrigerator, and a threadbare sofa with a low-slung rustic-looking coffee table in front of it.

Directly across from the doorway was the desk that Trek had been sitting at when he was killed.

Frank knew that the obvious clues—the bloodstains, body positions, bullet holes—had been investigated months earlier. What he was looking for was something less obvious, a clue to whatever might have been missed because there was no context at the time, no reason to suspect anything but the obvious. He began a methodical search of the room, moving furniture around, looking inside the oven and refrigerator, pulling out desk drawers, taking books off the shelves, and looking beneath the bed. But Frank found nothing. The place was as clean as Jimmy Carter's conscience.

"Dammit," he said, sitting down on the rust-colored sofa, which was made of a rough woven fabric resembling corduroy.

And that was when he saw it.

In the crack between the edge of the sofa's upholstered armrest and its cushions, there was a glimmer of reflected light that shouldn't be there. Frank pulled the cushion aside and saw a plastic card wedged there. He thought it was a credit card at first, but that would have been so easy that he would have suspected it was a plant.

It was, instead, a plastic room key card for a lodging place called the Hungry Horse Inn. It featured a sad-faced saddle-backed horse, its long ears drooping like a Labrador's, on a tan background. Frank had only seen the card because of the faint glimmer of its white edge.

The hand of God, Frank thought.

"Where is this place?" Frank asked Acker, showing him the card.

"That's a little inn in Hungry Horse, about twenty miles from here, near the entrance to West Glacier. It ain't fancy, but it doesn't need to be. Many of the hikers headed into Glacier stay there for a few days before going into the park. The cabins have washers and dryers, hot showers, and a little more space than a hotel room."

"Can you take me there?"

"Sure," Acker said.

The Hungry Horse Inn was just as rustic as Acker had said it was. Its cabins were scattered over a snow-covered hillside right along the roadside of US 2, with a parking space in front of each unit. The office was in a smaller cabin at the front of the complex, marked with a nondescript lighted sign that, appropriately, said *Office.*

Acker parked Frank's truck right in front of the sign. "Frank, listen. The old bird who runs this place is named Emma Scowbridge. She can be a real pill if she doesn't like you, so be nice to her. If she takes a shine to you, she's as good as gold, but don't cross her. You dig?"

You dig? Frank thought. *What is this, the '70s?* He nodded.

As they entered the Hungry Horse Inn office, they encountered a withered, gray-haired crone seated behind the registration desk with huge bags under a pair of beady black eyes.

"Can I help you boys? You need a room?" she said, without looking up. A half-smoked, currently unlit cigarette dangling from her lips flipped up and down when she talked.

"No, Emma. This here's Frank Winger. He's a detective from Georgia."

Emma looked up, her wrinkle-shrouded eyes as wide as she could get them. "Sorry, Bill. I didn't realize that was you. How can I help you?"

"I found this key card in the cabin where the murders took place several months back. I don't think either of the men staying there would have had occasion to stay here at any point. I'm curious. Do you know if any women might have been staying here back then? I have some reason to believe that a woman may have some involvement in this case," Frank said.

"Do you have a name?" she asked.

"I don't, but I have the dates." He rattled them off, and she typed them into her computer.

"You know, this computer won't sort reservations by gender. People don't seem to pay that sort of thing much mind anyway these days. But we only have six cabins, so I reckon pulling the reservation forms might tell you what you're looking for. Up here, winter storms will knock the internet out every so often, so I always take a Xerox of their driver's license and an imprint of their credit card so we can still charge them if something goes kerflooey. I'm old school like that and not apologetic about it one bit."

Emma stood up and pulled out an old brown accordion file from the shelf behind her.

After a moment of sorting through registration slips, she smiled. "You're in luck," she said. "Only one woman staying by herself was registered here during those dates."

Frank felt his pulse quicken. "Do you have a name?" he asked.

"Alice Tubman."

Frank felt his burgeoning excitement suddenly deflate, like a popped balloon.

"You know her?" Acker asked.

"I don't," Frank said. "You said you have a picture of her driver's license?"

Emma pulled out the full-color copy of a Montana driver's license for one Alice Tubman and placed it on the countertop in front of the two men. "There she is. Ah yes. I remember her quite well. She stayed with us for about a year. She worked as a nurse's aide at the hospital while she took classes at the community college in Kalispell to become a surgical tech. Smart as a whip. Took a double load so she could finish early. Alice got her degree and finally left after the summer semester ended back in August, right before the Going-to-the-Sun Road closed for the season. I haven't heard from her since."

Frank's eyes widened as he stared at the image.

The woman in the driver's license photo had short blonde hair cut in a pixie style, but her eyes gave her away instantly.

"You don't have any idea where she went?" Frank asked quietly.

"Nope," Emma said. "She checked out one day, said her goodbyes, and that was it."

Acker peered over Frank's shoulder at the blown-up driver's license image. "I bet she's wearing contacts," Acker said, shaking his head slowly. "Nobody's eyes are that color in real life. That shade of blue ain't natural."

"Yes, it is," Frank murmured. "I've seen it myself."

40

July 30, eight months later

Frank stepped off the train platform in Seward, Alaska, into a beautiful late-July morning. The waterfront reflected an aquamarine sky dotted with only a few fluffy white clouds. He had a little over half an hour until the boat tour departed.

The four-hour ride from Anchorage on the Gold Star train had been incredible. Alaska was everything he'd heard it could be—wild, mountainous, and clean, it was filled with wildlife he'd only read about or seen on video. Standing on the observation platform, he had watched as the train passed rivers and glaciers. He had gazed across verdant evergreen forests that stretched to the horizon in every direction. Once, a majestic bald eagle had soared beside them as they turned to go into a tunnel. Suddenly, it dove downward, returning moments later with a gleaming rainbow trout wriggling in its talons.

It's so beautiful here, Frank thought.

Alaska seemed unspoiled and pure, unlike the rest of the country.

The day cruise left Seward at 11:30 a.m. Their boat, a

steel-hulled sightseeing vessel about eighty feet in length, was escorted out of the harbor by a pair of seals, who were initially seen floating on their backs eating shellfish. As the boat passed them, the seals disappeared beneath the water's surface, only to resurface directly alongside the vessel, much to the passengers' delight.

The ship passed Fox Island on its way out of Resurrection Bay, passing by Bear Glacier, partially shrouded by mist. Rounding the Aialik Peninsula, it passed through the choppy waters of the Chiswell Islands, with their vast nesting colonies of shorebirds and barking families of sea lions sunning themselves on seaweed-covered rocky outcrops, before entering Aialik Bay.

The tour boat stopped at Holgate Glacier at long last. Chunks of ice floated around them as the blue-tinted river of ice before them flowed inexorably down to the sea from the vast expanse of the Harding Icefield.

Frank got up from his seat and walked to the front of the boat. There, he stood alone at the railing, feeling the brisk katabatic winds as they poured freezing air from the glacier's surface. He was dressed in a plain black knit cap and multiple layers of polar fleece, with a waterproof insulated outer jacket from some Swedish company whose name he could not pronounce. He placed two gloved hands on the railing and gazed across the water.

"Incredible, isn't it?" said a woman's voice to his right.

Frank glanced at the woman. She was wearing reflective Maui Jim sunglasses and a hooded jacket cinched tight around her waist. A few tufts of blonde hair peeked out from beneath the hood.

They were alone at the rail, staring across the frigid water.

"It sure is," he said.

Both were silent for a long time after that.

"How are you doing?" Frank said at last.

"I'm fine," the woman said. "Who wouldn't like waking up to this sort of thing every day?"

Frank, his gloved hands on the rail, stared across the water for a moment. He looked around and said in a low voice, "You know the whole world thinks you're dead."

"That was my intent," she said.

"How do you live with that, Dr. O'Connor? Your parents and sister went through hell after you went missing."

"My name is Alice, Detective. Janie O'Connor is dead, legally and otherwise. That chapter of my life is over."

A riot of seagulls and boobies flew about them from the adjacent cliffs, diving and weaving around the two of them like feathered missiles. Neither Frank nor Alice said a word for a pregnant moment or two.

"You know, I almost didn't answer when you called me," Alice said quietly.

"Why did you, then?"

"I don't know. I saw the 912 area code and knew it was from Savannah. Part of me has always expected that I'd be caught someday, and I'm getting tired of living in the shadows. I suppose I thought it was fate calling, in whatever guise it took. And I guess that guise was you."

She wiped away a tear.

"I miss everyone so much. Maybe part of me wants to be caught."

She sniffled once and straightened up her spine, gripping the ship's railing with both hands.

"So how did you find me?" Alice asked quietly.

"Almost by accident," Frank said.

"By accident?"

"I got to know your sister, Diane, during the investigation. After the case closed, that resolved any professional or ethical conflicts we might have had, so I asked her out."

"You're dating my sister?"

"Well, there's more to it than that. We're in love. We're living together."

"In my house?"

Frank nodded.

"Wow," Alice said, shaking her head.

"The world can be a crazy place sometimes," Frank said.

Frank told her about the bill from Proton Mail, the video from the dock camera, and the plastic room key he found in the cabin in Kalispell.

"Once I knew the name you'd taken, some of my new friends in the FBI helped me track you down under your new identity."

"You involved the FBI?" Alice asked.

"Only peripherally. I did not give them any specifics. I asked them if I could locate someone from an old case who had picked up an alias. They were more than happy to help me find Alice Tubman. I never mentioned to them who I was trying to track down, and they never asked," Frank said. "Anyway, after it was clear that you were here, I decided to visit Alaska to meet you."

Alice nodded, brushing away the tears that had once again welled up at the edges of her eyes. "You know we never would have been rid of them."

"The Carrutherses?"

Alice nodded.

"It would have been difficult," Frank said, nodding in agreement.

"Phillip was used to always getting what he wants. When I rejected him, he viewed the situation as an unacceptable outcome. He was never, ever going to let me move on with my life. When Trek attacked Diane, I knew what I had to do. The die was cast."

There was an ear-splitting *crack!* as if the gates of hell had opened. The two of them watched as a huge sheet of ice calved away from the glacier and crashed into the cold blue waters of Aialik Bay.

"My God," Frank murmured.

Frank turned to Janie then (although he supposed he'd have to get used to calling her Alice, she was still Janie O'Connor inside his head) and asked her the very thing he'd wanted to know after all this time. "How did you do it? And why?"

Alice looked around, trying to be certain no one was watching, and then sighed. "It's a long story," she said.

—

July 14, two years ago

Janie was running on adrenaline. She'd been up all night doing surgery and hadn't had much sleep. Her nerves were frayed and jangly, and her eyes were tired.

But her sister had been raped, and she had a job to do.

She called her friend David Byck, a gynecologist.

"David? Sorry to bother you so early on a weekend, but I need a favor. A friend of mine was assaulted but doesn't want to go into the ER. Can I have the access code for your office to do a pelvic exam?"

"Oh God, that's awful," David had said. "Of course you can use our office. Do you need my help?"

"No, thanks. I need to handle it. The victim is emotionally traumatized and doesn't want anyone else around, especially not a man. The fewer involved, the better. You know what I mean?"

"Of course," David had said.

Janie's thoughts about the events of that morning began to coalesce as the two of them drove in silence to David Byck's gynecology office.

The brutal attack on her sister had shaken her to the core.

Even though Phillip claimed that he had nothing to do with it, Janie would never be fully sure of that fact.

Dave Wommack had told her the name of the person who had set fire to his home. It was the same man who had broken into her garage the year before—and the same man who had raped Diane. His name was Trek Richards—and the police confirmed that he had indeed worked for Phillip.

Did Phillip order Trek to attack her? Or was the rape the result of a renegade acting on his own?

In the final analysis, it didn't matter. Janie blamed Phillip for the entire Trek Richards experience. While it might have been true that Trek was acting on his own, the nutjob who had broken into her garage and raped her innocent sister would have never even known about her if Phillip had not given Trek her scent to begin with. Phillip should have kept that psychopath as far away from her as possible. Instead, he had brought the wolf right to her door. Any way you sliced it, what had happened to Diane was ultimately Phillip's fault, and she was determined to make him pay for it.

Janie had come to a stark, painful realization: If she did not marry Phillip, he'd never stop his pursuit until he either ensnared her or destroyed her.

He'll stalk me, spy on me, and make my life an endless hell.

Like her mother had warned her, *Men like that are used to getting what they want.*

But she couldn't marry him, not ever. That option was completely out of the question.

And so now Janie was faced with the zero-sum-game solution, the nuclear option: the recognition that if she did not marry Phillip, the only way out of this was for one of them to die.

But killing Phillip would not be enough. Cutting off the head of the hydra would only allow others to grow in its place—specifically Erika, who she knew hated her. And the poison roots of the entire Carruthers organization penetrated deep into the dark earth beneath the town she loved, corrupting everything. The Carruthers organization was everywhere. There was no hiding from them.

The only way out, for Janie and her family, who she loved, was for Janie to sacrifice herself. And that sacrifice had to occur in a fashion that would ultimately dig up the roots and stem of the sprawling poisonous vine that was the Carruthers family. She had to find a way to destroy all of it, burning it all to the ground, so that there was nothing left but ruin.

The wheels in Janie's head were turning quickly now, gears meshing, as her plan began to come together. After years of dormancy, the warrior in her was stirring once again.

Janie's knuckles whitened as she gripped the Volvo's steering wheel. She glanced at herself in the rearview mirror and saw what her mother used to call her game face. It was a particular expression Janie had always displayed before every soccer match, basketball game, or track meet when she was growing up: eyes slightly narrowed, jaw set, shoulders back.

After Janie had scored three goals in the second half of the AAA state championship soccer match to lead St. Vincent's to an unexpected come-from-behind title, a younger version of Diane had run onto the field and tightly hugged her jubilant, sweat-drenched sister.

"You're such a badass," Diane had said then, her eyes gleaming admiringly at Janie. "I wish I could be more like you."

Going into general surgery, Janie had quickly learned a hard and unpleasant truth: As a woman, she was forced to sublimate her innate competitiveness beneath a veneer of gentility. Although the gender ratio of medical school classes nowadays was about fifty-fifty, surgical residency programs remained overwhelmingly dominated by men. As a result, the OR was a testosterone-laden environment filled with a great deal of supremely macho bullshit. Surgery attendings were fond of calling the operating room "the arena of truth." A favorite saying among surgeons was that most medical problems could be fixed with a dose of "hot lights and cold steel." Unfortunately, there was a double standard.

Aggressive male surgeons were told they had balls. Aggressive female surgeons risked being labeled bitches.

So Janie adapted.

She knew that men found her attractive. Armed with that knowledge, instead of allowing her gender to serve as an impediment to her success, Janie had forged it into a formidable advantage. She cajoled, flattered, and flirted with the men around her, ultimately beating all of them at their own game. She was so incredibly good at it that most of them either didn't notice or didn't care. It was only in moments of crisis that Janie let her core of steel show, reverting to the fundamental take-no-prisoners mentality that had so characterized her youth.

This was the Janie O'Connor who now stared back at her from the rearview mirror.

Janie had read Sun Tzu's *The Art of War* all the way back in high school. From that ancient text, she learned that a warrior quickly learns to assess her opponent's strengths and weaknesses. Janie's key realization here had been this: Phillip wanted her back, and he wanted her badly. Marrying Janie would represent his final triumph, a demonstration of the sheer, overwhelming force of his prodigious will. Janie knew that Phillip would take every opportunity to prove to her that he was worthy of her undying affection.

But Phillip's burning desire to win back her affection was also his weakness, and Janie would use it against him. It was her trump card.

There was an old saying: *All's fair in love and war.* Well, this sure wasn't love anymore. That ship had sailed long ago. But war?

Yes, indeed.

Janie stopped by the Memorial Hospital ER on the way to David's office. She picked up a couple of butterfly needles and a few vials to draw blood, a rape kit, and some suture material, then gained access to the gynecology office through the back door.

Thank God it's Saturday, she thought.

Janie completed the pelvic exam, gave Diane a morning-after pill, treated her prophylactically for STDs, and drew blood work for baseline HIV and hepatitis B testing. Before leaving the office, however, she also drew a few tubes of blood from herself.

"Let's go back home," Janie said.

Diane, her eyes swollen and her face bruised and battered, nodded in silent agreement.

After taking Diane back to Twin Oaks, Janie gave her a two-milligram Ativan tablet and put her to bed. Diane, exhausted, was asleep in minutes.

Once she was certain Diane was asleep, Janie went into her garage, the very place where she had first encountered Trek Richards all those months ago, in what seemed like another life.

Janie had remembered that Phillip had once left one of his hammers behind at Twin Oaks while he was helping her hang some pictures. She recalled putting it in the toolbox in the garage.

Opening the toolbox, she saw the hammer lying there in all its red-enameled Sears Craftsman glory. A chill went down her spine.

"Awesome," she said out loud.

She carefully extracted the hammer from the toolbox with a pair of surgical gloves and wrapped it in a faded, threadbare SpongeBob SquarePants beach towel. She then took the towel-wrapped hammer into one of the verdant flower beds in her backyard, choosing an area hidden from any prying eyes by a hedge of red tips and a dense row of tea olive trees. Janie splayed the towel open on the pine straw so that the hammer was in the center, unstopped the two test tubes, and poured her own blood all over the hammer. The bloody baptism had transformed the previously generic-looking tool into something else. The Sears claw hammer was now a bona fide "murder weapon," and it looked the part.

Janie dropped the now-empty pair of test tubes and their stoppers into a ziplock baggie, then put the baggie into her pocket. She walked out to her dock and dropped the baggie into the dark waters of the Vernon River.

She watched the ghostly glimmer of the test tubes as they sank into oblivion.

Wrapping the hammer back up in the towel, she placed it in a plastic garbage bag before stuffing the garbage bag in an expensive leather Shinola valise that Phillip had given her a while back. Phillip had often used the valise as a day bag for their trips to the Montana place. Janie had commented that a bag like that would be good for nights when she was on call at Memorial, nights when she might not get home and needed to take some toiletries and fresh clothes and underwear.

"Keep it, then," Phillip had said, smiling at her. "It's yours."

And Janie had indeed kept it, until today.

She placed the Shinola valise in the trunk of her Volvo.

That afternoon, Dave came over to stay with Diane while Janie drove out to Wilmington Island to confront Phillip.

"Just stay down here and listen out for her," Janie said. "I gave her an Ativan to help her sleep, but there's a whole bottle of it in the kitchen."

"Does she know I'm going to be here?"

"She does, but if you hear her rustling about, just announce that you're here. She's still pretty jittery."

Janie kissed Dave lightly on the lips and said simply, "Thank you."

When she arrived at Phillip's place, she found that Phillip's numeric keypad code, the one she'd always used to get in the gate at the Carruthers estate, still worked.

That was sloppy of him.

Knowing that Alphonso was off on Saturdays, she parked her Volvo behind the garage. She plucked the crawl space key off the hook board on the wall in Alphonso's unlocked office, opened the padlock, and hid the valise containing the blood-soaked hammer inside the garage crawl space, placing it right next to a cinderblock pillar so that it would be easily seen. She then replaced the key on Alphonso's hook board and pad-locked the crawl space with a new lock of her own. She would throw the padlock key out of the car window on her way home.

And that's where the evidence trail began on the mysteri-ous "murder" of Janie O'Connor.

Janie walked over to the front of Phillip's mansion, took out her cell phone, and called him. He answered on the first ring.

"Janie? This is a surprise. Is everything OK?" His voice was so sugary sweet that it made Janie nauseous.

"Phillip, we need to talk."

"Of course. Where are you?"

"I'm standing outside your front door."

"I'll be right out."

The door opened in about two minutes' time. Janie envi-sioned Phillip sprinting through the cavernous marble-floored foyer, its life-size statues staring imperiously down from their perches along the curved stairway, and she could not help but smile.

He wants this to work out so much it's killing him, she thought.

"Come in," he said.

"I'd prefer to stay here," she said. "Something has happened."

"What is it?" Phillip said in a voice desperately straining to sound concerned.

"My sister, Diane, was raped."

Phillip's face fell. "Good God, I'm so sorry! When did this happen?"

"Early this morning. I just got her home."

"Is she OK? Well, that was a stupid thing to say. Of course she's not OK. But at least she's not badly hurt, right? Diane is such a sweet person."

"She is a sweet person. That's why I'm here. I need your help. The rapist was Trek Richards. He told Diane he was your employee."

"Jesus Christ," Phillip said, his fingers kneading his temples. "I just fired him."

"I want to go to the police, but I don't want him to run. Can you help me find him?"

"It might be difficult. Trek doesn't work for us anymore. Like I said, he was let go just this week."

Sweat was beading on Phillip's temples.

There's something you're not telling me, Phillip, she thought.

"I was aware of that. Apparently, Trek blamed me for his being fired," Janie said. "That's why he came to my house. But I was on call last night and Diane was there alone, so he took it out on her."

Phillip put a hand on Janie's shoulder, but she removed it.

"Phillip, I need you to be honest with me: You didn't send him to hurt me, did you?"

Phillip recoiled sharply, a shocked expression on his face. "Of course not! I love you, Janie. I wouldn't ever want anything to happen to you. You must know that."

"Do you remember the time someone broke into my garage?" Janie asked.

"Of course I do."

"It was Trek. I'm sure of it. I recognized his voice, his face, his stench. Everything."

"So you saw him today?"

"I beat the hell out of him, and Boodles just about ripped his arm off. But he got away. That's why I'm here. He told Diane that if we went to the police about the rape, your family would make our lives a living hell, that you had insiders everywhere and that you'd protect him. Is all that true?"

Phillip looked down at the ground, avoiding eye contact. "Trek's a liar. You can't believe anything he says. You said you haven't called the police yet, right?"

"Based on what Trek said, we were afraid to. Diane made me promise I wouldn't."

Phillip looked at Janie then with a serious expression, his brow slightly furrowed. She'd seen that look before, during business-related conversations and social events when promises were being made and deals were being cut. In better days, she'd even made fun of the look, calling it his negotiation face.

"Janie, I promise you this: I would never send Trek after you or your sister. He's perpetually out of control. That's precisely why he was let go. But you were right to not go to the cops, at least not yet. Trek has friends on the police force who will help him run and who would assist him in hiding from justice. I know where he lives, and I know where he'd go to hide. Let me help you find him. If you send the cops after him, he'll simply disappear. I have to go to Atlanta for a few days, but I'll be back on Saturday, and we'll track Trek down. Then we'll bring him to justice together. Does that sound like something you can live with?"

Janie looked up at Phillip. "You'd do that for me?" she asked.

"Absolutely," he said. "I'll make certain Trek pays for what he did to your sister."

Janie leaned in toward Phillip, kissing him lightly on the cheek. "Thank you," she said. "That means a lot."

Later, Janie turned into her driveway at Twin Oaks. She was very conscious of the unseen bomb ticking away in the very center of everything. Going forward, timing would be critical. Too soon, and the plan would fall apart. Too late, and it might mean the death of all of them.

A steady breeze blowing in from the river rustled the palms and tousled the Spanish moss that bearded the many live oaks on her property. The driveway took her straight past the namesake twin oaks for which the house was named, two massive trees that flanked the brick walkway at the front of the house. Dave's massive black Denali was still parked at the end of that walkway.

Janie pulled into the garage and closed the door.

After she entered her home, she thanked Dave for staying with Diane.

"You know I'd do anything for you," he said. "I love you."

"Thanks," she had replied. "I love you, too."

Janie kissed him on the lips then, softly at first and then more passionately, allowing herself to luxuriate in the warmth of Dave's embrace one last time.

She knew she would remember that kiss for the rest of her life.

After they parted, Janie closed the door and locked the deadbolt, gazing at Dave as he strutted down the front walk back to his SUV. He waved a jaunty goodbye as he got into the vehicle. Dave's smile was completely filled with love for her. It made her chest ache.

Brushing a tear from her eye, Janie shook her head softly.

"I'm so sorry," she whispered.

She put Boodles on his leash and took the old dog out into the yard. After he had relieved himself, she walked with him down to the dock. The sun dappled the waves around her. A pair of snowy egrets took off from the dock house as she approached and climbed up into the pale blue afternoon sky.

Janie knew she had precious little time now. Everything had to be over before Phillip returned from Atlanta on Saturday. Moreover, it had to be done in absolute secrecy, with no help from anyone. That was the only way. On the surface, things needed to seem completely normal, even as the inexorable machinations of Janie's impending "doom" turned, invisible and silent, beneath the seemingly unremarkable surface of each passing day.

Janie O'Connor needed to be dead and buried before Thursday rolled into Friday.

—

July 19

Janie finished rounding with the ward team on Thursday afternoon a bit early, at around 4:50 p.m. Afterward, she walked back over to her office and sat down at her desk. She picked up the framed, gilt-edged photo of her parents and looked at it, tracing the edges with her fingertips. She thought about taking it, but then she realized she couldn't.

Everything must stay the way it always was, she thought. *If I take it, someone will notice.*

She gently placed the picture back on her desk. For a moment, she thought she might cry.

Janie spent a couple of hours wrapping up the administrative work of her office, refilling prescriptions and signing the residents' notes. That was the OCD surgeon in her. She wanted to leave not a single item unaddressed before she left.

As she wrapped things up, she realized that she had to get moving. Locking up her office, Janie noticed the faint aroma of coffee coming from the break room. There was a light still burning in the dictation area. Janie smiled. She knew what that meant.

Liz Buck, one of the nurse practitioners, was still sitting at a computer in the dictation area, her reading glasses having slid down to the end of her nose. She was eating some of her seemingly endless supply of fruit. A little pile of mandarin orange peels had accumulated next to her keyboard.

"Hey, Liz, I'm heading out. Are you about done? We could walk out together."

Liz glanced up. "I've got a few more notes to do, and a full pot of coffee. I'll be fine. You go on home," she said, waving her off.

Janie glanced at her watch. It was already 7:23 p.m., near sunset. "See you tomorrow!" Janie said cheerily on her way out.

But she would never be coming back.

The very finality of that realization felt like a fishhook lodged in her heart.

Janie had always thought that suicide was a selfish act, eliminating the pain for the victim while causing immense pain for those left behind. And yet here she was, plotting her own death. Was that not some form of suicide?

But there's no other way, she thought. *They'll never leave us alone.*

She would miss her parents, for sure. Her mother would be OK. She was resilient, like Janie. Her father would take it hard, though. The two of them had always been close, and like Diane, her father was sentimental. Rick O'Connor's waters ran deep and silent, like an aquifer buried in subterranean limestone, but he felt things to the bone.

Janie's departure would hurt him.

I'm sorry, Daddy, she thought.

She'd miss Diane, too. She'd thought about telling her, but that seemed risky. If their father was an aquifer, Diane was a stream: Everything was on the surface. There was no duplicity in her. Nothing was hidden. To ask her to bear the burden of that secret would have been impossible.

And then there was Dave.

It was ironic that she'd realized too late that Dave was the true love of her life.

As she drove home, Janie could see the plovers and kill-deer coming into the tree-shrouded shoreline from the marsh, like they always did at dusk. That sight nearly made tears come into her eyes. She'd miss that. She'd miss a thousand other things: Spanish moss draped over the limbs of trees, craggy oyster beds poking curiously from the depths of the dark, thick mud, and the curious lilting Low Country dialect the old folks spoke. These things were the texture of the woven fabric of her existence, all the tiny details that people ignored every day but remembered so explicitly once they were gone.

She glanced over at the squat black leather doctor bag in her passenger seat. She never really used that thing anymore. It had once belonged to her great-uncle, a family practitioner from Claxton, and she carried it around for a few years out of respect for him, but most days it just sat in her office, gathering dust.

Not today, though.

By the time she arrived home at Twin Oaks, a little before 8:00 p.m., Janie unlocked the back door and turned off the burglar alarm, which was always on these days.

Boodles greeted her at the door, his tail wagging, his huge sloppy tongue lolling out of his mouth.

"Hey, boy!" Janie said, squatting down to greet him. Largely recovered from his recent injuries, Boodles wiggled with delight as he licked her face enthusiastically.

"I was wondering when you were going to get here," Diane said.

Janie looked up.

Diane's face was still bruised—the left eye had a shiner that looked like she'd gone a round or two with Mike Tyson—but the swelling in her lips and nose had gone down considerably.

"I'm sorry I'm so late. There's no reason for it—just a bunch of stupid computer junk, all busy work, really, along with a few phone calls to patients. Have you eaten?" Janie asked.

"I nibbled some on a few leftovers. I'm still not very hungry, you know. And it hurts to chew. I think my teeth are out of alignment. They just don't feel right."

"We'll need to get you to the dentist next week," Janie said. "I'm sure I can get Daniel to squeeze you in. You've got an appointment with your therapist scheduled for next week, as well. I figured you might be more physically up for that by then. And the library is doing just fine. They said you can come back to work whenever you're ready."

"Thanks, Janie. I'm sorry to be so much trouble," Diane said.

"You're not any trouble at all, Diane. You know I love you. I'm just sorry you've had to go through all of this."

Diane dabbed at her eyes, which were filled with tears. "So am I," she said.

Janie hugged her so tightly that Diane's vertebrae made a cracking noise.

"Ooh! I didn't hurt you, did I?" Janie said.

"You've never hurt me, Janie," Diane replied.

Janie watched Diane as she walked slowly up the stairs. Her gait was still halting, as though she expected the ground beneath her to open and swallow her up at any minute. She paused on the landing and turned back to Janie, a thin smile creasing her face.

"I haven't really said this yet, so I want to say it now: Thank you. You've let me come into your home and taken care of me like you always have. You're the best big sister ever, and I love you. You know that, right?"

"I love you, too, Di. And I wouldn't think of doing anything else," she said.

After Diane went into her bedroom and closed the door, Janie realized that she was starving. She made herself a turkey and avocado sandwich, with Duke's mayo, on seedless rye and set it on a blue-and-white porcelain plate. She sat quietly on the sofa in the den as she ate.

The den was filled with memorabilia. There were display tables filled with fossils, seashells, and rocks culled from the collections of her childhood. Antique Chinese vases were crammed onto the white wooden bookshelves, along with a few antique books with exquisite leather binding. And then there were the pictures of her family, dozens of them, all framed and perched on the bookshelves like so many frozen memories.

I'm going to miss all this so much, she thought.

She considered pouring a glass of white wine but decided against it. She'd be driving later that night and needed to be razor sharp.

She put the plate into the dishwasher and went upstairs. She changed into a pair of old jeans and a faded Elton John T-shirt that she never wore anymore, then packed a plastic garbage bag with a couple of changes of nondescript clothes and some spare toiletries (leaving her electric toothbrush; it would be too obvious if it were gone). She turned off the surveillance cameras for a moment and walked out to the garage, placing all those items in the trunk of her car. She then got the black doctor bag out of the front seat and opened it. Inside, she saw the one remaining vial of her own blood, the dental pliers, the scalpel, syringes, needles, and a bottle of 2 percent lidocaine with epinephrine. She also saw the collection of bones she'd retrieved from the anatomy lab, each carefully cracked open to expose the marrow chambers, and bleached them so that all their former DNA had been washed clean.

She looked at her watch. It was nearly 8:30.

Time to get moving, she thought.

She turned the surveillance cameras back on and texted Phillip.

Inside her head, she heard the clock ticking like a metronome.

—

Janie's hand throbbed like hell.

Her jaw hurt, too. She'd thought she would have been able to pull more than one tooth, but the first one hurt so damned much that she stopped there, choosing instead to use the old wisdom teeth that she had removed a few years back. For years, she had kept them in a wooden box on a shelf in her office for reasons she never fully understood. She supposed she could not bear to just throw pieces of herself away. In any case, she hoped that people would just see them as molars and not look any further.

Her tongue traced over the gaping hole in her lower jaw, where her other molar had been. She tasted blood there, but a soft clot had formed. She swallowed a small amount of the blood that had welled up in her mouth, feeling it slide down her throat like some soft-bodied slug.

She was grateful for the thumbnail of the waning crescent moon, which provided precious little illumination, as she sank her shovel into the thick marsh mud.

A fine mist had crept in from the river, its wispy tendrils curling among the rustling clumps of Spartina like the ecto-plasmic web of a ghostly spider. The mist swirled around Janie and slowly swallowed her up as she plunged the shovel into the thick marsh mud, *chuff, chuff,* her shoulders burning, the deepening hole gradually filling with water at its bottom.

It was low tide, thank God. She hadn't thought about that, which was stupid, but she'd gotten lucky and had some time to work. The water was rising now. In a couple of hours, the place she was digging would be completely under a foot or two of water. To make matters more complicated, the mud she dug into was choked with tangled clumps of marsh grass roots, myriad oyster shell fragments scattered among the roots like calcific shrapnel, which made the dig much more arduous than she had expected.

How quickly can Phillip get here? she wondered.

Janie did a quick calculation in her head. He'd have to drive from Buckhead to PDK, which could be thirty to forty-five minutes, and flight time ground-to-ground was usually about forty minutes from Atlanta. Then it was usually a forty-five-minute drive to Rose Dhu from the airport. She'd texted him a little after 8:30, so she figured she had to be gone at the very latest by 10:30 p.m.

She looked at her watch.

Damn, she thought. *We're cutting things close.*

It was already 10:00 p.m.

The left pinkie finger amputation had taken longer than she had hoped. She'd done the nerve block in textbook fashion and had sliced cleanly through the ligaments right at the level of the PIP joint so she didn't have to saw through any bone, but stopping the digital artery bleed without a Bovie had been much harder than she had expected. She had lost about twenty minutes trying to stanch the pulsatile blood flow. The feeling was coming back now, and she needed her left hand to use the shovel, and it now hurt like a son of a bitch.

She finally finished the hole in the marsh by 10:15 p.m. She removed the old bones, the finger, the molars, and the shirt she had worn the day before from the paper grocery bag she'd put them in. Suddenly, a set of headlights played across the expanse of marsh.

Shit!

Janie ducked her head below the marsh line.

The headlights were round, high up, and close together, like a Jeep's. They didn't have the typical low profile of the LEDs in Phillip's BMW. Janie watched as the headlights trailed luminously through the mist curling along the edge of Rose Dhu Road, like ball lightning, before rounding the corner near the shrimp boat dock and disappearing into the night.

She stayed crouched down after the Jeep had gone. She emptied the bones and teeth into the shallow grave, then dropped the shirt in. She threw her gold skull-and-crossbones MCG medical school ring into the mud. She placed the amputated pinkie finger on top, then poured the remaining vial of her blood all over everything. Finally she closed the wound in the earth, leaving a small mound on top.

She dragged some uprooted marsh fronds over the spot, wiped her hands on the now-empty paper bag, and started to walk out of the marsh with the bag and the shovel.

Just then, Janie saw another pair of headlights coming. This pair was more familiar, with a telltale bluish halogen tint.

Her pulse quickened. She crouched behind marsh grass and glanced at her watch. It was somehow 10:25 p.m. Phillip had made good time. She cursed at herself under her breath for being so careless.

Phillip flew past undeterred, rounding the corner under the gentle alley of live oaks that led up to her driveway at Twin Oaks.

And then he was gone.

Should she make the move for her car? The Volvo was fully loaded and gassed up. She had parked it just around the corner, on an otherwise deserted stretch of Schley Avenue.

No, she decided. She couldn't risk it. She'd have to wait in the marsh until Phillip left. If he saw her, or even the Volvo, the whole scheme risked being blown up.

So she waited.

At 10:49 p.m., she heard the thrum of Phillip's V-8 engine

as he drove back down Rose Dhu, speeding even faster than he had the first time. In an instant, he was gone again.

Gone forever, Janie thought.

Janie walked out of the marsh with the shovel and the bag. Moving quickly through the halo of illumination cast by the streetlight, she walked through the woods to the spot two streets over, where she had parked her Volvo earlier that day, and threw the shovel and the bag into the trunk. Cranking the Volvo, she jounced down a little-used dirt road that cut through the maritime forest to access White Bluff Road.

Driving away from Rose Dhu for the very last time, her lights turned off, Janie O'Connor said a silent prayer as she journeyed into the rest of her life.

41

"You cut off your own *finger*?" Frank exclaimed.

Looking down at Alice's hands, Frank saw that they were covered up by a pair of soft leather gloves.

Alice gazed across the bay at the glacier, then fixed Frank with a steely glare.

"I would have sawed my whole arm off if I had to," she said.

Alice gazed off into the distance as if seeing something far, far away. Her exhaled breath drifted like a ghost around her head.

"How did you pick the spot for the grave?" Frank asked.

"I tried to think of what a killer would do if he was going to kill me at my home and hide my body. I picked a place close by, on a single-lane road not near any dwellings, with marsh on either side, largely hidden from view by palmettos and scrub cedars. That place was surrounded by acres of undulating marsh grass that stretched all the way to the river. There's only one active streetlight on that whole stretch of road. Once it's dark and everyone is in for the night, hours can go by without a single car on the road. And at high tide, the grave would be

covered by water twice a day, hopefully accelerating decompo-
sition. It was the perfect spot."

"Except for the camera on your neighbor's dock," Frank
said.

"Well, yeah. I didn't know about that," Alice replied.

"And how did you end up in Montana?" Frank asked.

"That's complicated."

"I've got time."

Alice sighed. "When Trek attacked Diane at Twin Oaks, he
left his gun, which I took. Later that same day, I found his truck,
with the SecuriCorp insignia on it, stuck in the marsh near my
home. On the ground next to it, I discovered a map to the cabin
on the Carruthers Kalispell property. I'd been to the Kalispell
property with Phillip, so I knew exactly where that was. I took
both the map and Trek's gun with me the night I left. Figuring
that Trek was headed to Kalispell, I drove to Montana. It took
me three days, but I was in no rush. Once I got there, I found a
guy in West Glacier who made high-quality fake IDs for people
wanting to cross the border into Canada. At that point, I offi-
cially became Alice Tubman. Staking out the Carruthers property, I confirmed that Trek was staying in the cabin at the back
of the property. At that point, I started planning my revenge.

"I was patient. I got a job waiting tables in Hungry Horse
and began classes to become a surgical tech at Flathead Valley
Community College in Kalispell. After a while, I got a better
job working as a nurse's aide in the local hospital. I paid cash
to live in that crappy little cabin in Hungry Horse, although I
eventually got a credit card to build up Alice's credit history. I
then bought a laptop and continued to observe the Carruthers
Montana property. I watched people come and go there for a
few months until I understood the rhythm of the place. After
enough time had passed that Janie O'Connor's buried 'body'
could have fully decomposed, I set my trap. I got a device to
disguise my voice and called the SPD tip line to tell them where

my 'body' was buried. I signed up for Proton Mail and sent Tina Baker the video of Phillip walking around my property the night I disappeared. I sent Tina another email telling the police where to look for the murder weapon I had hidden on the Carruthers property. And then, when the time was right, I went to the cabin, ambushed Trek, tied him up, and texted Phillip to come to the Montana property using Trek's phone. The rest worked itself out from there."

The boat had started turning away from the glacier, white-capped bow waves foaming ahead of the hull. A small herd of bighorn sheep galloped up the side of an adjacent slope. Suddenly, Frank heard a cheer from a group of onlookers erupt toward the back of the boat, on the starboard side.

Alice glanced in that direction and nodded. "Whale," she said. "Probably a big humpback, judging from the size of the blow."

The gray mist that had surrounded the vessel when they first entered Aialik Bay began to dissipate as the boat chugged back toward the open ocean. Frank watched as seagulls hovered and swooped around them, squawking garrulously as they looked for handouts. Sunlight dappled the waves around them with flecks of gold and silver.

"Janie?"

"My name is Alice, Detective, please."

"OK, Alice. One question: Did you kill anyone?"

Alice paused for a moment. "One person. I had no choice. It was the only way," she said.

—

April 15, last year

Alice had waited so long for this day.

The map of the Carruthers Montana property that Trek

Richards had fumbled away during his hasty exit contained one very important detail: a back way onto the property. It was a meandering unpaved road, likely an old logging trail, which paralleled the creek. Although the road was obviously rarely used (there were places where Alice had to cut thick branches away to allow a rapid exit, just in case that was ever necessary), it led directly to the cabin that Trek was now living in. Over the previous several months, Alice had driven down it several times. Once, she'd even parked her car next to a granite outcropping and hiked the last mile or so, coming within sight of the cabin itself. Alice knew she would be able to get to the cabin, and back out, when the time came.

At long last, that day was today. The final act was due to be played out.

Montana was spectacular in spring and summer. The area around Glacier National Park was like the Montana of old: heavily forested, with rocky moraines piled up in ancient glacial valleys between towering snow-capped mountain ranges. Creeks and rivers, engorged with snowmelt, twisted in serpentine fashion through dense forests filled with a mixture of evergreens and deciduous trees. Below them, the forest floor was choked with ferns and other hopeful forms of lesser vegetation straining to reach the sun.

Alice got up before dawn, as always. She made a pot of coffee and had two cups (Starbucks Veranda Blend, black, with two teaspoons of sugar), then ate a bowl of Cheerios topped with cut-up strawberries. She was anxious to get on with the day but knew that there was no rush. Things would play out the way they would.

She took a shower, put in her contact lenses, and brushed her hair, putting it into a ponytail before getting dressed in comfortable clothes: quick-dry slacks and top, with a sturdy pair of Timberland hiking boots and a baseball cap. She then filled her backpack with the things she knew she'd need: two rolls of duct tape, a pair of Revo sunglasses, bottled water, a handful of protein bars and Gu Energy Chews, a saw, a Bic lighter, her Swarovski binoculars (ironically, a gift from Phillip), a charger for her phone, a large pocketknife, the map Trek had dropped, and Trek's handgun, fully loaded. She had recently been rereading T. H. White's novel *The Once and Future King*, a story of King Arthur's youth, and she packed that, too.

As Alice stepped outside into the chill twilight of the pre-dawn forest, she heard the shrill cry of an osprey someplace. She took that as an omen, although she logically knew it wasn't. The first rays of morning sunlight were beginning to trickle through the dense forest canopy—and it felt like destiny.

As Alice locked her place up, she turned on the front porch light. She didn't know when she would return—or even if she would return at all.

This might be it, she thought.

There was some odd comfort in the fact that if she *did* die, there would be no one left to mourn her. To her parents, and to her sister, Diane, she was already gone. That realization stung. Rick O'Connor had died thinking that his beloved Janie was missing and presumed dead. That made her feel awful. The thought that her ruse might have contributed to her father's premature demise left a deep wound that she knew would never fully heal. She also missed her mother's sagacity, wit, and sense of humor.

Diane, poor dear, would have to fend for herself at last. But at least she'd be freed from the Carruthers curse.

Janie's relationship with Phillip Carruthers, and its horrific aftermath, was a cancer that had to be wholly excised from all their lives. That was the only way they'd all get through this. Ultimately, it was for Diane's sake that she had been willing to go through all this. Was there some element of retribution? Of course. But this was also a protective measure, a way to ensure that no harm would ever befall her sister from the amoral predators who had been brought into her family's orbit.

Because of me, she thought. *I brought this terror into our world.*

There was some small comfort in knowing that Diane would be OK. As the sole beneficiary of Janie's estate, she'd have Janie's 401(k) and other investments to live on. She'd inherit Twin Oaks, too, which was fully paid off. And she'd have Boodles, of course.

The thought of Boodles made her smile.

Dave thought she was dead, as well. Alice regretted that. He had been her true destiny, her North Star. She had lost her way and had lost Dave in the process, because she had been temporarily blinded by wealth, glitz, and magnetic charm. Having been seduced by the dark allure of material things, she was now condemned to this half existence, this hollow purgatory.

I suppose that this is the penance I must pay for my sins, she thought.

The entrance to the back road into the Carruthers property was partially obscured by underbrush. Alice drove right at it, just like she'd done during her practice run the previous week, and the pokeweed bush folded down and allowed her to pass unencumbered into the enchanted forest.

The road was rutted and root-filled, and her Volvo jounced up and down as she pushed deeper into the woods. The cold, clear waters of the creek burbled alongside her, spilling over a rolling tumble of refrigerator-sized boulders. The wildness of the place was such that Alice half expected to see a charging moose or looming grizzly at every turn.

She parked in a small clearing adjacent to a short rock wall. A thicket of rhododendron had grown up alongside the road so that her car would have been hard to spot there even if someone drove right by it. She covered the Volvo with some spare branches so that it was nearly impossible to see. She imagined that if she did not come back, no one would find the car for years—and maybe not ever.

She hiked the rest of the way down the road.

When the cabin first came into view, she noticed a thin plume of blue smoke trailing out of the stone chimney.

He's awake, she thought.

For months, Alice had thought this whole thing through again and again. She didn't know what the layout of the cabin was. She had no idea what sort of defenses Trek may have mustered up inside. Going into the cabin would be to engage him on his own turf—and that would give him an advantage.

She realized that she'd have to lure him outside.

Alice looked around the place. There was a pump house outside, which likely housed a well. An older-model Jeep Wrangler, forest green with a massive dent in the passenger-side front door, stood guard in front of the cabin.

Alice took out her pocketknife and cut a strip of cloth from the bottom of her shirt. She crept over to the Jeep, unscrewed the gas cap, and stuffed the strip of fabric into the gas tank. The tank was full, and gasoline promptly wicked up into the cloth.

It's a big-ass Molotov cocktail, Alice thought.

She lit the cloth, and it started to burn. She opened the unlocked car door, honked the horn twice, and then hid behind a nearby birch tree.

Trek came outside and threw up his hands. "What the *hell?*" he exclaimed, just about the time the flames engulfed the Jeep's entire left side.

Trek jumped down from the porch and watched helplessly as his car burned. Alice ran up behind him carrying a huge tree branch. She swung the branch like a pinch hitter taking a swipe at a high outside curveball. The blow struck him in the temple and dropped him to his knees. Alice then used the pocketknife to expertly sever the Achilles tendons on the back of each of his legs. Screaming, Trek toppled over like a sack of potatoes. Alice drove her knee into the small of his back and placed the barrel of the gun against the base of his skull. She leaned in close so that he could hear her.

"Hello, motherfucker. I'm back," she said.

She used the butt of the gun to hit Trek in the back of the head, hard.

It was at that exact moment that the Jeep exploded.

—

When Trek awakened, he was confused.

Alice had duct-taped him into the chair at his desk. The tape was tight as hell around his chest, arms, and legs. She was sitting in front of him, pointing his own gun right at his head.

"Who are you? And how did I get here?" Trek asked.

"I dragged you," Alice said.

Trek looked up at her, bleary-eyed. And then his eyes opened wide, as if he recognized her for the first time.

"You . . . you're dead," Trek said.

"So are you," Alice said.

His eyes opened wider. "That's my gun," he said.

"Bingo."

Trek winced as he tried to move. "Jesus, my head hurts," he said. "And I can't breathe." He wriggled, grimacing in pain. "What the hell did you do to my legs?"

"I cut through your Achilles tendons," she said. "You'll likely never walk again. Not that that will matter much where you're going."

She stared at him. Trek squirmed in the desk chair like an insect pinned to a corkboard.

"I've got to ask you something. My dog had torn you up pretty good when I last saw you. I found your bloodstained truck stuck in the marsh at Rose Dhu on the day you raped my sister, but you were already gone. And then you showed up here. How did you get here?" Alice asked.

"After I left your house, when I found my truck was stuck in the mud, I stole a boat and took it to Coffee Bluff Marina, then hotwired a car there and drove it to the airport. The Carruthers' jet brought me out here to Kalispell."

"Phillip had you flown out here?"

Trek nodded. "He wanted me out of Savannah. Told me to lay low and that he'd take care of me."

"The bastard," Alice said.

"So I have a question for you. How did you find me?" Trek asked.

"You dropped this next to your stupid-ass truck," she said, waving the map in front of him.

"Shit," he said.

She knelt down next to him, so close that she could smell his rancid breath.

"I've been planning your death for months," Alice said. "But now that the day is upon us, I realized that I do need something from you. If you help me out, I just might let you live. You see, I'm a doctor. We're not used to taking lives. This sort of thing is very hard for me. I'll be more inclined to show you mercy if you can give me an assist."

Trek looked upward, as if he were looking for something hidden among the exposed beams of the cabin's ceiling.

"What other choice do I have, Mama?" Trek said out loud.

"Don't call me Mama," Alice said.

"I wasn't talking to you," Trek replied.

Alice shook her head, a quizzical expression on her face.

"OK, what do you want me to do?" Trek asked.

"You're not my main target here. Phillip is. I need to text Phillip using your phone. I want you to tell him you need to meet with him, in person, as soon as possible. If he calls back, you need to tell him you must see him. It's urgent, life or death. Maybe even something to do with me. Can you help me do that?"

Trek nodded.

"My phone is plugged into the charger in the kitchen area over there," he said, nodding in the direction of a primitive-looking gas range and an ancient, rusting Frigidaire refrigerator across the room.

Alice picked up Trek's flip phone and unplugged it. "What's your password?" she asked.

"1234," Trek replied.

"Wow. How original."

"It's a burner. I'm only supposed to use it for emergencies. I don't think there's much risk of being hacked out here," Trek said.

She scrolled through and found Phillip's number.

"If he calls back, I'll need you to talk to him," she said.

"He won't," Trek said. "It's an old-school phone, and there's no cell signal here. The text messages will go through the Wi-Fi, but you can't make phone calls with it when there's no cell signal." Trek looked up again, squinting and blinking rapidly.

Alice wondered if he was having a seizure.

"OK, Mama, I'll ask her. Just give me a minute, will ya? Jesus," Trek said.

"Who are you talking to?" Alice asked.

"My mama. She talks to me all the time, from in here," he said, pointing to his temple. "She says you're lying, that you're going to kill me anyway just as soon as you're done with me, and that I need to be ready for that because it's coming soon, coming like a freight train. That's what Mama said. She actually sang that line. I think it's from an old country song."

Alice stared at him, dumbfounded. *Is he delirious? What the hell is going on here?* She looked back at Trek's phone. "I'm going to text Phillip that there's something you need to talk to him about, but it's something he must see in person. Phillip has always been paranoid about the NSA reading his electronic communications, so that would play right into his paranoid delusional complex," Alice said.

"Dr. O'Connor?" Trek said calmly.

Alice Tubman, answering to a dead woman's name, glanced up.

"Mama says I should play my trump card," Trek said.

"What does that mean?" she asked.

"I'll give you something else to tell him: Tell him that I have some information about the company and that I need more money not to turn it over to the authorities," Trek said.

"What do you mean?"

"Just do it. He'll show up here ASAP. You're a hundred percent right about his paranoia. And I really do have something I could blackmail him with. I have insurance."

"What insurance?"

"You see the laptop in front of me? That's my insurance. It's Phillip's private laptop. I stole it from his office on the day he fired me. The hard drive is filled with information about the Carruthers business empire—both the legit businesses and the illegal ones. There are spreadsheets in there about the drugs they sell, the human trafficking business, the whole works. I took it from him just in case I needed it. And I'm willing to give it to you, along with the password that unlocks it, in exchange for one simple thing."

"What's that?"

"Promise me you won't kill me. I'm done with all the illegal stuff. I've been in Montana for a while now. I kind of like it here. I want to live out my life, find a girl, settle down, and get a real job. That's all I want. I take you to be a woman of your word, so if you promise me you won't kill me, I'll believe you."

Alice stared at him. Her face felt flushed, although she

could not tell if it was from the Jeep explosion or from something else.

"So do we have a deal?" Trek asked. His voice cracked like a dry twig.

Alice thought for a moment, then nodded. "OK, I won't kill you," she said softly. "Now, what's the password?"

"It's long and complicated, but Phillip taped it to the bottom of the laptop," he said.

Alice picked up the laptop, took a picture of the password taped underneath it with her cell phone, and tapped it in on the keyboard. She nodded as she looked over the screen.

"There's a lot of stuff on here," she said. "This will be very helpful."

After closing the laptop, Alice sent the text just as Trek had described.

Within a minute or so, the phone vibrated. She stared at it. A smile dawned across her face. "He says he can be here around 11:00 a.m. tomorrow," she said.

"What happens now?" Trek asked.

"Now, we wait," Alice said.

"Dr. O'Connor?" Trek said.

"Yes?"

"Look, I know you don't give a flying fuck about me. After what I did to your sister, I can even understand you wanting to kill me. But you must understand that I was only doing a job. I was working for your ex-boyfriend. He's the real bad guy here. I'm just a flunky."

"He didn't tell you to rape Diane. That was all on you," she said.

"No, he didn't. But he wouldn't have cared if I did. All that stuff that went on—breaking into your home, tapping into your surveillance cameras, shooting the dog, harassing your surgeon boyfriend—came at his direction. Phillip Carruthers is not what most people in Savannah think he is. He and Erika are involved in so much illegal stuff it's unreal. They're criminals, same as me. And they'll kill you if you get in their way. I've seen it more than once."

Alice nodded. She unplugged the laptop and dropped both the charger and the computer into her backpack. She then pulled out a syringe and a vial of something.

"What are you doing? I thought you weren't going to kill me," Trek said.

"I'm not, but you and I are going to be stuck here together for the next day or so. I'll be damned if I'm going to listen to you prattle on for the next twenty-four hours. I'll give you a choice: Either I tape your mouth shut, or I inject you with this sedative and put you to sleep."

Trek thought about this for a moment. "What's the sedative?" he asked.

"Ketamine. It's an animal tranquilizer. Very effective, but it can cause some vivid nightmares."

Trek shook his head. "Fuck it. Tape me up," he said. "I'm done with drugs."

"Suit yourself," Alice said, drawing the silver duct tape tight across his mouth.

—

The next morning, Alice put on a pair of nitrile surgical gloves, took a seat in a wicker chair beside the front door, and waited.

The cabin decor was rustic and primitive. Alice recognized the decorating taste of Anderson Carruthers everywhere: mounted heads of elk and bighorn sheep, taxidermists' renditions of owls and hawks in flight, a bearskin rug in front of the fireplace, now scrunched up against the wall behind the relocated sofa. The prints on the walls were landscapes of the towering mountains around them.

Anderson had been a man's man, his life topped off by

flagrant excesses of armament and braggadocio. Anderson had thought his socially adept son was soft. A profound disappointment. That disappointment was the source of the snake that lay coiled in Phillip's head. Alice could see that now.

She was pissed she had not seen it sooner.

After spinning the chair around so that it faced the desk, Alice roughly ripped the duct tape from Trek's mouth.

"Shit! That hurt!" Trek said.

"You'll live," Alice said.

The clock ticked by with paranormal slowness. The sun seemed pinned to the sky.

The hollow knock on the cabin door, when it finally came, startled her.

Anderson Carruthers would have just walked in like he owned the place, she thought. Because he did own the place.

Alice pulled Trek's gun from her backpack and took off the safety.

"Come in," Trek said.

It was shortly after 11:30 a.m. when Phillip Carruthers strode into his cabin in the deep Montana woods for the last time. He was dressed in faded blue jeans, a dark-blue sport jacket, and a white button-down Oxford. Alice inhaled his odor as he walked by. Once, it would have excited her. Now, it repulsed her.

"Trek?" Phillip said.

"Hello, Phillip," Alice said from behind him.

She closed the door.

The gun was pointed unwaveringly at Phillip's chest. They were standing a mere five feet apart.

"Janie? You're . . . you're *alive*?"

The tears came to her then.

This was not like her. She was a surgeon, and a damned good one. Emotions never affected her. But she was out of practice these days. Or maybe this was something different.

Because this wasn't life or death, she could be objective about some of the more tangible things.

This was about betrayal.

He betrayed you, Janie, she thought. *That should just piss you off. Get a grip.*

The tears shut off abruptly like a spigot had been turned.

"Yes, I'm alive, Phillip. I faked my own death to get away from you. And from him," she said, nodding in the direction of Trek, who was still duct-taped to the desk chair.

She kept the gun trained on Phillip as she walked behind the desk. She knew Phillip usually carried a 9 mm Browning handgun in a shoulder holster, and he knew how to use it. She dared not take her eyes off him, not for an instant. A momentary lapse and she might end up dead.

Phillip stared at Trek, a blank look of utter astonishment on his face.

"This is why you texted me?" Phillip said.

"She ambushed me," Trek said. "She blew up my car."

"I saw that. Didn't know what to make of it. I suppose it should have tipped me off that something was wrong here—but I sure didn't expect this."

"*She* texted you," Trek said. "Not me."

"This man raped my sister, Phillip," Alice said. "And *you* helped him escape. You hid him away up here so that the cops couldn't tie him to you."

"When the police ID'd Trek for setting fire to Dave Wommack's house, I arranged his relocation to Montana. That was all in motion before the rape. He raped her on his own. I'm truly sorry that happened to Diane. She didn't deserve that."

"No, she didn't," Alice said, shaking her head. "Not at all. Nobody does."

Alice looked over at Trek, sapphire eyes blazing. Then she looked back at Phillip. "Phillip, do you really want me back?"

He nodded. "Of course I do, Janie. I want that more than anything in the world."

"Do you still have that pistol you used to always carry in your shoulder holster?"

"I do."

"Well, if you want me back, you're going to have to prove it to me. I want you to kill him," Alice said.

Trek's eyes widened.

"You promised me you wouldn't kill me!" he exclaimed.

"I'm not going to kill you," Alice said, motioning toward Phillip with Trek's gun. "He is."

Phillip drew his weapon and aimed it at Trek.

"Sorry, mate. You heard the lady. And Trek, just for the record, I wanted to kill you in the first place. You know what's ironic? Erika, of all people, talked me out of it. She said it would be too messy."

"She's got—"

Trek never finished the sentence as the left side of his head exploded.

Phillip reholstered his gun. "There, Janie. Are you satisfied? It's done," he said.

"Not quite," she said.

Alice fired Trek's gun twice. The first bullet struck Phillip in the left chest, driving him to the floor. The second hit him in the right thorax while he lay there, a stunned expression on his face.

She knelt down to face him.

"I'm sorry it had to end this way, Phillip," she said. "Sorry, but not sorry."

She stood back up.

Bloody spittle came from Phillip's mouth as he struggled to breathe. His neck veins bulged, and his nostrils flared. His face was turning purple.

"I shot you through both lungs. You'll die soon, but you'll

suffer a bit first. And you deserve that suffering, after all you put me through."

"You damned b-bitch," he gasped.

"Goodbye, Phillip," Alice said.

She wiped a few tears from her eyes as she watched the life slowly ebb from the man she'd once thought she loved, a man she was once engaged to marry.

Phillip, struggling to breathe, bubbled blood from his nose and mouth with each breath but said nothing further, his lips gradually turning more cyanotic, his face ashen. After a few minutes, he sighed, took one final breath, and closed his eyes, his body collapsing on itself.

When Alice was completely certain Phillip was dead, she took off the first pair of gloves and put on a second pair, then used a paper towel to place Phillip's gun back in his hand. She then carefully cut all the duct tape away from Trek's body, wiped his gun down with another paper towel, and pressed it into his right hand, letting it subsequently drop from his hand onto the floor beside him. She then wiped the exterior of the first pair of gloves over his shooting hand. Cleaning the entire cabin, she fastidiously removed any trace that she was ever there. Packing up the cleaning supplies, towels, and duct tape in a plastic bag, she stuffed them into her backpack and walked out the cabin's front door, leaving it open. As she was leaving, Alice left the laptop right where she had found it: plugged in on the desk in front of Trek Richards.

When she returned to her place in Hungry Horse, the first thing she did was take a shower. After that, she went to bed and slept until dawn.

42

July 30, present day

When the Seward boat tour ended, Frank and Alice disembarked separately. They walked to the end of the dock in the Seward harbor and entered a small gift shop that carried Alaska-themed T-shirts, polar fleeces, and stuffed animals. Frank picked up a plush eagle toy.

"Boodles would like that," Alice said.

"I'll get it for him," Frank said.

They walked outside and sat together on a bench near a marker for the Iditarod dogsled race, which had once started in Seward. The sun overhead was a brilliant jewel burning through a few wispy cirrus clouds in an aquamarine sky. Silently, they gazed across the rippling azure waters at rows of jagged snow-capped mountain peaks that stood like dragons' teeth on either side of the fjord. A pair of harbor seals frolicked in the shallows.

"Diane and I are getting married," Frank said at last.

Alice smiled. "I'm happy for the two of you. Maybe y'all can give my mama the grandchildren she has always wanted."

"I hope so," Frank said—and he realized that he meant it.

Alice glanced out across the bay, her eyes narrowed against the sun's reflection. She closed her eyes and leaned back on the bench. "I saw online that Clarence Brown was elected mayor. And you're the new chief of police, right?" she said.

"That's right. I don't know how long that will last, but I'm willing to do the job for a few years, at least."

"Do it as long as you can, Chief Winger. Savannah needs people like you."

Frank really did not know what to say after that, so he sat silently, gazing down at the plush eagle toy.

"So what happens now?" Alice said, breaking the pregnant silence.

Frank looked up, squinting into the brilliant sunlight reflecting off the water. "Nothing," he said. "I'm going to leave Seward on a cruise ship this afternoon. It'll drop me off in Vancouver in a few days, and I'll fly back to Savannah from there. Those are all the plans I have."

"You aren't going to turn me in?" she asked.

"No, I'm not," he said. "I decided that even before I came here."

Tears welled up in Alice's eyes. She dabbed at them, shaking her head in disbelief, and threw her arms around Frank's shoulders as she buried her head in his shoulder.

Frank patted her on the back. "It's OK," he said softly.

She pulled away from him abruptly. "I've worried about this moment every single day for two years. To hear you say that is like a weight lifted off my shoulders. Does anyone else know?"

Frank shook his head. "I'm the only one."

"So I suppose I should say thank you," Alice said.

"You don't need to thank me. It was the right thing to do," Frank said. Gently, he took her hand and clasped it in both of his own.

"Janie, I love your sister, and you do, too. You gave up your entire life to keep her safe. I won't blow up everything you did over some nebulous matter of principle."

Frank paused. A couple of kids were throwing a ball back and forth, playing fetch with a golden retriever that reminded him of Boodles. He smiled and glanced back over at Alice.

"I was a soldier once. War taught me many lessons, some good and some bad. Being a soldier made me realize that life's crises aren't always black and white. Sometimes, they're painted in shades of gray," he said.

Alice pointed to a large mountain that loomed over Seward's harbor. "You see that?" she said. "That's Mount Marathon. Every July 4, they run the toughest 5K in the world up the side of that mountain. I might just run that race here next summer."

"You do that, Alice Tubman. Make some plans for your life," Frank said.

Half a world away, in Rose Dhu, a pack of fiddler crabs scurried across a shallow depression in the marsh, the place where the remains of Dr. Janie O'Connor had once been found. Softshell clams buried themselves deep within it; scrabbling shorebirds flapped above it. For a few months after the grave had been discovered, mourners had made the site a place of pilgrimage, leaving bouquets of flowers at the spot. However, the pilgrims never stayed long enough to see the tide rise, as it always did, to drown the faded blooms in the turbid, olive-colored depths of Houston Creek and the Vernon River.

Rose Dhu was the stuff of memory now, another life from another time. Janie O'Connor was truly gone—a changeling, reincarnated as Alice Tubman, coming into a new life on a new shore in a land that seemed at once alien and familiar.

Leaning over, Alice kissed Frank gently on the cheek before standing up to leave, still holding his hand. "Take good care of Diane, Frank. She's yours now," Alice said. She stared down at him, sapphire eyes sparkling in the midday sun.

"I will," Frank said. "I promise."

Boats churned the sun-dappled waters, shorebirds squawked and scrabbled along the docks, and peals of children's laughter filled the air.

Without saying another word, Alice Tubman and Frank Winger parted ways, for the first and last time. Alice put on her sunglasses and walked down the pier toward the shore.

Frank strode in the opposite direction, walking briskly to the very end of the cement pier before clambering aboard the bobbing Zodiac launch that would take him to the cruise ship anchored in the harbor.

After Frank's Zodiac left the pier, Alice turned and gazed across the harbor. She thought he might have glanced back at her, just once, the rim of his sunglasses catching an errant ray or two of sunlight. But then the tiny vessel rounded a stone jetty and was gone, seabound in a flurry of prop wash and foam, an escort of hungry seagulls flapping awkwardly above it like those pesky deerflies back home.

He's going back to Rose Dhu, Alice thought.

"Goodbye," she said out loud, wiping away a single tear.

And then Alice turned once more, never looking back, as she stepped boldly into the sun-drenched promise of a brilliant Alaska morning.

ACKNOWLEDGMENTS

Stephen King once said, "I try to create sympathy for my characters, then turn the monsters loose." This is the distilled essence of this novel, which focuses on the most frightening sort of monster of all: a monster who hides its profound evil under a veneer of socialization. It's a new twist on an old tale, dating back to stories like Bram Stoker's *Dracula* (which may have been partly written in Savannah), but it is the sort of story that has a particular resonance in today's society.

The late Michael Palmer, another fellow physician-author, once told me that all novels begin with a *"what if"* moment. Without giving the story away, the "what if" for *Rose Dhu* centers on how much one is willing to sacrifice for the people one loves. In that sense, it has something in common with my first published novel, *The Shadow Man,* in which the protagonist, Malcolm King, was willing to sacrifice everything to save his family. For fans of so-called Easter eggs, Malcolm does make a cameo appearance in this novel.

In writing this book, I also wanted to capture the essence of my hometown of Savannah. As many have discovered, it is a beautiful and haunted place, and one I am proud to call home.

In terms of specific acknowledgments, there are a few folks I need to thank for helping me in the process of whittling my initial 140,000-word manuscript into its final form. First, as always, I have to thank my wife, Daphne, my best friend, personal muse, and perpetual first reader, who is always appropriately nihilistic in her criticism and who has put up with me for nearly half a century. Second, I'd like to thank Marlene Adelstein, my longtime editor, who helped me muddle through the first two iterations of this work. Third, I'd like to thank all the folks at Girl Friday Books, who transformed *Rose Dhu* from a sprawling, labyrinthine story into an actual novel. And finally, I'd like to thank my many interesting, eccentric neighbors in the Rose Dhu community, whose quirkiness inspired many of the scenes in this novel. We should make some T-shirts that say "Keep the Dhu Weird." I'll even take the orders for them when I get a minute.

Oh, and one last thing: My father, Jack Murphy, died while I was writing this novel, so he never got to read the finished product. I hope that he and my mother, Peggy, reunited at long last in the hereafter, can read it somehow, and that it will at least be pronounced "better than Lean Cuisine." The two of you made me the man I am. I will love both of you forever.

ABOUT THE AUTHOR

Mark Murphy is a native of Savannah, Georgia. He's had a lot of jobs in his life: fast-food worker, student marine biologist, orderly, ordained minister, and—most recently—gastroenterologist. He's met many interesting folks in those occupations, including aging sitcom stars, disgraced televangelists, political kingmakers, and serial killers. And when he's not working at his "day job," helping the sick and doing endoscopy, he's reading (a lot) and writing (not enough—but it's never enough). He pens an award-winning op-ed column for the *Savannah Morning News* and has published quite a few short stories, magazine articles, and textbook chapters. *Rose Dhu* is his third novel.